A PROSPECT OF VENGEANCE

When Philip Masson's distinguished career was tragically cut short in a South Coast sailing accident, there were nasty rumours, in spite of the careful inquest verdict. For Masson was in line for a security promotion which didn't suit everyone. An eavesdropped bit of gossip at an embassy party sets Jenny Fielding and Ian Robinson, a successful 'investigative reporting' partnership, on the trail of treachery and power struggles in Intelligence Research and Development. But the sinister past starts catching up with them and threatens to silence them for ever . . .

A PROSPECT OF VENGEANCE

ANTHONY PRICE

A New Portway Large Print Book

**CHIVERS PRESS
BATH**

First published in Great Britain 1988
by
Victor Gollancz Ltd
This Large Print edition published by
Chivers Press
by arrangement with
Victor Gollancz Ltd
and in the U.S.A. and Canada with
the author
at the request of
The London & Home Counties Branch
of
The Library Association
1989

ISBN 0 7451 7197 4

© Anthony Price 1988

British Library Cataloguing in Publication Data

Price, Anthony, *1928–*
  A prospect of vengeance.
  I. Title
  823'.914 [F]

  ISBN 0–7451–7197–4

For Terry Page and
David Proctor

A PROSPECT OF VENGEANCE

PROLOGUE:

OLD MRS GRIFFIN'S COTTAGE

The children had spotted the ruin of old Mrs Griffin's cottage that very first morning, years before, and from the one place in the farmhouse where it could be seen through the trees: a little low window, cobwebby and covered with dead flies, halfway down the narrow twisty back stair to the kitchen. And then there had been no holding them.

Rachel and Laurence had known about it already, of course. The estate agents' man had explained that it was part of the property, as a more-or-less unwanted appendage to the farmhouse plot below the orchard, also dead on the line of the motorway and not part of the fields which had been already sold to the adjacent farms. At the time this had rather aroused Rachel's curiosity, so that when Laurence had embarked on a second tour of their dilapidated (but, as they then thought, strictly temporary) new home, she had gone exploring for herself.

Actually, she had never quite reached old Mrs Griffin's cottage then. But she had seen enough, because what she had seen she had disliked even in the safety of the bright sunshine. Indeed, although long afterwards she maintained that her dislike—even then, even then—had been instinctive, or intuitive, it had also been something fiercer than mere dislike: it was in reality strictly practical and maternal, primarily safety-conscious. The children were still little then, but no longer restrictively little. Rather, they were adventurously active, and she knew from bitter experience that Melanie would surely follow where Christopher led; and Christopher, having once glimpsed that little

3

brick chimney and gable-end rising up out of the mossy ruin of fallen thatch, would somehow penetrate the great tangle of brambles and briars and seven-foot tall stinging nettles which had conquered old Mrs Griffin's little garden, and which utterly barred her own progress, but had not prevented her glimpsing the pond.

It was a foul place, she had thought, even in the sunshine: foul, because she could see beastly things in the water—rotting branches and vegetation, and even an old saucepan breaking the surface of the water with a circle and a handle, over which a cloud of insects buzzed and skittered; foul also, because, although by the standards of her town-bred, traffic-accustomed ears its silence was absolute, it was somehow deafeningly noisy, with the low buzz and hum of all those insects hunting and fighting and dying and eating ceaselessly around her; and foul, finally, because she could smell all this activity, of plants and insects and invisible animals competing with each other, and winning and losing—a sweet-rotten smell, the like of which she had never encountered before, a world away from the carbon monoxide and Indian take-away smells which had occasionally invaded their London flat on hot evenings.

'That's a horrible place, down there, darling,' she had said eventually to Larry, when she'd found him again, in the barn beside the farmhouse, staring up at the chinks of sunlight high above.

'Just one or two displaced tiles, Dr Groom,' the estate agents' man had been saying. 'The structure itself is absolutely sound—the timbers, and so on. In fact, as I've said, it's also a listed building—Grade Three—like the house. Late

4

fifteenth century . . . perhaps early sixteenth . . . the expert witnesses at the public inquiry argued about that.' He had given Rachel a quick smile then, acknowledging her presence, if not her words. 'In other circumstances we'd be thinking about a barn conversion, splitting the property into two, rather than about a few displaced tiles. It really is a great tragedy . . . Do you see that main beam, up there? Five hundred years old, that beam is. And—'

'What's horrible, darling?' Larry had overridden the salesman's automatic spiel.

'The old Griffin place?' The estate agents' man had been quick then, scooping up his error with another smile which embraced them both. 'Awful, isn't it? It hasn't been lived in for years, of course. But it's amazing how quickly those little places fall to pieces once they're untenanted. And, of course, nobody wanted to live there, after old Mrs Griffin died. It's too far off the main road. In fact—*in fact* . . . you can't even get to it from here. You didn't actually get to it, did you Mrs Groom?' He had paused then, but too briefly for her to do more than open her mouth. 'There *was* a path from here, through the orchard, I believe. But that's totally overgrown now . . . The *actual* access to the cottage—not that it is a cottage now, it's quite irreparable . . . the *actual* access is from a track on the hill above, through the spinney there. But that's pretty overgrown, too.' Another smile. 'If it wasn't for the motorway, I'd be advising you to have the whole place bulldozed into the pond, and the trees there cut down. Then you'd have superb views of the moor.' Another smile. 'But then we'd be talking about four or five times the present asking

5

price—maybe more, if this barn was included.' The smile had saddened genuinely at that lost prospect. 'It *is* a tragedy, as I say . . . the motorway.'

Rachel had ignored him. 'It smells as though something had died in it.' She had addressed the bad news to Larry alone. 'The children will be into the pond there for sure.'

Her husband's expression had hardened then. And she remembered too late that he was a country boy, country-bred, and she had known then that resistance was in vain.

'Well, darling—' For an instant he had looked up at the ancient beam above him, with a mixture of love and bitterness, because his ownership of it was to be so brief '—well then . . . they'll just have to do what they're told, and keep away from it. It can't be more dangerous than London, any day of the week, anyway.'

That had made it certain, even though they were a partnership of equal partners. But then he had made it easier by twisting one of his smiles at her, which she could never resist. 'I'll talk to Chris, darling—don't worry. And . . . while we're here . . . you can look for another place, without a pond—eh?'

But with a five-hundred-year-old beam, eh? she had thought lovingly, understanding that he felt he was coming home at last, even if only temporarily here, but at least away from his hated asphalt jungle in Highbury.

But, very strangely, it hadn't been like that at all.

Or, at first, it had been—

'Mummy, Mummy!' Mel had cried, as she came down the back stair into the kitchen that first morning. 'There's an old cottage in the trees down there—' She pointed vaguely in the fatal direction.

'What, darling?' Rachel had pretended not to hear.

Larry looked up from his yesterday's paper, which he hadn't got round to reading in the chaos of their arrival. 'That's the old Griffin place,' he had said, matter-of-fact and ready to fulfil his promise as Chris arrived breathlessly behind his sister. 'It's part of our property. But it's only a ruin.' He had looked down at his paper again. 'An old lady named 'Griffin' was the last occupant. That's why it's called "the old Griffin place".'

Chris had sat down without a word. And, as Chris played his cards close to his chest even then, that meant that Chris had his plans worked out.

'Was she a witch?' inquired Mel. 'It *looks* like a witch's cottage, Daddy—it's . . . yrrch!'

Chris had considered the choice between cornflakes and muesli with ostentatious innocence. 'There are no such things as witches,' he admonished his sister. Then he had selected the cornflakes. 'Can I have two boiled eggs, Mother?'

Rachel knew her son almost as well as she knew her husband. So she had waited for his next move.

And Chris had waited too until the second egg. 'I think I'll go down and have a look at it,' he addressed no one in particular. 'Is that okay, Father?'

'What?' Melanie, at the age of six, didn't know

anyone very well, but she knew her brother better than anyone else. 'Me too!'

Larry looked up from his paper. 'Not just you—all of us, Chris.' He grinned at Rachel, then at Melanie, and finally at Chris. 'After the washing up we'll all go down and look at old Mrs Griffin's cottage. And then we'll make the rules. Okay?'

And it had been much better than Rachel had expected, after Larry had slashed his way through all the obstacles with a terrifying weapon he had acquired from somewhere, which looked as though it had last been carried by an angry *sans-culotte* in the French Revolution.

So, finally, they had reached the mouldering wreck of old Mrs Griffin's home: all the paraphernalia of a humble, long-lost and once-upon-a-time existence had still been there, among the nettles and fallen bricks and timbers, and the coarse-leafed growth: broken chairs and smashed furniture, the bits of an immense iron bedstead; the shards of crockery, and bottles and broken bottles—bottles everywhere—and the rusty evidence of tinned food—tins of every shape and size, mixed with rusty springs from an antique armchair mouldering on the edge of the pond.

'What's this?' Melanie held up half of a chamber-pot by its handle. 'Is it for fruit salad?'

'I'll have this, for my bedroom,' Chris, eagle-eyed, held up a pewter candle-stick. But then he'd looked at his father. 'Father—let's go back now.'

Larry looked at his son. 'What's the matter?'

'I don't like the smell.' Chris had balanced

8

himself on a sheet of corrugated iron. 'It smells like
. . . I don't know what—drains, maybe?'

'*Yyyrrrch!*' Melanie threw her half-chamber-pot
into the pond, raising oily circles of water, to
disturb clouds of insects. '*Drains!*'

'Let's go back,' Chris had repeated his demand.
'This is a beastly place.'

'Yes,' agreed Melanie. 'And . . . I bet she *was* a
witch—old Mrs Griffin!'

★   ★   ★

So they had gone back.

And it had been all right—even all right while the
children ranged far and wide over the moor, and
under the hill and over the hill and beyond, on foot
and then on bicycle, as times had changed, and
public inquiry (and government, and minister) had
succeeded public inquiry, and the years had passed
over the moor, and overhill and underhill, and Dr
Groom's job had developed. And Rachel had been a
member of the Women's Institute, and then
treasurer, and then secretary. And, in the seventh
year, Madam President.

And all their plans had changed, as the motorway
had taken a different line, and Underhill Farm
survived.

★   ★   ★

Until that day when Chris—Chris with his voice
broken, out of the school choir and into the Junior
Colts rugger XV, but Arts-inclined in the run-up to
his A-level exams,—had cycled over to the
archaeology unit which was blazing the trail for the

new line of the motorway, beyond the edge of the moor—

'Mother—*Rachel* . . .' (Chris wasn't sure how a chap ought to address his mother: some chaps thought Christian names were OTT, some were still old-fashioned) '. . . you know the old Griffin place—?'

Long since, Rachel had stopped worrying about the old Griffin place. It was where it had always been, more-or-less. But after all these years it wasn't one of her problems, 'What about it, darling? The old Griffin place—?'

'I was talking to a fellow—a Cambridge chap on the dig over the hill, where they're working on that Romano-British village . . . which they *think* may have some Anglo-Saxon burials . . .'

'Yes, dear?' Rachel was just beginning to acclimatize to that harsh reality of her son's greater knowledge in certain areas—like matters Romano-British and Anglo-Saxon, as well as sporting.

'He was very interesting—what he said was, I mean.'

She must be careful not to irritate him with her stupidity. 'About archaeology?' She had driven past the excavations only the day before, and had admired the chequer-board regularity of the work in progress.

'About dustmen, actually.'

'Dustmen?' Now she really had to be careful. So . . . not another word.

'Refuse collectors—garbage men.' Suddenly he was serious. 'You know, *if* my A-levels go okay . . . a big *if*, I agree . . . but *if* they do, and I can get a place at a decent university . . . I wouldn't mind

10

reading archaeology. How do you think Dad would take that?'

Rachel felt assailed on two fronts. 'You'll have to ask him yourself. And it'll be your decision in the end. So long as you don't want to be a dustman . . .'

He looked at her seriously. 'Dustmen have got a lot to answer for.'

'You can say that again.' The weekly struggle to manhandle—or, all too often, to *woman*handle—the dustbins from the kitchen door to the roadside for collection was a sore trial to her. But at least he was changing the subject from a delicate area to a safe one. And, until she had had time to consult Larry—or at least to stop him putting his foot in it—the further away, the better. 'What's all this got to do with the old Griffin place, darling? You know more of it has fallen down since you went away for the summer term? It was in that dreadful storm we had in May—the one that brought down the old plum tree in the orchard.'

'Yes, I know. I had a look not long ago.' He brushed back his hair from his eyes, and looked the image of his father. 'Yesterday, in fact.'

'Yes, darling?' There had been a time when she would have worried about such an exploration, and when it would have been strictly Against the Rules in fact; although, in fact, that had been one rule which the children had never broken. But now he was a big boy. But now, also, she was interested. 'Why did you do that?'

He stared at her for a moment. 'Dustmen, Mother—Rachel. I told you—dustmen. That's the point.'

Rachel could hear her husband clumping finally

from the bathroom to the bedroom upstairs. In a moment or two he would be on the back stair, coming down past the little arrow-slit window from which the surviving chimney of the old Griffin place was still just visible through the trees. 'Well, the point eludes me, darling. Because no dustman ever came within half a mile of old Mrs Griffin's dustbins, if she had such things—that's certain.'

'*Yes*, Mother.' He looked at her a little sadly. 'That *is* certain. *She* didn't—and *they* didn't. And *that* is the whole point.'

Still unenlightened, Rachel took refuge in interested (if not intelligent) silence.

And her silence broke him finally. 'It's all still there. For the finding.'

That broke her. 'What is?'

'Everything. Or, anyway, everything she ever broke, or threw away. Or lost.' Suddenly his voice was eager. 'Remember that old pewter candle-stick I picked up there, years ago? That's still in my room?'

The light dawned, even blazed, suddenly illuminating all his designs. 'But . . . it's a horrible place, Christopher—a *nasty* place—'

'No, it isn't, Mother. It's the ruin of an old farm cottage. And there probably has been a farmhouse hereabouts since medieval times. And . . . maybe the site of the old Griffin place was the original farmhouse, because it has its own pond—the Cambridge chap said it might be. But, anyway, because there weren't any dustmen and garbage collectors in the old days, and it's way off the beaten track—*everything's still all there, you see!*'

'What is all there?' Larry spoke from the open doorway of the back staircase, stooping

12

automatically so as not to knock his head on the beam, years of practice having made him perfect.

'All the accumulated refuse of old Mrs Griffin, dear.' Rachel felt her lips compress. 'And your son wishes to dig it up.'

'Not "dig it up", Mother. *Excavate* it.' Christopher turned to his father. 'Archaeology isn't just Roman and Anglo-Saxon—and prehistoric, and all that. It's anything that's in the past and in the ground. Or above the ground—like . . . like industrial archaeology.'

'It's a perfectly horrible place,' snapped Rachel.

'People excavate Victorian rubbish dumps. And they find quite valuable things,' countered Christopher.

Damn 'the Cambridge chap', thought Rachel. 'And get tetanus, probably.'

Dr Laurence Groom considered his wife and son in turn, and came to a scientist's conclusion inevitably, as Rachel knew he would. 'It sounds interesting.' But at least he had the grace to look at his wife apologetically. 'And . . . I've always wanted to clear that place up. That pond is undoubtedly the breeding place for our mosquitoes.' Then he smiled at his son. 'I doubt that we'll cast any fresh light on the past, to upset the experts. But you never know what we'll find, I agree.'

That, as it transpired, was an understatement. Because, as regards the past and the experts Dr Laurence Groom was wholly wrong.

PART ONE

IAN ROBINSON
AND
THE GHOSTS OF '78

CHAPTER ONE

Ian knew that there was someone in his flat the
moment he opened the door. And then, almost
instantly (and with a mixture of relief and distaste
outweighing surprise and fear), not *someone*, but
Reginald Buller. Once smelt, the special mixture of
cowdung, old tarred rope and probably illegal
substances which Reg Buller smoked was
unforgettable.

As he moved towards the living room door he
wrinkled his nose again, and knew that it wasn't
altogether because of the tobacco, but also because
Jenny had undoubtedly conned him, he realized.
Not only were they already spending good money,
but with her instinct for winners and the
Tully-Buller reputation for getting results, the
pressure to go ahead would likely be irresistible.
Even while seeming to meet his doubts she had
painted him into a corner as usual.

'Hullo, Reg.' He observed simultaneously that
Buller had helped himself to a beer from the fridge
and that he was busy examining the typescripts on
the table. 'Picked the lock, did you?'

'Would I do that?' Buller replaced the papers
without haste, but not very neatly. 'You've got a
nice Chubb lock, in any case.' He grinned at Ian.
'Beyond me, that is. When it comes to
breaking-and-entering, I'm strictly amateur.'

'Well, you certainly didn't climb in.' There was
something utterly disarming about Reg Buller,

although he had never been able to pin it down. But perhaps that was all part of the man's stock-in-trade. 'The back's burglar-proof, I'm reliably informed by the local crime prevention officer. And the front's a bit public on a Sunday morning. Apart from which, the wistaria isn't strong enough—you've put on weight, Reg.'

Buller shook his head. 'Not weight—prosperity, this is. Like the Swedish lady said to me, "Much to hold is much to love." Sheer prosperity, my lad.'

'It looks more like sheer beer-drinking to me. How *did* you get in.'

'Ah . . .' Buller lifted his beer-glass. 'I hoped you wouldn't mind. It's almost sun-over-the yardarm time, and I was thirsty. Besides which, you always have stocks of this good Cologne beer—I remember that from last time. And . . . I am working for you again after all.' He drank. 'Always a pleasure, that is.'

The beer or the work? 'Have another. I'll have one too. When you've told me how you got in, that is.

'This is the other. But I'll have a third—they are *little* ones . . . I used my key.'

'Your . . . *key?*'

'That's the ticket. You lent me a spare last time, when I was in an' out, dropping stuff off. So I had another one cut, just in case.'

Ian felt himself being shepherded towards the kitchen. 'In case of what?'

'In case I had to come calling again. Like, for a rainy day. An' today is rainy, and I knew you'd be at church this morning, like always . . . an' . . . I wanted to catch you before Mr Tully arrives. An' he said 12.30. An' . . . ' He gave Ian a sidelong look.

18

'And?' Ian knew that look of old.

'I wanted to make sure the coast was clear.' Buller studied his beer for a moment. Then drank some of it. Then studied what remained with regret. 'What I always like about Cologne . . . apart from the art galleries, an' the museums, an' all the culture, of course . . . is that, every time your glass gets down to the last inch or so, they just automatically bring you another full one. An' that's what I would describe as a very *civilized* custom . . . Providing you're not driving—because the police are something cruel there, if you've had a couple.'

Ian opened the fridge door. 'Ein Kölsch, Herr Buller?' He waited uneasily while another bottle from his fast depleting stock disappeared. 'What d'you mean—making sure the coast is clear, Reg?'

Buller drank. 'You don't know you're being followed? But then, you wouldn't of course! The Lady might know better . . . but you'd just go walkabout without another thought—I know you!'

Ian thought bitterly of the 'Lady' and of her instincts. But he only thought of her for a moment. Then he started thinking of himself. 'I'm being followed?' He tried to imply a mere wish for confirmation, rather than the actual consternation he was experiencing.

'Oh yes.' Buller nodded. 'Meaning . . . I wasn't *quite* sure. But I looked up the time of your morning service on the board outside the church. An' then I had a careful look-around . . . using a couple of my thousand disguises, naturally . . . An' it seemed to me that you had one at the front, an' one at the back, trying to blend into their surroundings . . . In fact, I nearly phoned up the local nick and tipped 'em off, to see what would

19

happen. But then I thought, we can always do that in future—because I'd have to do it anonymously, see? But you can get the old girl downstairs to do it. An' then we can see whether they do anything about it or not, as the case may be. But we won't have revealed our own guilty interest, if it's official.' This time, as he drank, he rationed himself to one swallow. 'Which I'd guess it is. But it 'ud be nice to be sure, for starters. When you're ready—when you're ready, eh?'

Jenny had been right. But it was all happening too quickly, nevertheless. Which, of course and on second thoughts, made her even more right, damn it! 'What makes you sure—now?'

'When you were out, the chap in the front called up the chap at the back. It's like he's plugged into one of these bloody 'Walkman' things—but he's two-way plugged . . . So they both met up at the corner, down the road. An' then I nipped inside.' Buller put his glass down on the kitchen table. 'Of course, they could have in-depth cover. So that could have blown me, too. But, I thought, if they've got that sort of cover, then I'm probably already blown to hell, anyway—so what the hell!' He grinned again. 'Besides which, it was beginning to rain, an' I haven't got an umbrella—' he shrugged '—an' I remembered about your beer supplies, too. An' I'm not charging for Sunday work. Not until 12.15. Plus travel expenses. So . . . so, actually, you're still on my private time now, without the meter running.'

Ian's thoughts had become cold and hard as he listened, like thick ice over bottomless Arctic water: it had been like this in Beirut, when Jenny had been doing the leg-work as usual in the misplaced belief

20

that the fundamentalist snatch-squad didn't rate women (or, if they did, they couldn't handle the indelicacies of kidnapping one), and he had been holed up in the hotel.

'They're back in place now, getting nicely soaked. So you'll have to go out again later on, with your lady and my Mr Tully to draw 'em off.' Buller nodded into his silence. 'Which the three of you all together certainly will, goin' out all together—*no! For fuck's sake don't go and have a look—!*' Buller slid sideways, to block his path. 'Let's be nice and innocent for as long as we can, eh?'

Questions crowded Ian's mind. 'What made you . . . suspicious?' It was an inadequate word, knowing Buller. But it was suitably vague.

'Huh!' Short of another beer, Buller produced an immense gunmetal lighter with which to set fire to the foul mixture in his pipe, which surely resisted conventional combustion methods. 'As soon as Mr Tully mentioned Masson's name, I thought "Ay-aye! Watch yourself, Reg!"'

'Why?' Ian remembered what Tully had said the first time he'd mentioned Reginald Buller's name: that, whatever you do, wherever you wanted to go, Buller was halfway there before you started towards it.

'I never did rate that much—a senior civil servant lost at sea: "what a terrible tragedy!" . . . I never rated that, not even at the time.' Buller shook his head. 'I thought . . . here we go again, I thought—' A foul smoke-screen enveloped him momentarily, so that he had to wave his hand to disperse it '—I thought *aye-aye!*'

'But there was nothing ever known against Philip Masson, Reg.'

21

'Nor there was. And that was what I thought next—quite right, when that was all there was.' This time, a nod of agreement. 'But when he turned up again . . . an' miles from the sea, an' dry as a bone—' From shake, through nod, to shake again '—what sort of tragedy was that, then?'

That had been what Jenny had wanted to know. Or, anyway, it had been the beginning of what she had wanted to know. 'You tell me, Reg—?'

'Hmm . . .' Somehow they had progressed out of the dining room and past the study door (and Reginald Buller would have examined all the 'Work in progress' there, too, for a certain guess), into the living room again; but Reg was blocking off the approach to the glorious bow-window, just in case.

'Well?'

'No bugger's saying anything. And you can't get near where they dug him up.' Buller scratched the back of his head. 'They've got the local coppers out, both sides of the place, guarding it. There are a couple on the back road to it, never mind the front . . . And it was two kids who found the body. But you can't get to them, either. And the parents aren't talking to anyone.' Another shake. 'And I had to be bloody careful, because there were one or two people there I know, sniffing around, buying drinks—from the *Guardian*, and the *Mirror* . . . and so maybe from the big Sundays, too. And the *Independent*, could be . . . But, the point is, there's a *smell* about it—about Masson—is what there is.'

'So you didn't get anything—?' He knew Reg Buller better than that.

'Oh . . .' Buller bridled slightly, on his mettle '. . . there was this barmaid I chatted up, who knew someone in the coroner's office. And *she* said . . .

22

that *he* said . . . that Masson was *planted*. And—'

'Planted—?'

'Buried.' Nod. 'In a hole.' Another nod. 'He didn't fall out of the sky, or trip over an' hit his head, or shoot himself, or have a heart attack.' Final nod. 'The way some of the stories go, there was this pond, an' he was *in* it. So . . . I thought he could have fallen into it—or maybe even jumped into it . . . But that isn't the way it was, apparently. Because these children *dug him up*, it seems.'

'Why—*how* . . . did they do that?' Both questions pressed equally.

'God knows! But it seems that they did. So . . . someone buried him. So someone killed him first—that's what the barmaid said. And I paid her £50 not to tell anyone else. Although it's even money that I may have made her greedy, so I can't be sure that I haven't wasted . . . *your* money, my lad—eh?'

Ian winced inwardly at Tully's final bill, which would pile his VAT on Reg Buller's VAT, to complicate matters even if they could finally claim it back; although Jenny's friendly accountants would sort that out for them, also at a price. But he mustn't think of such mundane things now. 'And that was all you got?'

Reg Buller looked offended. 'That was all I thought it safe to try and get, the way things smelt. Besides which, I rather thought I had other fish to fry, on instruction. Or rather . . . not other fish—*another* fish . . . other than Masson, I mean . . .' He tailed off.

'*Another* . . . fish?'

'Well . . . not a fish, exactly.' Buller drew deeply on his pipe. 'More like a shark, if you ask me—' he

23

breathed out a foul cloud of smoke '—like, in that film: something you go out to catch . . . but you end up trying not to get caught yourself, maybe.' He drew on his pipe again.

'You mean the man Audley? David Audley' Ian remembered Jenny's original proposition: she had come to him late at night—or, more precisely, early in the morning, after one of her socialite nights-on-the-tiles—getting him out of bed when he was at his lowest ebb—

'Darling, I think I've stumbled onto something really quite interesting—have you got a drink?' (Jenny bright-eyed, even at that unearthly hour, happily burning her candle at both ends and only a little tousled even now, having progressed from a day's work to an embassy party, and then to an elongated dinner, and finally to some flutter 'on the tables' in some hell-hole; except that Jenny had the stamina of a plough-horse and an alcoholic capacity rivalling Reg Buller's, so it always seemed.)

'Jenny!' (At least he had been halfways respectable, face quickly washed, hair quickly brushed, dressing-gown carefully and decently adjusted: only Jenny dared to burst in on him in the smallest hours—she had done it before, and he was half-prepared for such eventualities now.) *'For heaven's sake, Jen! Couldn't it wait until the morning?'* (But, strictly speaking, it had been the morning, of course.) *'You shouldn't be walking the streets now—they're not safe. I'll ring for a taxi—'*

'I've got a taxi—it's parked outside. The dear man said he'd be quite happy to wait, darling—he said just the same thing.' (Running taxi-meters aside, Jenny

24

could get round any man to do her will
her mind to it.) 'So . . . *just get me that dri*
I have to make it myself?'

'*I'll get you a coffee*—'

'*Don't be such a fuddy-duddy, Ian darling!*
. . . have you ever heard of a man named A
Ian?'

'*Who*—?' (If she was determined to
alcohol, then he would pour it.)

'*Audley. AUDLEY—Audley? Christian n*
"David"—?'

'No.' (He had recognized the sign then: the
innocent eyes weren't alcohol bright, but excite
even, possibly, she hadn't had a drink since tha
sudden stumble-onto-something, whenever it had
occurred; and all the rest of the evening-into-
night-into-morning had been cold hard professional Jenny; which was why she needed a drink
now.)

'*No. But you have heard of Philip Masson, maybe?'*

'Yes.' (That had been insulting—and deliberately
so! But now he was hooked.) '*And who is . . . David*
Audley", then?'

'Mr David Audley—yes. Or, to give him his proper
title, *Doctor* David Audley.' Reg Buller sniffed,
wrinkling the hairs on his drinker's nose. 'But not a
medical doctor—a *philosophy* doctor . . . Cambridge
"Ph.D."—or "D.Phil", whichever it is.' The big
red-and-blue veined nose wrinkled again: Reg
Buller had a huge dislike-and-contempt for
Oxbridge products, derived from bitter experience
of Whitehall and Westminster in his policeman
days. 'Only, not a philosophy doctor, either—a
history doctor—' The nose seemed to swell as its

unded blob-end lifted '—*ancient* history, too.'

But Ian had progressed since Jenny's untimely escent on him. 'Medieval history actually, Reg.'

'Oh aye?' Buller accepted the correction as a further confirmation of cause-for-contempt. 'Looked him up in *Who's Who*, have you? But what about his book on the *Latin* kingdom of Jerusalem, eh? Because, in *my* book, "Latin" is bloody ancient—right?'

'No. "Wrong" actually. The Latin Kingdom of Jerusalem was eleventh to twelfth century, as it happens. Not that it matters.' Compared with Philip Masson it certainly didn't matter. But a long passion for getting facts right, and for sorting the golden nuggets of truth from Jenny's loaded conveyor-belt of hearsay, rumour and gossip, forced him to react before he could stop himself. And then he had to put matters straight, into their priorities. 'He's a shark, is he, Reg?'

Buller's face worked, as he came back from what didn't matter to what did, which he had presumably uncovered during his second day of fish-frying for Tully and Jenny. And that also transformed Ian's own imagery, from dusty manuscripts in university libraries to that fearful triangular dorsal fin cutting through the water, and then submerging as the killer disappeared, rolling underwater to open its razor-sharp jaws as it came to dine on its prey.

'He could be. Or . . . seeing how he's a big bugger—six-foot-two, or six-foot-three, in his stocking feet . . . and a rugger-player when he was young . . . maybe one of those bigger ones—black-and-white, and *clever* with it . . . not sharks, though—?'

26

'Killer whales?' Black-and-white were the Death's Head colours, he dredged the memory up from his subconscious: not only of killer whales, or of the murderous magpies which killed small birds outside his window in the country cottage where he always put the finishing touches to each new book; black-and-white had been the colours of all those famous regiments, with skull-and-crossbones badges, like military pirates—and even of Audley's medieval Knights Templar, in his crusading Latin Kingdom; and, for that matter, the young men who squired Jenny to perdition on her late nights wore the same non-colours too, damn it!

But something had intruded into the sequence: he had heard the bell, and Buller's face had closed up as he heard it. And he cursed himself for not reacting more quickly to Buller's warning, now that Tully had arrived—or Jenny, or Jenny and Tully together—now that *someone* was interested in what they were up to—

'*Damn!*' He tossed his head irritably at Buller. 'I should have put them off, Reg! We could have met somewhere else.'

Buller shook his head. 'Wouldn't have done any good. If they're on to you, they'll be on to them . . . Just so they're not on to *me*.' He grinned. 'And even if they are, I can lose 'em any time. And, what's more . . . they won't even know it: they'll think they've been careless.' The grin became confiding. Then it vanished. 'Mr Tully and your lady don't know how—they'd only give the game away. Better not to tell them straight off.'

'I've got to tell them; Reg.' Ian felt increasingly uneasy as he spoke. Because while Tully was sensible enough to be scared, this news would only

27

strengthen Jenny's suspicion, turning it into a certainty.

'Wait! Hold on a mo'—' Reg Buller sidled sideways to block his passage again '—all this rabbiting on about Latin Kingdoms, and sharks—' The bell rang again '—let 'em ring—*hold on!*'

'What?' Ian stopped. 'What—'

'Just listen.' Buller almost pushed him back. 'You've tipped me off, on occasion . . . And you've recommended me—given me custom— *I know* . . . So, then, I owe you—right?'

'You don't owe me anything.'

'Okay. So all the bills have been paid, for the tax-man, and the VAT man.' Buller nodded. 'And in a minute I'll be on my usual rate—okay . . . See?' He ignored the angry ringing behind him. 'But *this* minute I'm still on my own time. So this is for free, then—right? And just between the two of us.'

Ian frowned at him. 'You'd better be quick. Or they'll think—'

'This bloke Audley—' Buller overbore him. '—I've got a feeling in my water about him. You want to watch yourself. And don't let the Lady push you where you don't want to go—not this time. That's all.' He stared at Ian for a moment, and then tossed his head. 'Let 'em in, then—go on!'

Ian sprinted towards the now-continuous bell, which meant that it was Jenny out there, without a doubt.

'Sorry, Jen—' He caught sight of Tully beyond her— '—hullo, John.'

'I should think so!' She pulled off her headscarf and shook a tangle of half-combed red hair. 'You look positively guilty, too.' She scrutinized him

28

momentarily. 'In fact, if I didn't know you better, Ian Robinson—and if I didn't know that it was Sunday . . . it *is* Sunday, isn't it?' She sniffed Reg Buller's tobacco appreciatively.

'It is for me.' He returned the scrutiny. Without make-up but with dark smudges under her eyes, she presented a curious mixture of innocence and depravity. 'But you look like you've had your weekend already, Miss Fielding-ffulke. And lost it.'

'Very funny.' She turned to Tully. 'As I was saying . . . if I didn't know him better, I'd say he'd got a girl in the bedroom, hunting desperately for her knickers right now. But—'

'No such luck.' Buller spoke from the sitting-room doorway. 'Sorry to disappoint you, madam. But all he's got is me. And I'm only hunting for beer.'

'Reg!' The night before seemed to drop away from her. 'John said you might be here—that you'd agreed to come to our aid at short notice. It's great to see you again! And . . . we do *need* you.'

'Always a pleasure, madam.' In Jenny's presence, Buller always took refuge in the practised insincerity of his long-lost police constable self: for some reason her charm had always been lost on him, Ian remembered from the past. Which was all the more curious because in his case the charm was not consciously turned on, she had a genuine regard for his skill, and a huge soft spot for him to go with it. And now he himself must take account of that unrequited admiration in assessing the worth of Buller's warning.

'Don't keep calling me "madam", Reg, for God's sake!' She made a face at Buller.

'No, Miss Fielding-ff—'

29

'And *don't* call me that, either.' She cut him off quickly. 'If "Jenny" is too much for you . . . I'm not responsible for the absurdities of my ancestors . . . so I'll settle for "Fielding". Okay?' Under the soft, almost pleading tone, there was the steely ancestral Fielding-ffulke voice of command, at which generations of Bullers (and Robinsons too) had jumped to obey. 'Okay. So what have you got for us on Philip Masson and David Audley?'

'I have prepared a report, Miss Fielding.' Buller looked at Tully. 'A written report.'

'It's all right, Mr Buller.' Immaculate as ever and secure in his Winchester tie, Tully nevertheless jumped no less smartly. 'Just the salient points now.'

Jenny caught Ian's eye. 'Reg would probably like a drink, Ian. And I certainly would. The last lot of church bells I heard, I counted to twelve.'

'No.' It wasn't just that the Robinsons no longer obeyed the Fielding-ffulkes automatically, it was also to suggest that Buller hadn't been with him for long. 'I want to hear what Reg has to say first. Go on, Reg.'

'Right, Mr Robinson.' Buller played back to him exactly the correct note of disappointment. 'Masson was murdered—and Audley works for the cloak-and-dagger brigade. Ours, that is.'

'But Reg . . . we *know* all that—'

'No you don't, Miss Fielding. At least, you may know about Dr Audley—someone may have told you. But it's not written down anywhere. Officially, he's a civil servant on contract, serving on a liaison committee of some sort—no one seems to know quite what—advising various ministries on research projects. And no one knows quite what they are,

30

either. Right, Johnny?'

Tully nodded. 'Yes. More or less.'

'Yes. Well, I'm telling you that he works for intelligence *for a fact*.' Buller paused only for half a second. 'And the same goes for Masson: the rumour's all round The Street—and down Murdoch's place in Wapping—that he was murdered. But the Police haven't said any such thing, they've been shut up tight from the top now. Believe me, I can read the signs. So I'm just giving you what they'd be saying if they hadn't been shut up.'

'Actually, there have been quite a few rumours,' said Tully. 'There was one that he drowned—drowned himself, that is.'

'Oh yes.' Buller nodded. 'I didn't say they haven't said *anything*. First off . . . first off it was "probably an ancient burial". Because they're always digging up old bones round there, apparently. Then there was an old local story, that it might be some poor old bloke who'd lived there in the First World War, who'd gone missing in the trenches and laid low. And then got influenza—there was a lot of that about in the village at the time. So his old woman had just buried him nice and quietly—it's miles from anywhere, on the edge of the marsh there, so she could have done that quite easily, and no one the wiser. But then it all blew up in their faces, of course.'

'They got an identification, you mean?'

Buller grinned. 'Someone blundered, that's what.'

'How d'you mean—"blundered", Reg?' inquired Ian. 'The Police?'

31

'No, not the Police. Although I think there was rather more tramping around in the first hours than they'd like to admit—"Isolate the scene", that's Rule Number One. But then, of course, these kids dug up the body, playing about . . . so they'd already made a right mess of it.' Buller shrugged. 'After that, it would have all been routine. And they'd have twigged pretty damn quickly that it really wasn't an ancient body, too—that 'ud put 'em into gear, if they weren't in it already. Not exactly top gear, like with a fresh body, when getting quick off the mark is half the battle, often . . . but putting the forensics to work and checking the records—B14, Missing Persons . . . Salvation Army, Alcoholics Anonymous—they all come into it.' Another shrug. 'Bloody thousands of people missing. So it's always nice to find one.'

'Even a dead one?' Jenny frowned at him.

'Even a dead one. You ask a farmer about his missing sheep: he'd rather find one dead than one missing—leastways, if it's been long gone. At least he *knows* then. And maybe he can do something about it. And that's the way the Police have to think, to make the best of it.' He stared at her for a moment. '"Missing Persons" is a pretty thankless job, I tell you. And a gut-twisting one too, when you have to tell some poor middle-aged couple that their fifteen-year-old daughter—or son now, the way things are—is probably out on the streets, earning money the easiest way.' He paused again. 'A lot of heartache in "Missing Persons", Lady.'

Tully stirred, almost as though embarrassed by this revelation of a social conscience where no sort of conscience should be, inside Reginald Buller. 'Who blundered then, Mr Buller?'

32

'Some civil servant.' Buller brightened at the thought. 'Probably one of your Dr Audley's colleagues, hiding his light under some committee.' He brought his lighter up to his pipe, but then thought better. 'Or maybe someone was on holiday—like Audley is at the moment. And some poor bloody clerk standing in for him didn't get to the bottom of his in-tray before the weekend. And then another load of bumpf went on the top of it on Monday morning. So he's for the chop now—' He glanced sidelong at Jenny '—or she is, now that we're all equal.'

Jenny merely smiled. 'The identification?'

'That's right. Teeth, most like—they're always the best ID.' Buller returned the smile. 'If you're going to plant someone, Miss Fielding . . . take my tip: cut the hands and the head off, smash the jaw up, and drop the bits off in a few dustbins just before the refuse truck comes round. Then dig a deep hole for the rest, where it isn't likely to be dug up by kids.' As he spoke the smile utterly vanished. 'But, whatever it was tipped 'em off . . . and I don't know it was teeth . . . the identification got out before anyone could sit on it, and that's a fact.' He switched to Tully. 'And that put the newspapers on to it. Masson being in *their* "Missing Persons" file of course. And then the fat was in the fire.' The smile returned, but in a thinner form. 'All just routine—getting the right file, or the right print-out. But this time in the wrong order.'

'So where did my drowning rumour come from?' Tully's pale intellectual face was expressionless. 'I thought it came from the Police?'

Buller nodded. 'So it did. But not officially. Seems like it was a "tip-off", from lower

33

down—like one of the DCs feeding one of the local journalists, off the record, supposedly. But it wasn't that at all, of course.'

'Disinformation?' Having been disinformed many times over recent years, Jenny was quick on that particular ball.

'*Dis*information—yes.' Buller liked accurate passing. 'Could have been the same clerk, trying to shut the stable door after the horse was already meat in the knacker's yard, as best he could. Or she could.' Half-smile, half-shrug. 'There is a lake there . . . or a pond, so they say.'

'You haven't seen the place?' Tully pursed his lips. 'Actually *seen* it—?'

'Not a chance.' Buller returned slight contempt for this hint of disapproval. 'It's guarded round the clock—an' Special Branch from London as well as the locals. An' it's a bloody isolated spot, too . . . plus I'm not about to display myself, snooping around, to be photographed for the record. That wouldn't be good for business.' He looked to Ian for support. 'Yours as well as mine?'

'He wasn't found in the pond—the lake?' Ian rose obligingly. 'The children dug him up. And . . . all the initial rumours were . . . *digging-up* ones?' Remembering what Buller had said when they were alone, it was easy.

'That is exactly right, Mr Robinson.' Buller nodded formally. 'The original story was drowning—"drowned at sea". An' then the first story was "ancient bones" dug up. An' then his name slipped out—an' then it was "drowning" again. But that won't stick for ever.' He shook his head. 'Maybe, if they'd had time to doctor the evidence . . . or, at least, to confuse it . . . then

34

they just might have made a drowning stick.' He looked from one to the other of them. 'Although, with policemen, and coroners, and all the rest . . . that's not so easy, I can tell you. But they might at least have bought more time, anyway. But *this* time . . . they didn't.' He ended with Jenny. 'He was buried, Miss Fielding. Not very deeply—not deep enough . . . But *buried*, for sure.' Single nod. 'And the fact that they first tried to change the story . . . and now they've got the place, and everyone in it, buttoned up like Greenham Common used to be on Easter weekend—all that merely confirms everyone's suspicions that there's some sort of cover-up in progress.' This time, not a nod, but a sly face. 'Oh yes—the vultures are out, as you would expect: I recognized a few old acquaintances, trying to drink the pubs dry on expenses. And there were some young hopefuls, too—'

'And they recognized you, presumably?' Tully's lips tightened again. Then he sniffed. 'Or smelt you.'

Buller looked disappointed. 'Come on, Johnny—would I work for any clients of ours without a cover story? You know me better than that. Not on something like this, that's been in the papers. You're not the only one with a sense of smell.'

Ian caught Jenny's eye, and her smile. The last time Reg Buller had worked for them he had also had a 'cover'. And it had been so genuine that he had happily collected double fees and double expenses from it. But as he watched her, he observed that the smile was only on her lips, not in her eyes. And it faded quickly.

'Your old acquaintances, Reg . . . what lines are

35

they following, do you know?' She sounded almost casual.

'I don't honestly know, Lady. I was too busy being not very interested in their business. But I doubt they've got much of value as yet, the way things are. Not until the inquest is resumed, they won't have anything to get their teeth into. And you can bet they'll be delayed as long as possible.' Buller cocked an eye at Tully. 'It'll be the backroom boys digging out the old cuttings on Masson at the moment, in preparation for that. So you'd better watch your step there, Johnny, if you're thinking of asking to have a look at him in your favourite newspaper library. Because they know you've worked for your present clients before.'

Tully touched his tie. 'Don't worry, Mr Buller. That's already all taken care of.' He acknowledged Jenny and Ian in turn. 'I have a very fair dossier on Philip Masson. And there won't be any comeback.'

That was going to cost them, thought Ian. Because, although Tully's own highly-computerized filing system was pretty damn good in its own right (and expensive to get into, also), it still couldn't match the better newspaper libraries. But newspaper librarians wouldn't come cheap either, those of them who could be bought. Or their assistants. Or whoever had access, down the line. But more than that, and regardless of expense, Tully was very certain of himself today: certain, although this had been contractually no more than a quick reconnaissance of a possibility, that he had Fielding and Robinson as full-blown clients again.

He examined them both with professional interest: the well-laundered, Winchester-tied Tully,

36

very confident; and the crumpled, smelly old Buller, no less a pro, albeit in his own distinctive style. But now, although Buller had given him the gypsy's warning, they were both equally excited at the prospect of profit and enjoyment.

'Yes.' Tully looked at him, and he realized that all three were looking at him, willing him to show enthusiasm. Even Buller, after what he'd said, was willing it. 'I don't think you need worry too much about the newshounds at the moment, Mr Robinson.'

'Why not?' In a position of strength he could afford to be awkward.

'Well . . . firstly, because of the timing, I rather think.'

'The timing?'

'Of Masson's death. It occurred at the very end of the Wilson-Callaghan era, in 1978. So they can't pin this on the Tories, in general—or on our present dear Prime Minister, in particular. If there was a cover-up, that is . . .' He smiled thinly. 'That takes some of the fun out of it, you might say. And the urgency with it.'

There was a flaw in that reasoning, thought Ian: pre-Thatcher shenanigans in British Intelligence could always be dressed up as 'destabilization', post-*Spycatcher*. But he didn't know enough about Philip Masson yet to undress that possibility.

'And none of them are on to Audley yet.' Tully bowed slightly to Jenny. 'Your ace in the hole is still safe, Miss Fielding. You're way ahead of them all.' Then he remembered Ian. 'If you want to proceed, that is.'

Ian was glad that he had resisted the temptation to look at Buller whose buttocks were still firmly

37

seated on that unpalatable information about the watchers outside, which would prick Tully's bubble of complacency explosively. But that in turn presented him with an immediate dilemma: because *someone* was alongside them already, if not actually ahead of them, and that was a damn good reason for exercising his veto, and proceeding with the book they had planned to write, which presented no great problems, reasonable (and certain) profits, and absolutely no Beirut-remembered dangers.

So this was that 'moment-of-truth' Jenny always made him face up to, when they had to decide to go ahead with a project after the first reconnaissance, or to cut their losses and start on something else. Only this was already different from all their other investigations—and not different just because of those two men outside in the rain: it was different also because it seemed to matter personally to her, not just financially. So, if he said 'no' she'd not only never forgive him, but she might also go ahead on her own account, without his protective presence—?

He couldn't have that, no matter how much against his better judgement, not after Beirut.

'I think I'll get that drink now. Dry sherry for you, John?' He didn't need to look at Tully.

'Beer for me.' Reg Buller beamed at him. 'One of those little bottles of that German beer? Have you got any of them?'

He didn't need to look at her, either: for her there was their 'moment-of-truth' custom. All he saw was the pile of papers he'd taken out of the study that morning, slightly disarranged as Buller had left them. So now the future of British education would have to wait until this matter of the past of British Intelligence had been resolved, he thought sadly.

It was all conveniently in the fridge—John Tully's Manzanilla, Reg Buller's Kölsch, and Jenny's celebratory bottle (even though he didn't feel like celebrating).

'Oh Ian darling!' She pushed through the door just as the cork *popped*, and the champagne overflowed the glasses messily. 'Thank you, darling!'

'Don't count your chickens, Jen.' He watched the ridiculously over-priced stuff subside. 'I still don't like it. And I think we could be risking our necks.'

'Of course, darling. But . . .' She swayed towards him, both hands full but still holding the door half open with her shoulder. '. . . but—' her voice dropped to a wide-mouthed whisper, enunciated as though to a deaf lip-reader '—I-have-got-promises- of-absolutely-marvellous-deals . . . from . . . Clive Parsons . . . *and* Woodward—Richard Woodward?' She read his expression, and nodded triumphantly.

Ian reached out to push the door fully open, knowing that that triumphant nod would have had to be the clincher if he had been genuinely still in doubt: with Woodward controlling the serializations on the front page of his heavyweight Sunday's supplement, to coincide with publication, and Parsons' publishers' clout in the American press, they had the necessary ingredients for another best-seller before he had put one word on paper; and if Jenny's rarely mistaken nose for a winner didn't let them down they stood to make a

39

small fortune. Or even a large one. And that was more than could be expected from British education.

'John—Reg—' She took the two untasted glasses in with a glance '—I've just been twisting Ian's arm unmercifully—' She raised her own glass '—so I think we can now drink to . . . what?' She zeroed in on Reg Buller. 'Murder, for a start?'

Buller drank without answering, keeping his counsel dry as an infantryman's powder.

Tully sipped his sherry, and from the look on his face either approved of its dryness or was thinking of his fees. 'Treason, for choice, Miss Fielding. With murder in a chief supporting role, perhaps—?' Then (as before) he remembered Ian. *'Pro bono publico,* of course . . . But it isn't Masson who is primarily interesting, interesting though he undoubtedly is . . . even *very* interesting, if I may say so.' He smiled his thinnest, driest-sherry smile at Jenny. 'But Audley is the one who matters.'

'Why do you say that, John?' Jenny watched him over her glass.

'Don't you agree?'

'Back in '78—'79?' She accepted the challenge casually. 'Whenever it was, anyway . . . Philip Masson was more influential than Audley—at least, potentially, anyway.'

'Was he?' He let her steel rasp down his blade. Either, they had already rehearsed this for his benefit, thought Ian—or, if they hadn't, then they were manoeuvring to find out how much the other knew. 'I would have thought that was . . . arguable, at the least?'

Jenny shrugged, and refilled her glass: since Tully was their employee now, at his usual rate, she was not minded to play games with him, the gesture implied. 'Philip Masson's dead and Audley's alive.'

'A very proper conclusion.' Because he had picked up her signal, Tully agreed with her. But because he was Tully he couldn't resist talking down to her. '*However* dead, in precise and gruesome detail, is of no interest, now that Mr Buller has pronounced on it.' He hardly glanced at Buller. 'And by *whomsoever* dead—by whose actual *hand* . . . that is merely a police matter. And I think it exceedingly unlikely that they will ever put their cuffs on that particular hand . . . And, if they can't then we won't.' He only had eyes for Jenny now, in proclaiming his limitations. 'But it won't have been Audley, anyway.'

'Why not?' The question came, surprisingly, from Buller—perhaps because the emptiness of his glass made him irritable.

'Why not?' This time Tully gave Buller his full attention. And although there was no surprise in his repetition of the question, there was a matching hint of irritation. 'I hope you haven't exceeded your brief, Mr Buller.'

'Ah! My brief . . .' Buller sucked in his cheeks slightly, and gave Tully back scrutiny for scrutiny, like a man who knows his rights as well as his place. 'No, I wouldn't say that, Johnny—no.'

'No?' Tully smiled suddenly, almost proprietorially. But then, of course, each of them knew his man, Ian reminded himself: the Tully-Buller relationship went back a long way, to the days when neither of them was engaged in his present avocation. 'Then . . . what would you say?'

For a moment Ian was tempted to suspect that he might be a potential client treated to a piece of

41

rehearsed dialogue, to which Buller's earlier confidences had been a mere prologue. But now that he'd as good as taken Jenny's hook (and theirs) such dramatics were hardly necessary; and Buller's thoughtful expression and elongated silence served to remind him of the watchers in the rain outside.

'What exactly was your brief, Mr Buller—' Jenny cracked first '—*your* brief, Reg—?'

Buller kept both bloodshot eyes on Tully for another five seconds'-worth of silence before turning to her, as though the sound of her voice had had to travel across some unimaginable distance before it had reached him. 'Just like always, madam—Miss Fielding: I take off my boot, an' then my sock . . . an' I dip my big toe in the water, to test the temperature.' He gave her his ex-policeman's smile of false encouragement. 'An' of course, I do all that behind some convenient bush, so no joker can swipe my boot when I'm not looking. As a precaution, like.'

'I see.' Even when a client, Jenny was patient in the face of such stone-walling. 'And how was the water, then—in that pond, where Philip Masson didn't drown . . . which you didn't actually see, you said—?'

'Warm, Miss Fielding.' Buller accepted the sharp points of her little claws approvingly, as though not being punctured would have disappointed him.

'Warm.' Jenny had drawn blood from harder stones than Reg Buller. 'Meaning . . . warm-cooling-down? Or warm-hotting-up, Reg?'

Buller liked that too—her acceptance of his imagery. But that, by some special alchemy, was the effect she always had, even on the most unregenerate chauvinist-pig, one way or another,

42

sooner or later. 'It may not warm up much down there, now. It could be just the place where he finished up . . .' He shrugged. 'He didn't live there. He may not even have died there.'

'But—?' She picked up the vibration instantly.

'Somebody planted him there. So somebody knew it was there—that's a fair bet.' Another shrug. 'All these years . . . that may be hard to pin down usefully. But if I was running the Incident Room I'd be waiting for that to register on the computer, anyway.' Nod. 'Because, although that isn't so very far from London there, it's still country—*deep* country . . . Or, it was then. And it's amazing what long memories they have, the country-folk. Like, I told you: there was this tale about the soldier who went missing in the war . . . And *not* Dr David Audley's war—or even his father's war, which was the same one—the '39–'45 one. But the one before that, with all the trenches and the barbed-wire . . . And *that* is a long memory for you.'

'But that was a story, not a memory, Reg—' Jenny started, razorsharp as ever, but then caught herself. 'But . . . go on—?'

'That's all. For Masson, for my money, there's still something down there. But there's no way we can get at it at this moment—not without crossing the locals, never mind whoever else is nosing around. There just aren't enough bushes you can hide behind, to drop your boot.'

'Yes. I see.' She had what she wanted there. 'But . . . you put your toe in . . . I can't say "Audley's water" without seeming indelicate, Reg . . . but you did take your boot off for him too, didn't you—yes?'

43

'Took it off, aye. Didn't dip me toe, though.'
'Why not?'
'Didn't need to.' Buller paused. 'Didn't want to, either.' He cocked his head slightly. 'Remember that book you and Mr Robinson did a few years back, about the Vietnam business, and all that?'

Jenny frowned. *The Vietnam Legacy?* Yes, Reg—?' The frown cleared slightly. 'You and John did some of the leg-work for us, of course. You covered that Chicago reunion I couldn't get to—and you traced that amazing Green Beret man who ran that mission up in the mountains, out West.'

'That's the ticket. The Grand Tetons. Always wanted to see them, ever since I saw 'em in *Shane* when I was a lad.' The eye cocked at Ian. 'Didn't see 'em though, did I! Low cloud, there was, the whole time I was there—d'you recall me telling you about it?'

'I do, Reg.' What Ian chiefly remembered was Buller's explanation that 'Grand Tetons' meant 'Big Tits'. 'But what have the . . . Grand Tetons to do with Audley, Reg?'

'Not the Grand Tetons.' The ghost of a wink accompanied the name. 'After I'd finished with Major Kasik I had a day or two spare, so I drove up from Jackson Hole to Yellowstone, where there's this great big National Park, with all the "geysers" spouting and fuming. And it was autumn then, with a nip in the air, like it might start snowing any moment . . . And there are all these little pools of water, clear as crystal and fresh-looking, with lovely colours—pale blues, and greeny-blues . . . In the hot summer maybe they'd look cool, but when it's colder you might reckon they'd be just nice an' warm, to take the chill off your fingers—or your

44

toes.' As he spoke. Buller turned back to Jenny. 'But it 'ud do a bit more than that. Because it's bloody boiling, scalding hot, is what it is—one dip, and you're cooked to the bone. And no saying "Ouch! I won't do it again!" and "Next time I'll know better", and "Now I want to go home".' He flicked a glace at Tully. 'If it's Dr David Audley you're after, then it's in for a penny, in for a pound—no half-measures, Lady.'

For a moment no one wanted to break the silence which followed this latest gypsy's warning, the truth of which Ian knew that he alone shared with Reg Buller. And, when he thought about it, the only truly curious aspect of it was that, if it was true, Buller himself had turned up at the rendezvous this morning, in spite of his own well-developed sense of self-preservation. But then, when he took the thought further, there were a lot of contradictory aspects in Buller's character and *curriculum vitae*.

Then Jenny filled her glass again. 'Ian—?' She glanced quickly at John Tully's glass, knowing that it would still be half-full, before returning to Buller. 'Are you trying to frighten me, Reg?'

Buller held out his empty glass. 'Would I do that, Miss Fielding?'

'Champagne, Reg? On top of beer?' But she poured, nevertheless. '*Yes*—if you thought it would do any good.'

'Any port in a storm, madam—even fizzy rubbish.' The bulbous nose wrinkled again. 'And therefore . . . *no* . . . because I know you've already made up your mind.' He took another gulp, and

45

spluttered. 'But you have been paying for a "reconnaissance", and that's what *I* have given you.'

The emphasis on Buller's first person singular—and no one, not even John Tully, and not even Jenny herself, was a more singular first person—gave Ian his opening. 'Are you saying that we're already blown, Reg?'

'What?' John Tully was bristling, before he spoke.

'You said . . . we were "already" in for a pound . . . having spent some of our pennies, Reg.' He drew Buller's attention, overriding Tully. 'Does that mean someone is on to us—*already?*'

Buller concealed any gratitude he might have behind another gulp, and another hiccup. 'Well . . . maybe you've been up to something I don't know about, Mr Robinson—like having some young lady in your bedroom, and a jealous husband . . . like it would have been in the old days.' He grinned, and then nodded at the typescript on the table. 'But with the book you're writing . . . I don't see the National Union of Teachers—or the Department of Education, and that Mr Baker—hiring anyone to watch this place, to see who comes in, an' goes out, of a wet Sunday morning, anyway.' He carried on the nod towards the window, out of which only well-bred, or well-heeled, or otherwise upwardly-mobile local Hampstead residents might be observed at such times, down Holly Row. 'But someone is watching you, and that's a fact.'

To their credit, nobody moved to verify this information; at least, neither Jenny nor John Tully moved—and then Ian realized that, since he ought

46

to be less professional as well as equally shattered by this news, he *ought* to move—

'*Ian*—*!*' Jenny admonished him sharply. '*Don't look!*'

Ian halted, fixing her first, almost accusingly; and then John Tully, almost angrily; and finally Reg himself, with a mixture of emotions which he couldn't control, but which only Reg himself could guess at.

'There's one at the back, too.' Buller agreed with all the confusion cheerfully. 'They've got you nicely bracketed . . . unless you've got another exit, up over the roof, an' down through someone else's back garden—have you?'

'John—?' Jenny cut through Buller's cackle decisively. 'You said no one was on to us—?'

Tully stared at her, and then clear through her, as he computed the possibilities, one after another, trying to pin a probability among them. But then he frowned. 'I don't understand it, Miss Fielding. Because . . . I do know a little—a very little—about Audley. So I was damned careful with him: only the people I can *really* trust, I asked—' His face closed up tight round his mouth '—only the people who owe me.'

'Well, it wasn't me.' Buller knew he'd be next. 'Unless anyone who appears anywhere near Masson sparks 'em off—that's maybe it. But I was careful, too. And they didn't follow me here, either—you can depend on that: they were here already: I spotted *them*, they didn't spot *me*—you can depend on that, too.'

But that was a hard one, thought Ian—estimating the known Buller against the unknown Audley. Because his confidence was only one step away from

47

pride. And pride was always inches away from a fall, remembering Beirut—

'It might have been me.' Jenny's total honesty was one of her greatest strengths. 'I've asked one or two questions, just recently. And I can't vouch for everyone whom I've asked—' She embraced Tully with that admission, binding him to her even more securely with it '—and then they'd come to Ian, of course . . . So it might be me, I'm afraid.'

'Well, it doesn't matter who it was, Miss Fielding.' Delivered from all responsibility for failure, Tully became loyal again, as an employee. 'The question is . . . *who is on to us*?' He looked at Buller. 'Not Fleet Street—?'

'Sod Fleet Street.' Buller almost looked sad. 'I remember a chap on the old *Star* . . . and one or two more, on the heavyweights . . . who'd have had us by now, the way we've blundered around . . . But they're all into management, and new technology, and colour supplements—the good ones. Or the little magazines . . . and writing books—' The blood-orange eyes took in Ian for half a second '—sod Fleet Street!'

'So that would make it official—?' Tully wasn't quite certain.

'Even after *Spycatcher*—Peter Wright?' Neither was Jenny certain.

Buller's mouth twisted. 'There's still a few reporters I rate.' He held out his glass. 'If one of them was loose, then I'd be worrying. But I'd also be happy, too.' He pushed at the neck of the bottle as Jenny poured, until the champagne frothed over the top of the glass and the bottle emptied into it. 'But I ain't seen one of 'em on this lark yet.'

'So it's official?' Tully persisted, patiently.

'Oh yes.' Buller sniffed disparagingly. 'What we've got, out there in the wet, is *civil servants*. The only question is . . . are they *ours* . . . or are they *someone else's*, who can park their cars, an' claim "diplomatic immunity", and not worry about paying the fine—eh?'

That was combining the frightening with the more frightening, rather than the absurd with the ridiculous, thought Ian: whatever heated up the water in his Yellowstone pond it was already on the boil.

'But . . . we're not safe in any case—any more.' Jenny overtook him, as she always did; and, as it always did, the degree of difficulty and danger only encouraged her, setting her on to go further. 'Is that what you mean, Reg?'

'Yes. That is just about what I mean, I suppose.' Buller gave Ian a belated guilty look. 'Except . . . you could do a book, between you, about something else—like about Colonel Rabuka, and the Fiji Islands, maybe? And Mr Tully and I could go out there . . . and you could call it *The Imperial Legacy*—? And we could maybe take in the French nuclear programme as well, that you've always wanted to do, which no one else has done properly—right from the Sahara trials, in the old days, when they had those Germans working for them on the rockets . . . the ones they wouldn't talk about?' Buller tossed his head. 'Either road, we'd be a bloody long way from here for a few months, anyway, Miss Fielding. An' out of the rain, too.'

Jenny had long waited to do that. But Ian had always been against it because he was scared of the French; and, after the sinking of the Greenpeace ship, they had both been right and wrong; and

49

Buller knew it too. But he also knew more than that, unfortunately—both about Jenny and about David Audley, so it seemed.

'Yes. That would certainly be agreeable, Reg—you're right.' She smiled at him. But then she smiled at Ian. 'But . . . the French will wait for us, darling, I think. And David Audley obviously won't wait, will he—?'

The sort of time-span she was thinking about would produce an indifferent book, he thought—even if it would also divvy up a hefty newspaper fee, for pre-publication of extracts, as well as a whopping advance, and a good transatlantic deal. And, as she was always reminding him, they were only in the business of 'non-fictional ephemera', anyway.

'So do you want to go ahead—in spite of Reg?' Tully wasn't chicken: either for honest financial reasons (to keep his children in their private school, and his wife at that standard of living to which she was accustomed), or for noble freedom-of-information, freedom-of-publication, freedom-of-*know* reasons, John Tully was a fearless investigator. 'Right, Miss Fielding—Mr Robinson?'

'No.' Ian saw the ground opening up before him. What he couldn't bring himself to admit straight off (or not quite yet) was that whatever John Tully might be, Ian Robinson was no longer at heart a journalist, nor at any time a fearless one. And, of course, they all knew that (they hadn't even bothered to ask him whether it might be anything that *he'd* done which had alerted someone: they knew him better than that, by heaven!).

'Yes, darling—?' Jenny checked herself suddenly, substituting patience for enthusiasm. For

50

a guess, she was reminding herself that she needed him just as much as he needed her—and never more so than now, when they had to work fast if they were to stay ahead of the pack. And there was the rub.

But he still couldn't admit to his fear of what the rub meant, not openly. 'We don't know who they are.'

'No, Ian. We don't.' Her patience stretched. 'But that doesn't matter. Mr Tully . . . or Mr Buller . . . will take care of that.' She smiled at him reassuringly, as to a Bear of Very Little Brain whose special skill was limited to assessing the different varieties of honey she delivered to him. 'The point is, darling, that they're *there*. And *that* means . . . we really are on to something. So we've all got to get our skates on now.'

He had delayed too long. 'I'm not sure I want to get my skates on, Jen. It's been a long time since . . . I did this sort of thing. I'm a bit rusty.'

She couldn't conceal the flicker of contempt which he had hoped he wasn't going to see. 'Ian—' Then the flicker clouded, as she remembered Beirut, and couldn't reconcile past experience with present observation '—you're not *scared*, are you—?'

Tully coughed. 'Mr Robinson hasn't been . . . out much, these last two or three years, Miss Fielding. You have rather kept him chained to his word-processor.' He drank the last of his sherry fastidiously. 'And to good effect, if I may say so. But . . . one does get rusty, you know.'

That was surprising loyalty (or male solidarity, equally surprising), coming from John Tully, thought Ian. Or, it might just be that he, unlike

51

everyone else, had not misunderstood the Beirut episode.

'No.' Reg Buller sidled towards the window, choosing a place where there was a slight gap between the frame and the curtain, where a sliver of light showed. 'The Lady's right.' He put his eye to the gap, without touching the curtain. 'Because he's not stupid, you see.' He turned back to them, past Tully and Jenny, and nodded to Ian. 'Welcome to the club, Mr Robinson.'

'Reg!' Jenny sounded almost accusing. 'You're not scared, are you?'

'This bloke Audley . . . *Dr David Audley* . . .' Buller took out his pipe from his pocket and studied it. And then thought better of lighting it again, and put it back in his pocket. 'Mr Tully's right, too: it won't have been him, that actually topped Masson—he's getting a bit long in the tooth for digging his own holes, when he needs 'em. *If* he needs 'em—'

'*When.*' Jenny emphasized the word coldly.

'We don't know that, with Masson.' Buller shook his head. 'All we've got is a bit of gossip you picked up, that you weren't meant to hear. And there's one or two people he's crossed, you can bet, who might like to fasten something on to him, Miss Fielding.'

'But you said "when", nevertheless, Mr Buller.'

'So I did.' He studied her for a moment. 'But before I went out West that time, to see the Big . . . *Grand* . . . Tetons, you said to me, "Keep an open mind, Mr Buller: no matter what they say, or what they did, or why they did it . . . or what it did to *them* . . . keep an open mind, Mr Buller", is what *you* said, as you put me on that Greyhound bus.'

Jenny smiled at him sweetly. 'We were

52

economizing at the time, Mr Buller. And you still said "when".'

Buller gave her another long look. 'And you may have been talking to someone who's talked to someone I talked to.'

'That could be.' The sweet smile vanished. 'You tell me, Mr Buller.'

Reg Buller sighed, and touched the pocket in which his pipe lay. 'No names this time, Lady.' Then he nodded. 'All right, then. There have been one or two times, over the years, when there's been some unpleasantness involving Mr David Audley, so they say.'

'Not "unpleasantness", Mr Buller.' Jenny was Miss Fielding-ffulke now, with all her ancestors behind her. 'And not just "one or two times". David Audley has a long string of deaths behind him, so I am informed—*reliably* informed.' Then she weakened deliberately, as she remembered that they were both on the same side. 'Come on, Reg—you've been trying to frighten us out of our wits all along—even with the boiling water in Yellowstone National Park! So don't bullshit us now.' She brushed back the tangle of inadequately-combed hair. 'According to *my* source he presided over an absolute bloodbath, somewhere down in the West Country, a couple of years ago—' She shifted to Tully '—right, John?'

'Possibly.' Not for the first time as Ian looked at John Tully he was reminded of Clive Ponting, whose face was also designed for very dry sherry as well as distasteful revelations.

'But nothing in 1978—or 1977. And he was in Washington almost the whole of '78, into 1979.' Buller looked to Tully for support. 'He's got a lot of

53

friends in the CIA . . . so *I* am reliably informed—eh?' Then he registered Tully's expression. 'And that wasn't because I was "exceeding-my-bloody-brief"—I got that for free, as it happens.'

'*All right!*' Jenny called them all to order. 'So, then . . . *I* will take him right now, and see how the land lies at the moment.' She embraced both Tully and Buller together, but chiefly Tully. 'John . . . I think I'd like to know who is out there, getting wet at the moment, if possible.' She came to Ian. 'And, as you are the historian among us, darling . . . and as Audley *wasn't* doing anything naughty then . . . do you think you could dig up 1978 for us, Ian—? And, if you like, you can take Mr Buller with you, for protection.'

CHAPTER TWO

The possibility that he was being followed aroused in Ian what he assumed to be the classic symptoms of paranoia: a feeling of unaccustomed importance, verging on pride ('Better put a tail on Robinson: he needs watching!'), moderated by a much less comfortable disquiet, which might easily develop into a persecution complex.

Of course, he'd been followed before, almost certainly. But that had been in Beirut, which hardly counted, because everyone who was anyone was followed there, by someone or other, and it would have been an insult *not* to be followed; in fact, he'd probably been followed by the Syrians, who had been protecting them both, who had been

54

shadowing other and nastier followers, like the lesser fleas on the bigger fleas on the proverbial dog, and so *ad infinitum*.

Only, he hadn't much liked the possibility then, and he liked it no better now, with Reg Buller's final patronizing and belittling words of wisdom echoing in his ear—

'No good looking for 'em, because you won't see 'em—not if they know their job. So no good tryin' to be clever, peerin' into the shop windows. An' whatever you do, don't try an' lose 'em—that's Rule Number One. 'Cause, when you do need to slip 'em, it's gotta seem like by accident, an' all nice an' slow. An' I'll stage-manage that, there's a taxi-driver I know who'll fix it . . . An' anyway, your job today is to draw 'em off to let me get off. So you just walk round to the Lady's flat for your Sunday lunch like always. An' phone me tonight at 7—from a public pay-box. Okay?'

Not okay. Because now, with the Sunday streets emptied by rain, and the Sunday pubs filled, the temptation to look over his shoulder at every corner was like an itch in his brain. And all the little antique shops, the contents of whose windows had never much interested him before, seemed full of intriguing objects . . . which he mustn't stop and look at, just in case *someone* might think he was trying to be clever. And as there probably wasn't anyone, that made him feel like a right prick.

But then . . . if Reg Buller was *right* . . .

He decided to concentrate on it, partly to help him to forget that itch and its accompanying incipient paranoia, and partly because Reg Buller usually *was* right, when it came to such mundane matters. Which cleared the way in turn for the consideration of the more important matters with

55

which Jenny would hit him during her version of Sunday lunch—*yuk!*

Because Jenny, too, had been *right* this time—and not in any mundane matter, either: her little shell-like ears (sensitive appendages, always attuned to items of scandal and indiscretion, as sharp as the diamonds which customarily adorned each of them) had picked up a winner this time, like a blip on a high-tech radar screen which registered not so much 'Friend or Foe?' as 'Profit or Loss?' unfailingly—

★　　★　　★

'*What about Masson, then?*'

'*A turn-up for the book, you mean?*'

'*Not a turn-up. I never did believe that story. It was too neat.*'

'*Which story? The official one—? Or . . . ?*'

'*Neither of them. But I tell you one thing: David Audley won't like it.*'

'*David Audley? You don't mean—?*'

'*I don't mean anything. Except . . . people who don't suit his book have a way of being safely written out of it. And Masson was a front runner then . . . remember?*'

'*Yes . . . But, surely, you don't think—?*'

'*Not aloud I don't—no! But I think . . . if I was Audley . . . I might be remembering the banquet scene in that play the actors don't like naming—eh?*'

★　　★　　★

'*You're sure you've got it right, Jen—?*'

'*Don't be a bore, Ian. Of course I've got it right. I*

was listening to them.'

'To whom?'

'To these two men. And don't ask me who they were, because I don't know—yet.'

'They didn't introduce themselves to you?'

'Now you're being thick. They weren't talking to me. I overheard them. And the play's "Macbeth", of course—'

'Oh? Not "Hamlet", then?'

'Not—what?'

'You overheard them. But I can't think they wouldn't have noticed you. Because you're quite noticeable, Miss Fielding-ffulke. So presumably you were hiding behind some arras, like Polonius in "Hamlet". That's all.'

'I see. So now you're being clever. So at least you're awake . . . Well, for your information, I was partly behind an arras, actually. Or a curtain, to be exact . . . And Victor Pollard and Nigel Gaitch were regaling me with inane Palace gossip about Charles and Di, which I really didn't want to know, but which they thought was just up my street. So I stopped listening to them . . . and there must be some sort of acoustic trick just there, because of the alcove there, and the curtain—I don't damn well know. All I know is what I heard. And it's "Macbeth"—the one the actors won't ever mention. And the banquet scene, too. And you know what that's about, do you, Ian?'

'Yes—'

'It's about a murder that's gone wrong, is what it's about—'

★　　★　　★

So maybe Jenny was right. For certainly Jenny was

clever, and she was very often as lucky as she was clever, which was an unbeatable alliance.

But that still left them with the Unnamed Play expert, who had been *unlucky*, as well as indiscreet, beside the curtain at the embassy party; he sounded clever too, and maliciously so perhaps. But just how clever had he been with that throwaway Macbeth reference?

Just *generally* clever, with Macbeth's hired murderer reporting back on the bodged killing—

—*Is he dispacht?*
—*My lord, his throat is cut; that I did for him.*

Or *exactly* clever, with Philip Masson as well as Audley in mind, after Banquo's grisly ghost had broken up a pleasant dinner—

—*the time has been,*
That, when the brains were out, the man would
    die,
And there an end; but now they rise again,
With twenty mortal murders on their crowns,
And push us from our stools

Was that it?

Had Banquo/Masson risen again, in order that Jenny Fielding and Ian Robinson should push David Audley from his stool—?

Well . . . Jenny Fielding's castle was now just across the wet road, and he could hear no footsteps behind him, only his old tutor's warning against preconceived ideas which fitted so well that one bought them too easily, without feeling the quality of the shoddy material.

The road was safe, anyway—as safe as suburban East Berlin on a wet Sunday, never mind Hampstead; and he was probably as unfollowed here and now as he had been there and then—and Jenny could have simply heard two malicious Civil Service tongues chatting imaginative gossip—

He skipped the last few yards, from the road and across the glistening pavement, to the refuge of the flat's entrance, and stabbed the bell with a sense of anti-climax, feeling foolish because he was simultaneously relieved and disappointed. Because, if Jenny and Buller were *right*, it might well be that they didn't even consider him worth following—

'Yes?' The cool, disembodied voice was haughtiest Jenny.

'It's me. Who did you think it was?' He heard his own voice too late, as squeakiest Ian.

'Are you alone? Or already in durance vile, with the cuffs on and a gun at your back?' Now she was stage-Jenny, making fun of all the painted devils of his imagination.

'For heaven's sake, Jen—let me in!' He couldn't stop himself protesting. 'My feet are soaking, damn it!' He managed to lower the squeak to a growl. *Click!*

'Darling—I'm so sorry—I am *sorry* . . . But John Tully and dear old Reg insisted—remember?' She patted him like a child after relieving him of his raincoat and umbrella. 'Of course, John wanted my taxi. And he said we'd got nothing to lose, anyway . . . And Reg wanted you to lead the opposition away, so he could do his own thing.' She brushed ineffectually at the huge bird's-nest tangle of hair which she'd pinned up, but which was falling down on all sides. 'I do *love* Reg—don't you, Ian?'

'No.' He could smell an unfamiliar smell. And it was as far removed from the usual smell of her flat as what he felt for Reg Buller was separated from love. 'Reg Buller is not lovable.' He sniffed again. 'Have you been cooking?'

'He is so. Come and have a drink. And he's also one very smart operator. Did you read his report? You did bring it with you?'

'Yes.' He had to sniff again. 'Is that what I think it is?'

'Eh? Well, I don't know what you think it is. But the man in the butcher's shop said it was his very best Scotch beef. And he gave me all sorts of advice about what I should do with it—he seemed quite worried that I might not treat it with proper respect. I almost asked him to come and roast it for me . . . only I was afraid he might take me up on the offer.' She smiled her Scarlett O'Hara smile at him. 'But then he said it needed a good Burgundy with it. Only, I know you like claret, so I asked the other man, in the wine merchants', who sells me my usual plonk . . . and he said this would be about right—' She swept a bottle off the sideboard '—he said it had the *body* . . . which really sounded rather gruesome . . . But I do remember the name—it has to be named after an Irishman really—"O'Brien"? Because none of that area is "haut", it's all flat as a pancake. But it was one of Daddy's favourite tipples, so it can't be bad—can it?' She jerked the bottle to her nose. 'I think it smells rather fun—it reminds me of Daddy, actually. He used to make me smell all his bottles. Here—have a sniff! Is it okay?'

Ian clamped his hand on the bottle. What he had to remember was that he was almost certainly being

60

taken for a ride, as better men before him had been, and others after him would be. Because Daddy had been a power in the land (and that was part of Jenny Fielding's stock-in-trade, and his also by their literary alliance). And also because she was his only-and-favourite daughter, and a conniving chip off the same block.

It was Haut-Brion, and he had been in short trousers when it had been in its grapes. 'This'll do just fine, Jen. It's . . . okay.'

'Oh—good!' She turned away from him. 'I have to take the little man's beef out of the oven—if I don't, I think he'll come and demonstrate outside, or haunt me when he's dead . . . And there are the vegetables—but they're just out of the freezer, so they're no trouble . . . But I have also made a Yorkshire pudding, according to that recipe the man gave us in Belgium—remember? The one who said that the people in Yorkshire had got it all wrong, after the battle of Waterloo—? But you *must* come and help me, Ian—'

He followed her, towards the smell, with his arm and shoulder frozen, as though it was a bottle of Chateau Nobel, from the Nitro Glycerine commune, of an unstable year—

Waterloo was right, though: the kitchen resembled nothing so much as the farmhouse of La Haye Sainte towards the end of the battle, after the French had stormed it, and Wellington's troops had re-taken it at the point of a bayonet. And, quite evidently, the ex-freezer vegetables were already casualties, and the Belgian-Yorkshire pudding had suffered the same fate as the unfortunate Belgian regiments which had been exposed to the fire of Napoleon's artillery for too long—

61

'Jen! Let's eat the beef—' There was just enough space to bestow the Haut-Brion safely on the table. But then, as he rescued what looked like the better part of an Aberdeen Angus from her, he met her eyes '—all this on my account, Jen—?'

'Well . . . you don't eat enough, do you? All those fast-foods—*junk* foods—and take-aways?' She looked down at the beef, and then back up at him. 'The way to a man's heart is supposed to be through his stomach, that's all.'

She really wanted Audley's scalp. Or someone's scalp, anyway. Or, one way or another, she wanted some more Beirut-style excitement, anyway. And (more to the point) she'd expected him to cast his vote against the enterprise.

'But all a bloody waste of time?' Having already got what she wanted, she was perfectly happy, and the irritation was hardly skin-deep. 'Shall we throw it all away, and go round the corner to the pub, Ian?'

'Certainly not!' As always, the pain was his as he was reminded for the thousandth time of the difference between her need and his desire. 'I'm not going to let this beef—and that plonk of yours—go to waste. Get the carving-knife, Fielding-ffulke! And lay the table—go on!'

'Yes, master—at once, master!' As always, she was his humble and attentive servant in her moment of triumph, and never more beautiful. 'So what about David Audley, then? Isn't he *something*, eh?'

'The devil with Audley.' Predictably, her carving-knife was blunt. But the beef was superbly tender. 'Were you followed?'

'Don't ask me, darling. But if Reg says we're

being, then I'm sure we were. And—don't you think it's fun?'

'No. I don't think it's fun . . . Is that enough for you, Jen?'

'No?' She peered over his shoulder, and the smell of her and the beef aroused different carnal desires simultaneously. 'No, I'm absolutely *ravenous* . . . and look at all that lovely blood, too! God, I must take up cooking, I think—evening classes in *cordon bleu*, and all that—and *nouvelle cuisine*—that'll do, darling. What d'you think?'

What he thought was that she now had a heavy-manual-worker's plate of roast beef, which would make a *nouvelle cuisine* chef quite ill to look at. 'What I think, Jen, is . . . that being followed scares me. And David Audley terrifies me . . . since you ask.' He offered her the plate.

'Can I have a little more of that . . . sort of gravy-stuff.'

'Blood, you mean?' He accepted the spoon she was holding out to him in anticipation. 'Well, at least you have the right appetite, I suppose.'

'What?' Greed deafened her for a moment. 'Do you want some of my Yorkshire pudding? I did put cheese in it, like the recipe said.'

Ian's memory of the outcome of that experiment enabled him to concentrate on his carving, while pretending similar deafness.

'What d'you mean—"the right appetite"?' She had heard, after all.

'People involved with Audley end up dead, according to Reg Buller.' He might as well match her greed: what wasn't eaten here and now would probably be thrown away, and it would be a sin to waste this noble animal.

'Ah! I see what you mean—' She cleared a space for them on the kitchen table simply by throwing everything into the sink, higgledy-piggledy '—and that's what this friend of Daddy's I talked to said, actually.'

'And doesn't that frighten you?' He watched her fish cutlery out of a drawer, and glasses from a cupboard. The cutlery was beautiful bone-handled antique, tarnished but razor-sharp, and the glasses were the thick and ugly petrol-coupon variety, and none-too-clean. But he was past caring about that now.

'I don't see why it should.' She let him pour, and then raised her glass high. 'Here's to us—and crime paying, anyway!' Then she drank. 'Mmm! It *is* good—trust Daddy!' Then she attacked her beef. 'Mmmm! So's this!' She grinned and munched appreciatively. 'I mean . . . if you look at what Johnny and Reg dug up about him . . . it is all rather vague . . . sort of *gossip*, I mean . . . There were inquests. But there was always a perfectly reasonable story of some sort—like that young man who blew himself up, during that cavaliers-and-roundheads mock-battle—'

'After someone else had got murdered, at another mock battle?' The need to concentrate on what she was saying detracted cruelly from the paradisal meat and wine. 'And that case has never been closed, Reg says.'

'But Audley wasn't there, that time—'

'So far as anyone knows. But he was there the second time—'

'But nowhere near the explosion—' All the same, she nodded as she cut him off '—I do agree, though: he is rather *accident*-prone . . . Except that he's never been summoned to give evidence, or anything like that.'

'Or anything like anything.' He swallowed, and disciplined himself against eating and drinking for a moment. 'And the year before last, when that visiting Russian general died—Tully says he didn't have a heart-attack—that he was shot by someone.'

'But not by Audley, Ian.' Jenny didn't stop eating, but she had somehow become a devil's advocate. 'He's a back-room boy, not a gunfighter. He's too old for that sort of thing.'

'But he was there, somewhere—Tully also thought that—'

'No.'

Thus flatly contradicted, Ian returned to his food. Whatever crimes Audley had, or had not, connived at, there was no reason why he should compound them by letting his meat congeal on his plate. If Jenny thought Audley was innocent of the Russian general's death, so be it. And if he'd never come out into the limelight, so be that, too. Because Jenny quite obviously thought there were other things he had to answer for.

'No.' She pushed her plate away and then filled her glass again, like Daddy's daughter.

'No?' He pushed his own empty glass towards her.

'Johnny didn't think that. *I* told him that. But then he did some checking, and he says there was one hell of a shoot-out, somewhere down there in the West Country. Only it was all very efficiently hushed-up. And the Russians helped with the hushing, apparently.' She nodded at him. 'And Audley was probably mixed up in that.'

'Probably?' Jenny had a prime source—that was

65

both obvious and nothing new: Jenny had more sources than she had had take-away dinners (or expensive restaurant dinners, for that matter). But, what was more to the point, it would be easier to excavate a two-year-old scandal than a nine-year-old one. 'Probably, Jen?'

'Maybe. But who cares?' She shrugged. 'It's Audley-and-Philly-Masson we're after, not Audley-and-General-Zarubin, darling.'

'But Zarubin sounds more promising.'

'I don't agree.' She savoured her wine, as though she was thinking of Daddy again. 'Zarubin was just an effing-Cossack, by all accounts—*not* one of dear Mr Gorbachev's blue-eyed boys. Which presumably explains all the friendly co-operation.' Then she was looking at him, and she very definitely wasn't thinking of Daddy. 'I don't say that isn't interesting. And maybe we'll find a place for it eventually. Because once we start turning over stones then I expect all sorts of creepy-crawlies will start emerging and running for cover—that's the beauty of it. Because Audley goes back a long way. Long before poor Philip Masson. So God only knows what we'll turn up.'

Now it was *poor* Philip Masson. And just now it had been "Philly". But that could wait. 'And yet no one's ever heard of him, Jen.'

'Of Audley?' She shook her head. 'That's not quite true. In fact, it's entirely *un*true: lots of people have *heard* of him. Lots of people *know* him, actually . . . and he seems to know a lot of people, putting it the other way round. They just don't know what he *does*, exactly.'

'But you think you do know?'

'No—not yet. But . . . it's like, he's often in the

66

background of things, so far as I can make out so far. Like, with a collection of people in group photographs, when you keep seeing the same face somewhere in the back . . . Or, you're not quite sure, because he's always the one who's partly obscured by someone else—or he's moved just as the photographer pressed the button, so he's blurred.' She shrugged. 'Like Reg said, he gives advice to people—to committees, and suchlike. But his name never appears.'

'That isn't so, according to John Tully. He's listed in quite a few places—in *Who's Who*, for a start. With a CBE in the early 1970s. And an honorary fellowship at King Richard's.'

'Oh yes.' She wasn't put off in the least. 'But it's all so vague—isn't it? An "assistant-principal" here, in one place—Home Office, was it? Then a transfer to the Ministry of Defence. And writing those books . . . But, darling, it's all got nothing to do with what he *really* does, of course—it's all flumdiddle. Dear old Reg said it all, didn't he? "Cloak-and-dagger", is what he is. Only this time it was more like "dagger-and-cloak", maybe.'

'Reg also said "research".' There was something in her voice he hadn't heard before, and couldn't pin down now; almost a hint of underlying passion, of malevolence even. All he knew was that he had to argue against it. '"Advice and research"; was it? And the man must be close to retirement, damn it Jen!' But that hadn't been all Reg had said, he remembered. And that weakened his resistance to her will. 'If they retire in his line of work.'

'Yes. And that's interesting, too.' Her voice was back to normal: maybe he had imagined that hint of genuine feeling under the 24-hour insatiable

67

curiosity which powered her normally, without commitment to any cause other than the truth. 'And particularly interesting to you, as it happens, Ian.'

'To me?' What he was going to get now was one of the arguments she had intended to use in support of the Scotch beef and the Château Haut-Brion (which she had surely known for what it was), in the event of his welshing on the deal.

'Uh-huh.' She gestured towards the Haut-Brion. 'I think I may have some idea of what he does, actually.'

This was that source of hers again: a source she would never mention even as a source, unlike Reg Buller's vague. 'There's a bloke I know, in The Street/in the Met/down the nick/down the pub/in the business', or John Tully's notated references to 'Contact AB' and 'Contact XY' in his reports, whose identities would all be in a little black book somewhere.

'Go on, darling—don't mind me. I've had more than my share.'

'So you have.' So she had. And if she'd been his, and he'd been hers, he might worry about that; though, as they never would be (which was the old familiar spear in his heart, twisting but never killing), and as she never seemed to change, no matter how much she'd drunk, except that she burned more brightly still, he had no right to worry.

'I've got more—I bought a whole case, darling. And the little man gave me what he called a "case-price", so our bottle was absolutely *free*—'

'Jenny! For heaven's sake—!' He had to move, to block her passage towards her Aladdin's cave. 'Just sit down, and tell me about Audley, there's a good girl—*sit down!*' As he restrained her he thought . . . *and that's another thing: when it comes to money, she's got no bloody idea!* 'Just tell me—eh?'

She sat down. 'Oh . . . you are a bore, sometimes . . . Don't you ever let your hair down—?' To match the words, she tried ineffectually to recover some of the hair which was coming down all around her face.

He waited until she had done the best she could. 'Audley?'

'Yes—all right!' She abandoned the pushing-and-poking process. 'There was this man Daddy knew, who was just *incredibly* high-powered . . . I mean, Daddy is *high*-powered—he is like *God*—' She saw his face, and tried to rescue herself from the blasphemy '—I mean, he's *kind*, even though he knows everything . . .' She trailed off, grimacing at him.

That was half her trouble—or maybe all of it: no one could compete against such opposition. And that was also his problem, too. But not just at this moment. 'I don't think I'm quite with you, Jen. This man . . . he was Audley?'

'Good God, no! He was an acquaintance of Daddy's, I'm trying to tell you. He's dead now—but quite naturally, I think.'

Maybe she had had one glass too many. 'I see. And high-powered with it. But not as high-powered as your father, eh?'

She frowned at him. 'What?'

'I was always taught that there was only one God.' It was odd to speak so lightly when one meant what one said. 'So . . . like St Peter, say? Or St Paul—he was rather high-powered.'

She stared at him for a moment, then made a face. 'Very clever.' Then the face became serious. 'Maybe a bit of both of them, actually. Although Daddy just called him "Fred", as I remember. When I met him.'

'"Fred"?' At least this wasn't one of her unacknowledged, unnamed sources, anyway. 'I don't think there is a "St Fred" in the calendar of saints. But never mind . . . You met this "Fred"—' It was on the tip of his tongue to ask her what Fred had to do with Audley. But then he looked directly into her eyes and caught himself just in time, knowing that he had been wrong just a minute before.

'Yes, I did.' The eyes were stony, not stoned. 'I was eighteen—I was just going up to college. And he frightened me.'

'Frightened you?' It was so unexpected that he repeated the words. 'How?'

'He quizzed me. No—he *interrogated* me, more like . . . What I thought, what I was going to do . . . at Oxford, after Oxford . . . Why I thought what I thought—why I was going to do what . . . what I thought I was going to do.' She stared at him. 'He really took me apart. It was quite frightening.'

From her that was also quite an admission. Because there wasn't much that frightened Jenny Fielding-ffulke. Or, anyway, nothing that wore trousers. And there was also something else that didn't fit. 'Your father didn't stop him—?'

'Daddy had a phone-call. He told me to entertain his guest—Mummy was at one of her meetings.' Her eyes glazed slightly, as though she was no longer looking at him. Then they focused on him

70

again. 'He was *sharp*—not *interrogated*, more like *dissected*: I felt like a poor bloody frog in a biology practical.'

'Fred' had been nothing if not memorable. And a faint whiff of her original fear travelled across the years in her imagery.

'When Daddy came back . . . he said—*he* said, not Daddy—"We've had a most interesting chat, Jennifer and I".' She cocked her head slightly. 'And then the bastard told Daddy what a clever daughter he'd sired, and bull-shitted him so that I couldn't decently have hysterics, or burst into tears . . . In fact, he even gave me his card, and told me that if I didn't want to go on with my bio-chemistry when I'd graduated then I could always came to him for a job. And poor old Daddy positively glowed.' She sniffed. *'Fat chance!'*

It was getting more interesting by the second—just as she'd promised it would do, although in another context. 'So what did you do?'

She sniffed again. 'I couldn't say anything then—now, could I? Not to Daddy—not without appearing to be a wimp, anyway.'

'But . . . what was on the card, Jen?'

'God—I don't know! I went to the loo, and had a good cry—and tore it up, and flushed it down the pan—' She stopped abruptly. *'Clinton*, though— that was the name: *Frederick Joseph Clinton.'* Now she looked at him. '*Sir* Frederick Clinton—?'

That rang a bell from somewhere. But he couldn't place it. But . . . the way she was looking at him, she expected him to place it. 'Clinton?'

'Yes.' She nodded. 'I found him in an old *Who's Who*, but there wasn't much about him.' She drained the last dregs of her Haut-Brion. 'He

71

retired from the army as a brigadier in '47—no mention of any regiment . . . But the DSO was from 1940, Daddy said. So that fits in with a book he wrote, about Dunkirk, when we ran away from the Germans, and made a great victory of it.' She almost banged her glass down. 'And he got his 'K' in '58, when he was supposed to be a permanent something-or-other in the Home Office—or one of the other ministries they had then, before it was the Ministry of Defence. But, of course, it's just like Audley—all flumdiddle.'

Dunkirk, of course: there had been that very curious book on Dunkirk, way back . . . with all sorts of elliptical references to high policy, both British and German, which the military historians had taken with a pinch of salt; he had bought a copy in a second-hand shop in Charing Cross Road as a schoolboy, for his grandfather (who had been there) because it had been signed by the author, with a great flourish (or, rather, because it had been dead-cheap, anyway). '*The Dunkirk Miracle*—of course!'

'What?' She frowned at him again.

'The book he wrote—*The Dunkirk Miracle*, Jen. But . . . how does he fit in with Audley?'

'Audley?' The name made her demote *Frederick Joseph Clinton*, so it seemed for an instant. Then she concentrated on him. 'If what I've been told is right, Audley was his blue-eyed boy—his pupil, and his beneficiary . . . Only, it didn't quite work out like that, apparently.' The frown came back.

'What d'you mean?'

'I'm not quite sure yet.' The concentration became almost disconcerting. 'But I think we could—just *could*—be on to something *rather* interesting in its own right, even apart from Dr David Audley . . . although he is part of it—very much part of it, in fact . . .'

She trailed off, and this time he waited patiently, because he recognized that look from old. Normally, in their strange symbiotic partnership, she was the one who brought in the new information which could not be obtained by conventional and straightforward means, which she scavenged from all sorts of unlikely and—to him—inaccessible places and people; and it was his job not only to combine it with his own research and render it presentable and saleable, but also to crack its bones and extract the marrow within. But sometimes—rarley, but sometimes—she could do a lot more than that.

She looked at him suddenly. 'Quite a lot of people know David Audley—and *about* him, too . . . in a way. And you know what they say, Ian?'

He knew what Reg Buller had said. But that had been private. 'No—?'

She nodded. 'They say . . . "Oh he's something in Intelligence, isn't he?". Or even just "Old David, darling? In one of those MI-somethings—always popping down to that *awful* secret place at Cheltenham, with all those initials."' She paused, closing her eyes. '"But he does have *the* most delightful wife and daughter—both perfect *sweeties*, darling. Whereas, he's a great *bear* of a man—a perfect *Caliban*, compared with them, don't you know".'

That sounded more like one of 'Mummy's' friends than 'Daddy's'. But that, of course, was exactly what 'they' *had* said, word for word, from memory. Given a notebook, Jenny would have

73

either broken the lead in her pencil or supplied herself with a dead ball-point pen; or, if she hadn't, then she wouldn't have been able to decipher her hopeless handwriting. But the gods, to make up for that deficiency, had given her total recall of anything that was said to her, down to the last emphasis.

But she was looking at him again.

'He was connected with that fearful man Clinton.' The concentration was back. 'That I know. And Clinton was "in" Intelligence—very much *in*. But he was never one of the directors of any of the big departments—MI5, or MI6, and all that. Because everyone knows who *they* were . . . Yet he was a bloody-big wheel—a power in the land. That's for sure, too.'

Was that 'Daddy', being indiscreet long ago with his little darling? Or that source, being infinitely more indiscreet, for some other reason? But he could see that there was more to come.

'Clinton got a successor, at all events. Name of *Butler*. Christian name *James*, but always known as "Jack". Ex-career soldier in some little line regiment. And not too successful even in that, because he went on the General List as a major when he was quite elderly. Then he was made up to half-colonel, and in—*in*—Intelligence, apparently. But not military intelligence: "one of Fred Clinton's lot", thereafter.' Her face seemed to sharpen as she spoke. '"Nice chap, but rather dull".' Sharper still. 'Which just could be an unreliable assessment, because he's just got his "K"—*Sir* Jack now . . . Just like *Sir* Fred, before him.'. She nodded wisely. 'Like you're always saying, darling—*pattern*: "Look for the pattern" . . . okay?'

74

She wanted to be jogged—or maybe reassured? 'So now he's Audley's boss—?'

'Yes. But boss of what?' Now she was really there. 'So . . . remember what old Reg said—"research and advice"? And when Reg picks up vibes, then they're usually right, aren't they?'

She had asked him to remember. So, once again, he remembered what Reg Buller had said out of her hearing. 'Reg is good—yes.'

'But not quite accurate this time.' Scoring a point always pleased her. 'Because I think the official title of the Clinton-Butler organization is "Research and *Development*". Although, of course, that doesn't really mean anything—just a useful bit of jargon, to put you off. Because everyone's got an "R & D" section now—it's like having a "computer facility", with a "systems manager", even if you're putting beans into tins—all flumdiddle, darling.'

'Flumdiddle' must be a new word in Jenny's circle. But, nevertheless, he was beginning to smell the marrow from the broken bone. 'So what does it mean, then?'

'Well . . . I'm by no means quite sure, darling—as I keep saying.' Knowing him, she was properly cautious still, in spite of all her certainties. 'But suppose—just *suppose* . . . that alongside all the little old *secret* services that we know and love by their initials and numbers . . . alongside all of them, there was another one, that we didn't know was there. Like, say, a sort of parallel world, in those science-fiction stories, almost—?' She cocked an eye at him. 'Not very big—really rather small—? But more secret, more exclusive—? Say . . . just responsible to the Prime Minister—the Cabinet Office? Or the Intelligence Sub-Committee of the

Joint Chiefs? Or—'

She wasn't beginning to frighten him. She was frightening him. 'Doing what?'

She shrugged. 'Doing whatever it was told to do. Doing what comes naturally—I don't know . . . I tell you, I'm not sure yet . . . Trouble-shooting? Or maybe trouble-making.' She blew a strand of hair which had fallen across her face. 'Because . . . as well as being very secret, I do rather get the impression that it may not be too popular in certain circles, whatever it is—whatever it does, exactly—' She seized the fallen strand and tried to push it back on top, releasing a whole cascade in the process '—damn!'

Ian accepted the diversion gratefully. That last revelation at least told him something about her source. Indeed, it fitted into the original dialogue she'd eavesdropped on to make a familiar pattern. In any investigation, the enemies of the subject of the investigation—or even, if the subject was an organization of some sort, any disaffected members within it—were prime sources of information. And . . . although this source sounded more like an outsider than an insider . . . it was hardly surprising that the 'Clinton-Butler' organization had its enemies, even on its 'own' side, never mind among its proper and official opponents.

'Well?' Jenny abandoned the wreckage of her bird's-nest. 'What do you say to all that then, Ian?'

Its opponents! he thought, staring suddenly at the window with a stab of disquiet. He had somehow taken it for granted that those watchers (if they were there—?) would be Special Branch, if not MI5. But they could be—who?

'Yes.' She grinned happily. 'It does account for

76

our sudden popularity, doesn't it, darling?'

'That's not the word I was thinking of.' At least he hadn't betrayed his fear. 'Is this what you told Woodward? Or Parsons?'

The grin twisted. 'Oh, come on, darling! As our Reg might say, "Would I do that, Mr Robinson?". Of course not.'

'So what did you tell them?'

She sighed. 'What did I say to them? Well, I said to Dick: "Richard, darling . . . do you recall that nice Civil Servant named Philip Masson, who was tragically lost at sea, when he fell off his yacht in the Channel nine or ten years ago?" And he said: "Jenny darling, that wouldn't be the same fellow whose body has just turned up in a wood somewhere, without his lifebelt?"' She smiled. 'I was very circumspect, you see.'

'Get on with it, Jen.'

'All right, all right! So I said: "Yes, darling—the one all your chaps are running around in circles trying to find out about, to no avail . . . How would you like the serial rights for our book on what *really* happened, darling? Or shall I go to Rupert Murdoch instead—?" And that was when he patted his cheque-book. Plus, of course, darling Clive will put his cash up front, as usual.' The innocent face vanished. 'So what do you say to *that*, then?'

She was too damn sure of herself. 'I'd say he's wasting his money. And so are we—and our time, too.'

She frowned. 'What d'you mean?'

The trouble was, he wasn't at all sure of himself. 'If what you say is true . . . if there *is* a Clinton-Butler operation of some sort, on the level you suggest . . . and if the man Audley *was*

77

somehow involved with Masson's death . . . for heaven's sake, Jen! It's going to be buried deeper than we're likely to be able to dig—that for a start—'

'The hell with that!' She snapped at him. 'Who said we can't? Who's better than us—you and me?' The Fielding bosom inflated angrily, and pointed at him. 'Besides which, as you well know . . . once you *know* there's a secret, there's always a way of uncovering it—' She caught her anger as she observed his face. 'We've done it before, Ian. We did it in Beirut—didn't we?'

'Yes.' And it was a commentary on her that she still didn't understand what a damned close-run thing that had been—and how much the memory of it still scared him. And how much the same memory *ought* to frighten her. 'But this is different.'

'How—different?'

'For a start . . . because they won't let us publish. Even if Dick Woodward is willing to stick his neck out. Which he won't be.'

'Oh—*come on!*' The fire kindled again. 'Just because of Peter Wright, and all that . . . *We* haven't signed the Official Secrets Act—*we* aren't going to publish secret documents—at least, not unless we can get hold of any, that is—' She smiled grimly at him through the flames. 'The Peter Wright thing doesn't stop us: he's made it Open Season, more like—don't you see, Ian?'

'No. I don't see. There's still the law, Jen—'

'The law?' She stopped for an instance. 'Well, I don't know . . . But I've talked to Simon Lovel about that. And he says that practicalities are going to come into that now—or *im*practicalities, where they're dealing with people like us: he says that

78

"acquisition" can't be an offence, otherwise they'd have prosecuted other people long before. And then, if we're just the teeniest bit careful . . . and he'll vet every line you write, Simon says he will . . . then there's a hell of a lot we can get away with, under "Public Interest"—*Pro bono publico*, as John Tully would say.' The grim smile showed again, quite different from her more mischievous grin. 'Audley won't sue. Because they won't let him—they never defend their own. Not like the KGB . . . But, if we're right, he won't *anyway*—will he?'

They were back to one of his earlier thoughts. 'You know him—? Do you know him, Jen?'

'Never met him in my life, so far as I know.' She frowned, as though running memories backwards. 'Big ugly fellow, apparently.' The frown cleared. 'That's a pleasure in store, darling.'

For her, anyway: 'big ugly fellows' couldn't very well thump young lady investigative-writers, certainly—not without the direst consequences. But this time, with time so short, she needed her Ian up there with her, in the forefront of the battle. And that wasn't reassuring. 'So why are you so hell-bent on nailing him, Jen?'

'I'm not.' No smile, no grin, now: she looked as neutral as Switzerland. Yet there was a cold glitter in her eye he'd never seen before. 'But this is one book I really want to see published.'

It couldn't be avarice, surely? 'We don't need the money, Jen. Not that badly.'

'The money?' Sudden anger replaced the coldness. 'Don't be silly, Ian. You're the one who likes money. I don't need it—remember?'

That was hurtful— and all the more so because

she intended it to be. And that wasn't really Jenny. 'I'm sorry—'

She closed her eyes for an instance. 'No! I'm the one who should be sorry. That was dirty. And you weren't being silly—you just don't know, that's all. It was before your time—*our* time.'

'Our time?' Whatever it was, it had hurt her. And whatever it was she wanted, he was going to do it for her, he realized. 'What was, Jen? 1978—?'

'Korea.' She produced the name like a rabbit out of a top-hat.

'Korea?' One of their future possible subjects (which, now he heard himself repeat it, Jenny herself had floated) had been the Korean phenomenon, in anticipation of all the Olympic coverage, and the possible political nastiness which might attend the event.

Jenny nodded. 'Philip Masson was a lovely man. And he was also a Royal Marine, long ago, in Korea.'

'A Royal—?'

'In the war—the Korean War.' She seemed to lose patience with him, where the moment before she had conceded that he couldn't know what she was talking about. 'Philly Masson carried Daddy for miles, on his back, in the middle of winter, with the Chinese shooting at them all the time—Daddy wouldn't have survived without him: he would have frozen to death before he'd died of wounds, if the Chinese hadn't finished him off, he said Philly saved his life.' She looked at him. 'So you could say, he saved *my* life, too. Because I wouldn't have been born if he hadn't done that. And . . . he was my godfather, Ian. And I loved him.'

CHAPTER THREE

It was Reg Buller who put his finger on it. And he put his finger quite literally on it (and slightly drunkenly, slurring his words a little), as he stabbed the projected enlargement of the microfilmed newspaper page.

'*Thish ish it! You mark my wordsh, Ian lad! Thish ish it!*'

Ian had spent three good hours in the library by then, dissecting the anatomy of an almost perfect murder, albeit without ever getting close to the victim. Because, if there was one certain thing about the death of Philip Masson, it was that he'd never actually been on board the *Jenny III* on the evening and night of Friday/Saturday, November 17/18, 1978.

But, equally certainly, somebody who knew his job had been on the *Jenny III* instead of him.

The reliable *Daily Telegraph* had done its own job well, in reporting the eventual inquest at length on page 3. Maybe there hadn't been a good murder trial that day, to lead the page. Or perhaps some smart editor had calculated that there might be a great many yachtsmen among the *Telegraph* readers, who would study every line of three columns thinking all the time *this could have been me!*

Time: 3.35 pm, Saturday, November 18; Wind: South-West freshening; sea: moderate to rough—

The yacht *Jenny III* (no prizes for guessing why she had been so named) had been found by a fisherman, adrift ten miles south of the Needles.

There had of course been no one on board, but (or because of that) the fisherman had been observant: the mainsail had been sheeted hard home, as for close-hauled sailing, and reefed down; the working jib had been set, but was flapping; the jib sheets were lying on deck, shackle in place, but pin missing; the tiller was lashed amidships; the navigation lights and the instruments were switched on, but the battery was almost flat. And the inflatable dinghy was rolled up and still in its locker.

He hadn't understood a great deal of that, but it had become clearer as the experts and the friends of the missing man had added their evidence and their theories bit by bit.

The *Jenny III* had evidently been Philip Masson's pride-and-joy ('Mr Masson, a senior civil servant in the Ministry of Defence, and former Royal Marines Officer, who had won the Military Cross in Korea'—as an ex-Marine, it was no surprise that he had the smell of the sea in his nostrils, of course).

He had kept her at Lymington during the summer. She was an old Folkboat (overall length 25 feet, waterline 19.68, beam 7.22; displacement 2.16 tons), built in the '50s in traditional style, and made to last. Probably, he could have afforded something better (or so said Elwyn Rhys-Lewis, his grieving friend and a fellow yachtsman)—

'But she suited him. He often sailed her

82

single-handed, you see, and he had her fitted out accordingly, with all the halyards led aft to the cockpit, a downhaul on the jib, and a system of cleats to hold the tiller in place if he had to go below. But she was a good sea-boat—she'd stand up to anything the sea would throw at her. After all, Blondie Hasler sailed a Folkboat in the first single-handed race, back in 1960—'

Elwyn Rhys-Lewis had been a good witness; maybe even a bit *too* good, in building up the picture?

So he had underlined *Elwyn Rhys-Lewis* in his notebook, for possible further consideration.

But this pride-and-joy had been kept in immaculate order, anyway—with a fair amount of help from old George White, over at Hamworthy. George was apparently a shipwright of the old school, and what he didn't know about wooden boats wasn't worth knowing. So that was why Philip Masson always laid the *Jenny III* up at Poole during the winter, said Mr Rhys-Lewis.

* * *

'We shall never know exactly what happened. But thanks to the evidence which we have heard, a fair reconstruction of what may have happened is possible,' the coroner had concluded at last.

'That Friday evening, the deceased went down to Lymington, for his Rover car was found in the car park. He must have gone straight on to his boat, though no one remembers seeing him. But we have heard that he had made no secret of his intention to sail her round to Poole as soon as possible, having already left it a little late in the season owing to pressure of work in London.

'There was, we have heard, a stiff south-westerly wind blowing that Friday, with the threat of worse forecast. These were not ideal conditions for the passage he planned to take, but nothing that he and his boat could not handle. At all events, he probably heard the late night forecast of a low pressure area building up in the Atlantic, and he must have decided to make a night passage.

'In that event, he probably motored her down from Lymington to Hurst Point. Or (as we have heard) may have sailed, even though he would have had to tack all the way. But he would have had an ebb tide under him, at all events.' (This coroner sounded as though it hadn't been his first sea tragedy, Ian had noted there.)

'Mr Rhys-Lewis and Mr White are both agreed that he would then have hoisted sail, prudently putting a tuck in the main. And once round Hurst he would have proceeded on the port tack, taking the inshore channel to pass north of the Shingles. With a south-westerly wind he would have made good progress for two or three miles, and gone over to the starboard tack once he was sure of clearing the Shingles.

'It is at this point, one may suspect, that something went wrong, and we must attempt to recreate the situation from the little evidence we have.

'The deceased would most probably have been intending to head out to sea on a southerly course, and once clear of the Shingles to have gone about, and sailed across Poole Bay until he picked up the Fairway. By then the tide would have turned, so he would have had a fair run into Poole entrance.

Daylight would then not have been far away, so he would have timed it exactly right to arrive at Poole Bridge for the early morning opening. With a mooring waiting for him in Holes Bay, he would have intended to go ashore at Cobbs Quay, and then taken a taxi back to Lymington, as he had done before on such occasions.

'But this he never did. We must surmise, rather, that when he went on to the starboard tack, probably somewhere off Barton in Christchurch Bay, the jib sheet shackle came adrift. It is significant that when the boat was found the jib was flogging and the sheets lying on deck, with the pin gone from the shackle.

'That, for an experienced yachtsman, would have been only a minor annoyance. All he had to do was to find a spare shackle, clamber up to the foredeck to fit it, return to the cockpit, and then sheet in and carry on.

'Being perhaps a little further inshore than he cared to be, he would have lashed the tiller and sailed towards open sea under mainsail alone as he hunted out a shackle and fitted it to the jib.

'It is at this moment, also, that he should have taken those precautions which should have been second nature to him—'

(This was where the coroner had ceased to be a yachtsman, and had become all-coroner, sad and solemn and wise-after-the-event. But it had been good old Elwyn Rhys-Lewis who had been more convincing earlier.)

('Yes, of course he should have put on a lifejacket,

and a safety-harness—or both—before he went up on the foredeck. But there are times when you just go ahead and get the job done . . . And how long would he have lasted in a cold sea on a November night—dangling over the side and unable to climb back? I remember chaps in the navy who didn't want to learn to swim—they said it only prolonged the agony.')

(The coroner had reprimanded him at that point!)

('Yes, sir—that may be. But a single hander's motto is "Don't go over in the first place", sir.')

So there it was: at that point Elwyn Rhys-Lewis and the Coroner had both agreed on the 'freak wave' theory. Which Rhys-Lewis had more vividly described as 'the Sod's Law of the Sea'—'when wind-and-water hit you in that single unguarded moment, groping around to catch a flogging sail—and then you're over the side and alone, with your boat sailing on without you, to the Port of Heaven—'

'We may be somewhat surprised that the body of the deceased was not recovered in the search next day, or that it never came ashore as others have done. But we have also heard an expert witness from the RNLI testify that the ebbing tide would have carried it several miles into the bay. And if it finished up in the Needles Channel, in the shipping lane, then it may have been hit by a large vessel well before daylight.

'So, before I record my verdict, it is more than ever necessary for me to emphasize that, however experienced one may be, the necessary and prudent precautions must be paramount. One witness has spoken of what he called "the Sod's Law of the sea". But—'

That had given the *Telegraph* sub-editor his arresting headline '*"Sod's Law" Killed yachtsman*'.

*　　*　　*

But that had been a 'Sod's Law of the sea'. And it had been a quite different Sod's Law—a 'Sod's Law *of the land*' which had finally brought Philip Masson into the light, all these years afterwards; which, in his neat little report, Reg Buller had pounced on smartly:

'Why did they plant him there? It's a good question, because bodies have a way of turning up. HM prisons are full of people who believed otherwise. But these chummies weren't so stupid as that, they just had very bad luck. Because that old ruin, where they planted him—and the nice old farmhouse on the hillside above, where the kids came from—was all due to go under the line of the motorway. So the machines would have cut through the hillside above there, and piled the soil on top of the ruin and buried him deep. And what must have given the chummies the idea was that it was about that time that the "Motorway Murders" came to light: this bulldozer driver was murdering women in his spare time, and then covering them deep next morning at work. That was a year or two before, but it was a big talking-point. Only then the Government fell, so there was a new Minister. And they found a lot of rare flowers on the moor there, which didn't grow anywhere else. So they finally re-routed the motorway by a couple of miles in 1980, and left that bit out. This is what's

called "Green Politics" today, I believe. But I'd call it "bad luck" . . . for chummie.'

More like *very* bad luck, Ian had mentally added there. Because the alleged drowning of Philip Masson had otherwise been perfect. There had been no dangerous carrying of bodies (always a risky business; and, presumably, Masson had been intercepted and murdered close to where he'd been buried, in the middle of rural nowhere). And then a false Masson had taken his car on, and slipped aboard the *Jenny III* in the gathering dusk, either taking another inflatable on board to get ashore, or (in view of the weather) rendezvousing with one of his confederates just north of the Shingles.

But, otherwise . . . it had been damn-near perfect, with no tell-tale body (bodies also were always a risk, however neatly killed; and with Philip Masson the autopsy would have been very thorough, for sure); but, for the rest, it had been utterly professional—plausible and detailed, but not too detailed . . . just basically *ordinary*.

Those three hours hadn't been wasted; the deceptive half of Philip Masson's death would eventually make a good detailed chapter in the story—and if Elwyn Rhys-Lewis turned out to be as good-and-true a friend as he sounded; which, on mature reflection, he probably was; but even then he would supply more good copy, as he gnashed his teeth about the way he had innocently helped his friend's murderers. So it was already shaping up nicely—it would make a fascinating contrast even . . . the *false* inquest, before the real one—

And then the door had banged, and Reg Buller had

made his entrance.

'I've lost my bloody pipe.' He patted all his bulging pockets, ignoring the 'No Smoking' notice, and the worried hovering of Ian's favourite assistant librarian until she got round in front of him. 'It'sh all right, love—I wasn't going to smoke it. I was only going to suck it. An' . . . I know how to work the machine—an' how to wind the film back afterwards. Don't worry, love.'

'It is all right, Miss Russell.' Ian didn't think it was at all 'all right'. But Reg Buller had also been at work on 1978 elsewhere this afternoon, and he desperately wanted to know what had come out of the latest foray. And, in any event, since Reg was in no case to look after him, he must look after Reg. 'I know this gentleman. And I'll vouch for him, Miss Russell.'

Miss Russell gave him a disappointed-fearful look. 'Just so he doesn't make any *noise*, Mr Robinson. You can talk here—' She could smell Reg now, and didn't find him reassuring. '—but no *noise*, if you please.'

'No noise!' Buller put his finger to his lips. 'If you hear a noise—it's *him*, not me. Trust me!' He almost knocked over a chair, watching it rock without trying to rescue it before he sat down in it. 'No noise!'

Miss Russell had fled then. And Reg Buller hadn't made a sound, as he went about his business, after he had briefly explained where he'd been.

But now his chair scraped back noisily.

'Thish ish it. You mark my wordsh, Ian lad! Thish ish it!'

Ian looked up from his notes, but past Buller, not at him, to make sure that Miss Russell (never mind

89

her boss) was not within earshot of this over-loud pronouncement. His credit was good in this library, as it needed to be with all the work he did in it because of its excellent range of microfilmed newspapers; and, at a pinch, it might survive the brewery-fumes Reg was exhaling. But it would never survive that deadliest of sins, *noise*.

Buller sat back, staring at him. 'Well, c'mon an' *shee*—'

'*Sssh!* For heaven's sake, Reg!'

Buller looked round. 'It's all right—' The slur disappeared magically but the voice was still far too loud. '—there's nobody out there. I made sure of that. We're okay.'

'Nobody', of course, excluded librarians in Reg Buller's *dramatis personae*, and until John Tully came up with answers, that was the best they could hope for. But he had worked too hard here to obtain his special privileges to let Buller queer his pitch. 'I meant *you*, man—' He pointed at the other printed legend on the wall '—that means "No piss-artists and dossers-coming-in-from-the-cold", Reg.'

'There's no call to be offensive. An' inaccurate—' Buller adjusted his upper dentures with a callused thumb and index finger ostentatiously '—I've been having trouble with this new set of choppers. And it isn't cold. And anything I may have imbibed this fine Monday was strictly in the line of duty, as I carefully explained to you—' His voice fell nevertheless, from jubilant conversational to a penetrating stage-whisper. '—you just look at this, Ian lad. An' then I may accept your apology.'

Ian steeled himself against disappointment as he got up. It was just conceivably possible that he had

90

done Buller an injustice, but unlikely—at least, so far as the imbibing was concerned. What he had remembered from previous occasions was that Reg's 'necessary disbursements to contacts', which figured substantially in his expense account, chiefly related to alcohol, rather than to old-fashioned back-handers (although these figured also, in nicely round multiples of five in sterling, and of tens and hundreds in foreign monopoly currencies). But then, of course, 'contacts'—'contacts' back-handed when necessary, but alcoholically-oiled invariably— were the very stuff of Reg's *modus operandi*. And in this case it had been 'a bloke I know in the Street, who's a sub on *The People* now—but he was a young reporter on the *Northern Gazette* back in '78, and he's doing shifts now, to keep his ex-wife in gin-an'-tonic', and 'I had to fill him up in the Star before I could get him to talk, and not remember what I'd asked him about afterwards'. And because of all of *that*, it had seemed quite depressingly possible that Reg had been enjoying himself at Fielding and Robinson's expense, just for starters.

'All right, Reg—' But then he remembered also that Reg got results. And that Reg, in spite of his warnings, seemed to be excited by this one (false teeth or alcohol notwithstanding) '—let's have a look, then.'

Buller shifted obligingly, to allow him to peer under the canopy at the magnified projection of the reel of microfilm.

'I can't see a bloody thing, Reg—it's all out of focus.' It occurred to him insanely that Buller, seeing everything out of focus already, had had to de-focus it in order actually to see it. But, even out of focus, the main headline was still just readable.

91

'Oh—sorry!' Reg adjusted the focus, first swimming it into pale grey infinity, and then sharpening it into readability. '*There*—eh?'

DEATH OF A MAD DOG, Ian read again obediently. And was again repelled by the crude simplicity of the message in its tabloid form, however eye-catchingly true it might have been (he remembered also reading similar proclamations of this same event, in smaller type and more sober words, in *The Times*, and the *Guardian* and the *Daily Telegraph*, not an hour ago, on this same machine; but Reg had naturally chosen his favourite newspaper).

'So—?' Twisting back towards Buller, he caught the full reek of Reg's share of those 'necessary disbursements'.

'"Mad Dog O'Leary"—?' At close quarters Reg Buller's eyes were like nothing so much as two halves of the same blood-orange. 'Christ! I suppose you were a fucking student at the time, demonstrating because your grant didn't keep you in beer-money! Or what was it—Rhodesia? Or bleeding Watergate, an' poor old Trickey-Dickie—?'

'Watergate wasn't '78.' Having just been all through the papers of the time, Ian felt safe enough now: he could even place Michael 'Mad Dog' O'Leary in his brief nine-days' horror context. And he was not about to admit how little of what he had read had struck any chord of memory, even though he had lived through that November and had presumably read in the original what he and Reg Buller had now re-read on this machine. Truthfully, except for a vague recollection that those had been The Last Days of Labour, Before

92

Thatcher, with threatened bakers' strikes, nurses' strikes and car workers' strikes, he could remember very little of that 'Winter of Discontent', in which 'Mad Dog' had been just another horror story among many. 'Actually, I was just beginning to panic before my final examinations, Reg. But I do remember we weren't doing too well in Australia.'

'Australia?'

'In the cricket, Reg.' Knowing that Buller despised all sports, he felt he was somehow reasserting himself. 'It was rather depressing, as I recall.'

'You can say that again! That whole bloody winter was depressing—'

'I meant the cricket.' Quite deliberately, he decided to keep the man in his place by ignoring 'Mad Dog' for the moment. 'What did your chap on *The People* have to tell you, then?'

'Huh!' Buller licked his lips, as though he had just remembered that the pubs were open again (in so far as they ever closed in Fleet Street). 'He'd just seen his gaffer—Robert Maxwell in person—comin' down from on high *en route* to his helicopter pad . . . An' 'e looks around—Captain Bob looks around—an' sez: "Ah! probably the largest electronic newsroom in Europe!"' He grinned at Ian. 'Which is what he always says, apparently. An' no one takes the slightest notice of 'im—' The grin congealed suddenly, as he realized what was happening. 'You don't remember 'Mad Dog' O'Leary, then?'

'Of course I do.' Ian attempted a superior Tully-expression. 'He tried to blow up the Northern Ireland Secretary in Yorkshire, at some university ceremony. And then they cornered him,

93

and shot him. So what?'

'So what? *So what—?*' Reg Buller spluttered slightly. Then he pointed at the brightly projected headlines. 'It's all there, damn it!'

Ian had to study the words again—

Cornered at last in a remote Yorkshire beauty spot, 'Mad Dog' O'Leary died as he lived yesterday afternoon: in a hail of gunfire—

The only thing odd about that, it seemed to him, was that there were too many words in the first sentence, including a subordinate clause, for good tabloid journalism.

Tipped off by informants, British Secret Service agents gunned him down without mercy. But he killed an innocent girl before he died—

Nothing odd about that, either. Except another subordinate clause, anyway. 'I don't see what's all there, Reg. You tell me—?'

'Christ, man!' Reg Buller started rewinding the microfilm at break-neck pace, stopping and starting with other arresting headlines—BREAD: PANIC BUYING—HOME LOANS SHOCK . . . and OLIVIA NEWTON-JOHN SPEAKS OUT—swearing all the while. Then he stopped rewinding and swearing, and adjusted the focus. 'There, then!'

They were back to the abortive bombing of the University of North Yorkshire, when the Mad Dog had failed to kill the Northern Ireland Secretary, and half the university faculty with him, *'thanks to the selfless heroism of a British Secret Service agent*

94

masquerading as a professor, in mortar-board and gown'.

'So—?' For a guess, it was the same reporter—or the same rewrite man, and the same sub-editor, acting on the same instructions from an editor or proprietor who had either decided that the Security Service needed a bit of favourable PR, or had been successfully lobbied to the same effect; but, either way, that repetition of the legendary 'British Secret Service', with all its nuances of James Bond, was a dead give-away. Because no one on the spot would ever have used that description. And now, in the post-Peter Wright era, it wouldn't have been fashionable: most likely, it would have been 'SAS marksmen', if not the Special Branch's anti-terrorist squad.

Buller was shaking his head, though. 'You haven't really looked—have you?'

'At the papers?' He had read more responsible accounts than this one, of the same event. 'There's more in the *Guardian*, Reg—'

'This is the one that matters. This is *my* man, who was there before any of the big ones.' Buller grimaced at him. 'But you're also forgetting what I told you yesterday, before Johnny and the Lady disturbed us—an' afterwards, when they'd gone off.'

More accurately, when Buller had *ordered* them off, thought Ian: Jenny through the front door, to take off one watcher; and then John Tully, through the back way, to draw away his comrade. And then, after Reg had lunched on bread and cheese and a bottle of *Père Patriach* (the Cologne beer being exhausted), Ian himself had been ordered into the rain ('although I don't reckon they'll have put

95

anyone on you, seeing as you don't do much at the sharp end anymore ... But, just in case, anyway—?'); and, although that had been insulting, he had obeyed; but now he must remember what had passed between them before he had done so.

'About David Audley, you mean, Reg?' Buller had talked with 'a bloke I know', was what he remembered: with Reg Buller there was an inevitable succession of 'blokes', from dukes to dustmen, via policemen and journalists, all of whom seemed to owe him one favour for another; but in this instance it had been almost certainly ('No names—right?') one of his old Special Branch *mukkers*—

Buller nodded, only half mollified by such a simple correct answer. 'Look how it stacks up: "masquerading as a professor", eh? And "mortar-board an' gown"—? Who'd they choose for that—that's got the balls to do it, as well, in cold blood?'

There was more here than either Reg himself or his favourite newspaper had said. 'In cold blood?'

Another nod. 'Somebody carried O'Leary's bomb out of that building—the new library they were opening, or whatever it was ... When they didn't reckon they could get the people away from it, before the bugger pressed his remote control button.' Buller tapped the 'selfless heroism' passage. 'Who better than Audley? One of his mates was running that show, on the security side, apparently. An' Audley's the professor-type—*looks* the part. Wouldn't need to *play* it, though. Because he's already a visiting fellow at that Oxford college, see.' Buller gave him a sidelong look. 'Wouldn't need a cover story to be there, either ... An' no shortage of guts, so they say.'

It was all hypothetical, thought Ian. Or, alternatively, Buller knew more than he was saying. 'Who's "they", Reg?'

'Friend of mine.' Buller grinned.

'The one on *The People*?'

'No. The one I told you about yesterday—the one that tipped me off about him being tricky—Audley . . . remember?'

What Ian remembered was that Buller had been characteristically vague about his Audley-source. But what was more immediately important was to uncover the foundations on which this hypothesis was built. And those seemed to involve his other friend, the sub-editor on *The People*, rather than the Audley-source.

'So what was it that your chap on the newspaper told you, Reg?'

Buller tapped his nose. 'He was there. That's what.'

Ian looked down at the Yorkshire university bomb story. At a ceremony like that—a routine academic event until 'Mad Dog' O'Leary had singled it out for attention—there might or might not have been one or two education correspondents from the London papers, depending on whether they'd been tipped off that an important speech was going to be made. There would certainly have been reporters from all the local Yorkshire papers, taking down all the speeches whether they were important or not, and probably taking down the names of all the local dignitaries too—that was to be expected anywhere, and especially in Yorkshire, with its fierce local pride. And as Buller's Fleet Street friend had then been a reporter on one of those papers—which was it? But it hardly mattered, anyway—his presence at the ceremony was quite unremarkable. So why was Buller looking as though he'd made some great discovery?

Suddenly the light dawned. 'You mean . . . he was at—the *other* place—where O'Leary was shot—?' *'My man was there before any of the big ones'* he remembered belatedly. 'Your chap . . . who's on *The People* now?'

'That's right.' Buller stared at him. 'He was at Thornervaulx.'

So there was more. 'And—?' He tried to look intelligent.

'That's right.' For once Buller was deceived. *'He was there—right!'*

'He—' This time the light was blinding. *'Audley*—you're sure—?'

'Near enough. "Big ugly fellow—bit like a boxer . . . or a rugger player. Broken nose—that sort of thing." Pretty accurate description, actually. Because he did break his nose playing rugger, as it happens.'

'I thought you said he looked like a professor.'

'That's when he opens his mouth.' Buller amended his own description without shame. 'Take it from me, that's him right enough. No mistake.'

And that, of course, validated the bombed-university hypothesis, via the O'Leary connection. The security service must have been tipped off that O'Leary intended to assassinate the Northern Ireland Minister at the opening of the new library and the degree ceremony. They had foiled the bomb attempt, but it had been a close shave. And O'Leary himself had also escaped, only it had been a damn close shave for him, too: in fact, he hadn't really escaped—he'd simply broken out of the inner ring—?

'How far is Thornervaulx from the University of Yorkshire, Reg?' He couldn't place Thornervaulx on his mental map: it was one of that famous concentration of ruined abbeys in the North . . . Rievaulx, Jervaux, Byland, Fountains, Kirkstall and Thornervaulx: originally they'd all been in the wilds, and most of them still were, including Thornervaulx no doubt.

'Not far, as the crow flies. But you've got to go round the little roads, and up over the dale to reach it.' Buller had the facts at his finger-tips, as usual. 'Takes a bit of finding.'

That fitted, too. With all the main roads blocked, O'Leary would have been forced off the beaten track, and had then been hunted down like the wild animal he was in the wilds. 'And your man was actually there.'

'Not at the shoot-out.' Buller nodded nevertheless. 'But within minutes of it—aye.'

Again, that wasn't impossible: a smart local reporter (and Reg Buller's contacts were always the smart ones) would have his friends in the Police, and could often be so well in with them as to be just behind them. 'And he saw Audley there—actually *saw* him?'

'He saw more than that.' Buller started winding the film forward again from the North Yorkshire bomb to the Thornervaulx gun battle, compressing the last long hunted hours of the 'Mad Dog' to ten blurred seconds. 'Or, rather, there were things that he *didn't* see, you might say.'

'What d'you mean—"didn't see"?'

Buller stopped the microfilm, and then adjusted

99

the focus with maddening slowness until DEATH OF
A MAD DOG shouted at them again. Only then did
he turn to Ian. 'It wasn't like that. That's not what
happened.' He shook his head. 'Terry—let's call
him "Terry". Because that's his name—Terry
didn't write it like that. He flogged 'em the
story—and for a small fortune too. Because he was
the only one that was there. So all the other stories
are based on his—or, rather, what was *made* of his
. . . and the official statements, of course.' The big
mouth twisted cynically. 'Which just happened to
tally exactly, you see—the *official* statement . . .
and his *edited* story.' An eyebrow lifted in support
of the mouth. 'Is that plain enough for you?'

'All too plain.' So somebody had got at the
editor, Reg was saying. But that was a risky thing to
do, they both knew. Because contrary to left-wing
received wisdom, the D-Notice people couldn't give
orders. 'You're sure?'

'Oh yes.' Nod. 'He put that story out twice,
Terry did. To his own paper first—the *Northern
Gazette* . . . an' then he re-wrote it, an' flogged it to
them—' He tapped the projected front page. '—for
the equivalent of two months' wages an' the
promise of a job with them.' Buller paused. 'So that
story went to two newspapers independently, the
way Terry wrote it . . . just with a few slight
differences. And it came out *not* how he wrote it,
but with the same amendments. Okay?'

'Yes.' So it hadn't been some re-write man, or
some sub-editor: someone had got at *two* editors.
And that meant that someone had been very
persuasive indeed, at the highest level. Because
editors weren't nearly as easily persuaded (or
bullied, or blackmailed) as the people also liked to

think. 'So what really happened, Reg?'

'Ah . . .' Having at last arrived where he had always intended to be, Buller relaxed. And, having learnt a thing or two over the years about stage management, and man-management, Ian understood what was happening to him. But knowing that was at least a quarter of the battle, if not half of it.

'I've read all this.' He gestured into the machine dismissively. 'And I'm thirsty. D'you know a good pub round here, Reg?'

'Round here?' Although it was an almost-insultingly silly question, Buller pretended to consider it briefly. 'I think . . . yes, I *think* . . . there may be one just round the corner—' He looked round the Newspapers and Periodicals room as though it might be conveniently sign-posted '—just round the corner—yes. I think.'

'Yes?' It was time to assert himself—even though he was also actually thirsty. 'You bloody-knew, Reg—come on, then—'

'So . . . what *really* happened, then?' As he drank thirstily he registered caution. Because this was Abbott beer, and more than two pints would put him into orbit round the planet, while Reg Buller wouldn't even have lift-off, never mind escape-velocity. And, judging by the barmaid's greeting, Reg Buller was an old and valued customer here, too.

'*Ahhh* . . .' Most of that was genuine satisfaction-and-relief, as Buller downed half his pint: the distant swirl of the pipes at Lucknow, the first sight of the sails of the relieving fleet before

101

they broke the boom at the siege of Londonderry, the thunder of the hoofs of the US cavalry—all that, and Mafeking too, and Keats opening Chapman's *Homer*, and stout Cortez getting his first glimpse of the Pacific Ocean . . . all that historic experience was re-lived when Reg Buller opened his throat at Opening Time. But that wasn't the end of Reg, it was only his beginning.

'It was accident, of course.' Buller wiped his mouth with the back of his hand.

'Accident?' It wasn't that the man ever lied, when he was on the payroll; it was just that he always doled out the truth bit by bit, to keep the client eager for more. But then (and what made the technique bearable), *more* was usually worth the extra money in the end.

'Yes. Because . . . after that bomb went off, at the university, they didn't know their arse from their elbow. An' it wasn't this bloke who was a friend of Audley's—Colonel Butler . . . Apparently, he was a good sort, even if he was foisted on them at the last moment. All the coppers liked him—said he wasn't at all like the usual run of Sandhurst-types, an' superior Oxford-and-Cambridge civil servants . . . aye, an' the cloak-and-dagger brigade, making 'em feel like peasants at a big party . . . No, *he* was civil to them, an' efficient with it, an' knew his job. But he only arrived at the last minute, to take over. An' there was lots of new surveillance equipment—all high tech stuff . . . half of which was on the blink, see—?'

'But they knew O'Leary was there, somewhere—?'

'*Oh yes!* They *knew*—someone had doublecrossed

O'Leary, somewhere down the line.' Nod. 'All these different IRA off-shoots . . . O'Leary was 'ILA'—*Irish Liberation Army* . . . which was a short-lived splinter-group no one ever seems to have quite sussed out. But *not* to be confused with the INLA—the Irish *National* Liberation Army—see?'

After Beirut this was peanuts. But, nevertheless, he had always steered Jenny away from Irish entanglements whenever that possibility had arisen; and (probably because of her divided family loyalties) he had never had any trouble there. So heaven only knew what she would make of this complication, then.

'But he was IRA—ultimately, Reg?'

'God only knows! When you get far out, on the edge . . . you don't know who you're really dealing with: it could be the really top IRA boyos, with their big cars parked outside their big houses in Dublin . . . or it could be the Marxist-Leninists, pure in thought—an' put a bomb in an orphanage, if they reckoned it could further the workers' cause, long term . . . Or it could be the Mafia or the KGB, doin' what comes naturally—' Buller shrugged. '—if you want to know what Michael O'Leary was for . . . then you'd best ask Colonel Butler—or maybe David Audley. But don't rely on whatever they tell you. So don't ask *me*, for God's sake!' Grin. 'But somebody peached on him—O'Leary— anyway. Yes.' Out of the shrug, and the grin, came recovery. 'The point is, O'Leary missed his target—all he got was half-a-dozen ducks, on a duckpond, when the bomb went off.' Genuine grin. 'So fuck him, then.'

'But he got away.' Deep inside Reg Buller, within the cynicism, there was a core of old-fashioned patriotism, like a Falklands Factor, thirsty for victory after years of defeat. 'Didn't he? Until Thornervaulx, anyway.'

Buller shook his head. 'No. He got *clean* away. He was a pro, was O'Leary: he had his escape route all mapped out—they didn't get a smell of him, not a smell.' Shake became nod. 'He was a real pro.'

There was something not right here—something which *did* smell. 'What are you trying to tell me, Reg? He *did* get away, at first . . . But they *did* catch him—'

'No. That's just the story in the papers.'

And you never ought to believe what's in the newspapers. And Buller had already told him that, anyway. So that was the end of the questions: he would wait now, for the answers.

Buller tossed his head, accepting his silence. 'Accident, I told you . . . Terry was driving down this road, in the rain . . . Actually, he was goin' to interview this CND Vicar he knew, who was refusing to have a Remembrance Service, the next day. Because it was a Saturday—November 11. An' the next day was when they were all going to have the services, an' Terry reckoned there might be a demonstration against the Vicar, an' he might be able to flog a story to Fleet Street. So he was just sewing up the loose ends, in his spare time. Because he wasn't covering a football match, that Saturday afternoon.'

Ian drank another careful measure. It was now Saturday, November 11, 1978 . . . on a wet afternoon, somewhere near Thornervaulx Abbey in Yorkshire. And that was still a week away from Philip Masson's own last journey, to his shallow grave far to the south, anyway.

104

'So he was driving along, minding his own business—' Reg Buller drained his glass, and lifted it towards the barmaid, catching her eye instantly, as Ian himself never could '—an' he heard this Police siren, in the distance—' Down went the glass, but not the eye, which was fixed on the stretched black silk, and 40D-cups which barely restrained the advance of those splendid breasts towards them, past less favoured customers. 'Thank you, love. And my friend too, love.' Buller encompassed her, overhanging-bosom and all, as she swept away his empty glass and replaced it with a full one, leaving Ian's unfinished one contemptuously, and was gone. 'An' then he heard another bell . . . so being Terry—or *Tel*, as we always used to call him . . . an' being properly brought up . . . he turned his car round, an' followed 'em.'

That was right: that was the old style journalist, of Reg Buller's vintage, who followed the sound of the policeman's siren and the fireman's bell in the same way as the old-fashioned captains had steered their ships towards the sound of the guns, in the hope of bloodshed.

'Of course, the Police 'ud been out, all that weekend, running about like blue-arsed flies, after any word of O'Leary.' Buller shrugged. 'But the word was, they reckoned, he was long gone—Liverpool, or Glasgow, or Manchester . . . But long gone, anyway. But there was always a chance.'

That *was* the old style: the best stories were always the ones that came out of nowhere, very often. The trick was to pretend that they were no surprise, and that you'd expected them all along, sooner or later, having your finger on the pulse of events.

'So he followed 'em—round the roads over the top, down in the Thor Brook there, over the narrow bridge, where you have to back up if you don't get halfway across, an' some other car has just got there before you—it's the original old bridge, that the monks built, there.'

More and more, the picture was emerging: like, out of the original 1978 mist-and-rain, in darkest and most back-of-beyond North Yorkshire, under the dripping over-hanging trees in the deep valley of Thornervaulx Abbey, with the Police sirens shrieking anachronistically, to sound alarms which had not been heard there since the times of the wild Scottish raiders.

'So he got there with the Police, anyway.' Buller nodded. 'An' as they were hardly there before him, an' they didn't know who the hell he was . . . at first they didn't stop him—when he pushed his way in.'

That was also the old style: look like you belong there—plainclothes policeman, special branch man, doctor (serious-faced, bag-in-hand if you can find a bag)—John Tully always simply looked like himself, and waved an impressively embossed card with his photograph on it, which testified that he was a Count of the Holy Roman Empire; and that, with his superior manner, had passed him into all sorts of unlikely places. And, when it came to unlikely places, Thornervaulx Abbey—

He stopped in mid-thought as he realized

106

simultaneously that Reg Buller was looking at him expectantly, waiting for him to speak, and that he'd been following the wrong line of thought, from the wrong angle—Buller's Terry's angle. And Buller had told him all he needed to know about Terry, of course—

And then it was easy—

'It wasn't an ambush, of course—*of course!*' All the thrust of the newspaper stories had been that O'Leary had been 'cornered'—like the 'Mad Dog' he was: Reg's favourite newspaper had started its subordinate clause with that word, and two of the quality papers had used the word 'ambush' in their headlines. But siren-shrieking police cars coming from afar didn't attend ambushes. They would already have been there, or nearby, unmarked and tucked away unobtrusively.

'Right.' Buller leered at him for an instant, then raised Ian's empty glass for the barmaid to see, and then came back to him.'Or, rather . . . wrong.'

'Wrong?' He covered his own beer with his hand to stop her getting the wrong idea.

'It was an ambush all right.' Buller reached across him to surrender his glass for refilling. 'But it was O'Leary who was doing the ambushing, not Audley's lot.'

This time it was stronger than hypothesis. But it was still no better than circumstantial. And good old-fashioned incompetence could yet turn those circumstantial elements on their head. 'What makes you so sure?'

Buller waited until his glass was returned to him. 'Terry talked to someone there—there's two or three houses by the ruins. One of 'em was the custodian's . . . Ministry of Works, or National

107

Trust, or whatever it was then. An' he said there was a police car parked in the car park, large as life, on the forecourt, where the coaches and the day -trippers off-load—blue light on the top, day-glow orange-and-red strip along the side—from midday onwards. Plus other cars, that looked official. Not tourist cars, anyway . . . apart from the fact it was a November day—November 11 to be exact . . . An' that was why old Terry was round there: he was goin' to interview this CND Vicar, who was saying he wasn't goin' to encourage the British Legion in their militaristic practices—huh!' Reg Buller tossed his head derisively. '*Anyway* . . . it was a wet November Saturday—it 'ud been pissing with rain earlier, but it was down to a fine drizzle when Terry comes on the scene, just behind a couple of police cars. And there were several big home matches that weekend, too. So there weren't any tourists sight-seeing, to complicate matters.'

That was typical Buller understatement, after he had just enormously complicated what had seemed before to be a neatly open-and-shut episode of counter-intelligence anti-terrorist operations.

'Except the one girl, who was killed.' All this made the poor little thing's death even more poignant: her presence there, late in the afternoon on a wet November day, had been against the odds; and maybe the only target O'Leary had seen when he had failed to find his proper target for the second time in succession. But that raised a much more important question. 'So . . . who was he after, Reg—O'Leary—?' He frowned at Buller, as the more important question suddenly offered an answer which was dangerous because it was also much too quick, much too simple.

'Yes.' Buller had been there before him, and had also seen the same dangers. 'If it *was* Audley he was going for—if Audley *was* at the university, just before . . .' He cocked his head. And then straightened it to get at his beer. And then came back to Ian. 'A bit too easy—eh?'

Ian drank the last of his own beer. All this was following on their established technique: in any investigation; one had to start somewhere.

Sometimes it was easy, and one started at the beginning. But more often than not there was no clear beginning: the more one researched, the further back the beginning went, in that first month's careless Gadarene rush at the subject, open-minded. And out of that their line would come (usually out of Jenny's greater gathering of fact, and rumour, and fiction . . . and his own final interpretation of all that).

'What d'you think, Reg?' He mustn't let the man go off the boil.

'I dunno . . .' Buller stared down into his glass. 'But . . . even without that bugger Masson . . . we could 'ave a good one 'ere, y'know . . .'

That was another sign: Reg only dropped all his aitches either deliberately or *in extremis* with clients—at least, apart from when he also deliberately did so to annoy John Tully.

'A good one?'

'Aye. An' thass the truth.' Buller slurred again. 'We do O'Leary . . . and maybe we've got O'Leary gunning for Audley, an' Audley gunning for O'Leary—an' that's bloody good.' He cocked an eye at Ian again. 'But if we add Masson to it . . . O'Leary *versus* Audley—that's simple. But Audley *versus* Masson . . . that's bloody complicated, I tell

109

you.'

Suddenly there was no contest, no choice: always, and forever, doing the easy thing—dating the girl who'd say 'yes', in preference for the other girl, who'd already said 'no'—was never worth doing. 'Was Masson involved in the O'Leary killing?'

Buller shook his head. 'God only knows.' Then he looked at Ian sidelong. 'Old Johnny'll maybe answer that, when he comes in out of the cold. Because when that bomb went off, an' killed those ducks on the duck-pond . . . he was just a senior civil servant, Masson was. An' then, three days for O'Leary, an' a week for Masson . . . an' then they've got something in common, see?'

Then they were both dead, Ian saw. (But that had not been apparent at the time, except by eventual inquest verdict long afterwards. But that, also, was what had started all this now.)

He cast around for further objections, taking his accustomed role with Jenny, of Devil's advocate. 'In common with the girl—' He fished for the elusive name in his memory, from the follow-up newspaper reports '—Sandra—? Marilyn—?'

'Marilyn.' Buller set his empty glass down on the table. Then he looked up, directly and disconcertingly at Ian, challenging him. 'You know why I started with Thornervaulx—an' the bomb that killed the ducks—?'

No ducking that challenge. 'The timing.' They both knew the rules. 'We have to start somewhere.'

The challenge remained in place, like a gauntlet thrown down which he somehow hadn't noticed. 'The bloke I talked to first, about Audley—*he* said 'Look for anything that doesn't quite fit—anything

110

that's somehow out of the ordinary, an' doesn't quite have an easy answer . . . An' then take another look at *that* . . . if it's Audley you're after. Because he doesn't fit, either."'

The challenge was still there. 'How . . . doesn't Audley fit—at Thornervaulx?'

The corner of Buller's mouth twisted. 'Thornervaulx doesn't fit—in the bloody back of beyond.'

'But he was there.'

'Aye. And one or two others with him, that Terry remembers.' The mouth tightened. 'And Marilyn.'

Now the poor girl herself was a challenge. 'Marilyn—?'

'"*Marilyn Francis*"—"shorthand typist".' Buller nodded. 'Little slip of a girl—Terry actually saw her, stretched out like a little drowned rat, when they put her in the ambulance.' Another nod. 'That was just when they twigged who he was—an' bloody-near thumped 'im, one of 'em did . . . an' then they tried to arrest him, before the top brass came up an' threw him out.'

Ian waited.

'"*Marilyn Francis*".' Buller repeated the name.

Ian waited.

'There's no such person,' said Reg Buller.

CHAPTER FOUR

Ian felt pleased with himself as he left the churchyard: pleased, first and foremost, because he was not being tailed (if he ever had been); but pleased, second and professionally, because it was

111

just like old times, with the wind in his hair and the rain on his face; and he hadn't lost all his own skills, when it came to the crunch (or, anyway, it wasn't only Jenny who was lucky as well as smart!).

Although, to be honest with himself (and he could afford to be honest now, with all the hot-bath luxury of certainty), he had to give Reg Buller his due: Reg had not only zeroed-in on 'Marilyn Francis', but had added hard investigative graft and shoe-leather to his intuition to come up with British-American Electronics.

Odd though (he thought) *that it had been British-American's 'Research and Development' centre, of all its factories, which had recruited 'Marilyn Francis' as a temporary secretary all those years ago, out of nowhere: odd . . . or maybe not so odd now—?*

Not so odd. And not out of nowhere—or, not quite nowhere, even after Reg had tracked down the agency which answered Brit-Am's Rickmansworth factory's temporary needs (Reg passing himself off as the pushy manager of another agency, offering his own 'well-qualified young secretarial persons—we are registered with your local job-centre as a non-sexist, non-racial enterprise'—at competitive rates; and then Reg, having gleaned the name of Brit-Am's favoured agency, suborning its personnel clerk somehow to let him look at her records . . .).

That had been a dead end, in more ways than one: if she had ever lived (which she hadn't), 'Marilyn Francis' would have been long dead, and quite reasonably purged from what were once the agency books, and now the agency computer. But, in any case, that had been more than offset by his outrageous (though deserved) bit of luck, in uncovering the single newspaper reference to 'the dead girl, who worked for an electronics company in Rickmansworth, Hertfordshire'; which, significantly, had appeared only once (*'Someone didn't get the message—some copper who'd looked in her bag like, early on, an' didn't know no better . . . See how it becomes just "A clerical worker on holiday from London" later on? I'll bet they came down on him like a ton of bricks, poor bugger!'*). And that had been enough for Reg (although anyone could have carried on from there, given time; just, Reg was quicker on the ball, as well as off the mark), and then, while he had still been acclimatizing to the prospect of having to dig out information for himself again, at the sharp end, instead of sitting in his ivory tower and putting it all together, Reg had automatically taken charge—

'That inquest, up in Yorkshire, must 'ave been fucking dodgy—evidence of identification, an' getting the paperwork done, an' the right documents and the release for the body, after the post-mortem—somebody took the woman away, an' somebody buried her. So, most likely, *somebody* passed himself off as next-of-kin . . . That 'ud be the simplest way, if the Police were in on it, an' smoothing things, rather than asking awkward questions . . . Coroners aren't so easy—they can be right little Hitlers when they've a mind to . . . But the local Police, *they* wouldn't have liked it, if that was the way it was. An' that's what went wrong

113

with Philip Masson, when they found him . . . But up at Thornervaulx, the top brass were already on the spot—Audley an' his friends—so they were able to call the tune right from the start—'

Pattern, once again. But not history repeating itself in Philip Masson's case: in Philip Masson's case too much had been revealed too quickly when he'd turned up at last; whereas, in the case of 'Marilyn Francis' . . . apart from Audley's presence on the battlefield, she had seemed to be only a poor innocent bystander, and everyone's attention had been focused on 'Mad Dog' O'Leary—

'So who do you think she really was, Reg?'

'No sayin' yet, Ian lad. But she's got to be one of three things. Like she *could* 'ave been just what she seemed: a little nobody—say, a girl that 'ud run away from home years before, an' got herself another identity to keep her nearest an' dearest off her back. But then, as there weren't any pictures of her in the papers, it couldn't have been them that claimed her. Which leaves . . . either she was there with Audley . . . or she was there with O'Leary—and maybe it wasn't him that shot her. Although, again, maybe it was: maybe he reckoned she'd put the finger on him, when he'd thought she was fingering his target for him. But it's early days—'

Early days, indeed! All they had known then, just twenty-four hours earlier, was that 'Marilyn Francis' and Michael 'Mad Dog' O'Leary had been killed on November 11, 1978, almost (if not actually) in the presence of David Audley, and that

114

Philip Masson had been dead within a week after that; and that, while those deaths might or might not be linked, they had to start somewhere with their part of the investigation—

'So, if it's all the same to you, Ian lad, after I've had another little talk with old Terry, an' got a few names, an' contacts up north from him . . . an' checked up one or two more things down here . . . then I'll just take a little trip up to Yorkshire an' see whether they maybe didn't bury this "Marilyn Francis" any deeper than Philip Masson. 'Cause it could be that it was a bit *too* easy for 'em. In which case they might 'uv been careless round the edges. And as for you, Mr Robinson *sir* . . . how would it be if you went an' had a word with British-American Electronics down at Rickmansworth? See, I was thinkin' you might be a solicitor, or something legal like that, tryin' to trace "Marilyn Francis" to give her a bequest? You could blind 'em with all that legal jargon you learned at college? That was how you used to do it, in the old days, the Lady told me—?"

Early days indeed! And, indeed, he had more than half-suspected that Reg only had the faintest hopes of anything surfacing down at British-American (who quite properly were unprepared to discuss matters relating to former staff over the telephone 'as a company policy rule'); though, to be fair, Reg might also have thought that a gentle wild goose chase within easy reach of London would serve to blow away the cobwebs from those long-unpractised foot-in-the-door skills of those 'old days', and

115

prepare him for sterner tests to come.

But then, quite suddenly, the early days had become interesting.

*   *   *

'Mr Robinson—?'

'Of Fielding-ffulke, Robinson, Mrs Simmonds.' Her door had boasted the legend 'Mrs Beryl Simmonds, Administrative Personnel Office', so he'd reached the right person in British-American at last. He just hoped that his old nicely-embossed card (*Ian D. Robinson Ll.B (Bristol)*, plus *'Fielding-ffulke, Robinson'* with a legal-sounding accommodation address in Chancery Lane) would work its magic again. 'I telephoned from my office, Mrs Simmonds. It's good of you to spare me your time.' He adjusted the small gold-framed spectacles which Jenny thought made him look so absurdly young that he must be what he said he was. 'As I explained then, I am inquiring about a former employee of yours.'

'Yes.' Frowning came easily to Mrs Simmonds: the years had grooved her forehead for permanent disapproval. 'I had expected you to write, Mr Robinson. That is the customary practice with such inquiries.'

'Yes, I know.' An instinct suddenly contradicted her appearance: she was frowning, but she didn't want to frown. Perhaps she had a nephew, or even a son, in the law; or maybe she simply had a weakness for very young men trying to make their way in the world. But, whatever, instinct whispered *hard shell, soft centre*, so he touched his spectacles again, and gave her the ghost of what he hoped was

116

a disarming smile. 'I am . . . rather trying to cut a corner, Mrs Simmonds. You see, we have a very demanding client from overseas. And . . . I also have a demanding senior partner. So I am *rather* depending on your help—in strictest confidence, of course. And I will send you a confirmatory letter, naturally: I do appreciate that there must be company policies in these matters.' He allowed the ghost to materialize more visibly for an instance, and then exorcized it with a dead-serious-pleasing expression.

'I see.' She was holding the frown now only with considerable effort. 'And about whom, among our former employees, do you wish to inquire, Mr Robinson? How long ago?'

'About ten years ago—' Even before he observed her expression harden again it occurred to him that if she had any sort of weakness for young men she probably had the reverse for the young women who preyed on them. And that decided him to add doubt and embarrassment to what was coming '—my inquiry relates to a certain Miss Francis, Mrs Simmonds. Miss—ah—Miss Marilyn Francis—?' Would she remember the papers, from 1978?

The hardness became granite. 'But . . . Miss Francis is . . . deceased, Mr Robinson.'

Deceased? Or, more likely, *dead—and bloody good riddance!*—this time instinct shouted at him. So she knew more than either he did, or what the papers had said. 'Yes. I do appreciate that also.' He tried to imply that he also knew a lot more than that, even as he prayed that she wouldn't ask him why, if he knew so much, he wanted to know more.

'Why do you want to know about her?'

He hadn't really expected his prayer to be

117

answered. 'I was hoping you wouldn't ask that. Because, quite honestly, I'm not at liberty to say. But . . . all I *can* say . . . is that I would appreciate frankness—and I will respect it, so far as I am able.' All the old Rules of Engagement flooded back. 'What I do promise, is that nothing you say here will be attributed to you, Mrs Simmonds. I simply want to know about Miss Francis—that's all.'

She was on a knife-edge. So it was the moment to lie in what he must hope was a Good Cause. 'I have spoken to others before you.' Whatever he said, it mustn't sound like a threat. 'I'm sorry to sound so mysterious, but I have to respect confidences and I *do* respect confidences. It's just that I do need reliable confirmation of what I already suspect.' As he delivered this flattery he screwed up his face with youthful embarrassment.

'Yes.' She pursed her lips. 'You do appreciate, Mr Robinson, that Marilyn—Miss Francis—was a temp . . . That is to say, a *temporary* secretary, supplied by an agency. I did not appoint her.'

'Of course.' He decided not to congratulate himself on the return of his old skills: although she liked him, and believed him, she was more concerned to exculpate herself from the Marilyn Francis appointment. 'But you do remember her—?'

'I do indeed.' The purse shut tightly.

Marilyn Francis had been memorable. In fact, even assuming that Mrs Beryl Simmonds had a good personnel manager's memory . . . Marilyn Francis had been *very* memorable. 'She was incompetent, was she—?'

Sniff. 'On the contrary. Miss Francis was highly competent, actually.'

118

Ouch! thought Ian. For a man who knew all about Marilyn Francis, that was a mistake—even allowing for the fact that Auntie Beryl would shy away from speaking ill of the dead, which he should have reckoned on. But the rule was to capitalize on one's mistakes. 'Well . . . you do rather surprise me, Mrs Simmonds. But I'm extremely grateful for being corrected—'

'As a secretary, she was competent.' She had done her duty. But now she didn't want him to get her wrong. 'Her shorthand was excellent—she must have had over 140 words per minute. Even with Dr Cavendish, who had no consideration for anyone . . . This was before we went over to full audio-typing, you understand—and when we still had old fashioned typewriters . . . But her typing was also excellent—quite impeccable.' Duty still wasn't done, the nod implied. 'And her filing. And her paperwork in general: she had been well-trained . . . and she was . . . an intelligent young woman—of that I'm sure. Appearances to the contrary.' Something approaching pain twisted her displeasure at the memory. 'I blame the schools: they have a lot to answer for—doing away with the grammar schools, and letting children run wild—especially the girls. *Especially* girls like Miss Francis, in fact.' Nod. 'They can't even spell these days. But, of course, we have a spell-check now, so they don't have to.' Sniff. '*Rarefy, liquefy, desiccate, parallel, routing*—and the Americanisms we have to cater for: *focused, protesters, advisers* . . . But Miss Francis could spell, I will say that for her. Except those dreadful Americanisms. And she only had to be told once, even with them, when Dr Cavendish was writing to America . . . No, as a secretary she was perfectly competent. It was her behaviour—and her appearance . . . both absolutely disgraceful, they were.'

'Yes?' Ian's heart had been sinking all the while she had lectured him: poor little Marilyn's defects were personal and moral, and she had been an innocent bystander at Thornervaulx, by whatever unlikely chain of events. So this really was a wild-goose-chase.

'It was so tragic—how she died. We all thought so.' Curiously, she was on his own wavelength. 'But, the truth is . . . and I'd be a hypocrite not to say as much . . . she was quite *man-mad*, was Marilyn.'

All he wanted to do now was to get away, back to London. 'Yes—?'

'Anything in trousers.' Nod: duty done, now the truth. 'Deluged in *the* most revolting perfume . . . tight skirts, and transparent blouses—I spoke to her about her blouses. But, of course, there were those who encouraged her—just like they always look at the *Sun* and the *Star* in the common room, even now.' Ultimate displeasure. 'Dr Page, and Dr Garfield—Dr Page is at Cambridge now . . . and Dr Garfield is in America . . . *they* thought she was quite wonderful. And even that dreadful Dr Harrison, who ended up in prison—' She bit her lip suddenly, catching herself too late.

'Dr H—?' He started to repeat the name automatically, still acting his part, because honest curiosity was perfectly in order. But then it echoed inside his memory, attaching itself to British-American in its proper context; and in that instant he knew that he hadn't finished with Marilyn Francis—and also that he too had caught himself too late, because Mrs Simmonds was already registering his surprise. So now he had to extricate himself from his self-betrayal. 'Harrison? Harrison—?' Better to pretend to be halfway there first, with a frown. And then embarrassment, for choice? *'Harrison—?'*

'He had nothing to do with Miss Francis.' Faced with two unhappy names, Mrs Simmonds chose not to repeat the more offensive one. 'His . . . what happened to him . . . that was some long time after she left our employ.'

He let his frown deepen. Had it been some long time after? Marilyn Francis had been killed in November, 1978—the beginning of his final year at university. And the Harrison Case . . .? But, whenever it had been, now was the time for embarrassment. 'Oh! *That* Dr Harrison—of course.' Surprised embarrassment. 'But . . . you do a lot of Ministry of Defence work—of course!' What had it been that the 'dreadful' Dr Harrison had betrayed? The guidance system to the Barracuda torpedo, was it? But now he had to let her off the hook. 'No . . . no, *of course*, Mrs Simmonds.' Smile. 'You wouldn't have given any of your secret work to a temp to copy out—no matter how well she typed!' As he broadened the sympathetically-understanding smile he felt his pulse beat faster. It *had* been the celebrated Barracuda. And it had not been very long afterwards—weeks, rather than months, for choice. But meanwhile he mustn't lose Mrs Simmonds. 'I don't want to know about him, anyway—Dr What's-his-name . . . But . . . Miss Francis had a—ah—a weakness for the male sex, you were saying, Mrs Simmonds.' Losing her fast, in fact.

'Did she have a particular boyfriend?'

'I have not the least idea of Miss Francis's private life.' She broke eye-contact, and picked up one of the files on her desk at random. Which was a sure sign of his impending dismissal.

Damnation! 'But . . . is there anyone who might know?' Not *losing*: already *lost*, damn it! So now he had to extemporize. 'We think she may have had . . . a fiancé in this area, Mrs Simmonds.'

The eyes came back to his, as blank as pebbles. 'I said that I have no knowledge of her private life, Mr Robinson. And as she has been dead these ten years, I really cannot see that any useful purpose can be served by relaying tittle-tattle about her.'

God! The old battle-axe *did* know something! So now was the moment for the Ultimate Weapon in this line of extemporization. 'Mrs Simmonds—'

She started to get up, file in hand. 'I really do not have any more time to spare. I'm sorry.'

'Mrs Simmonds—' He sat fast '—now I must betray a confidence—'

She stopped. Betrayal of confidences usually stopped people.

'We think . . . we *think* . . . that there may have been a child.' This time he broke the eye-contact, to adjust his spectacles. And that gave him time to decide the imaginary child's sex and appearance. 'A little boy. Fair hair, blue eyes . . . He'd be about ten years old now. And his uncle, who is . . . very prosperous . . . and childless . . . would like to find this little boy.'

The blank look transfixed him, and for a moment he feared that he had gone over the top with a scenario she must have read in Mills and Boon more times than Reg Buller had said 'Same again' to his favourite barmaid. But having gone so far the only direction left to him was to advance further on into the realms of melodrama: if not Mills and Boon, then maybe a touch of *Jane Eyre* . . . except that Marilyn didn't sound much like Jane. So perhaps the hypothetical 'fiancé' would be a better bet to soften Mrs Simmonds' heart and put her off the scent.

'It's really the father we're trying to trace, Mrs Simmonds. Because we think he looked after the child. Because . . . Miss Francis doesn't appear to have been very . . . maternal—?' He looked at her questioningly.

'No.' She blinked at him. '*That* doesn't surprise me.' Then she sighed. 'I'm afraid we don't keep files on our temps, Mr Robinson—certainly not going so far back, anyway. And, of course, Miss Francis lost her life in that dreadful business up north, with that IRA murderer—we read about that. And it was a terrible shock. But that's why I remember her so well, even though it is something one would like to forget.'

She was implying that, if there had been a file, it would have been purged. So there probably *had* been a file. And she had purged it.

She blinked at him again. 'As I recall, Mr Robinson, she left our employ in November, just before Armistice Day. And I do remember that because I was working with her in the same office: I was acting as Dr Garfield's secretary at the time, and she was temping for Dr Cavendish's secretary, who was on leave of absence.'

He observed her lips tighten at the memory. And it was 'tittle-tattle' that he wanted. 'Yes.'

'Yes.' Slight sniff. 'I remember that because

123

when . . . when the person selling the British Legion poppies came round she insisted on his pinning her poppy on her blouse. Which was . . . quite improper. But quite typical, also.'

Tittle-tattle. 'Typical, Mrs Simmonds?' He cocked his head innocently, deliberately forgetting Mrs Simmonds' earlier reference to Marilyn's blouses.

Half-sniff, half-sigh. 'One of Miss Francis's affectations was to wear as little as possible. I could never understand why she didn't get pneumonia.'

Ian opened his mouth. 'Ah . . .'

'She left us shortly after that. She received an urgent telephone message . . . apparently her mother had been taken ill. So she left us immediately. And I remember *that* too, because it was mid-week, and I let her have £5 from the petty cash as an advance on the money due to her, for her fare home. Which I never saw again, of course—though I suppose I can hardly blame her for that, in the circumstances . . . Although what she was doing up in Yorkshire a few days later I'll never know—*I* thought her home was in London.'

'But you don't know where?' Instinct stirred: she didn't know, but something had occurred to her, nevertheless. 'Did she commute back home every day?' That would have been easy enough from Rickmansworth. But London was a big place.

'No.' She shook her head. 'I believe she had digs somewhere down here.' Slight frown. 'She never minded working late, I will say that for her. But that may have been because she was trying to ingratiate herself with Dr Cavendish, in case Miss Ballard didn't come back. And she'd stay to cover for anyone else—Dr Page, or Dr Garfield, or—or anyone else.'

Like Dr Harrison, maybe?

'She said she needed the money, so the extra hours were useful.' Mrs Simmonds pressed on. 'But she was a nosey young woman. Always chatting the men up, trying to insinuate herself where she had no right to be—' She snapped her mouth shut on herself suddenly, as if she'd heard herself. 'But there, now: I'm being unkind, aren't I—' She cut herself off again.

'No.' Maybe she'd misread his expression. But, at all costs he mustn't lose her again. 'No. You're just being honest, Mrs Simmonds. And I respect you for that. Because . . . not many people are honest.'

She stared at him. 'Honest?' The word seemed to hurt her.

'Yes.' If he could hold her now, when her defences were down, she'd give him everything she'd got. 'Thanks to you, I understand much better now what others have said. And what they haven't said.'

'Do you?' The pain showed again. 'I wonder.'

'Wonder . . . what?'

'Perhaps I should have tried harder to understand her. After what you've told me.' She looked away from him for a moment. 'It's a long time ago . . .'

'Yes. It is.' He waited.

'And yet . . . of all the temps we've had . . . I remember her so well—so well!' She looked away again. 'Better than any of them, you know.'

Was that surprising? Apart from Marilyn's see-through blouses, not many of Mrs Simmonds' temps could have been shot by the IRA. But, more likely, the doting mother/kind auntie inside her was

125

now torturing her with visions of Marilyn Francis working long extra hours not to chat up the men, but to support the fair-haired, blue-eyed baby he'd invented. And that, in turn, didn't exactly make him feel a great human being.

She looked at him. 'Deep down I think she was sad.'

'Sad?' The word took him by surprise.

'Yes. And a little desperate, perhaps . . . But I can understand that now, of course.' She nodded wisely. 'Many of these young women make the most terrible messes of their lives. Early marriages, or unplanned babies—just like Marilyn . . . We try to help them, naturally. And some of them take it all in their stride—quite amazingly resilient, they are . . . It's as though they never expected anything different.'

'Yes?' He controlled his impatience. 'Are you saying . . . Marilyn wasn't resilient?'

She thought about that for a moment. 'Perhaps I am—yes. Some of the most intelligent ones have the biggest problems—the ones who realize that it all could have been different: they are the sad ones.' Another wise nod. 'They don't like what they've become, so they pretend to be someone else. And now I think about Marilyn . . . yes, I'm sure that she wasn't really like that. She was just playing a role—' She blinked suddenly. 'But that isn't helping you, is it?'

'On the contrary—'

'No.' She sat up very straight. 'As regards Miss Francis, Mr Robinson, I think your best bet would be a certain Gary Redwood.'

'Gary—' His repetition of the absurd Christian name seemed to tighten her mouth. 'A boyfriend?'

'No.' Her expression belied the question even before she'd rejected it. 'Whatever Gary was to her, he most certainly wasn't that.' She turned away from him abruptly, to stare at a pair of steel filing-cabinets which seemed oddly out-of-place in an otherwise computerized office.

'Who is he?' It disconcerted him oddly that she didn't move to consult the cabinet's contents, but merely stared at them, as though their entire contents were already on disc in her memory.

'*Was*, as far as this company is concerned, Mr Robinson. Yes.' She switched back to him. 'He *was* our messenger boy, while Miss Francis was with us . . . and for a brief time after that. Gary Redwood—his mother, who was a perfectly decent woman, worked in our canteen. They lived in Albion Street, near the railway line. But you won't find him there.' She looked at her watch. 'If he has continued to stay one jump ahead of the Police, you should find him in Messiter's timber yard, Mr Robinson—'

'*Redwood*—?' He cupped his hands round his mouth to direct his shout at the man over the shriek of the circular saw.

'*Eh?*' The man tapped his protective ear-muffs.

This wasn't Gary Redwood, he was too old by a dozen years: even now the former Brit-Am messenger boy would only be in his mid-twenties. '*Gary Redwood?*' Ian's voice cracked.

An uneven piece of mahogany fell away from the saw. The man picked it up and pointed with it towards a stairway before tossing it aside.

The noise fell away behind Ian as he ascended the

127

stair. He still wasn't at all sure what he was really doing; or, at any rate, whether it really had any bearing on what had happened to Philip Masson. For the link between Marilyn Francis and Philip Masson was hardly more than a tenuous sequence of November days in early November, with David Audley in the middle of it. Dr Harrison, of British-American, had been jailed for passing high-tech secrets to one of Russia's East European colonies—Hungary, was it? Or Bulgaria? And Marilyn Francis had quit Brit-Am (and Dr Harrison) on November 7, 1978, to keep an appointment with 'Mad Dog' O'Leary's bullet (or somebody's bullet) in Dr Audley's presence four days later; and, as things stood at present, Audley was playing Macbeth to Philip Masson's Banquo, his victim, if Jenny had heard more than a rumour. But there lay a full week between those two deaths, and a week was a long time not just in politics.

'Mr Redwood?' There was only one person in the timber-loft, so it had to be Gary. And as the man turned towards him from the pile of planks he was sorting the identification was confirmed: the acne-ravaged face and the stocky build filled Mrs Simmonds' 1978 description to the life.

'Yeah?' Gary straightened up, balancing himself among the planks.

'I believe you may be able to help me, Mr Redwood.' He returned Gary's empty gaze with a smile of encouragement. 'You used to work at British-American Electronics just down the road, didn't you?'

'Yeah—' A fraction of a second after he began to answer, as though his brain was slower than his tongue, Gary's expression changed from the blank to the wary '—who says?'

Mrs Simmonds' name was not the one to drop, decided Ian. And, in any case, he had a much better name to open Gary up. 'You had a friend there—' As he spoke, Mrs Simmonds' parting words echoed in his head: *'She let them chat her up—even a dreadful ugly little beast like Gary. At the time, I thought it was disgusting. But perhaps I was wrong: perhaps she was just being kind to him!'*; but now he observed Gary in the pitted flesh neither conclusion quite fitted '—a Miss Francis—Miss Marilyn Francis, Mr Redwood—?'

A succession of different emotions twisted across the moonscape face, ending with a scowling grimace. 'Who told you? Not that fucking old bitch Simmonds?' Gary spoke with susprising clarity as well as bitterness. 'You don't want to believe anything she says—right?'

It would be a mistake to underrate Gary, in spite of appearances. 'She only said you were a friend of Miss Francis, Mr Redwood.'

Gary shook his head, as at some crassly stupid statement. 'About Miss Francis—*Marilyn* . . . she's who I mean. You don't want to believe anything the old bag said about *her—right*?' The corner of his mouth twisted upwards. 'It doesn't matter what she said about me. Who gives a fuck for that, eh?'

There had been a sum of unaccounted petty cash outstanding between Mrs Beryl Simmonds and Mr Gary Redwood, back in 1979. But who gave a fuck for that? What mattered was that, once again, Marilyn Francis had been memorable. 'But . . . Miss Francis *was* a friend of yours, surely?'

'Yeah—' Gary stopped suddenly. 'No. I just talked to her—that's all.' He looked past Ian, down

129

the length of the timber-loft. 'She was a smasher—a right little smasher! Bloody IRA—*bloody bastard sods!*' He came back to Ian. 'I was only a lad then. First job out of school, like . . . But she was a smasher, she was—Miss Francis.' He pronounced the smasher's name almost primly. 'Why d'you want to know about her?'

Ian was ready for the question. 'Not for anything wrong, Mr Redwood. I'm just a solicitor's clerk, and we've got this will to check up on—next-of-kin, and all that. And probate, and death duties, and all the rest of it—' He shrugged fellow-feeling at Gary, as one loser to another '—I just do the donkey-work for my boss . . .' For a guess, Gary wouldn't know probate from a hole in the road. But it might be as well to divert him, just in case. 'She seems to have been a decent sort—Miss Francis?'

'She was.' He looked past Ian again, but only for a second. 'Yes.'

'And pretty, too.' Ian followed Gary's eyes, and his own came to rest on a copy of the *Sun* which lay folded on top of a bomber-jacket beside the wood pile. 'Like Page Three—?' He pointed at the newspaper.

'What?' Gary squinted at him. 'Like—? No, not like that . . . That'll be that old bitch going on—like she always did. She just dressed smart—Marilyn—Miss Frances did. But she was a lady. More of a lady than old Mrs Simmonds. And not stuck-up, like some of 'em . . . She'd *talk* to you—really talk to you—not treat you like dirt, see?'

Ian wasn't quite sure that he did see. It wasn't just that Mrs Simmonds' and Gary's views diverged on Marilyn Francis, that was predictable. There was something here that was missing. But he nodded encouragingly nevertheless.

'An' she was *clever*.' Gary nodded back. 'She *knew* things.'

'What things?'

'Oh . . . I used to talk to her about the Old West . . .' Gary trailed off.

'The old—what?'

'West.' Gary's eyes lit up at the memory. 'Cowboys and Indians . . . and the US cavalry—General Custer . . . It's my hobby, like—I read the books on it . . . And she knew about it—knew who Major Reno was, for instance—I didn't have to explain about him getting the blame for Custer getting hisself killed—*she knew*. We had a good talk about that once, while she was helping me with the deliveries all round the office. Which she didn't have to do, either . . . All about whether the Sioux had used more bows and arrows than Winchesters an' Remingtons—she didn't think they had many guns.' He nodded vehemently. 'An', you know, she was probably right—there's a new book I got out of the library just last week that says that . . . She was *clever*, I tell you.'

So it hadn't been just the see-through blouse with Gary after all—or the peroxide hair and the red nails. It had been General Custer and the Sioux (and Major Reno, whoever the hell he had been!). But—

'An' she knew about guns.' Another decisive nod, which brought a cow-lick of hair across the bright-eyes. 'Knew more than any girl I ever met—repeating rifles, an' double-action revolvers . . . An' we talked once about the SLRs what the army had. 'Fact, she said I ought to join the

131

army—said I'd make a good soldier, knowing about guns like I did—' Gary's gargoyle features twisted suddenly.

Clever little Marilyn, Ian had been thinking. Mrs Simmonds had said it, and Gary had said it—on that they were agreed. And he was himself thinking it: *clever, clever Miss Francis!*

But Gary was staring at him. 'You didn't join up, though—'

Gary straightened up. 'Got flat feet—haven't I!' He scowled horribly. 'Went down to the Recruiting Office—went down the day it was in the paper . . . Flat *bloody* feet, is what I've got. *Bloody* stupid!'

Ian became aware that he was returning the scowl. 'What . . . paper?'

'That one.' Gary gestured toward the *Sun*. 'In all of 'em—about the IRA shooting her. Christ! I'd 'uv given 'em *shooting* if I'd 'uv got into uniform, and got to Ireland, I tell you—killing her like that, the bastards!'

Lucky Ulster! Ian's thoughts came away from *clever Miss Francis* momentarily. But now Gary would give him everything.

'She talked about Ireland once—funny, that.' Gary's eyes were still bright with Marilyn Francis' memories. 'It was when we were talking about the army—about my joining up, maybe . . . She said it was a better job than running messages, an' delivering the post an' that, in Brit-Am. "No future for you here, Gary," she says. "But you could be doing a good job in Ulster, keeping the peace, an' protecting people. And they'll teach you a trade too, most like—an' you can practise your shooting for free!"' One broad shoulder lifted in resignation. 'She didn't know about my flat feet . . . But, then, she'd have been sorry—she was . . . *all right*, I tell you—' He stopped suddenly again. But this time he had remembered Ian, not Miss Francis. 'What you on about, then—asking questions—?'

Mills and Boon came to the rescue again, like the US cavalry in Gary's old West, trumpets blaring romantically: Gary, feeling as he did about Marilyn Francis, would not be able to resist Mills and Boon either.

'Well, Mr Redwood, it's like this—' He looked around the empty timber-loft, and then advanced cautiously across the unstable planks so that he was able to lower his voice confidentially. '—Miss Francis had a child—a little boy . . . And I'm trying to trace him, so that we can give him some money, which is due to him—his inheritance, from his uncle.'

'What?' Gary frowned. 'I didn't know about—?'

Ian raised his hand. 'It was very secret—you mustn't tell anyone, Mr Redwood.' Actually, on reflection, it was as much Charles Dickens as Mills and Boon. But Dickens would do just as well. 'There are those who would like me not to find Miss Francis's little boy, Mr Redwood. Because then they'd get the money, you see—eh?' He gave Gary a sly look.

'Yes—?' Gary checked the timber-loft himself, but more carefully, before coming back to Ian. 'What d'you want to know?' Then he frowned. 'It was a long time ago . . . But—?'

'Did she have a boyfriend?' The trouble was, Gary was dead right: it was a long time ago, 1978. And it might all be a waste of time, anyway. But . . . somehow Marilyn Francis was alive again now, in her own right; and he wanted to know more

133

about her, quite regardless of David Audley and Philip Masson, and Jenny and Reg Buller and John Tully. 'Was there anyone who visited her—*anyone* you can remember—?'

'No . . . *yes*—' Gary's brow furrowed with concentrated effort. '—there was a bloke I saw her with once, one night, just down the road from Brit-Am . . . I was just going past, an' she didn't see me . . . I thought he was chatting her up, at first.'

'But he wasn't—?'

'No. Because she gave him something—an envelope, or a package, or something.' The frown deepened. 'Good-looking bloke, in a Triumph . . . But she didn't like him—I could see *that*—' He pre-empted the next question '—because she gave him the brush-off, as well as the packet, whatever it was, an' walked straight on without turning round, an' just left him there—see?' He brightened at the memory. 'So he wasn't any boyfriend of hers, anyway.'

'No?' She must have been hard-pressed to have taken such a risk, so close to Brit-Am. 'But . . . didn't she have any friends, Gary?'

'Naow, she was just a temp. So she didn't know no-one, see?' Gary shrugged. 'Each night . . . she just went back to 'er digs.'

Ian controlled himself. 'Her . . . digs?'

'Yeah.' Gary dismissed the question. ''Er digs. Old Mrs Smith.'

Old Mrs Smith! Ian warmed himself on the recollection of Gary's 'old Mrs Smith' as he came to the end of the low wall which separated the churchyard from Lower Buckland Village Green.

He stopped in the shadow of the huge old yew tree at the corner and studied the scene. It was purely a precaution, and an unnecessary one at that: if there *had* been any car behind him earlier he had certainly lost it at one of the three consecutive stretches of road works on the edge of Rickmansworth. And it still took an effort of will—almost a suspension of rational belief—to accept Reg Buller's warning. So now, when he was aware that he was basking in self-satisfied success, was the moment to guard against carelessness and over-confidence, and make doubly sure before he searched for a telephone—

'Mrs S—' In that instant, as he registered the tall, painted, blue-rinsed presence in the doorway, and married it with the legend on the painted sign (THE ELSTREE GUEST HOUSE—*Proprietress: Mrs Basil Champeney-Smythe*), Ian amended the question '—Mrs Champeney-Smythe?'

'Yahss.' The blue-rinsed presence looked down on him from the great height made up of two steps and her own extra inches. 'I am Mrs *Basil* Champeney-Smythe—yahss.'

'Robinson, Mrs Champeney-Smythe—' He had somehow expected an unobtrusive lodging-house in a back-street, not this genteel four-storey Edwardian yellow-brick survival, with its ancient genteel landlady (Dame Edith Evans playing Lady Bracknell, to the life). But now plain Mr Robinson wasn't good enough, anyway '—Ian Drury Robinson, of Fielding-ffulke, Robinson, Mrs Champeney-Smythe—Fielding-ffulke, Robinson, of

135

Chancery Lane—?' He repeated the contents of his card as he offered it to her as though he expected everyone to recall it from the legal columns of *The Times*.

Mrs Basil Champeney-Smythe (alias 'Old Mrs Smith') accepted the card with one skeletal hand while raising a monocle on a gold chain to her eye with her other claw. And . . . *this wasn't going to be so easy*, thought Ian, considering his various scenarios: how the hell did Marilyn Francis, either as a blonde man-eater or an expert on General Custer's Last Stand, fit in with *The Importance of Being Earnest*?

'Yahss?' She returned the card, wrinkling her nose at the pronounced smell of curry which emanated from the Indian restaurant-cum-takeaway just across the road behind them.

Ian decided to acknowledge the smell by wrinkling his nose back at her. 'If you could spare a few minutes of your time, Mrs Champeney-Smythe—on a matter which really only involves you indirectly—' This was important, he remembered: ordinary folk always felt threatened by strange solicitors on their doorstep '—in fact, in a legal sense, doesn't involve you at all . . . But you could be of great help to one of my clients. So . . . perhaps I might step inside, for a moment—?' He sniffed again, and glanced deliberately over his shoulder at the source of the nuisance, which must be wafting in through her open front-door even now.

She considered him through her spy-glass for a moment, and he was glad that he had selected his best charcoal-grey pin-striped Fielding-ffulke, Robinson suit and Bristol University tie. Then she

136

drew back, leaving an opening for him into the darkness beyond. 'Yahss . . .'

That was the first hurdle. Long before, in the old days, he could well remember trying to get past the porter of a minor Oxford college to interview the Master about an alleged sex-and-drugs scandal for the *Daily Mail*, only to be rebuffed by the loyal college porter with *'You just fuck off! We know your sort!'* (And, actually, he had been wearing a decent suit and his Bristol tie on that occasion, also.)

The darkness dissolved slowly, and the curry-smell was repelled by a mixture of furniture-linoleum polish, Mrs Champeney-Smythe's face powder and the steak-and-kidney-pie-and-cabbage, which had presumably been the Elstree Guest House residents' lunch not so long ago.

'If you would be so good as to ascend the stairs.' Mrs Champeney-Smythe indicated his route, but then pushed ahead of him after closing out the Indian invasion.

Ian followed her dutifully, up the stair and across the landing, into what was obviously the best room in the house; which, in commercial terms, meant that she wasn't down on her uppers for money, if she could keep it as her own sitting room.

And the tall windows let in the light, so that he could instantly make out all Mrs Champeney-Smythe's lifetime accretion of memorabilia and bric-à-brac, which was consciously arranged around him, on occasional tables, and sideboards, and bookcases, and windowsills: silver-framed pictures, and little boxes, and brasses, and paper-weights, and innumerable meaningless objects which meant so much to her.

137

It was the pictures which always told the most, and quickest: no children, naked on rugs, or self-conscious in shirts-and-ties and party-dresses, or gowned for graduation; only an extremely handsome man, posed again and again in carefully-lit situations, always immaculate and cool, and once with a cigarette in hand, the smoke curling up past his nonchalant profile, in a Noel Coward pose.

'You may recall my late husband.' Mrs Champeney-Smythe observed his interest with satisfaction as he bent over the cigarette advertisement. 'That is my favourite—the one Gabby Pascal gave me. But he always preferred Arthur's favourite—' She pointed, '—that one . . . which was taken for *The Dark Stranger* . . . Basil had only a small part. But he had all the best lines, Arthur said—J. Arthur Rank, of course.'

'*Basil Champeney as Harry de Vere*', Ian read dutifully. So he was in the presence of late pre-war and early post-war British cinema, not in 1978, but over forty years—maybe even half-a-century—ago!

'Yes!' He lied enthusiastically. 'Yes—of course!'

'Indeed?' She frowned at him suddenly, as though she had seen through his enthusiasm, to its insincere foundation. 'But that was . . . before you were born, Mr Robertson—?'

'Robinson.' He smiled at her desperately, and played for time while he took out his spectacles again, peering through them round the room. 'Yes. But those were the great days of British cinema, Mrs Champeney-Smythe—' He saw her more clearly now: the ancient remains of past splendour, plundered and weathered by time, like the Parthenon: or, if not an old Bluebell Girl, she had

138

the height for the front row of the chorus, certainly. So all he had to remember now was the list of those old films, hoping for the best. '*The Private Life of Henry VIII* . . . and *Things to Come* . . . and *Rembrandt*—' He cudgelled his brains, between Gabriel Pascal, and Alexander Korda, and J. Arthur Rank '—and *The Four Feathers*, with Ralph Richardson . . . and *Pygmalion* . . . and, after the war—I have many of those films on video now, Mrs Champeney-Smythe: those were the *great* days—' He bent towards Basil's picture, as though to a shrine '—I never expected . . . *The Dark Stranger*—of course!' He sat back, nodding at her, and terrified lest she quiz him further. 'But—I am imposing on you—' At all costs, he had to get away from the Great Days of British Cinema '—you see, it's about one of your former . . . guests . . . a young lady—a young lady—?'

'A young lady?' She had sat down, into her favourite chair, beside the table which carried the *Radio Times* and the *TV Times*, and her copy of the *Daily Mail*. 'Which young lady, Mr Robertson?'

He adjusted his spectacles, solicitorly. 'It was some years ago—nine or ten, perhaps . . . a Miss Francis, Mrs Champeney-Smythe—Miss Marilyn Francis—?'

She frowned at him again. And in that second he threw away all his planned explanations, on instinct. And put nothing in their place.

The frown cleared slightly. 'I remember Miss Francis—yahss . . .'

Yahss: they all remembered Miss Marilyn Francis. And, at a guess, Mrs Champeney-Smythe had once disapproved of Marilyn's appearance quite as much as Mrs Simmonds . . . Or, with her own chorus-line memories, maybe *not* quite as much? Mrs Champeney-Smythe in her time must have seen other bright butterflies and moths fluttering around flames; so Marilyn Francis might not have seemed quite so outrageous after all.

'Yahss—' Other memories intruded: Mrs Champeney-Smythe had read her *Daily Mail* back in 1978, and the recollection of her reading, which she must have shared with her other lodgers with shock-horror all those years ago, showed in her face now. '*Yes*, Mr Robertson. I remember Miss Francis.'

A gentle smile was called for. 'You wouldn't, by any chance, have any record of a forwarding address—if your records go so far back—?'

'No, Mr Robertson.' She fingered the strings of costume jewellery which accompanied the monocle's gold chain, and waited for him to continue.

She was time-biding, Ian decided. She must be all of seventy years old (with all that paint and powder, it was hard to say: she could be nearer eighty for all he could tell: a relic of the twenties, even!). But, just as with Gary, it would be a mistake to underrate her; and he'd already made the elementary mistake of combining two questions into one, so that he didn't know which one that 'no' applied to. 'Your records don't go back—?'

'My records go back to June 1960, when my husband and I bought this property, on our retirement from the profession, Mr Robertson.'

'So she didn't leave any address?' He chose to interpret her answer. 'Isn't that unusual—not to leave an address?'

'Not if you do not have an address. Miss Francis
140

left one place, where she was lodging, and came to me. That is all.'

It wasn't all. She remembered Marilyn Francis very well—so well, that even with Marilyn nine years dead she wasn't going to give any Tom, Dick or Harry . . . or Robertson, of Fielding-ffulke, Robertson . . . easy answers. 'Didn't she receive any mail?' He remembered Mrs Simmonds had let slip about Marilyn's hurried mid-week departure, with £5 out of the petty cash in her pocket. But perhaps she'd just been playing her part to the last. 'After she left, I mean—?'

'Miss Francis did not receive any mail.'

Well, that rang true, however uninformatively. But at this rate he'd be here all day, and still not be much the wiser. So he must push harder. 'But she did have callers, Mrs Champeney-Smythe.' He made this a statement, not a question. 'There was a boyfriend, I believe?'

'There was no boyfriend.' She rejected his ploy almost contemptuously. 'And there were no callers.'

They stared at each other like evenly-matched duellists.

'I find that hard to believe, Mrs Champeney-Smythe.' He allowed an edge of irritation into his voice.

'Then . . . you must believe what suits you, Mr Robertson.' She parried the first thrust easily.

'But she was an attractive young woman.' In their different ways, Mrs Simmonds and Gary had both been agreed on that.

'She was, yahss.' A hint of distaste: Mrs Champeney-Smythe would incline more towards Mrs Simmonds there, having no interest in General Custer and firearms and recruitment to the British

141

Army. But she still refused to be drawn any further.

Another thrust, then. 'She left you rather suddenly, I believe—?' Once on the attack, he had to go forward. 'Just before her very tragic death, that would have been, of course . . . And you read about that, in the newspapers, naturally—?'

The mask didn't crack. But this time he received only the slightest of nods, and no '*yahss*'. Yet that concealed pain, he judged.

Suddenly he saw a gap in her defences—or, if not a gap, then at least the faintest impossible hope of one. 'Did she come back to you, to say goodbye?'

No reaction at all.

Wait—or attack harder? The possible dividend of success was great, but so was the penalty of failure. Then, even though the mask still didn't crack, he knew that she was old and frail behind it, and he was young and strong. 'She didn't come back—did she?' *And there had been no forwarding address: she had already admitted that! And how many suitcases, and other minor pathetic luggage, were up there in the attic—or down there in the cellar—belonging to other 'guests' who had made the proverbial 'midnight flit', rather than settle their accounts? Belongings which were either festooned with cobwebs up above, or mouldy-green with damp down below—?* 'So her things are still here, then?'

She looked away from him, towards one bric-à-brac-choked table over which Basil Champeney (without the plebeian 'Smythe') presided out of another silver frame. But he could see nothing on it which was of the slightest interest—a wooden ashtray, with a mouse carved on it; a brass frog grinning foolishly; a crude rhomboid First World War tank in seaside souvenir china (which was probably worth a tidy sum in any auction!); a hideous piece of Venetian glass, from Murano Island . . . none of which had 'Marilyn Francis' imprinted on it. And then the washed out eyes (which, for a guess, had once been *ingenue* china-blue) came back to him.

'Tell me, Mr Robertson . . . what is all this about?'

He had won. Or, if he was careful now, and gentle with it, he could win. 'I am concerned with a legacy, Mrs Champeney-Smythe—' He touched his spectacles, as though slightly embarrassed '—one of those difficult next-of-kin family affairs, which could go on for years . . . which could swallow up most of the money in legal fees, and all the other costs. But, you know, I don't believe that's what my job ought to be about, you see—?' He gave her his most innocent look, which Jenny always said almost melted her heart. Only now, when he came up against all Marilyn Francis's contradictions, he found to his surprise that he was no longer quite pretending, even in the midst of this elaborate tapestry of lies. Because, if he'd been in the law and clever little Marilyn had had a blue-eyed Mills-and-Boon offspring, he really would have been fighting for its inheritance. 'Do you see—?'

She frowned so hard that the make-up on her forehead cracked. 'No.'

He was surprised as well as disappointed. Because she didn't seem to be rejecting his appeal. 'No?'

'Her brother took all her things . . . afterwards, Mr Robertson.'

'Her—?' *Damn!* He should have expected that.

143

'Her brother?'

She shook her head. 'She telephoned me—of course . . . but that was the next day, after she didn't come back from work. She said how sorry she was . . . She always phoned me, when she was working late, or when she had to go away—she was always thoughtful . . . Because she knew that I worried about her, when she was late . . . But she didn't phone that time—when she went away, the last time. Not until the next day, very late—' She stared at him, and then through him. And then at him. 'Such a *lovely* girl, she was—in spite of all appearances to the contrary—' The stare fixed him, demanding his agreement '—*so* intelligent—so *thoughtful* . . . She knew I worried. Especially when it was dark, at night.'

The image of Marilyn-in-the-dark jolted him. Because Gary had worried also for his darling Miss Francis, when she worked late. He had even followed her all the way back here, one late October evening when the mist was up, to make sure she got home safe: that had been how Gary knew about 'old Mrs Smith'.

'She phoned you—? The next day?' They had both loved her: in quite different ways *they had both loved her*.

'Yes.' She nodded. 'After her dinner—or, if she was late, after her supper, which she'd often take with me, in this room . . . after that she'd often stay, and we'd talk . . . About her day at work, sometimes. Or about what was on the 9 o'clock news, or in the papers—she was always *very* well-informed, about what was going on . . . And then we would read our books, until it was time to go to bed—' She inclined her head upwards '—her

144

room was right at the top of the house, and *not* really very comfortable—not for reading, anyway. So she'd stay down here with me. And we'd have a cup of cocoa—*so* much better than coffee, or tea, which are *stimulants*.'

From getting nothing, now he was almost getting too much. Or . . . *cocoa* and reading before bed-time mixed as inappropriately with see-through blouses and 'anything in trousers' as with Red Indians and the army's new rifles. But there was something much more important than all of that. 'She had a brother—? He took her things, you said.'

Her mask tightened. 'That was unfortunate.'

'How—unfortunate?'

'He came when I was out, Mr Robertson.'

'When—?' But, then, it wasn't unfortunate, of course: it figured exactly, that Marilyn's 'brother' would have watched for his moment.

'When I was out. She said he would be coming—' The mask softened '—and that she would be coming back to see me, some time. But she'd obtained this new position, up north—not a temporary one, but a permanent post, with a pension *and* opportunities for promotion, you see—'

Ian nodded. There had been no pension, and no opportunities. But it had certainly been up north. And it had been permanent, too. But, in those last hours of her life, Marilyn Francis had been nothing if not professional, sewing up all her loose ends tightly.

'My maid—my *house-keeper*—was here.' Mrs Champeney-Smythe corrected herself. 'Her brother cleared everything out . . . And, of course,

145

she—Miss Francis . . . she was paid up to the end of the month—she always insisted on that, even though it was quite unnecessary—' She stopped suddenly, as she saw his face fall.

Dead end! thought Ian. Just when he had thought he was there, too. But . . . it had happened before, and it would happen again. And maybe Reg Buller would still come up with something, from 'up north', where someone might have been careless—now that he knew, anyway, that there really was something to be careless about with the real Marilyn Francis, who didn't exist in Somerset House, or anywhere else except here, in the Elstree Guest House, and in the sad recollections of Gary and his 'old Mrs Smith'.

'Well . . .' He smiled at her sadly, and sat up in his chair. When one lost, one cut one's losses gracefully. And, in any case, he hadn't wholly lost. 'Well, I'm most grateful to you, Mrs Champeney-Smythe—for your time, and your help.' On impulse he decided to give her more than that, as he stood up. 'I'm glad . . . Miss Francis had such a happy time, before . . . before the tragedy occurred.'

She stared at him without replying, as though she hadn't heard what he had said. Then she turned away, looking again towards the table with its incongruous collection of souvenirs.

He coughed politely. 'Mrs Champeney-Smythe—?'

She pointed. 'There is something. You can't have it. But you can look at it, Mr Robertson. They belonged to her.'

He looked at all of it, already defeated: wooden mouse, or brass frog? China tank or spindly glass

146

horse (minus its tail)? Old ginger beer bottle, advertising 'Burbank', a 'High Class Chemist' of Oxford? Unless Marilyn had left a message in the bottle, it was all rubbish. But he had to humour her. 'Which object do you mean?'

'Not the table—' The thin finger stabbed irritably towards the table '—the bookcase, Mr Robertson, the bookcase.'

There was indeed a bookcase behind the table, its mathematically aligned contents also part of the room's ornamentation: she had been looking at that all the time, not the bric-à-brac.

'Which books, Mrs Champeney-Smythe?' *'We would read our books, until it was time to go to bed'*, he remembered. So what would Marilyn Francis's literary tastes run to?

'At the end there—at the end!' It seemed to irritate her that he needed direction.

There was a set of Dickens (which didn't look as though it had ever been opened), and a run of diminutive New University Society classics in red-and-gold bindings—and a wealth of better-read washed-out yellow Reprint Society volumes which Basil Champeney-Smythe had surely collected, and which customarily stood out on the shelves of a thousand second-hand bookshops . . . *The Robe, The Black Narcissus*, Bryant and Pepys, Churchill's *My Early Life* . . . But he didn't even know which shelf, which end: should he be looking for *The Life of General Custer*—? Or even *A History of the Repeating Rifle*?

'The fairy books—I told you—at the end, there!'

'The—?' *What*—? Then he saw them—one old, and hardback, the other new, and paperback—

The Fairy-Faith in Celtic Counties, by W.Y.

Evans Wentz—

Who had ever heard of 'W.Y. Evans Wentz', for heavens sake! Well ... evidently the Oxford University Press, for a start! And a Penguin book—*A Dictionary of Fairies, Hobgoblins, Brownies, Bogies and Other Supernatural Creatures*, by Katherine Briggs—

He opened the Penguin. The right date, anyway: first published, 1976—and in Penguin, 1977 ... And, on the flyleaf, 'F.F. '78'—but who the hell was 'F.F.'—?

He looked questioningly at Mrs Champeney-Smythe, then down again at the dictionary of fairies, which had fallen open in his hands at the point where the paperback binding had fallen apart with use, at page 175—*'Fin Bheara'*—was underlined.

And who the hell was *'Fin Bheara'*—?

He felt a cold hand on his backbone: Fin Bheara, *alias* Finvarra, was apparently more than just the Fairy King of Ulster, which was 'Mad Dog' O'Leary's old stamping ground, but also maybe King of the Dead (and therefore a recipient of many of 'Mad Dog's' customers—?)—

This foolish diversion of his concentration angered him. 'Who is "F.F.", Mrs Champeney-Smythe?'

'You are looking at the wrong book, Mr Robertson.' She closed her eyes as she spoke.

The paperback almost came apart in his hands as he juggled clumsily with Marilyn Francis's only known possessions to bring the stout OUP hardback to the top—

'Robbie, with love—Frances—16.7.72'

'Who—?' He realized that there was more than

148

an inscription, there was a folded piece of paper—

It was a bookseller's bill, with a name and an address—

★　　★　　★

He looked back one last time into Lower Buckland churchyard, in which the second of his future book's bodies lay. But, unlike Jenny's lovely heroic Philip Masson, his own lovely, heroic 'Marilyn Francis' would at least remain decently undisturbed. For she was buried properly—

FRANCES
his loving wife
1948–1978

—alongside her

ROBERT GAUVAIN FITZGIBBON
Captain, 39th (Royal Ulster) Lancers
1946–1974

Meanwhile, the Village Green was still as comfortingly empty as it had been when he had first arrived. Maybe it was just because it was the betwixt-and-between time of early evening, with the threat of rain from the low clouds which touched the trees on each side of the valley, which kept the inhabitants in their houses. But he might as well have been in Fin Bheara's country, in which Captain and Mrs Fitzgibbon now lived as of right. For the only living souls he'd seen so far were the old village-shopkeeper-cum-postmistress (who

149

looked as though she already had one foot in Fin's kingdom, although she had given him useful information) and (quite fortuitously, but more useful still; and who might be said to have some connection with Fin's business) the village priest. But the emptiness was reassuring, nevertheless.

So now he had his bearings again: he had parked the car prudently out of sight down *that* turning, just in case. So the post office must be down *that* lane, just to his left. And there should be a phone near that—

He had been lucky today, it had to be admitted. Lucky with the start Reg had given him, directing him to Rickmansworth . . . and lucky, in a way, *at* Rickmansworth, during each of his three interviews. But luck was not such a wild card as most people liked to think, it was quite often the just reward for effort, with the Lord helping those who helped themselves. But those roadworks had been pure luck; and he would in any case have sought out the priest next. Meeting him like that, right in the churchyard, had saved him time, undoubtedly, but—

And there was the phone-box. He should have noticed it first time round. And now, because he was lucky today, it wouldn't be vandalized. (Or anyway, phones didn't get vandalized in places like Lower Buckland.)

(Tracing Mrs Frances Fitzgibbon wouldn't be too difficult, at least up to a point: it was the sort of thing John Tully and Reg Buller did well and quickly, with their wealth of varied experience.)

He was barely half an hour late phoning Jenny, which by her standards was nothing. So she'd still be in (and today, anyway, he was lucky).

It wasn't vandalized. And he had plenty of change—

(Tracing Captain Robert Gauvain Fitzgibbon, of the 39th Lancers, would be even easier: Captain Fitzgibbon, in life and in death, would be a matter of record, public and military. Not, in this context, that he would be worth more than a passing reference or two or maybe a footnote, if his family was an interesting one; or—)

'Hullo? Who's that?'

That was Jenny, safe and sound and undoubtedly: Jenny never answered the telephone with her own name and number. 'Ian, Jenny—'

'Thank God for that! Where are you?'

'What? I'm at—'

'No!' She cut him off. 'Don't answer that. You're not at home—at your flat, Ian—?'

'No. What the hell's the matter, Jen?' He had never heard her so flustered. And that, in very quick succession, surprised him and then frightened him. 'Jenny—'

'Shut up, Ian. Don't say anything. Don't tell me where you are, or what you're doing. Just listen.'

He opened his mouth, and then remembered what she'd just said. But his fear overrode that. 'Are you all right, Jenny?'

'Shut up. I've got to be quick—you've got to be quick. Get out of there—wherever you are—and go to that place where the man dropped the soup . . . Remember that? And don't be followed. If you are, then go to my father's place, and don't leave it. And I'll phone you there. Okay?'

Although he tried to digest all that while she force-fed him with it, there was too much of it, and he gagged on it. Now he was just plain

151

frightened—Beirut-style frightened. Or perhaps even more frightened, because he didn't know what ought to be frightening him in Lower Buckland, or her in London.

'Okay. It'll take me an hour, Jen.' He estimated the journey from Lower Buckland to Abdul the Damned's restaurant as best he could. But he couldn't leave it at that. 'What's happened, Jen? You must tell me. Then I'll go.'

There was a fractional pause. 'Reg Buller's dead, Ian. And I can't raise . . . his friend—he doesn't answer. I think the police may be there.' Another heart's-beat pause. 'Watch yourself, Ian—for God's sake watch yourself!'

The phone went dead.

CHAPTER FIVE

There were times, under pressure, when everything around him ceased to exist—even he himself seemed disembodied—and the only reality was what was going on in his head.

Jenny was all right, his brain told him. *If she hadn't been all right, she wouldn't have spoken like that: when she'd spoken to him that one time in Beirut, when she'd been unfree, she'd been calm and matter-of-fact, almost confident. This time, she'd been free, but neither calm nor well-organized, and far from confident—certainly far from confident that her line was safe—*

He realized that he was still inside the phone-box in Lower Buckland, just down the lane from the Village Green; and he was staring at the dialling

152

instructions blindly, with the phone still in his hand. And his hand was sweaty—

Oh God! He closed his eyes on the blasphemy. *Reg Buller!*

He replaced the receiver, and disciplined himself to accept the world as it now was, both around him in Lower Buckland, and beyond it. Jenny was in her flat, and although she was dead-scared (and although she had been dead-scared she had waited quite deliberately for his call, in spite of that . . . either because she needed him, or because she wanted to warn him—either or both, it could be) . . . *although* she'd been scared, she still thought she could beat the odds, and get away to Abdul the Damned's, where she reckoned they'd both be safe—where little Mr Malik could undoubtedly be trusted: that gave more credence to her present safety than anything else she'd said.

There was nothing to be seen outside. And *nothing* included Reg Buller, for evermore in the world as it now was: Reg Buller, with his noisome pipe and drink problem, and his bulbous nose, and his suburban semi-detached villa, had moved from *evermore* to *nevermore*.

On that thought, he pushed open the door, and stepped out of the box, with Reg Buller at his back. Because Reg would have had no time for such futile sentiments, and he couldn't afford them either, now.

The lane was empty.

Of course the fucking lane's empty, Reg Buller would have said. *Just get to the fucking car and drive, like the Lady said—right?*

But it wasn't right. Because Reg Buller had been smart, yet not smart enough. Because Reg had

153

believed in danger before anyone else had done. But Reg was dead now, even though he'd been smart.

And the car was all that was left to him, whether he'd been as clever (or as lucky) as he'd thought, just a few minutes back: he just might have been clever enough (or lucky enough) . . . but Lower Buckland was undoubtedly in the middle of its own commuter-belt nowhere, with a bus once-a-week if at all. So, if he wasn't going to walk, then he had to drive—

It was different now, was Lower Buckland, as he progressed up the empty lane towards the Village Green: it really was Fin Bheara's kingdom, as briefly glimpsed in Mrs Frances Fitzgibbon's—now Mrs Champeney-Smythe's—*Dictionary of Fairies*: if you were still in the land of the living yourself, then all the people you met there were already dead. And he wished now that he hadn't read that—

Yet that wasn't so much *not right* as simply ridiculous: he had had a long day, and if he hadn't been so frightened then he'd be dog-tired after all the unaccustomed leg-work and interviewing, never mind the driving; and, as this day—this evening, this night—was now very obviously far from over he had to cool his unfounded fears here, and summon his reserves, and pace himself.

Also, the Village Green wasn't empty now. There was a woman pushing a pram, with two children and a dog in tow, on the far side. And there was a car—two cars—two lovely, ordinary cars, with drivers and passengers in them—passing just ahead of him. And Fin Bheara surely wasn't into prams, and children, and dogs, and cars full of passengers, to people his shadowy land.

He swung round the short stretch of road into the parallel lane where the car was, almost angry with himself for his over-fertile imagination. And then halted for an instant before reversing direction, to set off diagonally across the broad expanse of Village Green, towards the great old yew-tree, where he'd paused the first time, and the churchyard and the church behind it—

God! There had been a man bending over his car, while trying the door to see whether it was unlocked! And, as he'd paused fractionally, the man had looked up, and their eyes had met across fifty yards; but the man hadn't dropped his hand, he had gone on staring—! God—!

He accelerated his pace, almost to the beginning of a run, not knowing where he was going, only that he wanted to put distance between himself and the man, his follower—his follower who had caught up with him, to become his pursuer—? Or, after Reg Buller, something more fearful than that—?

God! He hadn't been so clever, or so lucky, after all! He'd been stupid—stupid to blunder straight here, on the track of Marilyn Francis, without taking proper stock of the situation . . . stupid to delude himself that he was clever . . . and stupid, more immediately, to have reacted as he had just done—to have halted for that fatal half-second, and then not shouted angrily like an honest man, but had acted like a thief himself, and given the game away thereby—damn, damn, oh damn—! Stupid! Stupid!

But the yew-tree was marching towards him by the second, and he was only compounding his stupidity with self-recrimination. Because when he reached it he'd have to know what he would do

155

next, where he would *go* next; because there were only two roads out of Lower Buckland, according to the map, and both of them were behind him now, on the wrong side of the Village Green, with maybe Fin Bheara himself in the way. And ahead of him . . . ahead of him was the churchyard wall again—

Damn it! All the citizens of Fin's kingdom would be waiting for him there with old Reg Buller grinning over Marilyn Francis's shoulder!

And he was there, now. And he must stop thinking this Fin Bheara nonsense before it reduced him to a helpless jelly: simply, he must turn round and face his pursuer. Because . . . because—for heaven's sake!—he wasn't in some Beirut wasteland now, like last time: there were no half-smashed tenements full of hooded women and Kalashnikov-armed trigger-happy bandits from half-a-dozen different militias: these were elegant Georgian-Regency-early-Victorian English residences around him on the other three sides of the green, with elegant stockbroker-merchant-banking-high-tech-yuppie wives (with little boys and girls playing computer games at their backs as they started to prepare dinner, while watching the early evening BBC/ITV news on the kitchen TV), waiting for their husbands to return from the high-return, high-risk fray—*shit!*

(*Shit? That was what Jenny would say. But Jenny was extricating herself from her flat; and he had a rendezvous with her at Abdul the Damned's; which he had to keep—or face her father—*)

He was right underneath the yew-tree now, where he'd been so few minutes before, in the age when he'd still believed himself *clever* as well as *lucky.* But it was as much the threatened prospect of having to explain himself to 'Daddy' as his own desperation which turned him round, at the last—

Shit! He had increased the gap to the full width of the Village Green, but there were two of them now!

From being in trouble, he was in big trouble now, in his own high-return fray, which had also suddenly become as high-risk: the closest of the Georgian houses was away to his left, beyond the corner of the wall, with its manicured box hedge and holly tree, and its owner's wife's big silver Volvo Estate outside; but could he really knock at the door, and say: *'Excuse me, madam . . . but my name is Robinson—Ian Robinson, of Fielding-ffulke, Robinson . . . And I'm just researching Mrs Frances Fitzgibbon, who used to live here, just across the Green, in Gardener's Cottage—Captain Fitzgibbon's widow—perhaps you remember her—? Only . . . there are these two men, just on the other side of the Green—one of them is wearing a check sports jacket, and he's tall . . . and the other is short and plump, in a grey suit . . . But I think they may have been following me. And now I think they may want to kill me—I know that sounds silly, but they may just have killed my associate, Mr Reginald Buller—formerly of the Metropolitan Police Force . . . So, do you think that I might use your telephone—or your lavatory—? Or could I please cower in one of your attics, perhaps? Can I take sanctuary with you—?'*

One of them was moving left, round the Green. And the little fat one was advancing across the grass, towards him—

Sanctuary—?

He did know someone in Lower Buckland: the old priest, in his long black cassock—the Vicar? the

157

Rector?—had spoken to him. And the church was right behind him—and the Vicarage—Rectory?—was just somewhere behind that, through the churchyard: he had glimpsed it round the back—and the priest himself had indicated it at the end of their encounter, after he'd pronounced on the Fitzgibbons, beneath their stone in his churchyard, and very lovingly—

With Check Sports Jacket and Grey Suit converging on him purposefully, the thought of knocking on strange doors and seeking safety no longer embarrassed him: it was no longer a question of feeling foolish, but of *which door*—? And Check Jacket decided that for him by accelerating towards the silver Volvo and thereby eliminating the door behind it (which might not, in any case, have opened up quickly enough). But Grey Suit (who was not so much short and plump as menacingly thickset and powerful at close range) had already reached the furthest end of the churchyard wall, not far from the lych-gate in it.

Ian ducked under the overhanging yew-tree branches and sprang on to the top of the wall with an agility which surprised him—it was as though his arms and legs, once released from their brain's indecision, knew damn well what to do when it came to physical self-preservation—

He landed awkwardly in a pile of grass-cuttings, but the arms adjusted his balance and the legs kicked strongly, launching him out and away at immediate top-speed among the gravestones. At the same time, nevertheless, his brain cautioned him that perhaps even now he was piling up mistake on mistake: back there, on the edge of the Village Green, he had at least been out in the open, where there might have been watching eyes in the houses on its other three sides to see whatever might have happened next. But here, among the stones—*Richard Glover, 1810–1894—Edmund Chapman, 1785–1847—Martha Chapman, 1821–1867—William Thomas Eden, 1712–1790*—this could be where *Ian Drury Robinson* might end up—*1958–1987*—and no one the wiser: this might even be where Check Jacket and Grey Suit had been quite deliberately driving him—*God!*

He jinked round an ancient weathered gravestone, and skidded to a halt, steadying himself on its finial, the gritty surface of which sandpapered his hand—

A grinning skull-and-crossbones, spattered with yellow-grey splodges of lichen, mocked him: *George Wellbeloved, beloved husband*—

They were both almost inside the churchyard now, so there was no question that he had been imagining persecution where there was none: he was their target, whatever their final intention—and, with this obscene confidence of theirs, half-hurrying, half *un*hurrying, he wasn't going to wait to find out what might be on their minds, in this too-private graveyard.

He pushed himself away from George Wellbeloved's stone, twisting on one heel in the soft rough-cut grass, and took three strides. And stopped.

He was trapped—

He swayed, beginning to half-turn. And then stopped the turn as its purpose became irrelevant: he knew what was behind him, because he had assessed it only a moment before. So now he knew what it was in front of him—and understood why

159

Check Coat and Grey Suit had been so confident.

He was caught—pin-pointed as a collector's butterfly: not pursued, but caught, beyond all hope of escape!

To Check Coat and Grey Suit he added *Combat Jacket*: a third style, naturally, so that there had been no uniform appearance to register among the followers he might have noticed, if he'd been more observant—if he hadn't thought himself so clever, and so lucky. Or . . . or, if he'd taken poor old Reg more seriously, maybe—?

But now he was caught, anyway. And caught finally and more obviously than before, and quite unarguably. Because, where Check Coat and Grey Suit concealed their weapons, Combat Jacket carried his own openly—openly, albeit casually, in the crook of his arm. But then, in Lower Buckland on a wet September evening, a shotgun was as good as a Kalashnikov and more easily explained.

He straightened up, accepting the inevitable even as he tried to reject it as something which didn't happen in real life, to ordinary people.

Or . . . not to Ian Robinson—?

Or . . . not to Reg Buller—?

Combat Jacket straightened up, too. But, as he did so, his free left hand came up, to steady the shotgun even as his casual right hand slid back, to slip its trigger-finger into position.

'Hullo there!' Combat Jacket smiled at him, even as the double-barrels swung from their safe downwards-point into the shooter's readiness position, for the clay pigeon, or the rabbit, or whatever sport was in prospect—whatever game: feathers-and-two-legs, fur-and-four-legs—or *skin-and-Ian-Robinson—*

This time his legs betrayed him: he wanted them to run, but his knees had thrown in the towel, and it was all he could do to stop them buckling, to bring him down to grass-level.

'Mr Ian Robinson, I believe—?' The gun was coming up. And Combat Jacket was smiling psychopathically, with enjoyment—

It would be an accident: one of those tragic shotgun mishaps—

Ian closed his eyes. There would be a terrible impact. And then there would be . . . whatever there was after that: probably pain, until communications broke down; but that wouldn't take long, with a shotgun at five yards. And then . . . *everything*? Or . . . *nothing*?

Nothing happened.

Or perhaps time was standing still for him, in his last second of it?

Only, time *wasn't* standing still: all he had felt, before that last thought, was blank fear filling his chest. But then he realized that he had breathed in deeply as he'd closed his eyes, and now he couldn't hold his breath any longer: it was the discomfort of that which was filling him—

He breathed out and opened his eyes again simultaneously, to find that there was no one in front of him any longer: there were only the greens and greys of the churchyard, swimming slightly for an instant and then coming sharply into focus as he blinked the sweat away.

He had been stupid, he began to think. And then the confusion in his mind cleared, just as the sweat had done, in another eye-blink, as he remembered that the man with the gun had called him by his name.

He turned round clumsily, grasping at the nearest grave-stone for support as his legs threatened again to give way under him, making him stagger slightly.

Combat Jacket was still in the churchyard, but was way past him now, up by the wall midway between the yew-tree and lych-gate and staring out across the Village Green, shot-gun still at the ready. For the moment he seemed quite uninterested in Ian.

But . . . *'Mr Ian Robinson, I believe?'* was there between them, validating the man's presence, making it not-accidental—and reconvening all Ian's fears in a clamorous disorderly crowd in his brain: the man was real, and his shot-gun was real. And those other men had been no less real—Check Coat and Grey Suit—but where were they now—?

Combat Jacket turned towards him suddenly, beckoning him.

There was no arguing with the invitation. If there had been a moment to run, and continue running, it was past now. And, anyway, the weakness in his legs dismissed the very idea as ridiculous, never mind that shot-gun in the man's hands.

The rough-cut churchyard grass was soft and springy under his feet, and there was a different cross-section of memorials to the long-dead inhabitants of Lower Buckland all around him. But he only had eyes for Combat Jacket now, as he approached the man.

Combat Jacket was no longer smiling (and maybe he'd never been smiling: maybe that smile had been inside his own imagination?).

'Well, I think they've gone.' Combat Jacket nodded at him, then re-checked the Village Green,

162

and then returned to him.

'They've gone?' Ian's husky repetition of the words betrayed him. But . . . Combat Jacket was fortyish, for the record: young-fortyish, but a little haggard; brown hair, short-cut but well-cut; brown eyes, regular features . . . the sort of man, if he'd been ten years older, whom Jenny might have looked twice at, once he'd acquired a touch of grey (older men, not younger, were Jenny's preference—)—

(*Philip Masson maybe? Is that it, Jenny? Is that it?*)

The thought of Jenny made him want to look at his watch. But he mustn't do that!

'Didn't you hear the car?' Combat Jacket was studying him just as carefully.

'No.' It was just possible that this man had saved his life. But, if he had done so, he had only been obeying orders, just like that Syrian major in Beirut. And it was Jenny who mattered now—and Jenny's orders. So he must keep his head and not let foolish sentiment get in the way of necessity. 'Who are you?'

'My name is Mitchell. Paul Mitchell—' Mitchell-Paul-Mitchell took another look over the churchyard wall: whatever Mitchell-Paul-Mitchell was, and *whoever* . . . he was a careful man. 'Paul *Lefevre* Mitchell. Almost exactly three hundred years ago one of my Huguenot-Protestant ancestors fled from Louis XIV's France, to England . . . and just a minute or two ago I rather wished he hadn't, Mr Robinson. But now, I think it's time for us to go, too.'

That was curiously interesting. Because a few years back (and before Jenny had vetoed the idea of it, in preference for the more saleable Middle East)

163

he had proposed a book on that anniversary of King Louis' expulsion of his Protestants, which had given England the Bank of England and Laurence Olivier; and Paul Revere to the United States.

But that was all also quite ridiculously beside the point now: the point was . . . he had to get to Abdul the Damned's tandoori restaurant. And to Jenny.

But the point also was that he mustn't seem too eager—however desperate he felt. So he must ignore the more important second statement in preference for the first. 'You wished he hadn't, Mr Mitchell? Why was that?'

Mitchell raised an eyebrow. 'You are a cool one, aren't you!' Then a hint of that original not-smile returned. 'But then, of course, you *were* a cool one in Beirut, weren't you? When they snatched your lady-friend, and you negotiated her release—? That was cool—yes!'

Mitchell was Intelligence, not Special Branch: it might be MI5 (it could hardly be MI6) but it was one or the other, to know so much . . . even though he'd got it quite pathetically wrong, about the coolness. But he mustn't spoil the illusion. 'Oh—?'

'I wondered why you didn't duck down behind the nearest convenient cover!' Mitchell nodded. 'But, of course . . . you weren't surprised, were you?'

He had to get away from this total misreading of events. 'You seem to know a lot about me, Mr Mitchell.'

'I know all about you, Mr Robinson: Miss Fielding-ffulke asks the questions, and has the

164

contacts, and negotiates the deals . . . and you sort out the sheep from the goats she brings you, and write the actual books. You are the brains, and she is the brawn . . . unlikely as that may seem.' Mitchell took another look over the churchyard wall. 'Shall we go, then?'

With Mitchell here beside him he was physically safe; that shot-gun, if not Mitchell himself, proclaimed that. So, with this *Mitchell-Paul-Mitchell* in a mood of indiscretion, he must forget Jenny and get all he could, while he could get it . . . no matter how his guts were still twisting. 'If I'm "the brains", Mr Mitchell . . . then I'd be obliged if you'd tell me what's going on—?'

Mitchell cocked his head. 'Are you going to be difficult? After what has just happened—?' Again he looked towards the Village Green. 'I think they've gone . . . But let's not push our luck—eh?'

Because Mitchell wasn't happy, Ian began to feel unhappy. 'But I still don't know who you are, Mr Mitchell—any more than I know who *they* were, actually.'

'But you ran away from them?' Mitchell's mouth twisted. 'You are being difficult—'

'Not difficult—' Actually, *not* difficult: for this instant he could be at least partially honest '—who were they?'

Mitchell stared at him for a moment, as though deceived by that partial honesty. 'You don't know him? Well . . . maybe you don't at that! But . . . you ran like a rabbit, across the Green—?' The moment of credulity faded into suspicion. 'Oh—come on, Mr Robinson! I've just gone through a very bad time on your behalf: this isn't when you should be playing silly games with me,

165

for God's sake!' He lifted the shot-gun meaningfully across his chest—and then broke it, thrusting it towards Ian. 'See—?'

What Ian saw was that the man's face was breaking up as he offered the gun for inspection, the mouth twisting bitterly.

'Empty.' Mitchell pushed the gun closer. 'See!' Ian had to look at it.

'Okay?' Mitchell snapped the shot-gun together again. 'Father John—Father John whom you've met . . . he *lent* me his gun. But he couldn't find any cartridges for it—not at short notice, he said—huh!'

That was indeed what Ian had seen: the twin-chambers of the shotgun had been just like the muzzles which he had imagined he'd faced, both black empty circles—

Mitchell nodded. 'I've just pointed an unloaded gun at Paddy MacManus for you, Mr Robinson. And that means that you owe me far more than you can ever repay: I got you one of your nine lives back—but we've *both* just lost one of our nine lives—okay?'

The empty shot-gun unmanned Ian. He didn't know who the hell 'Paddy MacManus' might be; but *Mitchell-Paul-Mitchell* knew—and that smile, if it had been a smile, would have been the Syrian major's smile, as they'd finally left the car at the rendezvous, of reassurance-pasted-over-fear, when they still hadn't known whether it was a meeting or an ambush—

He followed Combat Jacket towards the lych-gate.

'My car's across the Green, Mr Mitchell—' he began. Was it going to be as easy as that, though?

'We're not taking your car.' Mitchell pointed towards the Volvo. 'You come with me.'

He was still following Combat-Jacket-Mitchell-Paul-Mitchell. But his Rover Vitesse was as much his pride-and-joy as Philip Masson's Folkboat *Jenny III* has been. 'But what about my car—?'

'I'll send someone for it. If they followed you here, then they've bugged it. So we'll *un*bug it for you—not to worry!' Mitchell remotely unlocked his big silver Volvo. 'And we'll go out the opposite way—just in case?'

They had followed him here. In fact, *they* and *Mitchell-Paul-Mitchell* had both followed him here, when he'd thought himself so clever.

'How did you follow me here?' He still didn't really know who *Mitchell-Paul-Mitchell* was. But it didn't seem a time for argument.

'You were easy.' The Volvo rolled forward smoothly. 'At least, after Rickmansworth, you were easy.' The Volvo circled the peaceful square of grass. 'This way's longer . . . but, just in case . . . we'll go the longer way, I think.'

They passed the post office side-road, and then the side-road in which his own abandoned pride-and-joy lay. And then accelerated.

'What did Father John say to you, when you met him in the churchyard?' Mitchell pre-empted his next question as they began to climb the other side of Lower Buckland's peaceful valley, in which no one had just been killed.

'Father John' must be the old priest whom he'd met, and thought himself so lucky to meet: 'Father John', in his long black cassock, High Anglican and

167

old—old Father John, and old black cassock, as he'd thought . . . But now he had to think of Father John as part of the deception of *Mrs Frances Fitzgibbon*, of which *Mitchell-Paul-Mitchell* was another part.

'Can I help you?' (The old priest had appeared out of nowhere, so it had seemed to him.)

'Sir?' (He had been caught looking at the Fitzgibbon grave—*Captain Robert Gauvain* and *Frances*; and he'd been looking at it too long for comfort, with all the other graves around to look at.)

'Are you looking for anyone in particular?' (Father John had given the Fitzgibbon stone a little nod—almost a blessing.)

(That had shaken him. He had crossed out *Captain Robert Gauvain*, and concentrated on Frances, beloved *wife*; because *Frances, beloved wife*—formerly *Marilyn*, beloved 'smasher' of Gary Redwood . . . and maybe the long-lost, never-born daughter of Mrs Champeney-Smythe—but who, in reality? Only, whatever she had been, *Marilyn/Frances* had almost overwhelmed him then, as he'd seen her name on her tombstone.)

(And that tell-tale concentration on Marilyn/Frances had warned him off her, as Father John had looked at him.) *'I was just looking for Captain Fitzgibbon, sir.'* (The Father of Lies had jogged his arm then.) *'He was in the regiment, sir.'*

(Father John had nodded then, understandingly. *'Ah . . . Robbie Fitzgibbon was a splendid chap! The bravest of the brave . . . and a good cricketer, too.'* (The ultimate accolade!)

168

'*Did you know his wife, sir?*' (The ultimate question.)

'*Frances? Yes—*'

He caught a last glimpse of the church far below, and it brought back a memory of the look on the old priest's face then, which had said it all even before Father John confirmed what he himself already knew. But it hadn't been the moment to press for more, he had judged.

Or had it been that he had no heart then for more of his own lies? Not where Mrs Frances Fitzgibbon was concerned—?

The car jolted over a pothole as they left the valley behind.

'I was easy?' He knew so much about Frances—and yet he knew nothing really. But it was this man Mitchell who mattered now. 'After Rickmansworth? Why then?'

'When you came out of that old woman's house—that boarding house . . . you looked like the cat who'd found the cream, Mr Robinson.' Mitchell frowned at him quickly. 'So then I knew where you were going. But how the blazes did she know where to send you, though? Frances—Mrs Fitzgibbon . . . certainly didn't tell her. And I cleaned that place out myself, just in case.' He frowned at Ian again, but this time with all the underlying arrogance of a man unused to making mistakes.

'So you were the "brother".' It was good to prick that arrogance. And it was also good when things fitted so glove-like: Mitchell had been to Lower

169

Buckland before—and often, surely, to be on shot-gun-borrowing terms with the old priest. But . . . why did it hurt to think of Mitchell knowing Frances Fitzgibbon so well that her Christian name came to him first? 'But . . . who are you, Mr Mitchell? And *what* are you?' All he could do to soothe that unaccountable pain was to hug his own small secret close. 'And why were you following me?'

Mitchell drove in silence, still frowning.

Another question occurred to Ian, rather belatedly in view of its importance. 'Where are we going?'

This time the man grinned. 'To meet Miss Fielding-ffulke—right?'

That was a nasty piece of logic. 'Why should I want to do that?'

'Oh, come on, Mr Robinson! You've got a lot to tell her. And she's probably got a lot to tell you. Plus what Messrs Tully and Buller have rooted out of the dirt.' The grin faded. 'And now we both need to see her rather urgently don't you think, eh?'

The man didn't know about Reg Buller. But then how—?

'Come on, man!' Mitchell lost some of his cool. 'Those friends of yours back there—they went away smartly enough when they saw me. But that was only because I wasn't expected, and MacManus doesn't like the unexpected—not when it's a gun pointing at him. He didn't want a shoot-out, he was just paid for *you*, Mr Robinson. But . . . he isn't going to go away forever: he still wants his money. Or . . . if not him, then there'll be someone else.'

It was simple, really: Combat Jacket had been the unexpected for Check Coat and Grey Suit. But

Check Coat and Grey Suit had also been the unexpected for Combat Jacket: the borrowed shot-gun, the *empty* borrowed shot-gun—told all. *God!*

'What are you, Mr Mitchell? Special Branch? Or Security?' Ian saw a motorway sign ahead, offering them London or the West.

'I'm the man who's just lost one of his nine lives on your behalf, Mr Ian Robinson.' Mitchell fumbled in his pocket. 'Which way? London, I presume?'

Away in the gathering murk ahead of them Ian saw innumerable rushing headlights on the M25. Which way?

'It could be a forgery, of course.' Mitchell waited as Ian studied the identification folder. It didn't tell him much more than he'd already guessed, and he'd seen others like it. 'But then . . . if it was, you could already be dead, Mr Robinson. Because, by asking all those clever questions of yours, about Philip Masson and David Audley, you seem to have raised the Devil himself between you. Only it seems that the Devil wants you, instead of David, doesn't he?'

They were approaching the slip roads junction. 'London—yes,' said Ian.

CHAPTER SIX

Ian could never penetrate the labyrinth of Islington without remembering the Monopoly game he had been given on his eighth birthday, and his father, whose present it had been: Dad had been nutty about place-names (among so many other things), and *Islington* had been his own very first purchase, where the dice had transported his little silver car—

'*"The Angel, Islington"—buy it, boy! Buy it! Although there aren't many angels in Islington these days, I fear . . . No—the "tun" of the "Eslingas" once, it would have been . . . the people of some minor North Saxon chieftain, "Esla" by name . . . Funny that: "Essex" for the East Saxons, "Sussex" for the South Saxons, and "Wessex" the biggest—the West Saxons. And even "Middlesex" for the Middle Saxons. But no "Nossex", eh? Maybe they were Angles there—"Angels", maybe—?*' (Dad had thought about that for a moment, then had got up from the game and gone to his study, to 'look it all up', as was his disruptive custom; and Mum had cried out *'Eddie! Come back! We're playing a game—and it's your throw!'* and looked at Ian despairingly; and Dad had shouted back, from far away and quite unrepentant, *'Only be a minute, dear! Must look it all up. Because knowledge is power and power is knowledge—always set an example—only be a minute, dear!'*; and then, after a full eternity of five minutes, had returned shaking his head at Ian, as he usually did.) '*No angels in Islington, that I can find. But lots of the opposite—bad men in Pentonville Gaol, and wicked women in Holloway, my lad . . . And, frankly, I wouldn't rate the Polytechnic much higher—I expect the police patrol in pairs there too, at night . . . But you buy it, Ian—*'

And a sad-sweet memory of Mum and Dad followed on from that: they had never seen his
172

smart Hampstead flat, or his Vitesse (still parked in Lower Buckland). But, in any case, Dad would have enjoyed his reference library more, and Mum would have loved meeting Lady Fielding-ffulke and the Honourable Jennifer, however much they would also have terrified her.

But now—*now* . . . he wished Dad had been right, and that there had been numerous pairs of large Metropolitan policemen flexing their knees on every street corner as Paul Mitchell nosed the silver Volvo into the lucky space outside Abdul the Damned's tandoori restaurant.

But now—*now* . . . he had to trust Combat Jacket—just as Combat Jacket was trusting him not to scuttle away into the rain-swept half-light when he had the chance, instead of guiding him into the space.

'Am I all right—?' Mitchell poked his head out of the driver's window.

'You've got another two feet—left hand down—right!' There were people here, whom he could see—unlike those he hadn't seen in Lower Buckland, even when they'd been there; but he had to trust Mitchell's confidence in their safety, just as Mitchell was trusting him. 'Steady!'

'Phew!' Mitchell locked the car, and then turned on its burglar-alarm. 'Bloody great big tank!' He grinned at Ian. 'Not mine, you understand? But marvellously unobtrusive in the commuter belt—*all* the wives have got 'em to take the kids to school: and the dogs, wherever they take the dogs.' He looked round, up and down the street with deceptive casualness. 'Ah! There's a phone-box! If it's unvandalized, then I'll phone in from there. You go on in, Ian—be my John the Baptist with

173

Her Ladyship—okay?' The blue neon light advertising Abdul's tandoori delights illuminated his face diabolically. 'Tell it the way you do in your books, straight from the shoulder—the way it was—okay?'

He didn't want to like Paul Mitchell, for all that they seemed to have Mrs Frances Fitzgibbon in common. But there was something in the man which called out to him, which he couldn't add up, but which came to him across their conflicting interests. And it wasn't just that Mitchell had saved his life—indeed, it wasn't that at all; because that had been duty, so that counted for nothing. But . . . there *was* something else—

'There's a phone inside, Mr Mitchell.' He indicated Abdul's restaurant.

'Uh-huh?' The street received another up-and-down look. 'You call me "Paul", and I'll call you "Ian"—remember?' Mitchell came back to him. 'If we're on Christian name terms we can exchange home-truths without insulting each other, I always think: "Fuck-off, Paul" is so much more friendly than "No, Mr Mitchell"—eh?' The dark-blue lips curled fiendishly. 'Okay, Ian?'

The curry-smell recalled the street outside Mrs Champeney-Smythe's boarding-house too vividly for him to return the devilish grin. And Mitchell didn't wait for his agreement, in any case.

Then the smell engulfed him, as he opened the door.

And there was little Mr Malik himself, smiling with his own infectious humour and balanced on the balls of his feet like a boxer waiting for him.

'*Mister* Robinson—you have damn-well been up to no good this time, I think!' Mr Malik signalled towards a group of white-coated waiters, from which the two largest instantly detached themselves. 'But you don't worry. My little brother and my cousin will take a damn-good look outside—make damn-sure nobody is snooping around out there, see?'

The two waiters were already peeling off their white coats, and Mr Malik's gorgeous sister reached under her cash-till to produce two dark windcheaters: when Mr Malik had first launched his business in this tough area there had been several episodes of 'damn trouble', Ian recalled. But Mr Malik had dealt with his problems in a manner which the locals understood and appreciated, without recourse to the forces of law and order. So all was peaceful in Cody Street.

'No, Mr Malik—!' The thought of Paul Mitchell having a final snoop outside, and encountering the grinning six-foot 'little brother' in the process, hit him as the little brother slipped a cosh down his sleeve. 'No!'

'Oh yes, Mr Robinson!' Mr Malik waved him down. 'Miss Jenny says we take damn-good precaution—those are her orders, Mr Robinson.' He carried the wave on to his Search-and-Destroy squad. 'You go!'

'No. I have a friend out there—in the phone-box across the road, Mr Malik—' In desperation, Ian skipped sideways to block the doorway. When Jenny issued orders, men always jumped. But these two looked like men who had had a boring day up to now.

'A friend?' Mr Malik seemed surprised that Ian had any friends. But he snapped his fingers, and the squad froze. 'But . . . we have a telephone, Mr

Robinson. And Miss Jenny says to look.'

'Yes.' Jenny really was running scared, to give such orders. But, then, she was damn-right to run scared! 'My friend didn't want to impose on you. Is the phone okay, out there—?'

'Okay?' Mr Malik drew himself up to his full five-foot-five. 'Mr Robinson . . . we have no trouble in Cody Street—no damn trouble, sir.' He nodded towards his little brother. 'When Mr Robinson's friend finish his call, you bring him in. And then you take a damn-good look, like I said—okay?' He amended his cold-hard look of Absolute Monarchy to its original friendliness as he brought it back to Ian. 'Now I take you to Miss Jenny, sir—please?'

Ian followed the little man down the length of the Taj Mahal, between tables which were already crowded in mid-evening, and with people who acknowledged Mr Malik, and whom he in turn acknowledged with matching esteem, until they reached the curtained stairway at the end.

Mr Malik held the curtain for him. But then touched his arm, arresting his progress.

'All my regulars, this evening, Mr Robinson—all known to me, you understand?' He looked up at Ian and tapped his nose. 'Okay?'

'Yes—?' The trouble was, he understood all too well.

'Yes. No strangers out there.' Nod. 'And . . . all the damn tables taken tonight—until Miss Jenny leaves.' He grinned suddenly. 'Except regulars, that my sister knows—*they* get served, only.' The grin evaporated. 'You remember that night—when the damn-soup spilt—?'

'Yes.' That wasn't a night easily forgotten: it had been the crowning event of the Taj Mahal's first

176

week—very nearly literally—when the obstreperous drunk had jostled the waiter, and the soup had been spilt, and the drunk had moved to crown the waiter with a handy bottle of Malvern Water, and little Mr Malik (not yet *aka* Abdul the Damned) had squared up to the aggressor—and Jenny had decreed intervention—

'*Do something!*' (Jenny, outraged, Ian, scared.')
'*What—me?*' (Ian, appalled, to her . . . the drunk being large, and their table loaded with untouched dinner.)
'*You want trouble—?*' (Drunk to Mr Malik, overjoyed.)
"*You make damn trouble!*" (Mr Malik, disconcertingly unafraid.)
'*Ian!*' (Jenny, outraged with him now.)
'*I say—*' (Ian terrified, but resigned.) '*—steady on now, everyone!*'
'*Who asked you?*' (Drunk to Ian; then lifting the bottle, to all comers.) '*Anyone else for trouble—?*'
'*Yes.*' (Jenny, unflustered and lovely, taking everyone's attention as she squeezed out from behind the table to take centre-stage.) '*Me—if you think I'm small enough?*'

★　　★　　★

But Mr Malik was grinning at him. 'No problem this evening, Mr Robinson—no damn-soup, eh?' The grin almost split his face in two. 'You go see Miss Jenny—second door left, Shah Jehan Room. And I bring up your friend pretty soon. And no damn strangers.'
Ian did his best to return the grin, while trying

177

not to imagine what might occur if Mitchell's confidence was misplaced, and Abdul's retainers encountered this afternoon's hit squad.

'Thank you, Mr Malik.' What unmanned him, as he kept the false grin in place over his shoulder, was that there was no limit to his imagination after this afternoon, this evening. But then there was a limit to how much he could worry about, he discovered.

The Shah Jehan Room was to the left—one of the special private dining rooms, of course . . . next to the Mumtaz Mahal Room—Mumtaz, for whom all the wonder of the original Taj had been created . . . and now strangely celebrated in innumerable restaurants and take-aways long after the Mogul emperors and their British conquerors had receded into history.

'Jenny!' The room was dim, and disturbingly scented, after the relatively greater half-light of the corridor and the dominating curry-smell which had followed him up the stairs. 'Jenny—?'

'Well! You took your time, I must say!'

'Yes—I'm sorry, Jen.' Coming out from behind the silken hangings, she should have been dressed to match, with jewellery and a bare midriff; but, as she was, her voice went with her old sweater and jeans. 'I was held up.'

'Held up? You said an hour, for God's sake!' She took an inexpert puff from her cigarette, and then stubbed it out; and then picked up the glass by the ashtray, and drained it; and Jenny drinking was nothing unusual but Jenny smoking was demoralizing. 'What held you up, for God's sake? I've been worrying myself stiff.'

'*Who*—not *What*.' There were times when he wanted to slap her, and if things hadn't been so

178

serious this might have been one of them. Besides which Mitchell had said he wouldn't be long, so there was no time for recrimination. 'What happened to Reg Buller?'

'He's dead—I told you.' She took herself and her glass over to the well-stocked bar in the canopied alcove. 'And we killed him.' She filled the glass. 'Or, to be strictly accurate, *I* killed him.' She lifted the bottle. 'Credit where credit is due. Have a drink, Ian. I said we'd got a winner here, and you can't say I wasn't right. We can even dedicate the damn thing to old Reg now—that'll wow the critics: "*Dulce et decorum est pro Jennifer Fielding mori*"—how about that?'

She wasn't scared anymore—or, if she ever had been, she wasn't now. But if this was Dutch courage as well as self-pity, they were in more trouble now, with Mitchell coming.

'Don't worry—it's only Abdul's most innocuous plonk, which is practically alcohol-free.' She could hardly have read his expression in the subdued light, but she always read his silences. 'And I've spiked it with soda water. So I'm not pissed, Ian darling—or . . . what was it old Reg used to say, when he'd been on a bender—?' "Crapulated", was it? No—"*crapulous*"—I'm not *crapulous* . . . see?' She thrust the bottle towards him. 'Hardly opened.'

She *was* scared—of course she was scared. And he was scared too—but, less forgivably, he had been stupid—

'It's all right, Jenny.' He took the bottle from her and put his arms around her, brotherly-sisterly, thinking *brotherly-sisterly—and the first time since Beirut . . . but that had been different: that had been shared relief, not shared fear!* 'It's all right, Jen.'

179

She held him tighter. 'Oh Ian—it isn't all right—it's all *wrong*! What have I done—for God's sake, what have I done?'

'You haven't done anything.' What mattered was what they were going to do. And with Jenny so completely out of character he realized how much he normally depended on her to answer that question. So he had to straighten her out first—and quickly. 'Whatever's happened, Reg was just as keen to work on this as you were—he was dead-keen—' he grimaced at the wall behind her as he heard his gaffe, and pushed on hurriedly '—and so was John Tully—' he unwrapped her gently: however much he wanted to know about Reg Buller, that would have to wait (and Tully was more important now, anyway!) '—where is John, Jenny? Have you been able to get through to him yet?'

'No.' She blinked at him. 'No, I haven't. And . . . and we can't, I mean.'

Stupid, again: she had said something about the police on the phone, and he had automatically assumed their progression from a dead Reg Buller to a live John Tully, and then had clean forgotten that in the press of events.

'But, Ian—'

'No.' Even Tully wasn't the most important thing now. 'Listen, Jen: there's someone coming to see us—here—' He tried to keep one ear cocked for the sound of Mitchell on the stair as he spoke, against the sound of his own voice and the faint restaurant hubbub from below '—any second now.'

'Someone?' Her eyes widened momentarily, and then narrowed. '*Who*—'

'Just listen. I went to Rickmansworth today, to check up on the girl—the one who was killed up

180

north, just before Masson disappeared—'

'Yes, I know. John told me you and Reg were off on some wild goose chase somewhere.' She nodded. 'Marilyn-something—?'

'It wasn't a wild goose chase.'

'Francis—Marilyn Francis.' The nod became contemptuous. 'A typist.'

'Audley was there when she was killed.' She was irritated with him for acting on his own initiative, but he was also angry with her now: angry because she had closed her mind prematurely (which was unlike her) . . . but also angry at her dismissive contempt for Frances Fitzgibbon. 'I thought it was Audley we were after—isn't it?'

'It is.' From below him she somehow managed to look down on him. 'But, according to John yesterday—and John hasn't been wild-goose-chasing—Audley only got back from the States the day they shot the IRA man. And it's Audley and Philip Masson we're interested in, not Audley and Marilyn Thingummy-jig, or Marilyn Monroe, or any other Marilyn. You can put her in as a footnote, if you like—one of Audley's field-work casualties . . . But Philly Masson was top-brass, and nothing to do with field-work: Philly was going to be Audley's new boss, if he'd lived—*if* he'd lived.' She achieved another amazing contradiction, to match the physical looking-down one: her anger made her almost plain. 'But not for long. Because he'd probably have given Audley the push pretty soon, Philly would have done . . . Maybe a bit of ribbon, and a full fellowship in some Cambridge college, to go with it . . . But maybe not even that.' The ugliness vanished. 'But Philly died, of course.'

Was that a creak on the stair—?

'And so has Reg Buller, Jenny.' Almost, she had weakened his confidence with her Tully-Fielding heart-of-the-matter intelligence safely garnered while he'd been skirmishing so dangerously in Rickmansworth and Lower Buckland. But the ghost of Reg Buller shook his head at him—*and there was blood on Reg's face . . . and that had been a sound on the stair.* 'And I think I came damn close to following him, just this afternoon, what's more—'

'What—?' Without any matching distraction, she had taken in every word after he had hit her below the belt with *Reg Buller.*

He strained his ear into a sudden unnatural silence: even the pots and pans in the busy kitchen below them seemed to have stopped clattering, and the whole of Dad's ancient *Eslingastun* seemed momentarily still.

'Two men came after me, Jen. At least, I think they did—'

Tap-tap—the soft double knock on the door cut him off decisively. And then, as though the silence had been released by it, the pans started clattering again, and a car driver changed gears inexpertly and revved his engine outside. But Jenny was already turning towards the first sound.

Damn! thought Ian. 'And this man probably saved my life then—*Come in, Mr Mitchell!*'

In the stretched seconds during which the door opened, Jenny came back from it to him, with an angry expression he was glad he couldn't see clearly.

'Hullo there! Ian—?' Mitchell saw Ian first, and smiled hesitantly at him; then took in Jenny, holding the smile in place; and then swung round, away from them both. 'Thank you, gentlemen—for your help . . .' The smile began to droop as he got it back to Ian. 'I'd be obliged if you'd tell the Indian Army out here that I'm friendly. Because they're beginning to frighten me.' He opened the door wider, to reveal Mr Malik's fearsome brother at his shoulder and the equally terrifying cousin on his otherside.

Ian nodded to them. 'Thank you, gentlemen.'

Mr Malik's brother stood to attention. 'You want anything, sir—you just ring.'

'Phew!' Mitchell closed the door with evident relief. 'They were waiting for me outside the phone-box. I thought they were going to mug me. Then one of them mentioned your name . . . But he still looked as though he'd rather thump me—even after I'd told him I was a friend of yours.'

'And are you a friend of ours?' Jenny had recovered her glass but not her temper, from the cold hostility in her voice. 'Mr Mitchell, is it—?'

'I beg your pardon?' Mitchell smiled at her uneasily. 'Miss Fielding-ffulke, I presume?'

'Plain "Fielding" will do, Mr Mitchell.'

'Not "plain", Miss Fielding. And my friends call me Paul. That being my name.'

'Is that so? And we are friends?'

'I would have thought so—yes. I'm undoubtedly *your* friend, Miss Fielding. And you certainly need friends.' Mitchell was no longer smiling.

'But I already have friends, Mr Mitchell. Lots of them. And in high places, too.'

'Ah . . . yes.' Somehow, as Jenny had become less angry and more confident, Mitchell seemed to have become the opposite. 'But now you may need

183

one in a low place, perhaps—don't you think?'

'Meaning you, Mr Mitchell?'

'Meaning me, Miss Fielding.' Mitchell gave Ian a slightly puzzled glance.

'But I really don't know you, Mr Mitchell. I don't know who you are. And I don't know what you do.'

Mitchell's head inclined slightly, as though from weariness. 'Oh, come on, Miss Fielding—I know I was only away for five minutes. But I can't believe that you've been discussing the menu with Ian here. Or the weather. Or your last joint royalty statement. Or . . . even your next advance, on the book you're planning to write.'

'How d'you know we're planning to write a book?' Jenny knew she was winning.

'Isn't that what you do?' By the same token, Mitchell seemed to think that he was losing. 'You dig the dirt . . . or should I say pan the gold—?'

For the first time, Jenny smiled at Mitchell. But not sweetly. 'Isn't that where gold is found—in dirt? But we don't make the dirt, Mr Mitchell. People like you do that. We merely *find* the gold—' Then she gestured abruptly. '—I'm tired of metaphors, though . . . In answer to your question, Mr Friendly-Mitchell—*yes*, we are going to write a book. Because that is what we do. So what?'

'Unless someone stops you.'

'Stops us? Who's going to stop us?' Jenny seemed delighted that he'd picked up her gauntlet so quickly (Ian felt the metaphor shift from goldmining to single combat: and that would please her, of course!). 'Not you—you're a friend of ours, you said.'

'Not me, no.' Mitchell nodded towards Ian. 'He

184

does the writing, doesn't he? And someone damn nearly wrote "The End" to his book this afternoon, Miss Fielding. Ask him if you don't believe me.'

'I see.' She didn't even look at Ian. 'Would you like a drink, Mr Mitchell?'

'Thank you.' Mitchell didn't relax. 'I would like a drink—yes.' He watched her pour a generous glass of Mr Malik's plonk.

'So you're just here to frighten us—is that it?' She thrust the glass at him, spilling it as usual in the process.

'Am I?' Mitchell drank thirstily, swallowing and then making a face. 'I think you ought to be frightened.'

'But you don't mind us writing, though? And publishing—?'

Mitchell considered the question and the wine together, and neither seemed to his taste. 'It all depends on what you write, I suppose.' But he drank, nevertheless.

'Usually we settle for the truth, Mr Mitchell. Our lawyers find that less complicated to defend.' Jenny watched the man drink again. 'And we try not to be too economical with it.'

'Then, you've been fortunate to find such a lot of it. I've always found it somewhat elusive, myself.'

'Like gold?' Her mock innocence was transparent. 'Another drink—?'

'Sometimes like fool's gold, Miss Fielding. And even the real stuff . . . since we're into metaphor again . . . it can be just like a little knowledge—dangerous.' He nodded towards Ian as he presented his glass. 'As Ian here surely must have told you—thank you . . . I can't really believe that you haven't told Miss Fielding about our

185

adventures of this afternoon.' Then he frowned slightly over his glass at Jenny. 'Or has she had even more traumatic adventures of her own, maybe—?'

Ian felt himself frowning. The man was fishing, unashamedly. But he was also behaving as though he still didn't know about Reg Buller. So . . . who the devil had he been phoning from the box outside, who also didn't know? Could Intelligence really be so uninformed—so downright incompetent—?

'Only very briefly.' The voice inside his head giving the obvious answer seemed louder than his own voice.

'Yes. Too briefly.' Jenny followed him up quickly. 'So perhaps you would elaborate on what Ian said, Mr Mitchell. As a friend?'

'Ah . . .' Mitchell acknowledged the turning of the tables on him with the ghost of a smile. 'What did you tell her, Ian? No point in repeating . . . the truth, eh?'

'He thought you might have saved his life, that's all.' Jenny refused to give up her advantage.

'All?' Mitchell sounded a little pained. 'That seems quite a lot to me.'

'He wasn't sure it was what you did, though. Maybe not the truth?'

'Oh, it is—I did. And rather heroically too, I thought. Or, as some might say . . . foolishly?' He shook his head at Ian. 'You didn't tell her about Father John's gun—?'

'He did not.' To her credit Jenny resisted this irresistible red herring. But then weakened. 'There were two men—?'

'Ah? So he did say more!' But then Mitchell
186

weakened in turn. 'Actually, there were three—'

'Three?' Since no one had offered him a drink, Ian had been heading for the alcove. But the number stopped him in his tracks.

'Three, including me.' Mitchell took his nod from Ian back to Jenny. 'We were all following him. But I was . . .' He shrugged.

'The cleverest?' Jenny put her knife in with a sweetly inquiring smile.

'Undoubtedly—and fortunately.' Mitchell considered the proposition seriously for a moment before continuing. 'But I was actually going to say "better informed". So I got to Lower Buckland ahead of everyone else, from Rickmansworth. There's a little back road—'

'Why were you following him?' More red herrings bit the dust.

Mitchell frowned. 'Why—to see where he was going, Miss Fielding. Why else would I follow him?' Then he shook his head. 'I'm sorry—'

'Sorry?' Jenny had been about to snap at him. 'Why?'

'Yes. It was a silly answer.' He half-smiled at her. '"Why did the chicken cross the road?"—"To get to the other side" . . . But we're past the childish Christmas-cracker jokes, I think. And . . . the chicken had other reasons, of course.' Mitchell twisted the smile downwards. 'But the joke was certainly on this chicken, Miss Fielding: I had no idea how dangerous the road was going to be. And *that* is the truth, believe it or not.' Then he lifted his empty glass. 'Could I have a proper drink, please? Like whisky, say?'

Jenny stared at the man for a moment, almost as though she was seeing him properly for the first

187

time, before taking the glass and turning to the alcove. And Ian felt himself sharing the instant, and also seeing more clearly what he had glimpsed before: that, whatever and whoever he was, Mitchell was also flesh-and-blood, and no superman; and that in Lower Buckland they had both of them come upon their own life-and-death, equally unexpectedly. And that was certainly no joke.

'I think Jenny meant . . . how did you get on to us?' That was a fair question, with a useful answer—if Mitchell was so foolish as to give it. But also, after this afternoon and what he'd just thought, he felt obligated to Mitchell.

'Is that what she meant?'

'What?' Jenny looked from one to the other suspiciously as she handed him a new glass.

'Thank you.' Mitchell drank a little of his whisky. 'Well, if I may answer you with an ancient truth . . . *"when you sup with the Devil, you need a long spoon"*—is that right? I can't remember where it comes from. But your spoon just wasn't long enough, it seems.'

Jenny squared up to him. 'What the hell is that meant to mean, Mr Mitchell?'

Mitchell looked at her for an instant. 'I mean . . . at least, I think I mean . . . that if you ask particular questions . . . of *particular* people, about *other* people—?' He cocked his own question at Ian. 'Then someone's going to start asking questions about *you*—quite naturally, wouldn't you think?' Then he smiled at Jenny. 'And we don't want any harm to come to you, of course.'

The square shoulders lifted, as Jenny took a deep breath.

188

'We're talking about Philip Masson—and David Audley, of course.' Having been offered an olive branch, the Honourable Miss Jennifer Fielding-ffulke hit Mitchell in the face with it. 'Or is this another Christmas-cracker joke?'

Ian saw Paul Mitchell flinch as the branch slashed him—just as the Syrian major in Beirut had done, when he'd been expecting gratitude and had received the rough side of her tongue instead; the only difference was that the Major had saved her life, whereas Paul Mitchell had only saved *his*—

'Jenny! For heaven's sake!' He saw Mitchell *un*flinching. But that didn't blot out Major Asad's pilgrim's progress from incredulity to bitterness, which had soured their comradeship into contempt at the last. '*Jenny*—'

'No, Ian.' Jenny shook her head obstinately. 'Don't be wet. He's starting to bull-shit us now.'

'No I'm not.' Mitchell's jaw tightened. 'You asked me why I followed Ian. I followed him because *you* had been asking questions—and you asked one too many, of the wrong person. And about the wrong person.'

'Meaning Audley?'

'So I drew the short straw. Meaning Ian here. Fortunately.' Mitchell ignored the latest question. 'Because it would seem that you actually flushed out someone else from the undergrowth with your questions—someone who really doesn't want *any* questions being asked.' He stared at her for a long moment. 'I don't know what the hell you've been doing today, Miss Fielding. But, if our experience is anything to go by, you've been bloody lucky, anyway. Because you're still alive.'

Jenny licked her upper lip, and a trick of the

light revealed to Ian that there were beads of sweat above it. Which, since she knew about Reg Buller, was fair enough: whether Mitchell knew as much or not, those last words of his had hit her where it hurt.

Then she resisted the blow. 'These other two men—the ones who followed you, Ian—' but she wasn't interested in him: it was Mitchell she was looking at '—you known them—?'

'I knew one of them.' Mitchell frowned at him. 'God! You really didn't tell her much, did you?' He shook his head. 'Yes, Miss Fielding—Jenny: I *knew* one of them, from the old days. And that makes us all lucky—and maybe Ian and me luckiest of all. Because Paddy MacManus was a hard man when I knew him . . . Or, more accurately, knew *of* him, back in Dublin in the late '70s. A real *hard* man—even too bloody hard for the boyos, in the end, when they started to wonder who he was working for.' He drew a breath. 'You see, when you keep a tiger, you've got to feed him regularly, because he gets hungry . . . And when he's a man-eater, and he gets the taste for it . . . that's okay when you're in a killing-phase, because then you can feed him. But when you want to lower the profile—maybe for political reasons, or just for public relations in America, for *financial* reasons, say . . . then you've got a problem —' Mitchell opened his mouth to continue, but then closed it. 'Mmm . . . well, let's put it like this: when the postman comes up the drive, then he's delivering letters. And when *you* start asking questions, then you're thinking about writing a book—or writing for the newspapers . . . or both.' Another breath. 'But when you see Paddy MacManus striding
190

towards you in the middle of nowhere . . . then he isn't writing a book. And it's not the post he's delivering. Will that do?'

Jenny breathed out, as though she'd been holding her breath. 'He works for—? The IRA?'

'No. At least, not any more.' Mitchell shook his head, almost regretfully. 'He's privatized himself: he's strictly a contract man now—that I do know . . . I'm really rather out of that scene, in so far as I was ever into it.' He shrugged. 'I'm more like Ian here—a writer. I arrange other men's flowers, is what I mostly do now.' He turned to Ian. 'A much underrated job, not to say unglamorous. But very necessary. And also agreeably safe.'

'I see.' Jenny moved quickly, as though to discourage any idea of writers' solidarity. 'So you work for Research and Development, now?'

The unexpected question caught Writer Mitchell unprepared, in the midst of offering Ian false friendly sympathy, freezing his smile. 'I beg your pardon, Miss Fielding? I work for—?'

'Jack Butler.' Having achieved her desired effect, Jenny herself brightened into innocent friendliness in her turn. 'Sir James . . . but always *Jack*, of course?' Even a sweet smile now. 'Why didn't you say so straight away, Paul? It would have made things so much easier!'

Paul Mitchell's desperately-maintained smile warned Ian to attend to his own expression. But neither of them was looking at him, they were concerned only in each other.

'*Such* a charming man!' Jen was the Honourable Jennifer now, claws sheathed in velvet. 'One of the old school, my father always says—and those enchanting daughters of his . . . Which is the one

191

who's with Lovett, Black and Porter—Daddy's quite *adorable* lawyers—? Is that Sally? Or Diana—or Jane?'

In the car Mitchell had wondered what she'd been up to, while they had been having their own adventures—and so had Ian himself; and, latterly, they'd worried more than that, each of them, as they'd progressed agonizingly through the evening traffic into London. But now they both knew.

'Jack Butler was in Korea, of course.' She nodded knowingly. 'Daddy never met him—not *there* . . . not until long afterwards, when he came back from Cyprus.' The nod, continued, became conspiratorial. 'But he says—Daddy says—that his MC on that river there—where was it? But . . . wherever it was . . . Daddy says it should have been a VC, anyway.' She turned the nod into a shake, and then returned the shake to Ian. 'It was only because Jack didn't get himself killed there that they gave him a *Military* Cross, Daddy says.' She came back to Mitchell. 'But, of course, you must know that, seeing as you work for him.'

She had the poor devil on her toasting fork now, thought Ian. Sir Jack Butler might not have been quite as heroic as that, long ago, any more than he was 'charming' now, after having been so dull only yesterday (any more, too, than his three daughters might be 'enchanting' and—least likely of all—that those legal advisers were 'adorable'). But, when all her calculated exaggerations had been stripped away, Mitchell remained spiked on the facts which he must know were accurate, and on the real possibility that her father knew Butler, even if she didn't.

'I do?' Mitchell had managed to get rid of the

192

wreckage of his original smile. 'Do I?'

'And, of course, that really answers our question, darling.' Jenny gave Ian a brief nod. 'Jack wouldn't want anything nasty . . .' She trailed off as she turned back to Mitchell. 'But, then again, it doesn't quite . . . does it?'

In place of the smile, Mitchell's face was stamped with caution. 'It doesn't?'

'Mmmm . . .' Jenny eyed him thoughtfully. 'You are all rather elusive and mysterious, of course—in R & D . . . But, then, that's what you're paid to be, so one can't really *quarrel* with that, can one? Daddy said not, anyway.' She smiled at Mitchell as she turned the toasting fork, with one side of him nicely browned. 'I really wanted to talk to Oliver, you see—Jack's No 2 . . . I told you, didn't I, Ian darling—Oliver St John Latimer?'

'*Ahh*—' With his mouth already open, that was the only sound Ian could manage before she re-engaged Mitchell.

'But positively the *only* person connected with R & D I could track down was Willy Arkenshaw. And that was more by good luck than good management—in the chocolate shop at Harrods actually, buying a little birthday present for Oliver, would you believe it?' By the second she was becoming more and more her own most-despised self ('*The Honourable Jennifer Fielding-ffulke, the well-known author, chatting with Mr Ian Robinson, and Mr Paul Mitchell*', as *The Tatler* might caption her). 'And Willy's only a camp-follower, really . . . You remember Tom Arkenshaw, Ian darling—who was such a sweetie in '85—?'

'Yes.' This time he was ready for her: the very mention of 'Arkenshaw', which was a

193

uniquely-memorable name, had already alerted him. And the occasion itself had been memorable too, when Sir Thomas Arkenshaw, baronet, had descended on the embattled embassy in Beirut like the wrath of God: it had been Sir Thomas who had first made contact with Major Asad . . . *It had been Sir Thomas, through the Major, who had been instrumental in saving Jenny, not so much from a fate-worse-than-death, as from death itself, which was the only truly-worst fate of all!* 'But—he was R & D—?' The answer seemed to beg the question.

'No, darling—not *then*.' She rounded on Mitchell, almost accusingly. 'Jack's only just recruited Tom, hasn't he, Paul—?'

'What?' Mitchell wasn't nearly as ready. 'Tom—?'

'Oh, come on! Now it's my turn!' Jenny had dropped enough names (which were probably all she had; but which she thought ought to be enough, evidently). 'I'll bet you were at Willy's wedding—weren't you, Paul?'

'Yes?' Suddenly Mitchell was certain. 'But you weren't.'

'No. *We* were both out of the country at the time, as it happens.' The sharpness of the reply betrayed what was left unsaid; which was not so much pure *Fielding-ffulke* snobbishness as *Jenny Fielding's* stock-in-trade, which required her to be present, and seen-to-be-present, on such occasions, when useful old contacts could be renewed, and future contacts established. 'But . . . never mind Tom. Because Willy Arkenshaw—Willy *Groot*, as she was . . . Willy and I go back *ages*, my dear man. We were *finished* together, by the celebrated Madame de la Bruyère, the dragon-lady of Geneva, more years ago than either of us would care to admit now.'

Mitchell wilted slightly under this further avalanche of name-dropping—to *Jack* and *Oliver*, add *Tom* and *Willy* and *Madame de la Bruyère*. But then he looked mutinously at Ian. 'Yes . . . I suppose you would know Tom Arkenshaw, at that! In Lebanon, that would have been?'

That was another worrying straw-in-the-wind of British Intelligence inefficiency, thought Ian: Mitchell's homework had included Beirut, but it was homework only half-done if Tom Arkenshaw now worked for R & D but hadn't been consulted about his memories of Fielding-ffulke & Robinson. And that deplorable omission intruded into his own attempts to put faces to names: *Tom* he could remember well-enough (although not as well as Major Asad); but *Jack* and *Oliver*—and *Willy* (if he'd been invited to her wedding with *Sir Thomas* it was news to him!)—they were on the dark side of the Moon . . . unlike Mrs Simmonds, and Gary Redwood and Mrs Champeney-Smythe, and Father John—

'Yes, Beirut.' He heard his agreement come out as a growl, and tried, and failed to put a face to that other name, of someone he'd never seen and never would see now, in the flesh: *Mrs Frances Fitzgibbon, alias 'Marilyn Francis', Mitchell? Your colleague who was careless at Rickmansworth—and at Thornervaulx too, maybe? Put a face to her for me, Mitchell: tell me about her then!*

'Ian—?' Mitchell was frowning at him suddenly. 'What's the matter?'

'Mr Mitchell—' Jenny frowned also.

'Miss Fielding—pardon me—' Mitchell cut her off without looking at her '—*Ian*—? What's the

195

matter?'

'Nothing.' He blinked at Mitchell, and felt foolish: this too-long day, with its surfeit of information—re-animated experience, and experiences . . . and new faces *and* information—this long day was beginning to play tricks on him, stretching his imagination too far; and, on an empty stomach, the smell of little Mr Malik's succulent curries was making him light-headed.

'No.' Mitchell humiliated him further by seeming solicitous, as he had never done with Jenny. 'You look as if you've seen a ghost.' The next breath was worse than solicitous: it was understanding, 'But then, I suppose Beirut must have been pretty hairy, I guess!' He took the next breath to Jenny. 'You were both pretty damn lucky there, too.'

'*No*—' Ian was all the angrier for not reacting more quickly. There were other ghosts—*newer* ghosts—than Mrs Frances Fitzgibbon: even Jenny's Philly Masson was a week younger . . . and far more important; and Reg Buller was so newly-dead that he probably didn't even know how to haunt the living properly yet. (Or, anyway, Reg would be too busy now haunting his hundred favourite pubs, trying to catch a last sniff of beer and sending shivers up the spines of his best-loved barmaids as they remembered him across the bar, horrified by the evening paper headlines—)

'What?' Jenny sounded irritated: Jenny didn't believe in ghosts.

He faced Mitchell. 'Audley, Mr Mitchell—Audley?'

All the expression went out of the man's face: it was like watching a bigger wave wash away every footprint in the sand, leaving it smooth again.

196

'If you work for R & D, Mr Mitchell—*Paul* . . .' What was sauce for the goose was sauce for the gander. So he smiled at Mitchell. 'If you're here to help us—if we need *friends* . . . tell us about David Audley, then.'

Mitchell frowned. 'I'm sorry—?'

'No.' Jenny reached out, almost touching Mitchell. 'Ian doesn't mean . . . tell us *about* him.' She touched Ian instead, digging her fingers into his arm—little sharp fingers. 'Because . . . obviously, you can't do that, I mean.'

Mitchell shifted his position. 'No . . . Obviously, I can't do that.' He took them both in.

'Because he isn't even in England now, anyway.' Jenny added her total non-sequitur statement as though it explained what Mitchell had just said for Ian's benefit. 'He's on holiday, with his wife and daughter, at the moment, Ian darling—' Then she gave Mitchell her most dazzling smile '—Spain, I gather—?'

Another wave washed across Mitchell's face. 'Spain?'

'From Parador to Parador!' She nodded, as though he'd admitted everything. 'Fuenterrabia, Santa Dominigo de la Calzada . . . which was next? Benavente, was it? And now the Enrique Two at Ciudad Rodrigo?' She took the nod to Ian. 'Paradors, darling—remember those lovely old state-owned hotels the Spaniards have?' Back to Mitchell. 'Paradors, Dr Mitchell—right?'

Mitchell stared at Jenny for a moment, and then seemed to relax, even as Ian realized that he'd just witnessed an event as rare as it was unfortunate: *Jenny knew damn well who Paul Mitchell was—had known from the moment his name had been first*

197

mentioned, if not from the appearance of his face round the door; and she had just put her foot in her mouth, to forefeit that advantage prematurely with 'Dr' Mitchell.

'Hold on, now.' It was a long time since they'd worked together like this. But the old rules still held good, and they required him to cause a diversion. 'Jenny—how come I'm the only one without a drink?'

'Oh darling, I *am* sorry!' She came in on cue instantly, contrite—when her normal reaction to such petulance would have been contempt. 'It's Mr Malik's genuine British-German Pils you like, isn't it—?'

'Yes.' As she turned away, he looked deliberately at Mitchell. But the man was staring at Jenny's back with unashamed calculation. So all that he had gained for her was a little time, no more. But the charade still had to be played. 'You can laugh.'

'I'm not laughing, my dear fellow.' Mitchell scorned his game. 'I was just thinking that . . . your associate has been busy . . . while we've both been at the sharp end, eh?'

'There, darling!' She came back to him quickly—too quickly, with the froth from the badly-poured beer cascading over the top of the glass. 'One *ersatz* Pils!'

'Busy' was an understatement, thought Ian, torn between admiration for her coverage of both Audley and Mitchell somehow—and in a working day which had also included the Reg Buller horror somewhere in it—and irritation with her for blowing the Mitchell part of it unnecessarily. 'Thank you.' On balance the admiration won.

'Spanish state-owned hotels—you were saying, Jenny?' Mitchell showed his teeth.

'Yes.' She returned the compliment. 'So David Audley has fled the country for the time being, has he? But did he run? Or was he pushed? That is the first question, Paul.' She cocked her head at him, dislodging some of her hair. 'But, of course, you won't answer that—can't answer that. Because that's a secret, isn't it? "An *official* secret", well within the meaning of the Act. But then, *everything* is well within the meaning of the Act.' Now she smiled again. 'And every*one*, too! All of us—and poor little Mr Malik downstairs—we're all just one big Official Secret now, aren't we? And . . . all to protect *naughty* Dr David Audley! Who is the biggest Official Secret of all.' She paused. 'But now he's our *little* secret, as well as your big one—right?'

As she spoke, Ian had been drawn naturally to watch Mitchell, as she moved up the scale of challenges. And Mitchell was watching her very carefully, now that he had been warned.

'He sent postcards, didn't he?' He grimaced at her. But then he frowned. 'To Willy—? But no . . . Willy knows better than to tell you that.' All her more recent feints, and sharp-toothed threats, were calmly ignored in the search for an explanation for her special knowledge. 'So . . . it would be—*Mrs Clarke*, of course!' Mitchell nodded to himself. 'And she puts them up on her mantelpiece, amongst those lovely old mugs of hers, over the kitchen-oven—?' He nodded. 'For all to see . . . and he sends them to her because she loves them—because he loves *her*.' Another nod. But he was only thinking aloud because he wanted her to hear his thoughts, quite deliberately. 'Or were they from Cathy—?' He stopped suddenly. 'But you went down there, bright and early. And you chatted

Mrs Clarke up—' Mitchell's mouth twisted 'and you're pretty, and you're smart . . . and Clarkie's old now, of course.' His expression hardened. 'There would have been a time when you wouldn't have got through that door, Miss Fielding-ffulke: she'd have clobbered you with her rolling-pin first, I tell you!' Then he relaxed again, having betrayed himself momentarily . . . and perhaps not so deliberately this time. 'So . . . it was the postcards, wasn't it—? Fuentarrabia—Santa Dominigo de la Calzada, Benevente, Ciudad Rodrigo?' The man's certainty increased as he echoed the drum-roll of names. 'You really *are* good! Because . . . that's bloody ingenious—just from a collection of postcards? And poor old Clarkie?'

Jenny smiled at Ian. 'Dr Audley has this ancient retainer darling . . . his old nurse, I believe she is . . . And she's a perfect sweetie.' She transferred the smile. 'Don't worry, Dr Mitchell. I didn't tell her that her "dear Mr David" was a murderer—it would have been too cruel.'

'And it would also have been wrong, Miss Fielding.'

'Wrong?' Her lip curled. 'He's not a murderer? Of course!'

'Of course.' He nodded, and then considered her for a moment. 'Do you always start your books with preconceived notions about the goodies and the baddies?' Then he shrugged. 'But there! I suppose that's the nature of investigative journalism these days: don't spoil a good story with inconvenient facts, by golly! "I name this bandwaggon *Freedom of the Press*, and this gravy-train *The Right to Know*. And God bless them, and all who crusade on them, and do very-nicely-thank-you while smiting the wicked and putting down the proud, eh?'

'That's not true,' snapped Ian. 'We don't go about it like that.' All the same, he didn't want to look at Jenny. 'If Audley isn't—'

'*If* he isn't.' Jenny interrupted him quickly, but coolly. 'Then he's been quite remarkably accident-prone in his long career. Or . . . other people around him have been, wouldn't you say, Dr Mitchell?'

Mitchell looked at his watch. 'What I would say, Miss Fielding-ffulke, is that . . . now that we've met at last . . . is that I have more work to do this night. So I must leave you temporarily, I fear.'

'Temporarily?' The breath she drew belied her coolness. 'But . . . you were just getting interesting, Dr Mitchell.' The repeated *Dr* Mitchell, matching *Dr* Audley, was another straw in the wind.

'I'm always interesting, Miss Fielding-ffulke. But, what I mean is . . . it's my duty to protect you, so that you can traduce me in print in due course—if you can find a publisher—if—?' This time it was Mitchell's lip which curled. 'But, of course, you have found one—*post* Peter Wright that's only to be expected, isn't it! And especially with your record of heroic and responsible investigative reporting—' He embraced Ian in this embittered accolade '—foolish of me . . . yes!' The lips straightened and tightened. 'But you can't stay here, is what I mean. You need a safe house—a very safe house, as of Paddy MacManus's appearance on the scene, I'd say.' This time he lingered on Ian. 'Because he's still got his fee to earn, as I told you.'

'Paddy—?' Check Coat's name was suddenly like a lump in Ian's throat, which had to be swallowed as he thought of Check Coat out there somewhere in

201

the gathering dark of a London night. So he swallowed the lump. 'Still—?'

'You'd better believe it.' Mitchell nodded. 'It's just like your books, Ian: 50 per cent advance on signature of contract—is that it, for you? And then the rest on publication?' He paused to let the terms sink in. 'Which, in this case, will be the publication of your obituary. And failure to deliver, after signature, is bad for business—right?'

Ian looked at Jenny, and caught her drawing in her breath.

'We're safe here, Dr Mitchell.' She deflated with the words.

'You're not safe anywhere, Miss Fielding-ffulke.' Mitchell's voice grated on his reply. 'What you don't seem to understand is that you're in the big league now, Miss Fielding-ffulke: you're not just messing with old fuddy-duddy British Intelligence—not with chaps like me, who've got so shit-scared of their own shadows, in case they step out of line, that they swan off without protection, and have to borrow weapons from the local vicar.' Mitchell swung towards Ian. 'For Christ's sake, man: suppose Father John hadn't borrowed that shot-gun himself, to shoot those pigeons that were crapping on his bells in the belfry—? Or . . . never mind he wouldn't find the shells—in case I actually *shot* anyone, even in self-defence—?' His mouth twisted. 'So where the hell would you have been *now?*' He shook his head. 'Because I sure-as-hell wouldn't have gone out there to point my finger at that bastard, and said *"Bang-bang!"*—' Mitchell brought his hand up as he spoke, and squeezed his eyes shut as he pointed his finger. 'Because that's the way to get dead, forever after.' Then he focused again. 'You're in the big league. And the first mistake you make in that league is to think you're cleverer than the opposition. And that's the only mistake you make.'

Ian had been conscious of Jenny all the time Mitchell was speaking, drawing in breaths to interrupt; but first just failing to get her words in edgeways, and then failing altogether as Mitchell concentrated not on her, but on him, because he was more receptive to the message after their shared experience of Lower Buckland.

'But why *us*, Dr Mitchell?' She seized the first moment of silence between them. 'If you're not trying to stop us . . .' There was still doubt in that: she still wasn't giving him the whole benefit of doubt, even now—'. . . then who is?'

'Who?' Mitchell gave her his full attention. 'I wish I knew, Miss Fielding-ffulke!' He shook his head. 'I tell you—you were just a bloody inconvenience, as of forty-eight hours ago . . . Asking all your questions, in the wrong places—'

'About Audley—David Audley—?'

'Forget Audley!' Mitchell shook his head. '*Philip Masson*—d'you think we haven't been asking questions about *him*, too? Ever since he turned up—?'

She stared at him obstinately. 'Only if you don't already know the answers . . . about *him*—?'

Mitchell stared at her for a moment. Then he looked at his watch again. Then he looked at her again. 'Miss Fielding-ffulke—*Jenny*—?'

'Very well.' She nodded. 'Tell me about Philip Masson.'

Suddenly Ian felt like a fly on the wall, ignored by them both. They were each making terms now, and no longer pretending; and whatever Mitchell thought he could get, Jenny herself was as excited as she ought to be at the prospect of having someone on the inside, who was willing to trade with her.

'We don't know any of the answers.' Mitchell drew a matching breath. 'We didn't expect Masson to turn up. But . . . when he did . . . we didn't think Audley had anything to do with it—' he shook his head slowly '—because it's not his style . . . And, he hasn't the resources, anyway—'

'The Americans?' She cocked her head as she cut in. 'Or the Israelis—? He's been kissing-cousins with both of them for God knows how long! Since Suez—? Or, since the Seven Days' War, anyway: wasn't he the middle-man then? When the CIA doublecrossed the State Department—?'

Mitchell's mouth opened. 'My God! That was long before my time!' The mouth closed tight-shut. 'Who the hell have you been talking to? That's—for Christ's sake—!' He frowned at her.

'Ancient history? Medieval history?' She paused. 'Or modern history—modern *secret* history?'

Ian knew exactly what she was doing: if the man was here to make a deal, she wanted him to be under no illusions about the strength of her position, which he had been trying to weaken with his emphasis on the danger that threatened them. So now it was her turn.

'You said it first, Paul.' He nodded as to an equal. 'She's been busy.' And that crack of Mitchell's about 'investigative journalism', couldn't be left unanswered: it had to be nailed once and for all. 'It's what we "investigative writers" have to do, to earn our money: we have to earn it by being

204

busy. And, because we're self-employed, we *are* busy: it's what Mrs Thatcher calls "Private Enterprise". And the emphasis is on both words equally. So we can't afford to waste our precious time.'

Mitchell gave him a something-less-than-friendly look. But at least that was better than being regarded as part of the furniture of the Shah Jehan private dining room.

'But you were wasting your time today.' Mitchell looked like a man who found himself where he didn't want to be. 'And mine.'

'Was he?' Jenny picked up her private bottle again. 'And yet . . . there was that man—the man with the contract. And now we're not safe, even here?' She applied the bottle to her glass. 'Even here?'

'You're not safe anywhere. Not with MacManus after you—'

'"The big league"—yes! So you keep saying.' In spite of her best efforts, glass shook against glass. 'And yet, you don't know why—?' She got the wine into the glass at last. 'You only know that David Audley had nothing to do with Philly Masson's death, back in 1978?'

'Yes.' Mitchell watched her drink. 'And—yes, I *don't* know why. If I did I'd know better what to do next. All I know is, I'll be able to think a lot straighter if I don't have to worry about you two.' He looked from her to Ian, and then back to her. 'Just for a few days, anyway?' Deep breath. 'For your own sakes, if not for mine—' He looked at Ian almost pleadingly. 'For God's sake, man . . . MacManus isn't just a name in the index of some book, he's *real*. He's got *your* name in his own little book, which he keeps in his head—your name *until he crosses it out!*' Back to Jenny. 'Maybe he hasn't got *"The Honourable Miss Jennifer Fielding-ffulke"* in it yet. But there has to be big money on Ian's head. Because MacManus is taking a big risk to earn it, I tell you. Because . . . there's a warrant out—Christ! There are half-a-dozen warrants out on him—in half the countries in Europe, Ireland included . . . So neither of you are safe, as of now.'

The dishes were still clattering downstairs. And Paul Mitchell might be a good actor—he probably was a good actor. But (as in Beirut) Ian knew that he himself was a clerk at heart, not a man of action. And Jenny was looking at him.

'I think they call it "Protective Custody" darling.' She smiled at him. 'But we can consider it as part of the rich tapestry of life's experience—one of the hazards of "investigative journalism" in a free society?' She turned the smile on Mitchell. 'And it'll look jolly good in our book eventually, won't it? How the Security Service protects the citizen—even the fearless writer? The fearless *inconvenient* writer—? We could make a fortune out of your solicitude for our safety, Dr Mitchell. And maybe they'll promote you—' I could have a word with Daddy . . . and Daddy can drop a word in the Prime Minister's ear.' Having inserted the knife, she couldn't resist turning it. But then she pretended to return to Ian. '"Protective Custody", is not "Durance Vile"—shall we be good citizens . . . if only for "a few days, anyway"—and for our "own" sakes—?' Then she spoilt it by not waiting for him to agree. 'Very well, Paul! So . . . what do you want us to do?'

For a moment Ian thought she might have

overdone it. Because anyone who knew Jenny when she was as brittle as this wouldn't trust her an inch. But Mitchell didn't know her, he saw instantly: Mitchell only knew that she ought to be frightened, as he had intended her to be, and deluded himself consequently that she was hiding her fears behind her banter.

'You stay here, for the time being.' Mitchell was infinitely relieved by her surrender, so that he insulted Ian by not even looking at him.

'You mean . . . we *are* safe, under Mr Malik's protection?' She was so sure of herself now that she prodded Mitchell unmercifully.

'This is your secret place, is it?' Mitchell was still relaxing. 'Nobody knows about Mr . . . Malik—?' For the second time Mitchell tasted what was in his own glass, which he had hardly touched hitherto.

'Yes.' Suddenly she wasn't quite so sure.

'Yes. Well . . . there's a term we have for that: it's called "Making pictures".' Mitchell nodded, and tasted his drink again. 'Which means, believing what we'd like to believe.' He wanted to drink more deeply, but he resisted the temptation, and looked at his watch instead. 'So . . . maybe you've got another hour or two, at best.' He looked up from his watch. 'But you let me worry about that now. And when I come back . . . then we can maybe make a deal—okay?' He started to turn away, towards the door.

'*Paul—wait!*'

Ian agreed with her: now it was all happening too quickly. '*Mitchell—!*'

Mitchell turned. 'This is your secret place—isn't it?'

Jenny drew a deep breath. 'What's the deal?'

207

'How do I know?' He shrugged. Then he concentrated on them both. 'Well . . . let's say . . . if I have to throw David Audley to the wolves . . . then *you* can be the wolves—how's that, for starters—?' He paused for a second—two seconds—while Ian's mouth opened, but before he had time to look at Jenny. And then he opened the door and was gone through it before they could exchange faces. And then it was too late.

Ian stared at the door. *'Phew!'*!'

'Shit!' murmured the Honourable Miss Jennifer Fielding-ffulke.

'What?' He hated to hear her swear.

'Did he really save your life?' She was angry.

Ian pressed his video-buttons, rewinding fast and trying not to see the reversal, which always reduced reality to comedy; but then, as he played forward again slowly, frame by frame, without sound, the reality became frozen into a succession of unrealities, turning the horror film he had lived through into single pictures, like the stills outside the cinema.

'I don't know.' He tried to add up Mitchell—*Combat Jacket* to *Dr Paul Mitchell*. 'But I think he thinks he did, Jenny.'

'He was lying.'

'What?' He couldn't complete the addition. But there were certain pictures he couldn't forget. 'I don't know. But . . . I don't think so, Jenny—'

'I mean, he knows one hell of a lot more than he's saying, Ian.'

That was true! She hadn't been there, in the churchyard, or afterwards. *But Paul Mitchell knew one hell of a lot more about Mrs Frances Fitzgibbon—that was true!*

'About Audley—by God, he does!' She crossed over towards the heavy curtains at the window. 'Never mind Philly—Audley—!'

That was different—*Audley* was different. And . . . she knew more about *Mitchell*, too—more even than she had let Mitchell himself see.

'What about him, Jenny—Mitchell, I mean—?' He cursed their failure to communicate in the few minutes they had had, when they'd thrown away their advantages, so that they'd had to play the game cold just now.

'He's R & D from way back.' She touched the curtain, but then turned back to him. '"P. L. Mitchell"—doesn't the name mean anything to you, Ian? You're supposed to be the literary one—the *literate* one? Half of them are bloody authors, in their spare time—*P. L. Mitchell*?' She shook her head irritably. 'Or *Neville Macready*? You're not an economist, of course . . . but "*Hayek and Keynes*"—you must have seen Macready's book reviewed in the *FT*, or the *Sunday Times*, or somewhere. Because even I did . . . even though I didn't read the reviews. But Macready is R & D —he's their economist, actually. And Audley's their medieval historian . . . for all the good that does them!' She touched the curtain again. 'And P. L. Mitchell—' She peered into the gap '—*Dr Paul Mitchell*—'

'What are you looking at?' What she knew, which he didn't know, needled him more than what she was doing—which was obvious, now he thought about it. 'A big silver Volvo, Jenny. And it's parked right outside the door, on double yellow lines . . . But he could be back in the phone-box again—'

He saw the curtain tighten sharply, almost

convulsively, as she held on to it. And, for a foolish half-second, didn't understand why. And then he realized that she *was* holding on to it, as her knees buckled, to stop her falling—

'*Jenny*—' In the next half-second he was holding her, and she was a dead-weight as she let go of the curtain, and he took the strain. And the weight was nothing—she was light as thistledown, with her hair in his face, and what little there was of her in his arms; much more than the childish weight, he could *smell* her—he had seen her sweat before, as all red-headed girls always did, with those dark patches under her arms, when she hadn't changed her dress in Lebanon—when her dress had been sweaty and dirty, that time . . . But now, when she was in his arms and close to him—she might have been sweating before, but she was throwing it off like an animal now, mixed with her own additional expensive commercial smell, which was always with her '—*hold up, Jenny!*'

She stiffened, her legs suddenly obeying her will again, pushing her body upwards and then letting him manoeuvre her sideways towards the nearest chair.

Then, without warning, she started resisting him, trying to throw off his arms. 'No! Let me go—'

That was more like her: Jenny *never* fainted—that was her own boast. But she'd never been closer to giving the lie to that than just now, all the same.

'I want to look—let go, Ian!' She struggled weakly. 'I want—'

'No!' He pressed down hard on her shoulder, thumping her into the chair. '*I'll* look, damn it!' He twisted round her, to get his back to the wall as he

210

parted the inside edge of the curtain, knowing simultaneously that he wanted to look, yet didn't want to—and that this was the wrong way to look anyway—not extinguishing the light first, before he looked. But the hell with that!

'Well?' She whispered the question.

To make the best of an unprofessional job, and in order to see right up and down Cody Street, he pushed himself all the way in, letting the curtain drape round his shoulders like a cloak. It had rained since he had come out of the premature half-light of the evening, and the street lamps reflected a million points of light in every drop of water trapped in the unevenness of the road surface. Then he looked back towards her, frowning.

'Well?' Her face was chalk-white, emphasizing the dark smudges under her eyes and the remains of her lipstick: with her accustomed fall-down hair she looked even more like the wreck of the *Hesperus* than usual. And more beautiful to him than ever.

'There isn't anything—is there?' Something of the original Jenny returned as she clenched her jaw.

'There isn't anything there, Jenny.' He couldn't lessen her humiliation. Whatever she'd thought she'd seen, there was nothing now in Cody Street—not only not the scene of carnage he'd been half-expecting as he'd parted the curtain from the wall . . . but *actually* nothing, other than the reflection of the wetness on the street and the cars parked in it; and, most of all, no Mitchell and no Volvo—the man and the car had slipped away into the night together and quickly, without fuss, unheard against the Taj Mahal clatter.

'No. There wouldn't be.' She subsided into the chair, gripping its arms. 'I'm hungry—' She pushed

211

herself up, straight-backed, and picked up her glass from the table '—I haven't eaten anything since breakfast. You're always telling me that I don't eat enough . . . In fact, I'm bloody-starving, Ian. So let's have one of Abdul's specials, eh—? Ring the bell, darling.'

Excuses? But . . . *excuses*—from Jenny? 'What did you see, Jen?'

'I didn't see anything, darling. Ring the bell.' She pointed at the bell-push by the light-switches at the door. And then picked up his beer, from where he had put it down beside her glass and offered it to him. 'You haven't touched your drink, darling. And . . . knowing you . . . did you have lunch—?'

He reached for the glass automatically. But as he did so, there came a sound from behind him: not so much a knock, as a finger-tapping scraping noise on the door-panel—quite unnatural, because it was quite different from Mr Malik's sharp-knuckled signal.

Jenny spilt beer over his hand as the door opened, and a hideous apparition appeared in the gap.

''Ullo there!' said Reg Buller.

CHAPTER SEVEN

There were so many things outrageous about Reginald Buller's appearance that the fact that he very obviously wasn't deceased was almost the least of them.

Most obviously, he wasn't deceased because the newly-dead had no need of large theatrical beards.

212

Or, if they did, they had no need to pull such beards down to reveal their faces as they came to haunt the living. Or, if such a revelation was part of the haunting, they had no call to grin quite so happily before releasing the ridiculous growth so that it sprang back slightly askew, under one ear.

And, anyway, in the next moment, Reg Buller was all-too-abundantly flesh-and-blood as he removed the equally-ridiculous trilby from his head, and then unhooked the beard, finally adding his voluminous Sherlock Holmes cape to them on the chair beside the door.

'That's better!' Reg Buller nodded to Jenny, and then advanced on Ian, larger and cruder than life, and took his glass from his hand, momentarily holding it up. 'And that's even better! Untouched by human lips—?' He drank noisily. 'Gnat's piss! But, like the bishop said to the actress, *"my need is greater than thine!"*' He finished off the beer, and returned the glass to Ian with exaggerated courtesy. 'Is there a back way out of here?'

'Mr Buller—' Jenny hissed his name '—*Mister* Buller . . . don't you *ever* do that to me again!'

'Do what, m'lady?' Buller caught Ian's eye, and nodded at the bar in the alcove before coming back to her. 'It was you at the window, wasn't it—? Very careless, that was . . . But—you knew it was me?' He wiped his mouth with his sleeve, and then gestured towards the heap in the chair. 'That's a disguise, that is—twenty-five quid's worth . . . if I get it back tomorrow, anyway. And cheap at the price—seein' as what I got with it.'

Ian observed her weaken. Of all the men Jenny knew, gilded and ungilded, she could resist Reg Buller least. 'What did you get with it, Reg?'

213

'I got professional advice, Mr Robinson. Which is worth more than gold-dust.' Buller nodded at the bar again hopefully. 'And I got the lady who gave it for free.'

'What lady, Mr Buller? What advice?' The colour was coming back into Jenny's face, 'I thought you only knew barmaids?'

'Theatrical costumier—"*costumier*"—?' Buller tried to will Ian towards the bar. 'She's only a barmaid part-time, in the evenings . . . And she said, "What you are, Mr Buller, is *unobtrusive*—you move like a shadow in the night . . . So, they'll be looking for shadows-in-the-night, the blue-bottles will be. So, we'll make you a bit of local colour—like an actor from the Hippodrome, down the road, where they've got the music-hall on . . . And I'll walk with you, on your arm, an' they'll look at me, not you!"—she's got a heart of gold, that woman has.' He concentrated on Jenny. 'But how did you know it was me?'

But Jenny wasn't looking at Buller. '*Is* there a back way out of here, Ian?'

Her stare caught him struggling with more important matters. But then, maybe they weren't more immediately important, he thought. 'I don't know, Jen. We've never had to get out of here—' And that, in turn, concentrated his mind. 'I'll ring for Mr Malik.'

'You do that, darling.' She had been there before him, so she was back with Reg Buller now. 'You're supposed to be dead, Reg. Why aren't you dead?'

'Why ain't I dead? It's a good question, Lady.' Buller scratched his nose abstractedly. 'Well . . . you could say that I ain't dead because Mr John Tully stood in for me—'

214

'*John*—' Jenny swayed suddenly.

'Or, then again, maybe it was poor old Johnny they wanted in the first place, an' not me. I don't rightly know, you see, Lady—'

'For God's sake, Reg!' As Ian caught her arm the full impact of what Buller was saying hit him: they were back in a nightmare again.

'Oh aye.' Buller was unrepentant. 'There's an easier way of breakin' the news, is there? Now that it ain't me?'

'I'm all right.' Jenny's face was white again, but her voice was steady as she shook Ian off. 'What happened, Mr Buller?'

'You don't know . . . anything, then?'

She shook her head. 'There was just the rumour . . . that it was you, Mr Buller. A man in the crowd outside said so . . .'

'An' you didn't wait around?' This time Buller sounded more understanding. 'Well, I can't say I blame you.' He nodded to Ian. 'I could use another drink, lad—with a chaser this time, if the bar runs to one. An' whisky for choice.'

John Tully was dead: Ian's relief at seeing Buller alive seemed like a dream already. *Buller alive was John Tully dead*: that was the appalling reality he must accept, now. And, more importantly, he had to get Buller a drink.

'I didn't wait to ask, neither.' Buller shook his head, after reassuring himself that Ian was moving. 'They've got clever young coppers trained to remember people who ask questions, when there's a crowd outside . . . An' I ain't got any real friends in the Met, now—not that wouldn't shop me, to get promotion.' He shook his head again, as Ian clinked the bottles while trying to watch him while looking

215

for something better than 'gnat's piss'. 'But, as to makin' a mistake . . .' He sniffed derisively. '. . . I took the BMW last night, to drive up north. An' John—'e 'ad my little Metro, with the"Disabled Driver" sticker—they don't clamp them so quick, in case the newspapers make a scandal out of it. So we always swap when I go out of town.' Buller's expression hardened. 'An' when I was probably somewhere else, an' 'e was up to something . . . 'e used to leave 'is credit cards at 'ome, an' carry only cash-money—losin' cash isn't a problem, they just takes it off you, if they've a mind to . . . But 'e'd have my calling cards on him, maybe. And those premises are in my name, too . . . if it happened there, that is.'

'Here you are, Reg.' Having put the glass and the opened bottle on the corner of the table, Ian just had time to move Mitchell's half-drunk whisky alongside it, for want of anything quicker, if not better, before Reg Buller looked at him. 'You're saying . . . they got the wrong man?'

Buller swept the smaller glass up, and drained it. And then poured the 'gnat's piss' carefully. And then looked at him over it. 'The wrong man—? Maybe the wrong man. Or maybe *not* the wrong man.' He sank half of the piss. 'They got John Tully, is what it looks like. And, with all his faults . . . which were many . . . *Mister* John Tully wasn't a bad bloke. Because . . . if he didn't pay twenty shillings in the pound . . . at least he paid fifteen of 'em. Which is better than most.' He shifted from Ian to Jenny as he swallowed the rest of the piss. 'So now we owe for *him*, as well as that one of yours, Lady—'

This time it was a genuine knock at the door, not
216

a ghostly scratching.

'Come in!' Jenny reacted more quickly this time, recognizing the knock.

'Madam!' Abdul took them all in almost as quickly, half-smiling first, and then smiling hugely as he saw Reg glass-in-hand. 'Mr Buller—you know Mr Buller—*I* know Mr Buller: I am not wrong, to admit him?'

'No—yes, Mr Malik.' Jenny brushed at her hair. 'Can we have three of your special take-aways, Mr Malik, please.'

'An' then your special "get away" to go with 'em' supplemented Buller.

'Please?'

'Back-way. Out-the-back—an' then scarper . . . *vamoosh*—?'

'Ah! Tradesman's entrance? Fire-escape? Both in passage—at the side, Mr Buller—council regulations: orderly damn departure, no panic, one minute.' Then the little man stared at Buller. 'But then you go out the front again.' The stare became a frown. 'Nothing out front, my cousin says. But I send him out again, maybe—'

'No.' Buller shook his head. 'What's out back—gardens?'

'No gardens.' Matching shake. 'Back-yard—back wall. Damn great high back wall, broken glass on top. No *back*-way, Mr Buller, sir.'

'Back-way over bloody wall, mate.' This time Buller nodded. 'Got a ladder, then? An' a bit of sacking—?' He grinned at Jenny. 'No problem.'

'Big problem.' Mr Malik shook his head. 'Other side—damn railway line, Mr Buller.'

'Railway line? Fine! They keep telling us we should use the railway more often.' Buller sank his

217

big nose into his glass. 'An' I got the car over the bridge down the road, by the cutting. If no one's nicked it.' He returned to Mr Malik. 'Ladder up the wall. An' plenty of sacking on top, over the glass, mind you . . . An' plenty of hot lime pickle an' chilli pickle with the special. An' some eatin' irons, just in case—an' six bottles of Tiger, my lad. With an opener . . . an' all on the Lady's slate—got that?' He advanced on Mr Malik as he spoke, shepherding him towards the door. 'Orderly damn departure—no panic—five minutes from now—*ack-dum* an' *pip-emma*—an' then no nasty questions for you, after . . . see?'

As the door closed on the little man Reg Buller was already heading for the bar again. 'It's a nice motor, the BMW—very easy to drive.' He delivered this intelligence to Ian, over his shoulder. 'So you can drive it, then.' He studied the stock. 'Troubles enough we got, without me bein' stopped by some little nipper in blue in the line of duty when we're doin' a bunk, before we can ditch it.' He cocked an eye at Jenny. 'They'll 'ave the number out soon enough. But I reckon we're safe until morning. An' you got your passports and Eurocheques with you, like always? You 'aven't changed your rules, since last time? 'Cause I don't want to 'ave to put those whiskers on again, an' chance my arm going back to your place, I tell you!'

Ian looked at Jenny unhappily as he heard the odds being so casually raised through the roof in this appalling mathematical progression.

'Are you proposing that we flee the country, Mr Buller?' Even Jenny sounded a bit shaky at Buller's clearly implied proposition.

'Well, you don't want to stay to face the music,

218

do you?' Self-released from the necessity of having to drive his—or the late John Tully's—'nice motor' while far over the limit, Buller was helping himself to another beer and another chaser. 'You don't think that Mitchell's goin' to let you play games do you?' He poured the beer expertly, with a steady hand. '"P. J. Mitchell"—*Doctor Paul Lefevre Mitchell*, as ever was—"one of our foremost young military historians", no less—' he held up the glass for inspection, and sniffed. And then drank. And then looked at them both. ''Ow the 'ell did you let *him* get on to you, then?' The look became accusing.

The look stung Ian. 'Mitchell saved my life this afternoon, Reg.'

''E did?' Another drink—another sniff. 'Or was 'e like the man who saved a maiden from a fate worse than death—'e changed 'is mind?'

That was the maggot in the apple: it all depended on whether Mitchell was telling the truth. 'Does the name "MacManus" mean anything to you, Reg, "Paddy MacManus"—?'

'Never 'eard of 'im. But then I never 'eard of Dr Paul Lefevre Mitchell 'till this morning. So that don't mean anything. So . . . who's he then, when he's at home? MacManus?'

'He's a contract killer, Mr Buller. Ex-IRA—?' Jenny had seen the maggot too. 'So Paul Mitchell says.'

'Does he, now? Well . . . he should know, I suppose.' As tell-tale as the maggot was Buller no longer dropping his aitches: the seriousness of their situation and the drink together reverting him momentarily to his more educated self. 'Mitchell . . . mmm . . .'

219

Ian looked at Jenny. 'He's a historian . . . as well as—?'

'Oh, yes.' Buller fielded the question. 'And he's done time in Ireland, in Dublin. *Watch by the Liffey*—"A history of the Irish Guards in the Great War" . . . and I'll bet he wasn't just researching the Guards when he was watching the Liffey.' He looked at Ian. 'And then *The Forgotten Victory*—same war, but a different river. The Ancre, in France. But you can look at that in the car—and that's £14.95 on your bill, too. "Necessary expense", that comes under. I had to buy the hardback.' Buller's features creased. 'How d'you think I recognized him? It's got his picture on the back flap. "P. L. Mitchell", it says, for all to see.'

There was more to it than that. More in Buller's face than he could read—and more in everything Buller had said and done since he'd arrived. And more, not least—more *most*—in his insistence on their using the "back way" to leave the Taj Mahal.

'"P. L. Mitchell", Reg—?'

'Funny that—putting his picture in.' Buller nodded. 'Like . . . careless? But then, they're all a law unto themselves, they are, in "R & D". They make their own rules, it seems.'

'He's supposed to be finding a safe house for us at the moment, Reg.' Jenny had also been reading the signals. 'He said we weren't safe here.'

'He did?' Buller almost seemed preoccupied. 'Well, I'd say he's right there. If *I* thought of here . . . when you didn't go to your dad's place—as maybe you ought to have done . . .' He crossed over to the door and applied a big blunt finger to the bell, leaning on it unmercifully. 'He couldn't have touched you there.'

220

Ian didn't look at her. 'What d'you know about Mitchell that we don't know, Reg?' But then he looked at her. 'Or what do you know, Jen?' He struggled for an instant with his own knowledge. 'He's a colleague of Audley's—or maybe a friend, even?'

She was staring at Reg. 'He's up-and-coming— isn't he? Jack Butler and St John Latimer . . . isn't he one of their blue-eyed boys?' Now she turned to Ian. 'I rather think we should be flattered—or, you should be, anyway, darling: they put one of their top men on your tail today.'

'*Huh!*' Buller chased down the last of his beer with one hand, and then stabbed the bell again. '"Top Gun" is more like it, Lady! *Come on! Come on!*' He edited his face as he returned it to them. 'You'd think little Abdul 'ud be glad to see the back of us!' He gave Ian a mildly inquiring look. 'An' what 'appened to this Irish bloke—Paddy MacWhat's-it—? Did you actually set eyes on 'im, then?'

'Yes.' Where Jenny sweated, he felt cold, contrariwise. And now he was freezing. 'But only at a distance—'

'An' now 'e's playin' 'is Irish 'arp—like on the Guinness labels—?' The inquiry became harder. 'But you don't look that scared, I must say!'

The door opened before Ian could reply, just as what Reg Buller was plainly implying and what had actually happened at Lower Buckland began to diverge confusingly, and Buller himself sprang away from it to one side, with surprising agility.

'Madam—' Mr Malik addressed Jenny, and then flinched from Reg Buller as he became aware of him '—Madam—you come, eh?'

221

'We come.' Buller gestured at them both. 'Double quick, we come!' And double-quick, they came, with Reg Buller's urgency transmitting itself to them, into the warm happy curry-smells on the landing, and round the banisters, and down the stairs.

'Your coat, sir—your hat . . . your—' The false whiskers baffled Mr Malik '—Mr Buller, *sir*—!'

'A lady'll come for them—' Buller was already pushing them '—which way—the back-way—?'

'The lady's coat—it is *raining*—damn cats-and-dogs—' The little man shouted something in his own language, suddenly no longer despairing but commanding.

One of his smaller waiters, who had been smiling encouragingly at the bottom of the stairs, stopped smiling and began to search feverishly among the coats hung above him.

'Your dinner, sir—' Another waiter presented Ian with two large plastic bags, one after another, with a similar smile firmly in place. 'Three *extra*-special—double hot lime, double chilli—' He offered the bags to Ian '—you come *this* way, please—'

'Where's the beer?' From behind Reg Buller had sorted out his priorities, grabbing the bag which had *clinked* from Ian. 'Lady—just take the next coat—they're all the same—'

Ian lost the rest of the exchange as he entered the kitchen, half in a daze as its heat and steam and concentrated smells-and-sizzling overwhelmed him: and bright light and stainless-steel and great bowls and frying pans—*and there was a door open down the end, offering escape—but what was he escaping from—?*

222

'Go on, Ian lad.' Buller's voice shouted from behind him, urging him forward down the aisles between the huge tables and the cooking ranges, even as the question answered itself, but then still left itself unanswered: *he was running away from Paul Mitchell—from Paul Mitchell, who was worried about his safety—?*

He issued out of the kitchen, past a series of rough-painted doors into a small yard lit by a single bulb which seemed all the dimmer for the huge canopy of darkness above it. A thin drizzle shimmered in the yellow light, far removed from Mr Malik's cats-and-dogs' rain.

Then he saw the 'damn great wall': it was certainly well-furnished with broken glass set in concrete, but otherwise it had been even more exaggerated than the weather, being only waist-high to the waiter who was even now draping sacks over the jagged glass topping it. Behind it, through a thin screen of bushes, he could see the lights of the houses backing on the opposite side of the invisible railway track.

'This is ridiculous, Mr Buller.' Jenny caught his own unspoken thought exactly. 'Why do we have to go grubbing around in the dark out there—?' She waved at the wall and their latest grinning waiter, whose white teeth shone yellow in the light of the single bulb on the side of the house above them. 'What's so terrible out there in front, for God's sake?'

'You tell me, Lady.' Reg Buller sounded cheerfully unrepentant. 'I've been up the street once all the way, with my kind lady-friend on my arm, an' kissed her goodnight at the bottom, whiskers an' all. And then come half-way back, an'

Abdul tells me you've got company—company *I* don't care to meet just yet. So I did a bit more walking an' window-shoppin', till Dr Mitchell removed himself—' He stopped suddenly. 'How did you know it was me?'

'It's the way you walk.' She shook her head irritably. 'But he's gone, Mr Buller—*Reg*—' She scowled at him in the drizzle, the first strands of hair already dampened against her face. '—*for God's sake, Reg!*'

''As 'e? Or is 'e just waitin' for you to run?' Buller was role-playing again. 'Though o' course, the blokes down at each end of the street now, parked in their cars on the double-yeller lines, bold as brass—*they* may not be *'is* blokes, I grant you. They could be local villains waitin' to do a job? Or villains at one end, an' plain-clothes lads at the other, waitin' to nab 'em? An' you want me to go an' *arsk* 'em, do you? 'Cause, I tell you, I ain't goin' to—' He pointed into the darkness, clinking the bottles in the bag in his other hand as he did so '—'cause *I'm* goin' over the wall, is where I'm goin'.' He swung round, clinking again. 'We won't be needing your ladder—just that box'll do, my lad!' He nodded at the wooden box which had been conveniently positioned below the sacking.

'Oh no! Ladder damn necessary!' Mr Malik skipped past them to the wall and on to the box, and addressed the darkness on the other side in his own language.

'What—?' Reg Buller strode forward and peered over. 'Bloody hell!'

'Walls have two sides, see?' Mr Malik addresed Ian this time. 'This side—little wall. Other side—damn great wall. All the same wall, but you

224

break your neck jumping it, if not careful. Ladder *damn* necessary!'

'Right then!' Buller drew back and gestured towards Ian. 'Over you go. There's a little bloke down there holding the ladder, so don't drop on him, eh?'

Going over the wall was uncomfortable and awkward, even with only one bag. But the other side was purgatory, one-handed on the slimy-wet rungs, brushed by sodden branches—the 'bushes' he had observed from above were in fact the tops of fair-sized trees—in almost total darkness . . . or, almost total darkness twice frighteningly broken by the passage of trains, each of which turned the dark into a nightmare of noise and light through the foliage. And the bloody ladder seemed to go on for ever: if anything, the little man had understated the size of his great wall.

But then, to make him feel feeble and effete, Jenny came down after him like a cat, in half his time. And even Reg Buller made light of his descent, only worried for the safety of his beer.

'Well, that's blown away the cobwebs!' Buller puffed slightly as he turned to the attendant waiter, whose white coat belied the darkness. 'You do this often, do you?'

'Please—?' The single word sounded curiously unIndian: second generation London-Indian, different not so much because of its pronunciation as for its simple politeness . . .

'Never mind, lad. We got down. Now, how do we get out? Are those lights I can see up there the ones on the bridge?'

A sniff came from Jenny's direction. 'Now you ask!'

225

'Don't fret, lady. I've been alongside more railway lines than you've 'ad 'ot dinners—as a nipper *and* as a copper, chasin' nippers. There's always ways in, an' there's always ways out.' Buller drew in a breath. 'Well, lad?'

'Oh yes, sir. Those are the bridge lights, sure. You just follow the wall—you take my little torch, okay? People throw junk—very dirty people—and you maybe trip, see? But no difficulty . . . just the rubbish.'

'And then we scale the wall again?' Jenny's voice was admirably calm.

'No, miss. The bank comes up by the bridge. The wall is very little there—very easily, you go up. Just the broken bottles of the dirty people, you got to watch for them. Then only little walls, like I say. No difficulty, Miss.'

'Well . . . thank you.' She prodded Ian inaccurately in the almost-darkness. 'In your wallet, darling—for services rendered?' She hissed the command.

'Oh no, miss.' The young waiter moved towards the ladder like a ghost. 'Service charges all included in the bill, my father says. I must go now—we've got to pull up the ladder damn-quick now, he says—okay?'

'Okay. Up you go, lad,' agreed Buller. 'And hide the bloody thing too, just in case—if you can—?'

'Don't you worry, sir—' The voice already came from above them, through the branches '—we padlock this fire-escape ladder back in the passage. Then my father loses the key, I think . . . Good night, sir—miss—' The voice faded.

'Artful little monkey!' murmured Buller admiringly.

'But well-brought up,' said Jenny.

'Ah . . . well, they still bring 'em up, don't they! Model bloody-citizens they'd be, if it wasn't for their religions, makin' 'em all hate each other—' Buller stopped abruptly. 'But we didn't ought to stand gabbin' sweet nothin's—'

As he spoke, the sound of another train rose, drowning the rest of his words as it increased, until it filled the cutting deafeningly. But, more than the noise which reverberated around him, Ian was filled from within with an almost-panic-stricken feeling of unreality, which worsened as he glimpsed the train's occupants sitting and strap-hanging in safety and comfort in their brightly-lit carriages—late city-workers going home to suburban wives and husbands, girl-friends and boy-friends, families and friends . . . or (since he didn't even know which way he was facing, up or down) going out happily for a night's West End entertainment, taking their real world for granted . . . *while he was cowering illegally on railway property in the darkness, with heaven-only-knew what vile refuse crunching underfoot!*

The noise fell away into echoes, which the wind of the train seemed to suck after it, down the line—up the line? *And worse—*

'Come on, now!' Buller moved into the deafening silence which the vanished train drew into the cutting, within the enormous hum of that same real world above them, and all around them. 'We gotta get out of 'ere Lady—Ian lad—?'

And worse! (The drizzle, working down through the leaves above him into single larger drops of rain, spattering irregularly on his face now.) *And worse: the whole of that world, real or unreal, had turned*

227

against him. Ever since Reg Buller had first changed all the rules with his bad news, so few hours ago, but which seemed like forever now—now—

'Come on!'

He didn't want to move. This day had started unhopefully, yet then it had fed his ego deceptively, when he'd thought himself so clever. But from the moment he'd got through to Jenny its true nature had been revealed, albeit through a glass, darkly: the whole world out there was hostile, and full of dangers which he could no longer dismiss as imaginary.

'Come on—' Buller had moved, lighting his own way first with the boy's inadequate pocket-torch, and then helping Jenny as she had followed, leaving Ian behind in the actual dark, as well as his inner darkness. So now the voice came further off. '*Mister Robinson!*'

'I'm coming.' The feeble glow illuminated a great buttress, dark on his side and dirty yellow-brown on its railway side: the Victorian bricks in which London had burst outwards in its great days, in their untold billions; but now his feet were skidding and crushing on filthy modern detritus, of bottles and cans and plastics, up against the wall and the buttress, all mixed with the leaf-compost of a hundred years.

'What's the matter?' Buller shone the torch into his eyes challengingly. 'We 'aven't got all night, y'know . . . You got the bag, 'ave yer?'

That was it! Ian felt the last strand of his patience snap, with the addition of the bag of congealing curries and rice and pickles to Buller's assumed 'working class' voice, which was designed to jolly him along, challenging him to behave like an officer and a gentleman, and not let the side down.

228

'No.' He rounded the buttress, and then set his back against it, as though exhausted. 'This is far enough.'

'What?' The torch came back to him.

'Darling—when we get to the car—' Jenny supported the torch—'—and I'm getting *wet*, too!'

'Damn the car!' When they reached the BMW, he would be driving it. And then it would be too late, because he would have to concentrate on his driving. And . . . maybe they were both relying on that. 'I want to know what's happening to me.' As he spoke, he knew that he had the whip-hand: even apart from her unwillingness to drive and Reg Buller's careless intake of alcohol (and consequently even greater unwillingness), they couldn't leave him behind now, with whatever they each had in mind—not with Paul Mitchell out there . . . whoever else was out there.

The light continued to blind him. But behind it, in the absolute darkness, they must each be coming to the same conclusion. So he leaned back, and let the enormous weight of brick support him, just as it had held up the whole of Cody Street for a hundred years, above all the trains which had used this cutting.

'Fff—' Buller cracked first, but then remembered Jenny.

'What are you playing at, Ian?' Jenny was not so inhibited, so she sounded unnaturally shrill. 'My God! Aren't things bad enough already? With—' The rest of the words were cut off by the rumble of another train, which approached them more slowly so that, where before her face had been only flickeringly illuminated, disco strobe-lighted, now he saw its anger and intensity as the noise enveloped them again.

'No . . . *no!*' Buller came back first. 'He's right. You got to level with him, Lady—that's only fair. And now's as good a time as any.'

'What?' She sounded incredulous, as well as angry.

'About Mitchell, Lady.' *Clink.*

'*What*—?' From incredulity-and-anger to doubt. 'But . . . I told him about Mitchell, Mr Buller: he's their blue-eyed boy—and he knows Audley—?'

'Ah! And then—?' Buller paused. And the torch went out, and the pause elongated.

'I don't know what you're talking about, Mr Buller.' She stopped him sharply on her own full stop. 'Ian—*Ian* . . . we had a three-way talk this morning—Reg, and John Tully and I, on that gadget of John's—the phone-thing—?'

'I was still up north, coming back, on the motorway,' supplemented Buller. 'And then, after what I told 'em, the Lady was going to check out Dr Mitchell.'

'Yes. And so I did, as far as I could.' Jenny's voice strengthened. 'And you were off checking on that woman—the one who got shot . . . so we couldn't warn you about Mitchell. And it never occurred to us that he would be after *you*, darling.'

'Yes.' It occurred to Ian that Jenny hadn't reckoned too much to 'the woman who got shot' when they'd spoken to each other last night. But maybe it hadn't just been the dogsbody job they'd given him: maybe, more simply, they'd just wanted him safely out of town, where he couldn't come to much harm while drawing off some of their followers on his wild goose chase. 'Go on, Jenny.'

'Well . . . that's all there is to it, as far as I'm
230

concerned, darling: I *did* get some more, about all of them. Including Dr Paul Mitchell. Including the fact that Willy Arkenshaw thinks he needs the love of a good woman to sustain him—or even just look after him, like Paddington Bear: *"Please look after this Mitchell"*—'

'Huh!' Reg Buller emitted an unPaddington Bear-like growl from his own darkness . . .

'And I only got that out of her because she's *very* pregnant with the next little Arkenshaw baronet, and all dewy-eyed about marriage and motherhood. And even so she clammed up then, and started quizzing me about where I'd met him . . . which she'd assumed had been at some party, and that I'd fancied him there. So I had to concoct an elaborate tale which I'm not at all sure satisfied her. Not that it matters now, anyway.' She paused. 'But that's all I got about Mitchell since we talked on the phone, Reg. But now you've got more, obviously—?'

'No.' Buller remained silent for a moment. 'I had more *then*. I just didn't want to give it to you over that line, for all to hear.' The next silence was broken by a *clink*. 'A lot more.'

Another *clink*. And then a tiny scraping sound. And then a *glugging* sound: Reg Buller was at the Tiger beer already.

'Couldn't we go on?' Jenny advanced commonsense tentatively. 'I mean . . . we could talk more comfortably in the car, Ian—couldn't we?'

'No.' Buller sounded as though he was more comfortable: Buller's main in-battle worry would have been—and was—the source of his next liquid refreshment. 'I think . . . maybe we'll leave the car where it is, an' call for a taxi. It might be safer. An' there's a pub I know, not far away. And there's a bloke I can phone from there who's into instant travelling, an' no questions asked, too.' Another *glug*. 'I reckon we're about as safely lost as we can be, right now. An', whoever's out there . . . by the time he comes to ask questions up above, an' gets the wrong answers—' Buller chuckled '—'cause, little Abdul—he'll be good with the wrong answers, to drive 'em up the wall—' Another chuckle. Then another *glug*. And then a soft empty *clunk* as he dropped the bottle, adding himself to the 'very dirty people' '—but not *our* wall . . . *his* wall, eh?'

'And then?' Jenny just got the question in before the next train.

Buller waited for the noise to hurry after its cause. 'Then they'll get their skates on. Because they'll know we've rumbled 'em. And they'll reckon we've long gone . . . And there won't be time for committee meetings then: they'll be wetting their britches, an' doubling-up in Hampstead—or at your dad's place, most likely. An' that's *really* goin' to worry 'em, by golly!'

'Yes?' Jenny sounded doubtful suddenly.

'Right!' Buller caught her doubt. 'That's where you'd have gone, eh? Home to daddy—all nice an' safe? An' then maybe a phone-call to one of daddy's friends in the Government? Or a call from the House of Lords to the Home Secretary—?'

'You know I wouldn't do that.' Jenny bristled with outrage.

'Wouldn't you? *I* would—if I was you. Bloody right, I would!' Buller paused for only a fraction of a second. 'All right—*you* wouldn't. But they don't know *you*, Lady: they'll only know that they don't know which way trouble's comin' from, while

232

they're tryin' to find where you've gone—now that they know you're on to them—see?' Another pause. 'If it's Mitchell . . . then he'll be running scared too, I reckon. With Audley out of the country, eh?'

'He can always run to Jack Butler.'

'Can 'e though?' Buller paused as though in doubt. 'That's one of the things that doesn't add up—I reckon *that*, too.'

'Why not?'

'Because Jack Butler—*Sir* Jack Butler, as 'e is now, from the last Birthday Honours . . . he's not a dirty player, they say.'

'Yes.' Jenny came in quickly. 'They do say that—yes! But—?'

'But Mitchell?' Buller came back even more quickly. 'Ah! Now we're into Mr Peter Wright, an' his dirty tricks, an' his young Turks.' Buller paused. 'An' . . . *Philip Masson*, maybe.'

This time it was Jenny's silence, with no train coming, and only the distant continuous hum of the city above them holding down the lack of sound in the cutting.

'Philly wasn't part of R & D then,' she said finally. 'And Philly would never have been into dirty tricks.'

'Wouldn't 'e?' Buller goaded her cruelly. 'Not like Audley? Not like Mitchell?'

'We're not discussing Philly, any more.' She refused to be goaded. 'It's Mitchell we're running away from, aren't we?'

'Oh aye?' Buller harumphed derisively. 'Well, he'll do for a start, Lady. But—'

'But he saved Ian, Mr Buller. Now why would he do that—for a start?'

Ian was already beginning to regret his obstinacy.

233

Most of all he wanted to question Buller about Frances Fitzgibbon. Yet he didn't want to do that in front of Jenny, although he didn't know why. But then, even as he tried to conjure up the girl in his imagination, his thoughts suddenly ignited. 'He was there, Reg—wasn't he?'

'There? Where?' Buller played for time. 'Who?'

'At Thornervaulx. Don't play silly buggers with us, Reg. In '78—Mitchell was there—right?'

Now, when it was least required, a train from the opposite direction announced itself; and then (obeying a variant of Sod's Law), took an unconscionable time to pass them, unlike its predecessors, stopping and starting convulsively just in front of them.

'Was Mitchell at Thornervaulx, Reg?'

'I heard you the first time, old lad.' Buller had used the interruption more profitably. 'They were *all* there—at Thornervaulx. Except Masson, of course.' Silence—mercifully unpunctuated by another *clink*. ''E was probably ordering 'is new suit, with 'is new badges-of-rank, on bein' promoted to command Research an' Development, most likely.' Silence. 'But the rest were all there—*yeah!*'

Contempt from Jenny was par for the course. But from Reg Buller—that was over the top. 'And Marilyn Francis—? Mrs Frances Fitzgibbon—? Are you including her, Reg?'

'You mean the woman?' Buller sounded surprised at such sharpness, coming from him, like a ferret bitten by a rabbit.

'Yes—the woman.' It was time Frances Fitzgibbon got her due, outside Lower Buckland. '"The woman who was killed the week before",

234

Jenny—? The "innocent bystander"?'

'Yes.' Buller recovered. 'Yes . . . the one that blew it—her too, *yes!*'

'Blew it?'

'Got 'erself killed. That's blowing it, in my book.' Buller didn't give him time to bite back this time. 'She didn't ought to have got herself killed by "Mad Dog" O'Leary— "Mad Dog" my eye!'

'He wasn't mad?' Jenny cut in quickly.

'Oh . . . 'e was mad right enough. 'E was mad to stick around after 'is bomb went off, an' 'e got clean away . . . But, of course, 'e *stayed*. An' that was what took 'em all by surprise—'im staying, an' 'avin' another go. Took the police by surprise, certainly. But they were bloody fed-up by then, anyway—the way the Intelligence lot had sodded 'em around, tryin' to run things, an' then throwin' O'Leary into their lap when things went sour.' Buller paused. 'Not Colonel Butler, though—"Sir Jack" as 'e is now. Got a lot of time for 'im they 'ave.'

Reg had been talking to the Police. Or, at least, to some contact he had inside the force up north: Reg always seemed to have an old mate, or a mate of an old mate, in whatever Police Authority he found himself. 'Why was that, Reg?'

''E was brought in late, to the University—where the bomb went off. And . . . they said 'e wasn't too pleased with what 'e found. But 'e didn't waste time complainin'. An' 'e didn't blame anyone neither, at the University there. But then they—*his* bosses—they took O'Leary off him, more or less, apparently. Like . . . well, the last bit, after the bomb and before the shooting at Thornervaulx—all that was pretty confusing, after that, by all

235

accounts.' Buller paused, but Ian knew of old the mixture of resignation and cynicism which he couldn't see. 'Everybody got praised for everything, but that was to keep 'em quiet. Because crossing O'Leary off the "Most Wanted" list made all the Top Brass—the cabinet ministers, and the judges, and the rest—it made 'em sleep a bit sounder at night. And saved a lot of taxpayers' hard-earned money, too: *"Efficient police-work in preventing the suspect from escaping from the cordoned area"*—although they didn't know where the hell he was. And *"vigilance on the part of the security services and the anti-terrorist group"* . . . meaning "Thank you very much for shooting the bugger dead. So let's not have any arguments to spoil the good publicity, eh?"' Buller sniffed. 'Never quarrel with the bloke who pins the medal on you—not when there's been a happy ending: that's the rule.'

'But it wasn't a happy ending for Mrs Fitzgibbon, Reg,' Ian couldn't keep the bitterness out of his voice.

For a moment, Buller didn't reply. '"Fitzgibbon", was it?' Another pause. 'You had an interesting day, did you, Ian lad?'

He had to keep his cool. 'But *she* had a bad day—November 11, 1978?'

Another pause. 'What was she doing in Rickmansworth?'

'What was she doing in . . . where was it?' Surprisingly, it was Jenny who came to his rescue. 'At Thornervaulx—the ruined abbey there, wasn't it?'

'You know the place, do you?' Buller had obviously decided that he was giving too much and receiving too little in exchange.

'I know the place. Daddy used to shoot near Thornervaulx—or hunt, or something.' Jenny also knew Buller's game. 'Or maybe it was racing at Catterick . . . What was she doing in Thornervaulx, Reg—this Mrs FitzPatrick?'

'Ah . . .' With Jenny, Buller usually surrendered more quickly than this. 'Well, it's like they always say with makin' omelettes: you 'ave to break the eggs now an' then. Only . . . it's always the cooks an' the omelette-eaters talkin', isn't it? Never the eggs and the chickens.'

'So she was just doing her job.' It was impossible to say whether Jenny was more irritated by Buller's obstinacy or by the fluctuating extremes of the accent he tended to assume with her. 'But was she Police, Mr Buller? Or was she Intelligence? And . . . if she was Intelligence, In R & D? Because they do appear to pretend that they're "equal opportunity", it seems.'

Equal opportunity to die, in this case, Ian added silently.

'I tell you one thing, Lady . . .' But Buller trailed off maddeningly as the sound of another train came down the line towards them.

'One thing—?' Jenny urged him on, her voice rising against the sound.

'Aye. She was . . . *brave, Lady*—' The rest of his shout was cut off by the train, the noise sucking the words away with it again.

This time she waited until the noise had gone, and the hum of the city had reasserted itself as a background to the silence in the cutting. 'Brave, Mr Buller?'

'She was the one that picked up the bleedin' bomb at the University.'

237

Frances? thought Ian *Frances!* 'How do you know that, Reg?'

'I thought it was Audley, first. But he wasn't there—at the University.' Buller addressed him deliberately in the darkness. 'An' then I thought it must 'ave been Mitchell. But it was *'er—*'

'How do you know?' That it had never occurred to him before seemed like a betrayal, almost: like Buller, he had never dreamt of equating the 'heroic secret services officer' of Reg's favourite tabloid newspaper with its 'innocent bystander' at Thornervaulx a few days later. *'How do you know, man?'*

'I talked to a bloke that was there—what d'you think?' Buller was guarded about his police contacts once again. 'An' I've just put two-an'-two together. An' they make four, just like always.'

'She sounds a bit stupid, to me.' Jenny spoke to no one in particular. 'But . . . she was R & D, then—is that what you're saying, Mr Buller?'

Suddenly Ian didn't want to talk about Frances any more. And he didn't want Jenny to talk about her either. 'I thought we were talking about Mitchell, not Mrs Fitzgibbon.'

'And we know that he's R & D,' agreed Jenny. 'But . . . what's Thornervaulx got to do with Philip Masson, Mr Buller?' There was doubt in her voice, and she wasn't arguing now: she was conceding a point while seeming to ask for an explanation.

But Thornervaulx was Frances Fitzgibbon to Ian. 'He wasn't there—you said, Reg?' (If there had been the slightest possibility of that, Jenny wouldn't have asked her question: it would have been all Thornervaulx then!)

'No, 'e wasn't there.' Buller dismissed the idea

238

scornfully. 'The bleedin' generals don't go into the front line, lad—'

'Mr Buller!' Jenny snapped him off. 'Just answer the question, please.'

Buller crunched the dirty people's refuse under his feet. 'It's time we got out of 'ere, Lady. It's not too far to that pub I know. An' I can phone from there—'

'*Mr Buller!*'

'Okay, okay!' He drew a noisy breath. 'I don't know for sure. But if I'm right . . . then Thornervaulx wasn't just the death of O'Leary an' the woman: it was the death of your bloke, too, Lady.'

CHAPTER EIGHT

It was always another pub with Reg Buller: it was a mystery to Ian how the man had found enough opening hours in all the days of his life to be so intimately friendly with so many landlords and landladies, barmaids and barmen, so that they were willing to spirit him away into their small back rooms on the nod, safe from prying eyes.

'Not one of my usual watering 'oles—not since the brewery done it up,' Reg had murmured in his ear as he propelled them through the noise and smoke towards a door at the back of the bar-room. 'But the bloke 'ere owes me a favour, anyway . . . Up the stairs, door straight ahead, an' I'll join you in a mo', when I've fixed up our travel arrangements—okay?' Then he ducked back into the noise again, leaving them staring at each other.

'What travel arrangements, Jen?' Ian felt that he had left the wet outer darkness of the street outside for a brightly-lit but greater inner darkness.

'Don't ask me, darling.' She shrugged while attempting to repair the ruin of what had probably started out as an expensive hair-do. 'Mr Buller seems to have taken over, that's all I know. Don't you know?'

'You spoke to him this afternoon, Jen.'

'But only on the phone, darling. And he didn't say much then, except that he wanted me to ask around about Paul Mitchell . . . which I had already started to do on my own account, actually . . . But I thought *you* knew all about his trip north—?' She gave up the repair-attempt. 'I'm not going to argue the toss with you here, darling, in public. So just do like the wretched man said—get up those stairs.'

The only thing he knew—or the only *additional* thing he knew—thought Ian wearily . . . was that, however scared Paul Mitchell and others might be running now, or soon, Reg Buller was running scared already. And after John Tully, never mind what had happened at Lower Buckland this afternoon, that made sense. So getting up the stairs also made sense.

But the room at the top of the stairs in no way resembled the Shah Jehan room: it had foul red-plastic covered tables and an even fouler smell of stale tobacco-smoke, complete with overflowing ashtrays: it was a meeting-room of some sort, and all that could be said for it now was that it was empty.

'What about Mitchell?' He faced her again.

'Darling—you know him better than we do.' She
240

returned to her repair work, letting the whole elaborate ruin down in a red cascade. 'If only I had an elastic band! You don't happen to have one, do you, darling?' She glanced at him a little too casually. 'No—of course you don't! But . . . he did save your life—didn't he? Mitchell, I mean . . . No . . . well, of course, we don't know that for sure, do we? And you were busy with that woman of yours . . .'

He had to hit her back. 'Whom you didn't think was important?'

'I still don't think she's important.' She spoke through several hairpins.

'And Reg Buller going north—?' Buller had come back with information about Mitchell. So she damn-well couldn't argue with that. 'What—'

The door burst open, and a large young women with a tray swerved through the opening. 'One large gin-and-tonic—one low-alcohol lager—?'

Jenny dropped her hair. 'Mine's the gin—' She seized the glass from the tray, letting her hair fall again.

'Thank you—' He took one of the three glasses which remained: not the pint in the straight glass, and not the large whisky chaser, and looked interrogatively at the barmaid.

'Those are for Mr Buller—if you don't mind, sir?' She didn't even look at him.

Ian took Buller's share, and waited until the door had closed again. 'But you don't think that was a wasted journey now, do you, Jen?'

'No.' She drank deeply, like Reg Buller. And then set her glass down on the nearest table and returned to her hair. 'I think that was all part of the scene—the run-up to Philly's murder. But your

241

woman was out of it by then.'

He hated that—and almost hated Jenny with it. 'She's not "my" woman.' But he hated that, too: he heard the cock crow as he spoke. 'But I think you're wrong, Jen. And . . . I think she's interesting . . . I mean, I think she may be important—' But he didn't want to argue about Francis Fitzgibbon. 'What "scene", Jen—?'

The door opened again as he spoke, and Reg Buller came through it this time.

''E's goin' to call me back.' Buller looked at them briefly, his radar having indicated where the drinks were. ''E knows there's something dodgey goin' on . . .' He drank. '. . . maybe 'e's 'eard about poor ol' Johnny. But I twisted 'is arm, so 'e'll divvy up, you can bet on it . . .' Another drink. '. . . Kidlington, most likely—if 'e can 'andle the paperwork. But he may prefer us to take the hovercraft from Ramsgate, an' then lay on a plane from the other side, see—?' He wiped his mouth. 'What "scene" was that, then?'

'1978, Mr Buller.' Jenny answered him coolly. 'Where are we going . . . from where was it?' She frowned. 'Ramsgate, I know . . . But "Kidlington"—?'

'1978!' Buller tossed off his chaser in one swallow. 'A soddin' bad year for the Labour Party! '78–'79 put Mrs Thatcher in. An' she's never looked back since then—eh?'

'Where's Kidlington, Mr Buller?'

'Just outside Oxford, Lady.' Buller grinned at her unsmilingly. 'It's the largest village in England, they say. So it's got its own airfield.' The unsmiling grin vanished. 'But you're right about 1978: that's the key to the door, of course.'

There was nothing very clever about that. But, if she chose not to be very clever, he must play their game. 'So what really happened in 1978, Reg?'

Buller looked at Jenny. But Jenny was suddenly pretending to concentrate on her hair again, to their exclusion.

'Reg—?'

'All right.' Buller dismissed her, and drank more of his beer. 'There was one of their internal bust-ups . . . like the bloke who ran R & D was going, because 'e was sick . . . an' 'is No 2 'ad just died with 'is boots on, of a heart-attack—what was 'is name, Lady—?'

'Stocker—' The name cut through the hairpins.

'Ah! Just so . . .' Buller shrugged off the name. 'So they were all tryin' to fix things, so it came out right for 'em, an' they got the bloke they wanted to sign their expense accounts—okay?'

Jenny half-turned away from him, as though regretting that she'd even given him a name, pretending to fight again with her hair.

'Okay.' Buller turned to Ian. 'So Audley an' all the rest of 'em wanted Jack Butler. Because, better the devil you know than the one you don't know . . . An' the one they *didn't* know was the Lady's bloke—Mr Philip Masson—see?'

He had already seen that much. 'So—?'

'So Butler was their front runner. Because he was there—he knew the form.' Buller forgot to drop his *aitches*. Which was a sure sign that what he was saying was more important to him now than how he was saying it. 'An' Butler was a crafty choice because he was working-class—not Eton and the Royal Marines . . . but grammar school scholarship, an' commissioned-in-the-field, in some

243

second-rate North Country infantry regiment in '45 . . . An' 'is dad was a big trade unionist, who'd been a mate of Ernie Bevin's in the TUC in the old days, before his boy had learned to be an officer an' a gentleman—' He swung towards Jenny '—so you may think your bloke was the greatest thing since sliced bread, Lady . . . But Jack Butler was a front runner while Chief Petty Officer Jim Callaghan was still Prime Minister, an' running the show—*right?*'

Jenny tossed her hair aside. 'Philly was the man for the job, Mr Buller.'

'Oh aye?' Reg Buller's lip curled. 'More like . . . "Philly" was the man in the Civil Service who could fix things so Butler fell on his face—how about that then?'

Jenny held her hair up with one hand, while finishing her gin with the other. 'What do you mean by that, Mr Buller?'

'What do I mean?' Buller had consumed enough alcohol to be unafraid of her now, even apart from the fact that he appeared to be running their show at the moment, however temporarily. 'I mean we just tipped all the pieces of the jigsaw out on the table so far. An' we don't even know we got all the pieces yet. In fact, we certainly *ain't* got 'em all . . . But that don't mean we can't try an' put the bits together that look like fitting, eh?'

'I see.' Her lips compressed. 'So you've just picked up some dirty little rumour about Philip Masson—is that it?'

'Oh aye? An' you didn't pick up some dirty little rumour about David Audley, Lady? I thought that was what started us off. Correct me if I'm wrong, Lady—?'

'But we've already had confirmation that it was a

244

strong rumour going around Audley played dirty back in '78, Mr Buller. John Tully and I both picked that up, quite independently: there was going to be a big shake-up in R & D. Fred Clinton was coming up for retirement, and his deputy had already gone. And Audley was backing Jack Butler. But the Cabinet Secretary and others were backing Philip Masson.'

'Ah?' Buller emptied his beer glass and instantly stamped heavily on the floor, like a magician summoning up spirits from the underworld. 'So the smart money was on your bloke, then. But Audley's a man who likes to get 'is own way—'

'That's precisely it, Mr Buller: Audley likes to get his own way. So Philly had an accident—and Audley *got* his own way, didn't he?'

Buller stared at her for a moment. Then he stamped again, more heavily than before. Then he sniffed. 'You don't think killin' someone on 'is own side . . . or 'avin' 'im killed . . . you don't think that's comin' on a bit strong—even for 'im?'

Jenny's lip twisted. 'Audley? Aren't you being a bit sentimental, Mr Buller? His side—*our* side . . . we don't do such naughty things? Only the lesser breeds—the KGB and the CIA . . . and the Israelis . . . do naughty deeds?' The twist became more pronounced. 'They say Audley's left a trail of bodies behind him over the years—remember?'

'But they were his enemies, Lady, by all accounts.'

Or innocent bystanders, thought Ian bitterly.

'If Masson had been a traitor now—' Buller started to develop his thesis unwisely.

'Don't be ridiculous, Mr Buller. If you think that then we'll settle your bill here and now. I have my

245

cheque book with me, as well as my passport. You can even have a Euro-cheque, if you prefer.'

'I wasn't saying that, Lady. Your bloke was clean. If there'd been any doubt about 'im—any slightest doubt . . . I grant you that.' Buller hastily changed his tack. 'What I mean is . . . it would 'ave been straight murder, killing him. An' if you think about it, they didn't even arrange for old Peter Wright to 'ave an accident, when they knew 'e was goin' to cause 'em all that trouble—now did they? An' why not?' He paused. 'Because for a private murder you need a private murderer. So Audley would have had to get hisself a man, and a good one—someone, in fact, like "Mad Dog" O'Leary—' He nodded towards Ian '—or your bloke MacManus. An' there's a lot of risks involved in hiring that sort of talent. You really got to 'ave someone you can trust. And you can't never trust a private murderer, I don't reckon.'

Jenny shook her head. 'That's a pretty thin argument, Mr Buller.'

Buller made a face. 'I wasn't really talkin' about that, anyway—not yet anyway.'

'No. You were talking about Philip Masson. And some dirty little slander.' Jenny was like a terrier dropping a dead rat in preference for a larger one whose back she also intended to break before it could get away. 'So what was that, then?'

The door opened suddenly, and the same large young woman entered again, with more drinks. Buller had indeed summoned up spirits from the deep.

They waited until the re-fuelling had been completed, and then Buller turned back to Jenny. 'All that trouble they had up north, at the

University, with the bomb, an' then O'Leary turnin' up at Thornervaulx, when Jack Butler was on some other job . . . There's those that might say it was Jack Butler who was being measured for an "accident" there. Only the woman that was killed an' Dr P. L. Mitchell spoilt the accident between 'em—'

'Mitchell?' Jenny wasn't interested in 'the woman'.

'Oh aye.' Buller nodded. 'Old "Mad Dog" was a top man in his profession—he was *good*, Lady . . . Even goin' to Thornervaulx like that, which was a mad thing to do, it seemed . . . But 'e'd got a car waitin' in a barn about a mile away, over the top, complete with a police uniform and identity papers. An' then another car about five miles away, with another identity—an' the uniform of a major in the Royal Signals, from Catterick. An' a real major, too—only 'e was on leave at the time. An' the number-plate on the second car was the same as the major's car. They didn't even find those cars for a fortnight, neither. So 'e'd 'ave got away, you can reckon.'

'You were talking about Mitchell, Mr Buller, I thought.'

'I *am* talking about Mitchell, Lady. Because old "Mad Dog" was a real pro. But Dr P. L. Mitchell is another. An' maybe a better one, too.'

'How so? What are you trying to tell us, Mr Buller?'

Buller drew a breath. 'By all accounts, 'e 'ad no more than two seconds flat, that day at Thornervaulx, after O'Leary started shooting. An' O'Leary had a long gun—a rifle of some sort. An' Mitchell—*Doctor* Mitchell . . . he had a little gun.

247

A hand-gun, that would be. Probably an automatic pistol, that would be, so as not to spoil his jacket . . . But it don't really matter—that it was a *little* gun. Because it was big enough for what was needed, see?' He looked at them in turn. 'O'Leary gets off one shot—bang!' His free hand came up, with a finger pointing at Jenny. 'An' *bang-bang—bang* goes the little gun. An' 'e never even got a second shot off—down like a pole-axed steer, 'e went . . . "never", as they say in the old westerns, "to rise again". A proper little Wyatt Earp, our *Doctor* Mitchell is. Or maybe more like Doc Holliday.'

As Jenny digested all this in silence, Ian was conscious of a shiver down his own back because of Buller's chance imagery. Almost, that might have been how Gary Redwood would have described that shoot-out, with his own dear Marilyn Francis down in the dust—the wet hillside bracken at Thornervaulx—after that first-and-last shot of O'Leary's.

'Who told you all this?' Jenny had indeed noticed the curious imprecision of Buller's account, which ruled out one of his police contacts . . . even supposing that he'd been clever enough and lucky enough to find one so imprudent to say so much. And even then—

'Ah! Now that would be telling!' Buller savoured his memories for a moment. 'You know what I've got—eh?'

'An eye-witness.' Ian snapped the words as they hit him, in the instant that he recalled Buller's powers of conversation-recall from past experience, when these could be checked against played-back tapes for comparison.

'And clients paying for your time,' added Jenny tartly, but oddly out of character. 'Come on, Mr Buller—don't piss us around: you've got an eye-witness.'

'Strictly speaking . . . *no*, Lady.' Buller drank deeply. 'Meaning . . . you won't ever be able to turn this into one of your lovely bits of dialogue, Ian lad—like with that Yank we found up in those mountains—remember?'

'Why not, Mr Buller?' Jenny was less hampered by any imperishable memories of the Grand Tetons in Wyoming, never mind the horrors of Vietnam.

'Because my eye-witness is dead and buried. So I never got to talk to—'

'*What?*' Ian gulped air.

'Hold on, lad!' Buller cut him short. 'At ninety-one years old she has a perfect right to be dead—and decently buried, too! you don't need to blame me: it was pneumonia, after she broke her hip getting out of bed, an' fell over, see? An' . . . she was always gettin' up—they never could stop the old girl, that's what her daughter said . . . An' the daughter's nearer seventy now, than sixty . . . But she heard all the commotion, the old woman did, so she got out of 'er bed an' went to look—see?'

The repetition of *see?* was maddening. 'You're saying, Reg . . . a ninety-one-year-old woman . . . saw Mitchell shoot O'Leary? At Thornervaulx—?'

'She wasn't ninety-one then. She was . . . what's ninety-one minus eight?'

'Eighty-three.' Jenny answered automatically, before she could stop herself. 'You're pissing us around again, Mr Buller. And in our time.' She was beginning to get angry again. 'She was . . .

249

bed-ridden. But she was an eye-witness. And . . .
now she's dead?'

'That's right—you got it, Lady.' No one could
shrug off Jenny better than Reg Buller. But, then,
no one but Reg Buller dared to shrug her off.

'Got what, Mr Buller?'

Buller half-grunted, half sighed. 'Got the whole
thing. The story of your life an' mine—how we
make a crust, an' something to drink with it,
between us. Like . . . no matter 'ow clever they are,
or 'ow careful . . . there's always somethin' that
they *'ave* thought of. But it still scuppers
'em—see?'

Ian didn't see. And he knew that Jenny couldn't
see, either. But, in the next instant, he knew exactly
what Reg Buller meant, all the same—in general as
well as at Thornervaulx, on November 11, 1978:
Sod's Law was out there, waiting for everyone.

'You've been to Thornervaulx?' When Jenny
remained silent Reg simply nodded at her. 'A lot of
old ruins, that Henry VIII knocked about a bit?
Chucked out the old monks—privatized the abbey;
an' pinched all their savings . . . An' now they
charge you a dollar to see what's left, all neat an'
tidy. An' half-a-dollar for the guide-book—right?'

Jenny wasn't meant to interrupt, and she didn't.

'You go up the steps, an' the path, from the
car-park, by the road—by the "Thor Brook", the
little river there—when you've paid your money,
an' got your ticket . . . an' you never notice the
cottages there, on the other side of the path,
alongside the ruins.' Pause. 'Farm-labourers'
cottages, they are—God knows how old . . .
They're all listed as "historic buildings", because
they're built with the stones from the old abbey,

250

anyway. But no one notices 'em.'

There was a picture forming in Ian's head.

'So they were all there, that day.' Buller warmed to his own story. 'It was pissing down with rain—it was a Saturday, an' it was in November, an' it was pissin' down with rain. An' then the cars started to arrive.' Pause. 'An' then *they* started to arrive—first Butler and Mitchell, an' Audley—*Dr David Audley* . . . an' some more.' Pause. 'An' the woman—'er too, eventually.'

Ian opened his mouth, but then shut it tightly.

'An', of course, old "Mad Dog" was there too, somewhere . . . Up on the hillside, in the bracken an' the trees—good cover there.' Pause. 'So he was there, too.' Pause. 'An' then a police car comes along, over the bridge—soundin' 'is siren, the silly bugger, just to show off.' Pause. 'They *will* do it, 'owever much you tell 'em not to, when there's no need—silly bugger!'

'Why was Audley there?' The question burst out of Jenny as though she couldn't contain it.

'God knows.' Buller seemed to dismiss the question. 'It was Butler who was in charge. My bloke that I talked to first didn't know anything about Audley. Or about Mitchell, either . . . Never even got their names.' Pause. 'Good descriptions, though. An' from the old lady too, second hand . . . Bloody shame, that. But even second hand, she was good, though.' Pause. '"The bloke in charge wore a deerstalker hat, an' carried a golfing umbrella, an' 'e 'ad freckles an' a red face"—how's that then, for memory?' Buller grinned. 'When it comes to mindin' other people's business, an' peering through the curtain, an' seein' strangers up to no good, you can't beat a countrywoman—specially

251

North Countrywomen. And they knew that, of course.'

'They?'

'The local cops. Maybe Butler, too—he's North Country, so he'd have known . . . So, after it was all over, they went into the cottages an' put the fear of God into the women there. The men an' the boys were all at the matches, see—there was the football and the rugby, it being a Saturday afternoon. So there were only women an' girls home. An' the Police put 'em through it.'

'What did they want to know?'

'What they'd seen. *Who* they'd seen. Every last detail.' Buller drew a breath. 'Frightened the life out of 'em—twice. First time, it was a uniform man, Mrs Rowe said—Mrs Rowe being the old woman's daughter . . . But not their own local man. A senior officer, with lots of silver braid on his uniform, and talked posh. Then, later on, a civilian, with their own local bobby in attendance. Same questions . . . only he talked even more posh. An' he wore a beautiful suit, she remembered—Mrs Rowe did. Because she'd been in one of the mills in Bradford when she was a girl, so she knew good cloth when she saw it. I reckon the suit frightened her more than the man. But then, of course, she was already scared stiff by that time.'

'Why?' Jenny had decided to be chief questioner.

'Huh! Because she knew by then that she'd deceived 'em something shocking the first time, Lady.' Buller chuckled grimly. 'She an' the old witch between 'em.'

'How?'

'She'd told 'em she hadn't seen anything. Just the police car, anyway . . . An' then a policeman had told her to stay indoors. An' the wall by the cottage is too high to see right into the ruins from the ground-floor, anyway. So he half-believed her the first time. But even then they also told her not to speak to anyone—meaning the Press, of course.'

'But she *did* see something—?' Jenny frowned.

'No. *She* didn't see anything. But, when they asked her if there was anyone else in the house, she'd said "Only my old mum, who's ill in bed upstairs". An' then the bloke with all the silver braid went up an' checked, she said. An' *that* frightened her, too . . . But, of course, all he saw was a frail old lady with the sheet drawn up under her neck, pretending to be halfway to heaven. So that satisfied him, anyway.' Buller chuckled again. 'Silly Bugger!'

Ian recalled his own grandmother vividly to mind. 'She saw everything—from her bedroom window, Reg?'

'Near enough, lad. Near enough!' No chuckle this time. 'When the daughter went back up, after the silver-braid bloke had gone . . . she started to tell the old witch about him. But she didn't get far, before the old witch started to tell *her* . . . near enough everything—aye!'

'And she didn't tell the second man—the man in the suit—?'

Buller sniffed. 'Too scared, she was.' Another sniff. 'The first one told her, if she'd not been telling the truth, or had withheld evidence, then she'd be in serious trouble. And her eldest boy was a prison officer, at Northallerton or somewhere then. So she thought he might get the sack, an' lose his pension. So she stuck to her story, same as before. An' fortunately the old girl was still in bed.

253

So the whole story stuck, same as before.'

Sod's Law: no matter how clever you were, there was always something waiting to catch you by the heel. Frances Fitzgibbon's book had gathered dust in Mrs Champeney-Smythe's shelf, waiting for its moment. And now an old woman's eye-witness story had found its moment too—even after the death of its eye-witness narrator.

'But she talked to *you*, Mr Buller—the daughter.'

'Ah, she did that, but 'appen I'm not a silly bugger in a uniform. An' my suit's Marks and Spencer, off the peg.'

And Philip Masson had been waiting also, in his shallow grave, for his moment, to catch someone—Audley? Mitchell? Someone, anyway—by the heel—

'Very true, Mr Buller.' Jenny wasn't about to let Buller's arrogance remain unpunctured. 'But you also slipped her a few of those nice crisp banknotes you always keep, to loosen honest tongues? Which you charge to expenses.'

'The man with the freckled face had a golfing umbrella.' Buller cut his losses. 'Red, white an' blue . . . or, red, *green* an' white—that's what the old woman said . . . An' she'd never seen a golfing umbrella before. But the old witch 'ad a telescope to spy on people, an' a good memory. Because Sir Jack Butler, KBE, MC . . . 'e's got ginger hair, an' a red-brick face, an' freckles. An 'e plays golf.'

'Yes?' Buller was making his point. But Jenny was after other game. 'What about Audley?'

'A big bugger. Like . . . her old man, who was long-dead . . . 'e was Rugby League. So she said there was one of 'em built like 'im: six-foot an' more, with broad shoulders an' long legs, an' a

254

broken nose from way back—?' Buller paused to let the next identification sink in. 'An' that's Audley, to the life, by all accounts.' Shorter pause. 'Rugby Union, 'e played—not Rugby League . . . But that's *Audley*.' Even shorter pause. 'But he was late: it was all over when he arrived. It was Butler first, with his umbrella—'

'*Why?*' Jenny snapped the question, before Buller could continue. 'What was he doing there?'

'Doing?' Buller gave a snort of derision. 'I'll tell you what he *wasn't* doing, Lady: he wasn't expecting to meet O'Leary.'

'Why not?'

'F—!' Buller swallowed the obscenity. 'If you were goin' to meet an IRA marksman . . . would you carry your golfing umbrella, to help him aim?' He let the thought sink in. 'An' besides . . . Butler had been told to give O'Leary back to the Anti-Terrorist Squad—an' the Special Branch— after the bomb at the University: it was them that were after O'Leary. An' they thought he'd long gone, too.'

'You don't know why Butler was there?'

'Christ Almighty!' Buller simulated outrage. 'Twenty-four hours—thirty-six hours . . . an' you expect me to know what British Intelligence was up to in 1978? An' not just MI5—but Research and Development? An' not even MI5 knows what R & D is up to, most of the time. Lady—you don't want much, do you!'

'I'm sorry, Mr Buller. I was just asking, not expecting.' Jenny recovered quickly. 'Tell me about Mitchell.'

'Yes.' Buller accepted the name, but stopped on his acceptance. Because 'Mitchell' wasn't just

255

another name any more: he echoed distant gunfire now, and maybe more than that.

'He was with Audley?'

'No. Audley was late—I told you. The woman was with him.'

'Yes—of course! Ian's woman.' Jenny dismissed Frances Fitzgibbon once more. 'So . . . Mitchell was there with Butler, was he?'

Ian's woman, thought Ian: in a curious way, that was what she had become now—just that. And the need to know more about her obsessed him again suddenly.

'Go on, Mr Buller.' Jenny's patience was beginning to stretch again. 'What—'

'Tell me about the woman, Reg.' Ian overrode her. 'Mrs Fitzgibbon.'

'Ian! For heaven's sake!'

'Tell me about the woman, Reg.'

'Yes.' Buller ignored Jenny. '"Just a slip of a girl", the old witch said—Mrs Rowe said she said. A pretty little thing, too—'

'She had good eye-sight, did she? At ninety-one?' snapped Jenny.

'Eighty-three. An' yes, she did.' Buller's voice strengthened. 'But I told you: she had this old telescope. An' she used to sit in her room, by the window, an' spy on everything—on all the people that came to visit the abbey ruins. Like, it was her hobby: see the coaches come over the narrow bridge, down the road, where they used to get stuck. An' then the kids climbin' on the ruins, an' their mothers pullin' 'em off an' thumpin' 'em—' He stopped suddenly. 'A pretty little thing. An' she saw 'er first when the car came. Like a racin' car, slitherin' on the gravel in the car park. An' out she

256

comes like lightning—didn't even close the door after 'er, before she started runnin': *that's* what the old woman saw first, that took her eye—the way she went off runnin'.'

Buller paused there, and Ian thought for a moment that he was challenging Jenny to interrupt again. But Jenny didn't speak, and in the next instant he knew why—and why Buller had stopped, as the final picture he was painting for them in words began to form again in his own mind—and to move, like a suddenly-animated film.

'It was rainin'.' Buller confirmed that second thought with extra information, to complete the picture. 'It 'ad been rainin' all day, off an' on. So there 'adn't been any visitors much, before then. An' it was November, in any case.'

November 11. Next day, there would have been the Armistice Day Sunday parades, with everyone wearing their red poppies up and down the country, and the Queen televised at 11 o'clock, laying her wreath at the Cenotaph, before the veterans' march-past.

'An' then . . . it was the way she ran.' Buller's voice was matter-of-fact, as it always was when he was totally-recalling what had been said to him. 'Like a boy, the old woman said: with 'er short hair, if she 'adn't noticed 'er skirt when she come out of the car, she'd 'ave thought it *was* a boy, when she ran up the path by the wall . . . Until she came out at the top, where you turn through the little gate into the ruins—remember?'

Buller was addressing Jenny, as one who knew what he was talking about, quite forgetting Ian now. So Ian had to build his own picture for himself, out of a jigsaw of other pieces, from other

257

places, other ruins: Tintern and Bylands, Fountains and Rievaulx—all the old ruined abbeys . . . And *Rievaulx* for choice . . . because, hadn't there been cottages nearby there—?

'You know, the old woman actually saw O'Leary—*saw* 'im?' For an instant Buller's matter-of-factness became incredulous. ''E must 'ave got there late—like Audley . . . Or, *not* like Audley. Because Audley would 'ave been VIP, an' 'alf the police in England was lookin' for O'Leary by then, so it wouldn't 'ave been easy for 'im, by Christ!' The next intake-of-breath was incredulity mixed with admiration. 'They must 'ave been payin' 'im premium rates, for whatever 'e was paid to do—even with all the escape disguises 'e'd got set up behind 'im. Because, 'e was really chancin' 'is arm, that last time—gettin' to Thornervaulx, over the top of the moor there . . . Silly bugger!'

'Yes.' Jenny weakened. 'But . . . what *was* he doing there, Mr Buller?' The logic strengthened her. 'It had to be Butler, surely—?' Then doubt intruded. 'Or . . . whoever was meeting him there—?'

'Aye. That's more likely. Because he must 'ave 'ad a clear shot at Butler—just about, anyway.' Buller sounded as though he'd been there before her, but was still uncertain. 'What about your Philip Masson, though?'

'No.' Jenny was decisive. 'Philly was out of the country that week. He was abroad—' As she spoke her voice came from Buller to Ian '—he was talking to the French in Paris. And he must have had all his R & D interviews by then. That's what I think, anyway.'

'So he'd got the job—deputy first . . . an' then

the gaffer, when Sir Frederick Clinton retired—?'
Buller stopped short, but just a shade too
innocently.

'I didn't say that.' Jenny also stopped there.
Because the reality was that they had both been
busy calling in their debts from their best
sources—Jenny from her friends, and 'Daddy's
friends', or even from Daddy himself, while Buller
had tapped his 'blokes' in Fleet Street, or the
Special Branch, who owed him favours (and who
hoped to owe him more in the future?); but, with
John Tully *dead*, this was a situation neither of
them would ever have faced before, anyway: with
survival at stake, they both had more urgent
imperatives.

'You know too much, Reg Buller,' said Jenny.

'Too much?' Buller snapped back at her.
'Lady—I don't know 'alf enough.' Deep breath.
'But Audley was in Washington too, that week—I
do know that. So someone tipped 'im off that Butler
was in trouble—right?'

'But he got there in time for the fun, all the
same—*right*?' Jenny still didn't know how much
Reg Buller knew, but she wanted all he'd got.

In time for "Mad Dog" O'Leary! thought Ian. *But
not in time for Frances Fitzgibbon.* 'Mrs Fitzgibbon
reached the ruins, Reg. She reached the ruins,
Reg—?'

'Ahh—' Buller breathed out again, through the
silence between his two questions '—yes, she got
there, lad—your "slip of a girl"—yes! She came out
there, at the top, through the gate—the gate,
there—?'

'Where was Mitchell then? Paul Mitchell—?'
Jenny's interest in the final picture still

concentrated on Mitchell.

'He was right there.' Buller agreed with her. 'He was up top, gawpin' about in the main part, under the hillside, where the high altar was, an' the big window at the end—the big round window they all admire—? That's in all the postcards?'

'The rose window.' Jenny supplied the rest of the tourist information.

'That's right. But there isn't any glass in it now—'

'*Reg!*' He lost patience with Buller. 'What happened then?'

'It was all rather quick, lad.' Buller sniffed. 'Mitchell was there—coverin' Butler, most likely. An' Butler was there . . . down in the lower part of the ruins, keepin' the rain off 'im, under 'is big umbrella. An' O'Leary—'e came down the hillside, over the bracken, an' through the trees . . . An' she shouts at 'im—the woman does—'

'Shouts what?' Jenny burst out, suddenly abandoning Mitchell.

'God knows.' Buller stopped. 'But 'e shot 'er dead, then—as she shouted at 'im. An' then Mitchell swings round, from watchin' Butler . . . an' *bang-bang-bang!*—with 'is little gun! An' bowled 'im over—O'Leary—like 'e'd been pole-axed.' Pause. 'Which at that range—an', I tell you, I've been there—at that range, that's target shootin', that is: like, two bulls, an' one inner, at thirty yards or more, before 'e could take over, O'Leary—like bloody lightning, that was!'

Ian thought of the two empty barrels in the shotgun at Lower Buckland; and of Mitchell's barely-suppressed passion after that, which he'd not understood.

260

'And then?' Jenny, once again, was unencumbered by that first-hand experience of Paul Mitchell. '*What happened* . . . Reg?' This time she softened the question finally.

Still no reply. So, there was something here which Reg Buller couldn't quite handle. And that struck Ian as strange, even disconcertingly strange, almost worrying. Because Reg Buller, drunk or sober (or, more-or-less permanently, midway between those extremes), was never a man to be lost for words.

'That is what the old woman *saw*? What she told her daughter?' Jenny had to be experiencing the same doubts: those were not so much questions as encouraging noises, jollying Buller along with her acceptance of what he was saying. 'Tell us, Reg.'

'Aye. What she saw.' Buller agreed with her reluctantly. 'Of course . . . it's early days yet. So we didn't ought to jump to conclusions an' then stay there. Because you never have before, anyway.' Sniff. 'Which is why you're worth more working for than some I could name.'

The man's reluctance and his change-of-subject fazed Ian completely for a long moment—and, obviously, Jenny also: their surprise flowed together in mutual silence.

'*Reg*—' Jenny broke first, albeit in a whisper.

'*Jenny*—' Ian reached out to restrain her, but misjudged the distance and caught only a handful of nothing.

'It's all right, darling.' She got the message, nevertheless. 'Of course it's early days yet. But we . . . it does rather look as though we don't have a lot of time. So do please jump to a conclusion for us, Reg dear.' As near as Ian had ever

261

heard—nearer by far than at any time in Beirut—she was pleading now, to get what she wanted. *'Please—?'*

'All right.' Reg Buller couldn't resist her, any more than any man could when she pushed so hard. 'So O'Leary went down—like 'e'd been pole-axed . . . an' that's probably exactly what the old woman said, because she was country-bred, so she's seen 'em kill their beasts stone-dead, with just the legs kickin' . . . But what she meant, I reckon, was that Mitchell knew 'e 'adn't missed, maybe. But 'e didn't care, anyway—not about O'Leary.' Reg Buller drank, and they waited for him. 'It was the woman 'e went for—to where she'd dropped down when she was hit.'

Ian was aware that his mouth was dry. He'd hardly touched his non-alcoholic lager. And he had another full glass, untouched, waiting for him.

'It was pissin' down with rain by then. But . . . Jack Butler came up, an' 'e 'ad 'is umbrella down, she said. An' 'e tried to stop Mitchell pickin' up the woman—the girl . . . But Mitchell pushed 'im away, an' cuddles 'er, an' 'olds 'er. So then Jack Butler puts up 'is umbrella again, an' 'olds it over 'em both, while all the rest of 'em comes runnin' up.'

Frances! thought Ian. And then . . . *Mitchell—?*

'An' 'e wouldn't let go of 'er, Mitchell wouldn't—not when the police came up, an' some others not in uniform . . . An' not even when the ambulance men finally came, with stretchers: 'e shoved 'em off, an' Jack Butler backs 'im up, an' points to where O'Leary is—' Buller moved from the past tense to the historic present '—so they goes to' get 'im. An' brings 'im down first, with a

262

ground-sheet over 'im, or a blanket . . . an' 'is arm 'anging over the side, like dead-meat—' Buller sniffed '—no proper scene-of-the-crime police-work for *'im*, with photographs: just get the bugger away quick, an' 'ave done with 'im! Okay—?'

Ian realized that he had made a noise of some sort, because Buller was looking at him suddenly, frowning. 'Go on, Reg.'

Buller stared at him. 'What is it?'

'It's nothing. *Go on!*'

'Okay . . . So in the end it was a policeman comes up, because Mitchell won't let go of 'er—like we used to do when there was a road accident . . . I've seen it happen, when they won't let go of 'em, just like that . . . when they know's too late.' Buller nodded at him. 'But Jack Butler—'e stops the copper, an' talks to 'im. An' then 'e talks to Mitchell—with the rain still pissin' down, an' Mitchell an' the girl are like a couple of drowned rats by then, with the rain, while Butler's been talkin' to the copper . . . So finally Mitchell picks 'er up in 'is arms, an' carries 'er down 'isself . . . with Audley be'ind 'im, an' then a copper that's picked up O'Leary's rifle, carryin' it like it was gold-dust, so as not to smudge the prints on it, with a pencil down the barrel, an' a string through the trigger-guard—she even remembered *that*, the old woman did.'

Ian saw it all, detail by detail, on the hillside he'd not yet seen, among the ruins of the abbey he'd also never seen yet—*not yet! But which he would see, by God, as soon as he was free again!*

'Yes?' He almost added, for Jenny . . . *this is one we have to write, Jen!* But then he suddenly wasn't so sure. 'Go on, Reg—*go on!*'

263

Another frown. 'Well, that's all there is, lad: they took 'er away—an' O'Leary with 'er . . . An' then they started to make bloody-sure no one ever printed the truth about what happened there.' Buller watched him. 'So what else do you want, then?'

Ian couldn't really say anything. But Jenny saved him from admitting so much. 'But . . . you haven't really told us the ending—have you, Reg?'

Buller picked up his chaser, but didn't drink it. 'Yes . . . But maybe that's the bit you won't like, Lady. An' I'd only be guessin', anyway. An' maybe it's too early to start guessin'? Not when you've got your cheque-book at the ready?' He looked at Ian.

For once Ian knew that he not only knew more than Jenny did, but also understood better what he knew: knew that he had lost forever what he could never have won anyway—*knew utterly and forever that his best book couldn't be written.*

'Go on, Reg.' His knowledge didn't set him free: it chained him. But he wanted Jenny to feel the weight of those chains.

'Okay.' Buller dropped him. 'Your bloke Masson, Lady—he may have been the greatest thing since bread an' alcohol. But he'd still have played his game the only way he knew—the way the clever buggers in the Civil Service always play it. Which is only the way everyone else plays it, anyway, if they're clever: you use the weapons you've got, that the other bloke hasn't got—okay?'

The man was trying to wrap up his can-of-worms in pretty paper. 'For God's sake, Reg—*tell her!*'

'Okay—okay!'

Jenny looked from one to the other. 'Tell me what—?'

Out of nowhere, Ian suddenly understood why Buller was delaying. And that was remarkably to Reg Buller's credit, when he was so shit-scared of 'Dr P. L. Mitchell'—enough to make them go over that wall in the rain and the dark into the railway cutting so uncomfortably and so recently. But, for his part, he couldn't let himself identify so exactly with Dr Mitchell—not yet, not yet!

He faced Jenny. 'Philip Masson wanted the job, Jen. And . . . maybe he didn't think Jack Butler was right for it—' Partly on impulse, and partly to help her accept what he was about to say, he sugared the bitter pill '—more likely . . . So he fixed a test for Butler to prove himself—handling all the different pressures, up north: not just O'Leary, but the Special Branch, and MI5, and the local police up there—and the Chief Constable—right, Reg?'

Buller nodded gratefully. And then faced up to the truth. 'It was a maybe fair test—' Then he faced Jenny in turn, to repay his debt. '—but it was a fucking dirty trick, Lady—if you'll pardon my French!'

'It was a fair test.' Ian chose to disagree. 'Because Butler pretty-well passed it at the University: he didn't catch O'Leary . . . but O'Leary's bomb didn't kill anyone.' He still tried to sugar the pill—even after Reg Buller's French. 'But then O'Leary went on to Thornervaulx. And . . . Mrs Frances Fitzgibbon died because of that, you see—?'

'You got it, lad!' Buller didn't want to owe him more than that. 'But that's where we 'ave to start guessin', Lady. Because it still could be Audley who did for him, after that. Or . . . it could be 'e

265

just turned a blind eye—see?'

The blind eye seeing confused her for a second. 'Audley—?'

''E could 'ave turned a blind eye.' Buller emphasized himself. ''E could have just pointed Mitchell in the right direction. Or he could have gone to Mitchell straight off, an' said "This bugger Masson—if 'e fell under a bus now . . . or, maybe, if 'e fell off 'is boat, an' drowned, an' no question asked . . . wouldn't that be nice, now?" An' after what 'ad 'appened to the woman 'e wouldn't 'ave needed to ask twice: 'e'd got the perfect murderer. Or almost perfect.'

Jenny stared at them both. *'Mitchell?'*

''E's got the balls for it, Lady.' Buller nodded. *'An' she was 'is woman, Lady—don't you see?'*

With a terrible certainty, Ian understood why she was so slow now, when she was usually so quick. And then he saw how he could make her understand. 'You want vengeance for Philip Masson, Jen. So Paul Mitchell wanted to even the score for Frances Fitzgibbon.'

She frowned at him. 'But Philly didn't kill her.' She looked at Reg Buller.

'"Mad Dog" O'Leary?' Buller shook his head. ''E just snapped a shot off—it could 'ave been at anyone—it could 'ave been at Mitchell . . . or it could 'ave been at Butler . . . or it could 'ave been some poor bloody copper, Lady: they're the ones who usually get the bullet.' Another shake. 'But it was *'er* . . . an' if it was your bloke Masson who put it all together, then it was *'im* that got 'er killed—that's the way I might 'ave seen it, if she'd been my woman, I tell you straight.' He cocked his head. ''Ave you ever loved anyone? Your mum and

266

dad, maybe? Or this bloke of yours, Philly—?'

Jenny had got it: it was pasted across her face, white under falling-down red.

'If it 'ud been my woman I might 'ave done it, anyway,' repeated Buller simply. 'Or . . . if I was "Dr P. L. Mitchell"—yes. Because then I'd 'ave known how to do it, too—'specially if I'd 'ad "Dr D. L. Audley" to help me.' He stared at Jenny. 'But, then again, I'm not sure about Audley to tell the truth. Because, 'avin' 'eard a thing or two about 'im, I reckon 'e'd 'ave fixed Masson some other way, short of murder.' He cocked his head at her. 'Wasn't it you said on the phone today that 'e likes to out-smart people? That 'e gets 'is jollies that way more than any other? An' she wasn't *'is* woman, after all—was she?' He shook his head finally. 'No . . . if I was bettin', then I'd say the worst 'e might 'ave done is to 'ave looked the other way. An' my money would all be on Mitchell, Lady.'

Jenny looked at Ian: she had been looking at him ever since she'd got it, he realized. 'Ian—?'

He had to face it, too. 'She was quite something, Jen. Everyone who knew her—' He thought of Mrs Simmonds for an instant '—everyone who knew her as she really was . . . she must have been quite a woman, Jen.'

'I don't mean *her*—' She brushed irritably at her hair '—I mean *Mitchell*, Ian.'

'Yes.' Ian had to face that, too. And with Paul Mitchell there was the matter of the empty shot-gun between them, as well as Frances Fitzgibbon. But it was Frances who made the decision easy. 'Actually, I think Mr Buller has got it wrong, Jen. It's clever . . . but he's wrong. Although . . . it's early days, of course.'

'Oh aye?' Buller frowned at him in surprise.

'Yes.' Never writing this marvellous book was bad enough. But helping Paul Mitchell to escape was a more immediate problem. And then, quite suddenly, he saw the easy answer. 'Or is Mitchell a saint, Reg?'

'A—?' The frown deepened.

'Only saints have the gift of bi-location, Reg: they can be in two places at once. But the rest of us can't.' Annoying Reg Buller would also help. 'Even if Mitchell wasn't saving my life this afternoon, I really don't see how he could have been killing John Tully—do you?' There was, of course, a major flaw in that dismissive argument: he didn't really know that Mitchell had been behind him, watching him, until quite late in the afternoon. But Reg Buller couldn't know that. 'I'm his alibi, Reg.'

'Oh aye?' Buller stared at him belligerently as they both faced up to John Tully's death, about which they knew next to nothing. But . . . if that had also been Mitchell, then his own ethical problems multiplied hideously. But he would think about that later: it was early days—everyone seemed agreed on that.

Buller grinned suddenly. 'You could be right at that, lad—back in '78.'

It was Ian's turn to frown. 'What?'

'Someone hired O'Leary. So someone was up to something.' Buller dropped him, almost contemptuously, in preference for Jenny. 'So now Masson's turned up again, an' there's a great big can of worms goin' to be opened up . . . An' if you want me to try an' guess what's 'appening—Lady, I can't even *begin* to guess.' He made a face at her. And then remembered his whisky chaser on the

268

table beside him, and picked it up and downed it. 'But I tell you one thing: there'll be others as well as Mitchell tryin' to stop up the rat-holes. An' the rats are all runnin' scared, bitin' whatever gets in their way—like us, for a start, maybe?' He looked at Jenny for a moment, and then nodded. 'So I'm runnin', too. An' not just from Dr P. L. Mitchell, neither, Lady.'

Mitchell himself had said it, thought Ian with a swirl of panic: *they had raised the Devil between them! And now the Devil was after them!*

Now he found himself looking at Jenny— looking, and trying not to look at her bitterly, without recrimination. Because it had been Jenny who had wanted vengeance for her beloved Philip Masson, against his own better judgement, and that had been what had started them off on this ill-judged enterprise. And from their present experience he now came upon an unpalatable truth belatedly, which his judgement and instinct hadn't been quite strong enough to formulate exactly, before it was too late—

The door opened again, without any knock, as before—

Oh God! Ian thought. *Not more drinks! Not when Reg Buller's bulbous red nose seemed even larger than usual, and they needed him stone-cold sober, as never before!*

The large barmaid was somewhat breathless, and she didn't smile at Buller this time. 'Call for you, Mr Buller—on the phone downstairs—okay?'

'Thank you, love—' Buller addressed the door as it closed again. Then he looked at them in turn. 'Well, "the bell invites me", as the bard says—eh?'

That was Reg Buller to the life, thought Ian: all

those dropped 'aitches', and half-genuine, half-false common speech. But Reg Buller had always been more than he seemed to be. So now, when Jenny had started them off with *Macbeth*, Reg Buller was quoting *Macbeth* back to them: he either knew it from old, or he'd looked it up after Jenny had quoted it at him. And now he'd quoted it back at them, when it was too-damn close to the bone for comfort.

'Wait!' Jenny surfaced first: Jenny was never better than in danger. 'If we're running, Mr Buller—*Reg*—?' She half-looked at Ian, as though to remind him that even Paul Mitchell had wanted them to run.

That was their old technique: one picked up the unasked question from the other. 'Where are we going, Reg?' He moved slightly, so as to block Buller's passage towards the door. 'We're running . . . where?'

Buller grinned at him. 'We ain't exactly *runnin'*, Ian lad.' He replaced his empty beer-glass on the table, beside the empty whisky-glass, 'Because I don't reckon there's an 'ole deep enough for us to run to, not now—not even if we go an' call on the Lady's dad, even—' He started to move towards Ian.

'*Where*, Mr Buller?' Jenny moved too, alongside Ian.

'Not "where", Lady.' Buller stopped. '*Who* is the name of our game now, I reckon—*where* just takes us to him. And we know where.'

Now they were shoulder-to-shoulder in the way, just like in the old days. Only now . . . Frances Fitzgibbon was between them, somehow, thought Ian: now they were just business associates, and

270

allies at need.

'Spain, Mr Buller?' Jenny drew a breath.

'Audley, Lady.' Buller's expression hardened. 'The only bloke who can get us out from under is Audley. Because . . . if 'e knows, then we can maybe make a deal with 'im. An' . . . if 'e doesn't know . . . then 'e'll know what's what when we've told 'im. An' then 'e'll 'ave to be on our side, to save 'is own skin.' He started to move towards them. 'Okay?'

Ian didn't know which of them moved first. But they both moved, anyway.

And he completed that belated truth then: *as with lies, and with all the sins, great and little, so with vengeance and revenge: you never knew, until too late, what a great work you'd started out on—until too late!*

PART TWO

JENNIFER FIELDING
AND
THE GHOSTS OF SALAMANCA

CHAPTER ONE

Although the sun had nowhere near reached its full
strength Jenny already felt a prickle of sweat
between her shoulder blades. And, as she sensed it,
another spike of corn-stubble gouged her ankle
painfully, reminding her again that she had chosen
the wrong shoes this morning. She had planned to
look cool and elegant for this encounter, and she
was going to end up a perfect mess, sweaty, injured
and angry. And it was all Ian's fault—bloody,
bloody Ian!

'Ouch!' She stopped to examine the damage.
There was a glistening dark-red globule marking
the injury, not far from the unsightly smear of its
predecessor, which was mixed with red dust.
Sweaty, injured, angry and *dirty*—bloody, bloody,
bloody Ian! 'Wait for a moment! I'm hurt,
Ian—Ian?'

He hadn't even stopped. He was striding ahead,
quite oblivious of her. And now she couldn't even
see the rocky plateau towards which he started for,
when they'd left the car on the edge of that
fly-blown village: there was a long undulation of
lethal corn-stubble blocking the view. And she was
wearing the wrong shoes.

'*Ian!*' (They weren't really the wrong shoes: they
were her bloody *best* shoes . . . or, they had been,
anyway; it was because he had insisted on leaving
the car there, bloody-miles from where they were
going—that had made them wrong. '*I can see his
car,*' he had said, lowering his binoculars, speaking
in his strange new voice. '*It's up the track, just by*

275

that hut—a silver Rover Sterling. But we'll go from here. I want to walk . . . I want to think. There's plenty of time. Come on, then.')

He had stopped at last, silhouetted in the glare at the top of the rise against the pure blue cloudless sky. But he still wasn't looking at her: he had his binoculars glued to his eyes again, still oblivious of her.

Well, that bloody-settled it, thought Jenny. This was the new Ian—a problem Ian, and a difficult one; and all the more of a problem, and all the more difficult, because the old one had always been easy and simple, and just tedious in the usual obvious ways, like a dumb-clever brother—

'*Ian! Sod you!*' she shouted at his back.

Now, at last, after he'd observed what he wanted to check on, he turned towards her. 'What is it?'

'It's all right, darling.' She realized as he turned that the greatest mistake of all would be to whinge, like a man. Indeed, to whinge as Ian himself did (or, had used to do; but this was a different Ian, she had to remember). 'It's just . . . your legs are longer than mine . . . Have you spotted him?'

'Yes.' He turned back, away from her, lifting the binoculars again.

'Yes?' She was conscious of looking at the new Ian with new eyes, now that he wasn't interested in looking at her. That 'wimp' image had always been unfair, of course: he had been very far from that in Beirut that time, everyone had said afterwards; more like a hero, they'd said, but she'd taken that with a pinch of salt (or, anyway, taken it for granted: in wars and emergencies, scholars and poets down the ages had rarely been among the skulkers . . . and a scholar and a poet was what the

276

poor darling really was—or, in a better world, might have been). 'Where?'

'On the Greater Arapile.' He lowered the binoculars, and then pointed. 'See where his car's parked—the Rover? Just beyond that hut. Imagine that's the centre of a clock, and the hour-hand is pointing at eleven—follow that line up to the top, Jenny. He's standing just to the right of that monument. It must be a battle memorial of some sort.'

Jenny shaded her eyes and stared.

'"The Greater Arapile".' The binoculars came up again. 'That's where the French were, when the battle started in 1812. And the Duke of Wellington came along behind us, from the "Lesser Arapile" to the village. He must have had his lunch just about where we left the car: that was when he saw they'd over-extended their line of march, and threw his chicken leg over his shoulder and said "That will do!". So the story goes, anyway.'

Either it was the glare, or perhaps she needed glasses, but she couldn't see a damn thing in the desolate parched landscape. 'I really don't need to know about the battle—do I, darling?'

'It's an interesting battle.' He spoke distantly, as though to a child. 'When people think of Wellington they think of Waterloo . . . like, when they think of Nelson, it's Trafalgar . . . But Nelson's finest victory was the Nile—or maybe it was at St Vincent that he really showed what he was made of . . . So this was maybe Wellington's "finest hour" . . . ye-ess: *That will do!*"'

Jenny squinted hopelessly at a blur of boring fields and boring rocks, and knew that it wasn't her own finest hour. Or, anyway, not yet. 'I didn't know it was the Duke of Wellington we were interested in, darling. I thought it was David Audley.'

'We could do a book on Spain instead, you know.' The new Ian was impervious to sarcasm. 'All those people on holiday on the Costa Blanca, and the Costa Brava . . . and now Spain in the Common Market. And the ETTA link with the IRA . . . And we could take the history all the way from the Black Prince, and the War of the Spanish Succession, and Wellington . . . *and* the Civil War, with the International Brigades—' The binoculars went down, and then up again '—and the phenomenon of peaceful transition from fascism to democracy . . . I met a woman recently who is an expert on Spanish economic development, and what she had to say was *extremely* interesting—*ahh!*'

The new Ian was also becoming sassy in pushing alternative projects to the one which mattered to her. Although the one plus-factor was that at least he seemed for a moment to have forgotten Mrs Frances Fitzgibbon, *alias* Marilyn Francis, about whom he had obsessively taxed poor Reg Buller all the way from London to Madrid to the exclusion of almost everything else.

Reg Buller—? The thought of Reg (and of Reg complaining about Spanish beer, even more vociferously than about Spanish food) momentarily diverted her: in Spain Reg Buller was much less of an asset than in London; he seemed somehow to have withdrawn into himself, as though he no longer approved of what they were doing in seeking out Audley; although it couldn't be Audley whom he was worrying about—more likely he was torn between self-preservation and his duty to his

278

paymasters on the one hand, and a sneaking identification with Paul Mitchell, their new suspect, on the other hand—could that be it?

'"Ahh"?' It probably was it. Because Reg and the Police Force had parted company long ago not so much because of his drinking (that would have been no great sin, the way he held it) as because of his sneaking sympathy for underdogs and minor villains versus authority. But it was still an added burden now, when Ian had gone funny on her too. 'What is it, darling?'

'I think I've spotted the wife.' He concentrated on the lower part of the plateau.

'Where?' Reg Buller was all the back-up they had, somewhere behind them in the car, and probably drinking already from his hip-flask. But Ian was her immediate problem.

'Or it may be the daughter . . . They're both tall and thin and blonde . . . But what on earth is she doing—?' He concentrated for another moment. Then he lowered the binoculars and pointed. 'Just down there, left of the car—in the ploughed field . . . Come on, Jen—let's get going.'

'Hold on.' It was still a long and uncomfortable walk to where he was pointing and she felt mutinous. 'Why are we walking all this way?'

'Eh?' The bloody binoculars came up again. 'I told you, Jen: I want to think a bit. And I also want to look at the battlefield.'

'You want to—?' She bit off her anger, and looked round instead to help her count to ten: it was (she could see at a glance) a most excellent and absolute, and suitable and tailor-made . . . *battlefield*: apart from the modern railway-line which ran diagonally through the valley between the two rocky plateaux, with a couple of grotty station-buildings halfway along it in the middle of the open fields, and that single even grottier hut where Audley's car was parked, there was absolutely nothing to be seen. So, once upon a time, the British and the French could have killed each other in their thousands quite happily, without inconveniencing anyone or damaging anything of value. But that 1812 suitability still didn't answer the question. 'Why do you have to do that, Ian darling?'

'I don't have to. But I want to.' Now he was studying a more distant ridge to the right of the Greater Arapile. 'It's what Audley's doing today, Jen. I told you in the car—remember?'

What Jenny chiefly remembered from the short journey out of Salamanca was that he had been irritatingly masterful and matter-of-fact and decisive. But then he had been like that for the last thirty-six hours, ever since Reg Buller had sold them his theory about Paul Mitchell and that wretched woman.

'So what?' What cautioned her was that he had also been efficient with it, in coaxing information about David Audley's whereabouts from a series of slightly bewildered Spaniards while she had stood on the sidelines like an idiot girlfriend whose main function was to stare at the ceiling of a series of bedrooms.

'I told you, Jen.' Now he wasn't so much masterful as quite damnably long-suffering. 'The daughter prattled to that man the receptionist found for us in the hotel after we checked in—the one who spoke English? They were here all yesterday, but they were "doing" the English side of the battle,
280

and that ridge over there—' he pointed. 'So today
they were going to do the French side. And the
French were up *there*—' The pointing finger was
re-directed towards the Greater Arapile '—and
that's where Audley is. But I wish I knew *why*.'

'Why . . . what?' If he'd wanted to make her feel
even more stupid, he was succeeding.

He sighed. 'Why is he studying the battle of
Salamanca?'

She mustn't lose her temper. 'Does it matter?
He's supposed to be a historian. Don't historians
study battlefields?'

'But he's a medievalist. The Peninsular War just
isn't his period.'

She *mustn't* lose her temper. 'I expect he'll tell us
why, darling, if we ask him nicely.' But now he
wasn't even looking at her again, damn it—*and
damn him*! 'I'll ask about Philip Masson, darling.
And you can ask about the battle of Salamanca . . .
and Mrs Fitzgibbon too, if you like—'

He looked at her then, even as she was already
regretting what she'd just said. And the way he'd
looked at her made her regret the unnecessary
words even more, however much he'd asked for
them. 'I'm sorry, Ian—'

'Don't be sorry, Jenny dear. I shall only ask him
one question about Frances Fitzgibbon. And I
think I already know the answer to it.' He shook his
head slowly. 'But it's of no importance to you, I
agree. So shall we go, then?'

The hateful corn-stubble ended eventually, but
with a deep drainage-ditch (as though it ever rained
in this parched landscape!). And Ian leapt the ditch

281

and went on again without a backward glance, leaving her to take the longer route beside it to the track, while he struck off on his own—

Hateful, hateful Ian! It isn't as though I haven't prayed that you'd meet some nice girl at one of your Christian Fellowship meetings, rather than making hopeless sheep's eyes at me! But now you have to go and fall for some crazy dead woman who wouldn't have given you a second look in life—a bloody ghost-woman! And now she's going to be the death of our partnership. Because I'm not going to play second-fiddle to any bloody ghost-woman for evermore—damn you, Ian Robinson! And damn you, Frances Fitzgibbon, too!

She reached the dusty track at last, sweating like a horse and with her hair coming down. And she reached it ahead of him, because he had stopped for another of those exclusive binocular-sweeps of his.

What was he thinking about? Was he 'doing' his battlefield, like David Audley—imagining himself a poor sweating redcoat advancing towards the great unclimbable rocky prow of the headland with French cannon-balls whistling past his ears? Or was he back, not in 1812, but in 1978, with his ghost-woman—his ghost-woman who had been Paul Mitchell's real woman—? Was he practising his question—the question to which he already knew the answer?

She walked up the track to intercept him, forcing herself to recover her breath, and some shreds of dignity and self-respect.

282

It was the daughter, not the wife, she could see now: a tall blonde child mooching up and down the furrows of a newly ploughed field on the edge of the fallen scree from the Greater Arapile plateau, head down and intent on the red earth at her feet, as though she was looking for something she'd lost.

She had been foolish. Ian Robinson no longer mattered, any more than Frances Fitzgibbon had ever mattered (let alone Ian Robinson's question about Frances Fitzgibbon). And Paul Mitchell didn't matter. And even David Audley didn't really matter—even he was only a means to an end. It was only Philly, dear beloved Philly, who had always been there when she needed him—always there until some bastard had decided otherwise! And now some bastard was going to pay—that was all that mattered now—

She had a plan.

And she even had time to put back her hair. And it even went back easily.

'I want to talk to the child first, darling. Okay?'

The new Ian frowned at the old Jenny. 'What about Audley?'

Maybe she had done him an injustice. But now wasn't the time to think about injustice and Ian Robinson: this was justice-time and Philly-time now. 'Audley's not going to go away. Not while I'm talking to his daughter.'

'No . . .' Even the new Ian couldn't argue with that. But the new Ian didn't like being thwarted. 'But what's the use of talking to her?'

'It's what I want to do.' The old Jenny frankly didn't give a damn. 'You wanted to "do" the

283

battlefield of Salamanca, darling. So I want to "do" David Audley's daughter.' She could even smile at him now. 'We're still partners, aren't we?'

'Yes—of course—' He stopped suddenly. 'If you want to . . . okay, then.'

So now you know, too! thought Jenny. And it was strangely like that first moment of falling-out-of-love, when what one already suspected in oneself was confirmed by the sudden doubt in the no-longer-loved-one's eyes, rather than by any outright lie.

'I want to, then.' But now she also wanted more than that. 'What's her name? How old is she?' It irritated her that she knew so little: that she was asking these questions now, and not before, when there had been plenty of time. 'What do you know about her?'

'Her name is Catherine, with a "C". Because he calls her "Cathy".' He nodded towards his Arapile. 'Like in *Wuthering Heights*.' Then he shrugged. 'I don't know anything else. Except . . . she talks to Spaniards. So she isn't shy . . . even though she is only fifteen—or maybe sixteen, I suppose—' A faint memory of the old diffident Ian animated him suddenly. 'Why d'you want to talk to her, Jen? Audley's up there—' The Wuthering Arapile received another nod '—in fact, I rather think he's watching us, actually.'

Yes, thought Jenny cruelly: *you don't want to talk to any fifteen-year-old girl, do you! Fifteen-year-old girls probably frighten you. So at least you won't interrupt me!*

It was easy to ignore him. There was a wide-open gap in the fence inviting her towards the child, who was no more than fifty yards away among the furrows, staring intently down at the ground, pretending to ignore them both.

But Ian had got her right, exactly: mid-teens, tall and very blonde . . . and thin, almost flat: she'd never be a Page Three girl, for sure!

'Have you lost something?' On the strength of her own great age, and Catherine Audley's alleged 'not-shyness', she called out confidently.

The child had already observed them covertly, while keeping her head down. But now she straightened up and stared directly at them from behind the protection of huge sunglasses which emphasized the thinness of her face, first at Jenny, then with a small movement of her head towards Ian, and finally back at Jenny. 'No.'

Jenny felt herself being scrutinized woman-to-woman, from hair to unsuitable shoes, via her sweat-stained dress, and returned the compliment automatically: *jeans* (but designer jeans), *royal blue sweatshirt* (bearing the legend 'Buffalo Bar—Murdo—South Dakota', but without any sign of sweat), *and a Givenchy silk scarf artfully knotted*: the shoes alone were ordinary—*ordinary schoolgirl's uniform-issue, square-toed* (but that only served to remind her of her own sore feet, damn it!).

The child continued to stare at her, giving nothing away from behind the darkened lenses. And Jenny felt a trickle of sweat run down from her throat to lose itself between her breasts, and adjusted 'not-shy' to 'self-possessed' as the gap between their ages was critically narrowed.

'You're looking for something?' She realized too late that the question was a stupid one. Even though there plainly wasn't anything to look for in the newly-turned red-brown earth, Catherine

285

Audley had quite obviously been looking for something. 'What have you lost, Miss Audley?' She threw the name in deliberately, to regain the upper hand as though it was a fight between equals.

The child frowned, nonplussed by her recognition.

'It's Catherine, isn't it?' Jenny smiled sweetly. 'I'm a friend of Willy Arkenshaw's—Lady Arkenshaw?'

'Oh!' The frown dissolved. 'Willy—yes!'

'What have you lost, dear?' Jenny tried to open the age-gap again.

'I haven't lost anything.' Catherine Audley relaxed perceptibly for a moment. But then she began to frown again. 'I'm looking for bullets . . . Are you looking for my father?'

'Bullets?' The counter-punch caught Jenny unprepared, so that it took her a second to recover. And then she decided to leave the second question. 'Bullets?'

'Not *bullets*, actually—*musket balls*, I mean.' Catherine Audley touched the frame of her glasses with a nervous gesture. 'Do you know my father? I mean . . . if you know Willy—?'

If this was the teenage daughter, what would the father be like? Jenny wondered uneasily. 'No, dear. But—I've heard a lot about him.' Another sweet smile was called for. 'Musket balls?'

'Yes.' The child seemed to accept her lying-truth: it would take another year or two for her to learn that grown-ups were liars. 'There was a battle here, Miss—? Miss—?'

Saved by good manners! thought Jenny. 'Oh, I'm sorry, dear! I'm Jennifer Fielding—Jenny?' *Smile again Jenny*. 'And you are . . . Catherine?

286

Cathy—?'

'Cathy.' The child nodded. But then cocked her head. 'Fielding—'

'"Jenny", please.' She felt the smile painted on her lips as she wondered if the child watched television, and how good her memory was from not so long ago. Because after the Beirut business, when they'd had all the television coverage, the TV people had made a big thing of 'Fielding-ffulke', making a joke of it all the way back to 1066 and all that. 'Yes, I know there was a battle here—1812, was it? And have you found any musket balls, Cathy?'

'No.' Cathy looked at her steadily. 'I'm not having much luck. In fact, I'm not having *any* luck, to tell the truth.'

Jenny felt firmer ground under her feet. 'Did you expect to find any?'

But now Cathy was looking past her, at Ian.

'Oh—Cathy, I'm sorry!' She had clean forgotten about Ian herself. And she had done that in the past, and felt guilty about it; but now all she required of him was politeness. 'This is Mr Ian Robinson, dear: he's a friend of mine.' She looked down at the broken earth at her feet, and couldn't see any bullets (*why the hell should the child look for . . . bullets, for God's sake!*) 'Ian—Miss Catherine Audley—?'

'Yes.' His voice came soft and cold, and quite without interest. 'Hullo, Miss Audley.'

'Mr Robinson.' The child stared at him.

Jenny felt her doubts increasing. Because Mr Robinson had also appeared on the damned television programme, even if only briefly: Ian typically self-effacingly, even though he'd been the

287

real hero, and she'd not really been the heroine at all. *Damn!*

But if Cathy Audley remembered him, and recognized him, his lack of interest froze her out now—just as it had frozen Jenny herself out, these last few hours. Ian was only interested in one woman, and she wasn't here. Indeed, she wasn't anywhere.

'Did you expect to find any . . . musket balls, Cathy?' Jenny controlled her fears carefully. Because Ian's *Frances Fitzgibbon* obsession was all very well, in its place, however unhealthy. But now, when this eccentric child could lead them straight to Audley, Ian and his obsession were an inconvenience—even, a quite unnecessary obstacle, which made her wish that he wasn't here with her, when she had more urgent questions on her mind. So—*sod Ian*!, as she looked down at the earth at her feet. 'Musket balls—here?'

'Oh yes!' Cathy Audley matched her move. 'On the Somme I found lots of them. Or not musket balls, actually—lots of shrapnel balls, I mean. But musket balls must be just like shrapnel balls—like round—?' Her head came down so close to Jenny that she exchanged a strong whiff of childishly over-applied scent '—and there should be *lots* of them hereabouts . . . because the poor Portuguese charged up here . . . and then down again . . . and then the French charged after them. And finally the British charged. So there *should* be lots. But I just can't find any . . .'

Cathy trailed off, and they both concentrated on scanning the field together for a moment, to the exclusion of all other matters.

Jenny straightened up finally. 'No—I see what
288

you mean. Perhaps they've just been ploughed into the ground, Cathy?'

'Oh no! It doesn't work like that.' Cathy shook her head vehemently. 'There's someone I know who's an expert, and he says that ploughing brings them up to the surface, it doesn't bury them. And I'm sure this is the right place.' She reached into the back-pocket of her jeans, producing a crumpled piece of paper which she then unfolded with grubby fingers. 'This was practically the centre of the battle—at the start, anyway.'

It was a map, neatly hand-drawn, but now rendered incomprehensible with its profusion of little red and blue squares, and diagonally red-and-white and blue-and-white rectangles, which followed the criss-crossing arrows of the rival armies' advances and retirements around and beyond the Greater Arapile.

'We're *here*—' Cathy stabbed the map, and then shook her head. 'I simply don't understand it. It's most *vexing*.'

'Yes.' It was curious how, when Cathy Audley had stared at her she had seemed grown up, but now she was a child again. 'Do you collect . . . bullets and things, Cathy?'

'No . . . not really.' The child-Cathy grinned at her. 'But, it's interesting *finding* things—isn't it? I got some super barbed-wire at Verdun. My father says it's German. It's got very long barbs on it, and they're much closer together than on modern barbed-wire.'

Jenny felt her jaw drop open.

'People in America collect barbed-wire, you know.' Cathy Audley nodded seriously. 'There are hundreds of different varieties, going back to the middle of the nineteenth century, almost. Some bits are worth hundreds of dollars, my father says—the first bits they used in the Wild West, I suppose.'

The repetition of 'my father says' recalled Jenny to reality. She had established herself with the child. And now the child would lead her to the father, complete with an introduction of sorts. 'And your father collects battlefields, does he?'

The child's eyes sparkled suddenly, and she laughed. 'Oh . . . he collects everything—he's like a great big jackdaw, Mummy says: he never throws away anything.' She shook her head, becoming older again as she shared her mother's despair. 'But . . . yes, he *does* collect battlefields. In fact, this is a "battlefield holiday"—at least, the first two weeks are.' She grinned fondly. 'Medieval ones coming down: Crécy, Poitiers and Chastillon—that's the place where the French finally beat us, in the Hundred Years' War, you know—did you know?'

'No.' Jenny sensed Ian chafing nearby. But Ian was wrong to chafe: so long as they had the daughter, then they couldn't lose the father.

'Oh yes! There's even a monument to poor old John Talbot, who got killed there, by the river. And my father says . . . losing the American colonies was no great loss—no one minds losing *them*. But losing Bordeaux, where the wine comes from—that really was the most rotten luck. Because it's much too good for the French, he says.' She giggled again. 'And he said all that to a French couple and an American couple we met at the Parador at Ciudad Rodrigo—honestly, I thought Mummy was going to *kill* him . . . But that was later on. Because from Chastillon we came over the Pass of Roncesvalles—where Roland was killed . . .

that was *super* . . . And then down the other side, to a lovely old Parador, in a medieval hospital—that was so he could show us the battlefield at Najera, where the English longbowmen wiped out that Spanish-and-French army in five minutes—like machine-gunners, Father said—*wow!*'

Suddenly, Jenny understood: this poor child had been holidaying for nearly a fortnight now, with her overwhelming father and disapproving mother, between whom she hadn't got a word in edgeways. But now she'd met a sympathetic English-speaking stranger, so the floodgates of pent-up speech had burst, just as they had done with Spanish waiters.

'But this isn't a medieval battlefield surely, Miss Audley?' Ian intruded suddenly with the same silly question which he had put to her.

'Oh *no*—' Cathy Audley fielded the statement almost joyfully. 'But we did the medieval battles the first week, you see—and Mummy's having a week in Paris, for shopping, on the way back—' The grin twisted. '—and so am I . . . Father's going back to work and *we* are going shopping, Mummy and I!'

'So "Mummy" wasn't so stupid, thought Jenny: Audley himself paid for his idiosyncrasies—and quite properly, too!

'The middle week's the Peninsular War,' Cathy Audley concentrated on Ian. 'We've just come from Ciudad Rodrigo: another *super* old Parador . . . except Father hated the food there—' She cocked her head at him suddenly, almost shyly, yet unchildlike. 'Are you staying at the Salamanca Parador, Mr—Mr Robinson?'

Ian nodded, matching her shyness. 'We just checked in this morning, Miss Audley.' Then he blinked. 'The . . . Peninsular War?'

'Yes.' Nod. 'We stormed Ciudad Rodrigo in 1812. And my father . . . he wanted to see where "Black Bob" Crauford was killed—and where they buried him in the ditch there . . . I mean, he used to flog them, and hang them, but they loved him, my father says . . . He's a great admirer of General Crauford.' Cathy Audley nodded seriously. 'He wanted me to see Badajoz too, where our army did a lot of raping-and-pillaging. But Mummy said we didn't have enough time for that.'

'Why the Peninsular War?' Ian, when a 'why' eluded him, was as persistent as any child, regardless of raping and pillaging.

'Oh, not the whole of the war.' The child accepted his curiosity as quite natural. 'It went on for years and years, you know. But my father is only interested in 1812. And really he's only interested in *here*, because Salamanca is our *special* battlefield, Mr Robinson: my father has been talking about coming here for ages and ages.' She blushed slightly. 'This is a sort of reward for my A-levels—' The blush combined with a grin '—this . . . and Paris.'

A-level exam results were a blow below the belt: she had waited herself for them, through endless days a dozen years ago, to find out whether she had been accepted by the university of her choice, and it had been Philly who had been there, waiting for her at the last, as she'd scraped through by the skin of her teeth, with champagne ready for congratulation or commiseration! Philly, oh Philly—damn them all!

'So . . . you passed then?' Now it was her turn to
292

grit her teeth and concentrate on the matter in hand, all sweetness and light. (*It had been mid-August then, a month ago now; so, to travel safely from Parador to Parador, Audley must have booked ahead, planning this holiday-reward; so that meant he hadn't prudently removed himself from the country, to avoid awkward questions after Philly's body had been found—? Or had it been just luck, and not just confidence in his clever daugher?*)

'What's so special about Salamanca, Miss Audley?' Ian, having decided to be involved, was even more single-minded in seeking answers to questions which were bugging him—quite oblivious of the child's awkward modesty about her results (*straight bloody A-grades, with distinctions in the special papers, the clever little beast? But she mustn't let her sour grapes betray her smile!*).

'Oh yes!' The child seized on the question eagerly again: it saved her from immodesty, for a guess; but also (if she was normal) she properly preferred men to women now, for another guess. 'My great-great-great-grandfather was killed here, you see. In 1812, at Salamanca, Mr—' She floundered momentarily.

'"Ian",' Jenny supplied the Christian name tartly. 'He answers to "Ian", Cathy. But . . . your great-great . . . grandfather was killed . . . *here?*'

'Oh?' The child blinked at her for another moment. But then her years increased again as she measured Jenny up, and took in her slightly battered condition to even up the reckoning. And then turned back to Ian coolly. 'Not actually *here*, I mean.' She smiled at Ian and then swung on her heel and pointed away past the rocky headland of the Greater Arapile towards the distant ridge behind it, on which a long line of scrubby trees marked the skyline. 'That's where the British cavalry charged. And my great-great-great-grandfather was in the charge: he charged right through two whole French divisions . . . before he was killed, right at the end. So this is our special family battlefield, do you see?'

Wow! thought Jenny: Ian had wanted an answer to his 'why'—and he had got it to the last syllable. 'Like . . . the Charge of the Light Brigade—?'

'No—not at all!' Ian's voice was stiff with contempt. 'He must have been in General Le Marchant's charge—' He began by addressing her, but then dismissed her, to turn the words back to Cathy Audley '—and General Le Marchant was killed up there, too—in the moment of victory—?'

'That's right—gosh!' The child was quite enchanted by this supremely useless piece of information. 'You *know* about the battle, Mr Robinson?'

'I know about Le Marchant, Miss Audley.' Whether Ian really knew about 'General Le Marchant' hung in the balance for an instant: it could be either that he had always known, because it was the sort of thing he knew: or it could be that he had just done his homework last night, to know just enough, but no more than that. 'He was the one man in the army who was a scientific soldier—? A Guernsey man—from the Channel Islands?'

'That's *right*!' Cathy Audley positively bubbled with pleasure. 'You really *do* know about the battle, don't you!' Then she frowned. 'But that's silly, isn't it!'

'Silly?'

Not silly, thought Jenny, amending her previous

contempt abjectly as she realized what Ian was doing—and what he had done, which she hadn't even thought to do—

'I don't mean *you*—gosh! I mean *me*.' Cathy hunched her shoulders. 'I mean . . . you wouldn't be here, traipsing around like this, if you weren't interested in the battle. So . . . you're probably a historian—are you a historian?' She cocked her head at Ian, but not coquettishly: it was a simple, straight question, as unfeminine as it was unshy, but with logic behind it. 'Or are you a dragoon?'

'A—?' Ian was good, having done his homework. But he wasn't *that* good. 'A . . . dragoon, Miss Audley?'

'My father was a dragoon, in the war . . . Not the Peninsular War, I mean . . . but *his* war.' Cathy threw out her inadequate chest with filial pride. 'He wasn't on a horse, of course—he was in a tank . . . He doesn't even *like* horses . . . But, then, he doesn't much like tanks, either. Even though he's always talking about them.' Pride quite vanished beneath honesty. 'But . . . my great-great-great-grandfather was a horse-dragoon, you see. And he was shot right beside General Le Marchant—in "the moment of victory", just like you said . . . And my father says all British dragoons should come here, because this was one of the best charges they ever made. But, of course, he wanted me to see it because of great-great-great-grandfather . . . Are you a historian, Mr Robinson?'

'Not a historian, Miss Audley. Or a dragoon. But we *are* writers, Miss Fielding and I.' Ian smiled and nodded at the child. 'And we are thinking of writing a book on Spain—aren't we, Miss Fielding?'

'Possibly, Mr Robinson.'

'And if we do, we shall certainly mention the battle of Salamanca, Miss Audley—General Le Marchant's charge.'

'And the dragoons, Cathy.' It was Jenny's turn to smile. 'At least, we will if your father will tell us all about them—would he do that, do you think?'

'Oh . . . yes—' Cathy looked up towards the Greater Arapile '—well, I don't see why not.' She came back to Jenny. 'So long as you make allowance for him not being in a very good mood, I mean.' She made a face at them both. 'He's been like that ever since—' She stopped abruptly.

'Ever since—?' *Ever since they tipped him off that there was trouble back home*, thought Jenny. It was only to be expected. And with Fielding and Robinson on the loose it was doubly to be expected. 'Something he ate, dear?'

'Oh no!' Cathy was quite disarmed by the fatuousness of the suggestion. 'He just got a phone call from home. And he hates being bothered by the office when we're on holiday, you see.'

'Don't we all, dear!' Jenny laughed. 'But . . . is that him up there, watching over us? Up by that . . . what is it? It looks like a sort of monument—?'

'Yes.' Cathy followed her glance. Then she waved suddenly. 'All right—let's go and see him, then—'

Once she had her second wind the climb wasn't so bad, really: even, it was preferable to the corn-stubble, so long as she took care to avoid the occasional thistle.

'See these walls, Jenny?' Ian had stopped to let her catch up, while the child bounded ahead. 'They must have cultivated this land right up to here in the old days—' He spoke loudly, but then dropped his voice as she came level with him '—if Mitchell's phoned him he'll know who we are, and what we're up to. So he may even be expecting us, Jen.'

She waved at Cathy, who had also stopped now. 'Surprise, surprise. So he's expecting us, then.' She turned, as though to admire the view, and saw that the deceptive undulations of the fields had already flattened out far below her. It was hard to imagine that flesh-and-blood could ever have been so brave (or so stupid?) to march all the way she'd come, buttoned-up and constricted in silly uniforms and weighed down by weapons and equipment, and through a hail of Cathy Audley's elusive musket balls. But then, it was also fairly way-out, the process which had brought her so far from home, to this unlikely place: she was here because Philly had once carried Daddy on his back in far-off Korea (another unlikely place, by God!)—and because an Audley ancestor had once charged to death-and-glory here, to find his unmarked grave.

Philly had almost had an unmarked grave of his own, she thought. And the thought turned her round again. 'Come on, Ian. We've got work to do.'

Cathy was waiting for them.

'See there, Miss Fielding—Jenny—?' She pointed at the ground.

'What?' Behind the child the final tumble-home of the Greater Arapile rose more steeply, in a jumble of rocks. But it would be no more exhausting than climbing up to Piccadilly from the Underground without the benefit of the moving escalator.

297

'Autumn crocuses, Miss Fielding.' The child pointed again.

Jenny looked down. And there at her feet was a tiny delicate pale-mauve flower with a bright white-into-yellow centre, thrusting out of the dead grass like a promise of life-in-death.

'Isn't it beautiful, Miss Fielding?'

'Yes, dear.' Jenny stepped carefully around the crocus. And then she saw another, and another . . . and some were already wilting in the fierce Spanish sun, as ephemeral as butterflies. 'Very beautiful.'

'Here, Jen—' Ian reached down to help her up over a steeper place, almost like the old Ian.

Now they were on the edge of the summit, with bedrock and tumbled rock all around them.

Their hands and their eyes met. And it wasn't strange that he looked sad: they were at the beginning of their long goodbye; which had always been going to come one day, inevitably; but that didn't make it any sadder, now that they could both see it ahead of them: maybe they would write a Spanish book together, but it would be their last book; or maybe he'd write it, while she was frying some other and very different fish.

But this was Philly's day for her, anyway—

She felt his strength as he hauled her up, and mourned the loss of it already. But then she saw Audley, waiting for them.

And this was Philly's hour.

The sun beat down on her head, hotter than ever, behaving as she always felt it should now that they were closer to it, melting her as it had melted the wax holding Icarus's feathers to his wings. But there was a lump of ice-cold resolution in the centre of her which resisted the heat—which even seemed to expand as she stared past them, at Audley—

Audley waiting for them: he knew who they were, and what they were, and why they were here. So he was sitting there, on the plinth of the monument, on its cooler shadowed side: Audley still unhappy this morning, after last night's phone-call, but cool and calm and collected now, and ready for them—

'Wait a minute, Ian.' She used the last ounce of her waning influence over him in her voice. 'Please wait!'

He stopped. 'What is it, Jenny?'

'There's no hurry. He's not going away.' She looked round deliberately, taking her time; at first seeing nothing, then seeing everything with sudden clarity in the crystal air.

The Greater Arapile was shaped like a ship, exactly: long and flat-topped, and barely a dozen yards wide. And they were standing halfway down the deck, between the super-tanker prow and the slight rise to the monument; and the deck itself was covered with a carpet of dead grass, brown and withered, through which an astonishing profusion of Cathy Audley's delicate autumn crocuses burst out defiantly.

'What an amazing place!' It wasn't particularly amazing, actually: it was just another piece of the great yellow openness that was so much of Spain, with nothing to betray the great and terrible event which it had once witnessed. In fact, *nothing* had happened here since that moment when the rolling fields below had been black with marching lines and columns, and screaming horses, and thundering cannon. But there wasn't the slightest echo of the past up here now, any more than of the future.

But she had to say *something*.

And, by God! something was going to happen here now!

'Look!' She saw a sudden flick of movement in a jumble of rocks on the flank of the ridge.

'What—?'

'There—' She pointed. 'It's a fox—with long pointy-ears—*see*!'

Obligingly, the fox moved again, and became visible for an instant before it vanished into the hillside.

'Yes—!' In that same instant Ian's face lit up, with pure pleasure, and he was just like the old Ian at the sight of any small interesting thing, like a new postage stamp on a letter, or an old building which caught his eye. (Had he welcomed the sight of that first autumn crocus? Or had he had eyes only for Audley, and thought only for his Frances Fitzgibbon?) But then he frowned at her, and was the new Ian again. 'What are you playing at, Jen?'

Now they were at last facing each other in the face of the enemy, and facing their moment of truth. 'Audley's mine, Ian—he's not for you. I want him.'

He breathed out. 'Because of Philip Masson?'

'Because of Philip Masson. And because this was my idea, not yours—*my* truth . . . not yours, Ian.'

'Your revenge, more like. And that's the wrong way to look for truth, Jen—it's a *bad* way, Jen.'

300

He was right, of course. He was always *fucking*
right—going to church on Sunday, and giving to
charity, and never getting drunk on a Saturday
night, or any other night! But she wanted to hurt
him, not to argue morality with him. 'And you want
the truth about some silly woman who forgot to
pack her gun when she went to arrest a terrorist? A
woman you've never met—who wouldn't have
given you the time of day if you had met her?
That's *stupid*—' The image of Philly came back to
her: *Philly smiling his big slow smile at her, when they
met—Philly hugging her, godfatherly—the smell of his
pipe-tobacco and his malt whisky, Philly strong and
safe—Philly praising her, Philly laughing as the
champagne cork popped . . . even Philly in that rare
unguarded moment, looking at her with that
ungodfatherly look, of naked-desire-well-controlled . . .
which she'd shared—oh! how she'd shared!—but
which she hadn't truly understood until it was too
late—*

Too late! Too late!

But she had hit him hard. And that was all that
mattered. 'He's mine, Ian. Even if we don't write
this book . . . he's *mine*.' She corrected her own
thought: all that mattered was that *someone was
going to pay in full*; that was all that mattered. 'You
can have your bloody Spanish book instead.' She
swept a hand over the Greater Arapile. '*But I want
Audley, Ian!*'

Ian bit his lip. With Ian—or, at any rate, with the
old Ian—there had been times when commonsense,
and confused affection, and old-fashioned
journalism (never mind self-doubt!), had played the
very devil with his Christian imperatives! 'Well . . .
we'll see, Jen—we'll see!'

301

'Yes—we'll see, darling.' If she'd got that much back, to make him question his irrational obsession with the Fitzgibbon woman, then that much was better than nothing.

'Miss Fielding—?'

'Oh—?' Jenny turned quickly towards the question: she had halted Ian, but Cathy Audley had progressed towards her father before she'd realized that she was alone, and had had to turn back to them '—we're coming, dear . . . This *is* an amazing place—isn't it? All these lovely little flowers!' She grinned at the child. 'We saw a fox, Cathy—down there—' She pointed '—with great big ears . . . he's in the rocks down there, somewhere—'

'Did you? Gosh!' The child scanned the hillside. 'A fox—?'

'He's gone, dear—'

Audley was still waiting. Although now, after they'd taken such a time to reach him, he had managed to stand up, and had moved out of the shade of the monument into the full sunlight, so that she could see him clearly at last.

'Daddy—!'

What he looked like, length-and-breadth-and-face, was no great revelation: there had been that picture, which John Tully had uncovered, of David Audley in a line-out—*Cardiff* versus the *Visigoths*, on some dreadful rugger-playing day, when they'd all looked as though they'd been mud wrestling: and Audley had been wearing a dirty head-band, and a look of excited brutality, like an eager Saxon in the shieldwall at Hastings.

(But—*God!* the real-life image, of the man

302

himself, jolted her as though she'd touched a live wire—)

'Daughter?' Standing up under the monument, Audley could look down on them, with the huge sky behind him: a sky shading down from purest blue to palest blue-grey, where the distant green line of trees on the next ridge divided it from the yellow cornfields, and he seemed ten-foot-tall for a moment, above them. 'What's this, then?'

But it wasn't that—

'What's this, then?' Audley smiled at his daughter as he repeated the question. And then he looked directly at Jenny. 'Hullo, there!'

That made it worse. Or . . . not just worse—much worse!

'Daddy—this is Mr Robinson . . . and Miss Fielding. They know Willy Arkenshaw. And they write books, Daddy. And they want to talk to you.'

'Yes.' Audley stared at Jenny. 'I know.'

'Dr Audley—' The jolt of the shock was still there: it shook her voice, just as it had shaken her hands that time, after she touched that wire beside the ancient Victorian light-switch in the cellar at home. 'Dr Audley.' The husky faltering repetition was almost worse: it was so far from the way she had intended to face up to him that it was almost laughable. Except that, if she started to laugh, she was afraid she might go off into hysterics.

'Daddy—?' As Audley continued to stare at her—as they both continued to stare at each other—the child picked up the vibration of something strange happening.

'Miss Fielding.' Audley spoke at last, drawing her back to him even as relief suffused her. 'I do recognize you, actually. I saw you on the television

303

once. That time you escaped in Beirut. And, of course, I've read your books.'

He had a nice voice. And, although the pictures of that rather battered face hadn't lied in any factual detail, he seemed much younger than Willy Arkenshaw had suggested: *old* was as much a slander with David Audley as it had been with Philly: *old* was in the mind—

God! She was betraying Philly now—

'Oh, *Daddy*!' Cathy Audley exploded.

Jenny was aware that more of her hair was coming down; and there were beads of sweat crawling down the side of her face, and elsewhere—

But he was so very like—so very like, even though he was quite unlike—so very like Philly! And she bloody-well fancied him! And—what was so ultimately worse: what rocketted that betrayal into unimaginable orbit—was that he fancied her, too!

'Mr Robinson knows all about the battle, Daddy.' Cathy Audley's patience ran out. 'He wants to talk to you about General Le Marchant.'

'He does?' Audley let go of Jenny unwillingly. 'Does he?' The letting-go stretched itself until it had to snap. 'Mr Robinson . . . You are the writer, of course.' He smiled at Ian. 'And you have a rare grasp of good English. A quite unjournalistic grasp, if I may say so—?' All the smile went out of Audley's face. 'But that would be because you were at Princess Mary's Grammar School, and brought up on the classics? Like Gibbon having the Bible hammered into him?'

Jenny looked at Ian, and caught him with his mouth open.

Audley nodded. 'Hennessey—Henworth—? *Henworthy* . . . he was your High Master, of course.

And he was taught by my old Latin Master, as an inky child, before he gravitated to higher things.' He nodded again. 'There's a descent in such matters, among schoolmasters. Not quite as good as breeding through pedigree bulls, perhaps . . . but it leaves its mark, nevertheless, I'd like to think.' Another nod, but this time accompanied by a terrible cold smile. 'I particularly enjoyed your book on the Middle East. It had several interesting insights, as well as some quite deplorable flights of fancy.'

Jenny felt her own mouth open—*Audley wasn't perfect: the 'rare grasp of English' and the Hennessey/Henwood one-upmanship was fair enough at a smart cocktail party; but if Audley thought he could patronize Ian Robinson, he had much mistaken his man!* But then it was too late, because Ian was reacting—

In fact, Ian was smiling. 'Your daughter has told us about your ancestor, Dr Audley—who was killed in the charge here?' He gave Audley back a nod. 'But . . . was he just another bone-headed English dragoon? Or was he one of Wellington's 'Research and Development' officers—the 'exploring' officers, were they called? Andrew Laith Hay—? Or John Waters, or Somers Cocks? Or Colquhoun Grant? Or Dr Paul Mitchell?'

Christ! That was giving him both barrels! thought Jenny. *Ian, being Ian, really had done his homework!*

'You're interested in the battle of Salamanca, Mr Robinson?' Audley, being Audley, was taking Ian's measure now.

'Not in the least, Dr Audley.' Ian smiled at Audley. 'But—'

'Daughter!' Audley interrupted Ian rudely. 'Go

and see how your mother is—' He nodded past the monument, into a stone-quarried gap behind him, which divided the *Greater Arapile* super-tanker into two parts, fore and aft on its port side here, below the tall stone shaft. 'She's reading her book . . . or sunbathing, or something . . . down there—yes?'

Cathy Audley stared at her father, the huge sunglasses concealing what would certainly be a frown.

'Go on, Cathy.' Audley's voice was gently level now, neither pleading or commanding.

The sunglasses turned towards Ian for an instant. But now the tightened lips and the anger-lines around the mouth told their own story.

'Off you go.' This time he actually smiled. 'There's nothing to worry about.'

Cathy came back to him. 'I told them you received a phone-call, I think they pretended not to be interested in it. I'm sorry.'

Audley shrugged. 'So I received a phone-call. That's nothing to be ashamed of, love. So—'

'Yes—"Off I go".' The child started to go, but then stopped. 'But I'm forgetting my manners—aren't I!' She swung towards Jenny. 'They all say "Don't talk to strangers—forget about good manners!" But, I forgot my lesson, didn't I, Miss Fielding?' No child now—not for her, and not for Ian, in his turn: for Ian, a look which, if he'd been a British dragoon, and Cathy Audley a Frenchman sighting him along her musket, would have knocked him stone-dead from his saddle, beside her ancestor and General Le Marchant. 'And goodbye, Mr Robinson.'

Wisely (although she didn't give him time, anyway) Ian didn't try to answer, as she twisted

306

away again, and dropped down gracefully into the rocks below the monument, leaving the echo of his name on her bullet in the silence.

'Yes . . . well, I don't really need to enlarge on that—do I?' Audley watched her go, and then turned back to them with the vestiges of his smile still in place, but with a mixture of pride and contempt edging it. 'But, then, perhaps I am indebted to you both—for teaching her a lesson about the Great British Press, to go with "Don't talk to strangers"?'

Now it was war to the knife! thought Jenny. 'We're not the Great British Press, Dr Audley. We're just . . . *us*, actually.'

'"Us"?' Looking at her (rather than at Ian), his expression twisted. And the bugger of it was that she knew that look, having seen it on other men similarly caught between suspicion and desire; but she had not felt about them as she felt about him—*and she must stop feeling like that, right now!*

'We're in trouble, Dr Audley.' Self-preservation came to her rescue, adding tactics to inclination. 'We need your help.'

'My . . . *help* . . . ?' His confusion helped her. 'But . . . I thought *I* was the one who was supposed to be in trouble. Aren't you supposed to be investigating me, Miss Fielding-ffulke?'

'"Fielding"—' Everyone who wanted to shit on her waved that ridiculous name in her face '—just "Fielding", please, Dr Audley.'

'No "ffulke"?' He cocked an eyebrow at her. 'But that's a fine old name, Miss Fielding-ffulke: Rudyard Kipling chose it in *Puck of Pook's Hill*—which is one of our favourite books. "ffulke"—*Fulke* . . . he was the double-agent—the

307

traitor. He was the one whom the Lord of Pevensey "turned round" to save England from Robert of Normandy, Miss—Fielding-*ffulke*!' The eyebrow lowered. 'So . . . whose side are you on now?'

Ian loomed up at her side—like the old Ian, at need: like the *older* Ian, when they'd worked together. 'Didn't your telephone-caller of last night tell you all about us, Dr Audley?' Ian-like, he didn't try to give a smart answer to a silly question.

'He did—yes.' No expression for Ian. 'He said you were investigating me. And he didn't suggest that I should be flattered, either.'

'We're only trying to find out the truth about Philip Masson's death, Dr Audley.'

'Only the truth? Well-well!' Audley sneered at the word, just as Mitchell had done before him. 'I wish you the worst of luck then, Mr Robinson.'

'You don't fancy the truth?' Against Audley's sudden unpleasantness and the sense and the thrust of his own question, Ian was as respectful as a curate with a bishop nevertheless.

'My dear fellow! I've spent two-thirds of my life looking for the truth. But only in relation to other people, of course—just like you. The truth about *myself* . . . and my many wicked deeds . . . is quite another matter.' Cutting his losses, Audley became pleasant again. 'But you must forgive my bad temper—or make allowances for it, anyway. Because I am on holiday. And with my family—' He raised a big blunt-fingered hand '—and *yes*—I do realize that Dr Goebbels and many other villains—probably Attila the Hun, too—were good family men, who loved their children, and their wives, and also went on holiday . . . I realize that, Mr Robinson!' He smiled a terribly ugly-smile, not at all sweetly, in spite of his best efforts. 'But . . . would you like all your little secrets dragged into the harsh light of day? Or of *print*—in some book, or some yellow tabloid rag?'

'No.' Ian shook his head, still curate-respectful. 'Especially if they involved the death—or the murder—of another human being, Dr Audley . . . *No*—I certainly wouldn't like that.'

'I didn't mean that, Mr Robinson. I meant exactly what I said.' Audley twisted slightly, peering down beside the monument where there was a gap in the rocks, as though to make sure that his wife and daughter were not within earshot. 'As it happens I have been "involved", as you put it so delicately, in the death of a number of human beings over the years. Since before you were born, in fact, Mr Robinson.' The sneer was back. 'I started young, when I didn't know any better, with anonymous Germans in Normandy, saying "shoot" to my gunner—second-hand work even then, you might say.'

He was that old! thought Jenny. But of course he was, and Cathy Audley had said as much; and even Philly himself had been killing Chinese— anonymous Chinese in Korea only a hand's-breadth of years after Audley's war; and Audley hardly looked older than Philly had done, that last time, when he'd turned up out of the blue at the end of her Finals—*Philly! Oh Philly!*

'Ian—Mr Robinson—isn't talking about ancient history, Dr Audley,' she said sharply.

'Neither am I, Miss Fielding.' Audley almost sounded hurt by her sharpness. 'But . . . old men have a habit of remembering the wounds they had on Crispin's day.' He shrugged. 'As it *also* happens

. . . I had no hand in your godfather's death, for what it's worth—' He raised his hand as her mouth opened '—oh yes: I know all about him . . . And by "all" I do mean *all*, Miss Fielding. Because I investigated him, once upon a time . . . Or, rather, *twice* upon a time: first, before he died, because we needed to know who he really was . . . and then afterwards, when we wanted to know *why*—or *what* . . . and then *who* and *how*, as well as *why*.' He stared at her for a moment. 'He was quite a man, was your godfather . . . But, then, you know that already.'

He was quite a man, too! She started to think. But then she fought against the thought, amending it mutinously: *whatever he was, he was also a clever man—and even that instant of mutual recognition might be part of his cleverness, like a python hypnotizing its prey before swallowing it! So now he was trying to make her think what he wanted her to think, perhaps?*

'I know it suited you when he died, Dr Audley.'

'Did it? Well . . . perhaps it did. And perhaps it didn't. Who can tell?' He shrugged again. 'What I know is . . . that it doesn't suit me now to be bothered by you. Because I have other work to do—more important work than having to worry about you.' Now, at last, she got his purely-ugly face. 'Which is why I asked "whose side are you on?", Miss Fielding.'

'But you're on holiday now, Dr Audley. So we're not wasting your official time, are we?' Ian came in again, playing uncharacteristically dirty.

'I don't suppose it would do any good if I told you I have an alibi?' Audley ignored Ian. 'I flew back to Washington the Tuesday after we killed

O'Leary—the Tuesday after the Saturday when my very dear Frances died—?' He switched to Ian suddenly. 'No—?'

It was the wrong appeal, to the wrong person.

'No.' Audley nodded. 'I didn't think it would.' He sighed. 'And you're quite right, of course! It's like an old friend of mine is always reminding me, about what the centurion said to Christ, according to St Matthew: "I am also a man under authority, having soldiers under me; and I say to this *Go*! And he goeth".' He gave them both a twisted grin. 'It's what he calls "one of the hard sayings". Meaning that authority and action and responsibility are all the same thing in the end. So that won't do will it?' He smiled at her. 'So we have a problem. Because you won't believe me unless I tell you what I'm not at liberty to tell you. And even if I do tell you, then you may choose not to believe me. So I'm into a Catch-22 situation, it seems.'

'And so are we, Dr Audley.' If Ian had liked the St Matthew throwaway line, he didn't show it. 'Didn't he say—on the telephone?'

'Oh yes!' Audley bowed slightly. 'You've "raised the devil"—? And now he's after you—is that it?'

Suddenly Jenny wanted Reg Buller badly. Audley was playing with them, and Ian was still too screwed-up about Frances Fitzgibbon to think as straight as he usually thought. And even she was having trouble with Audley's sharp image imposed on her memory of Philly.

'Where's Reg, Ian?' What they needed was Reg Buller's no-nonsense brutality: Reg had no hang-ups about Philly or Frances, let alone Audley.

'Yes—' Ian raised his binoculars again '—he has rather taken his time. But—yes, he is coming now,

311

Jen—see?' He lowered the glasses and pointed at a distant dust-cloud in the valley between the Greater Arapile and the lower ridges opposite, across the intervening cornlands which had once been another foreign field that was for ever England. 'Actually . . . we've begun to think that it may not have been you, Dr Audley—see there, Jen—?'

'What?' The information casually dropped after Ian's advice to Jenny, that Buller was approaching at last, caught Audley flat aback. 'What d'you mean?'

'Mrs Fitzgibbon—' Ian squared his shoulders, while pretending to concentrate on the foreign field, like a French general watching the advance of the British Army '—she was Paul Mitchell's girl, wasn't she, Dr Audley?'

That couldn't be the question—there had to be more than that!

'What?' Audley frowned.

It *couldn't* be the question—even though it fulfilled the 'I-already-know-the-answer' criterion.

'Frances Fitzgibbon was Paul Mitchell's girl—was she, Dr Audley?' But Ian stuck to his gun like a brave Frenchman with the dragoons upon him, nevertheless.

'No.' Audley shook his head slowly. 'Actually, she wasn't. Although he would have liked her to be. But . . . she wasn't anybody's girl. Not even her husband's, I rather suspect . . . But . . . I don't really see what Frances Fitzgibbon has to do with you, Mr Robinson.'

'Or Paul Mitchell, Dr Audley?' Jenny came in on his flank.

'You asked us which side we're on, Dr Audley.' Ian came back on cue. 'But we don't know for sure

312

whose side *anyone* is on, now. All we know is that we're in trouble—like Miss Fielding said. And we think you're the only person who may be able to help us.'

That really was the truth. And, of course, who better than Ian to pronounce it?

Audley relaxed, suddenly. *'Mitchell—Paul Mitchell—?'* Then he laughed, but not happily. 'Oh yes—that would be it, of course! We laid the trail—and you picked it up . . . even after so many years—is that it? Now I see! You think that Mitchell—? Because of Thornervaulx—?' He completed the unhappy chuckle. 'It's what my dear wife always says: "too-clever-by-half"—and not half clever enough!' He looked at Ian, and then Jenny, and then away from both of them, down the hillside.

Jenny waited.

'Well, Miss Fielding—Mr Robinson—' Audley came back to them, with a slow shake of the head '—if you think that, then I think you're both in big trouble now.' He pointed down the hillside. 'So now we'll see?'

And then there was suddenly Reg Buller, stamping up out of the dead ground among the rocks.

And then there was Paul Mitchell with him—

CHAPTER TWO

Reg Buller was puffing like a grampus, from his climb: Reg would be sweating now, even worse than she had done before the sun had dried her, here on the summit of the Greater Arapile.

But Paul Mitchell wasn't puffing: he was striding easily, swinging up a long black case—half briefcase, half violin-case—as he surmounted the last of the rocks.

'Paul.' Audley seemed neither surprised nor pleased. 'You took your time.'

'David!' Mitchell trod disgracefully into the midst of the crocuses, quite regardless of them. 'I'm sorry, David—' He cradled the not-violin-case in his arms, to his breast, still crushing the flowers. 'Where's Faith? Where's Cathy, David—?'

'They're down below.' Audley nodded back towards the monument. 'Among the rocks. Sunbathing and reading. And possibly topless . . . Faith, anyway. Do you want me to call them?'

'No. They'll do well enough where they are.' Mitchell clambered up on to the uneven rocky platform on which the monument had been raised, setting the case down at his feet. 'No problem, David.'

'No problem,' Audley growled the words. 'You'd better be right.'

'Now, David . . .' Mitchell continued to scan the landscape, quartering it segment by segment '—when have I ever let you down?'

Audley stared at him, then shook his head resignedly. And finally came back to Jenny. 'You've caused us a lot of trouble, Miss Fielding.'

'Correction: she's caused *me* a lot of trouble.' Mitchell stepped down from the platform. He looked untroubled, but decidedly rough and quite unlike his previous rather smooth self, thought Jenny unhappily: unshaven, with the beginning of a pronounced designer-stubble and an open-necked shirt inadequately tucked into a pair of shapeless old trousers, he might just have passed for a local. And, oddly enough, the net effect of this was to make him look younger and much more sexy (at least, for those who might be into younger men; but still not in the same class as Audley). 'You've caused *me* a lot of trouble, Miss Fielding-ffulke— and that's a fact!'

'I'm sorry, Dr Mitchell.' It was hard to think of this ragamuffin as *Doctor* Mitchell. 'but . . . you caused *us* some trouble, too. In fact, you frightened us.'

'So I gather.' Mitchell flicked a glance at Reg Buller, who was mopping his face with an enormous and very dirty handkerchief. 'So—I—gather!'

Jenny looked at Buller accusingly. 'Mr Buller—?'

'Don't blame me, Lady!' Buller wiped his face even more vigorously. ''E caught me on the road, not long after you left me. An' . . . 'e was very nasty, I tell you.'

'Oh yes?' There would be no help from Reg Buller now, that wonderfully authentic whine indicated: Reg knew which way the wind was blowing, and he always adjusted himself to his circumstances, which was the secret of his survival from many past disasters. So, in his new role as their unwilling employee he could no longer be

315

relied upon. But that, in turn, freed her from employer's responsibility. 'So, do you still think Dr Mitchell is a murderer, Mr Buller?'

'I never said that, Lady—I never did!' Buller rolled his eyes, driven to over-play his role even more by such a direct accusation. 'It was Mr Robinson, more than me: I just reported what I found out—like you told me to.'

That shifted the whole weight to Ian, who hadn't said a word since the world had changed for them.

'That's not true, Mr Buller—'

'It's all right, Jen.' Ian watched Mitchell.

'It was Mr Buller, Ian—'

'It's all right.' He dismissed her, having eyes only for Mitchell. 'And it's true, also.' He blinked for an instant. 'Maybe we made a mistake. Or . . . *maybe we didn't*—?' he faced Mitchell unashamedly. 'What was she really like, Dr Mitchell? Tell me?'

Mitchell stared at him. Then he turned away and reached for the case.

'What was she really like?' Ian pursued Mitchell remorselessly.

'Let him be, Mr Robinson.' Audley took a step down from his eminence, to join them. 'This isn't the place—or the time.'

'Isn't it?' Ian didn't look at Audley: he watched Mitchell apply his thumbs to the two catches on the case, still concentrating on him. 'What was she like?'

'She was quite a girl—quite a woman.' Audley annexed the question gently, but firmly. 'But we didn't kill Philip Masson, Mr Robinson. I didn't give the order—and Dr Mitchell didn't carry out the order I didn't give.'

All the same, Audley was frowning: Audley was

316

frowning, and Mitchell was working on the contents of the case—the bits of dull metal, which *clicked* and *screwed* and *snapped* together, as they had been carefully turned and crafted to do—the bits (which were worse than useless by themselves: just bits of metal) became the usual *things*, custom-built and delicate and ugly: a long-barrelled rifle, slender and deadly.

'But you're quite right: she was something special.' Audley saw that he was losing, and raised the stakes accordingly. 'But how the devil do you know that? You never met her—did you?' He shook his head. 'No! You couldn't have done.'

Mitchell had completed his work. It was designed to be completed quickly, and he knew his job.

'No.' He lifted the completed thing up, and squinted through the telescopic-sight which had been its last attachment, staring first up into the sky, and then away across the valley, towards the railway station. 'I'll never hit anything with this—not at any sort of range, with the first shot.' He took another squint, and then selected a little screwdriver from the case and made an adjustment. 'I ought to have a couple of sighting-shots, at five-hundred, and a thousand.' He looked up suddenly, and smiled at Jenny. 'But you can't have everything, can you?' He lowered the rifle, resting it carefully on his thigh, and picked out a long steel-nosed, brass-jacketed bullet from a compartment in the case, and opened the breach and snapped the bullet home. Then he set the rifle down and stood up.

'I was the one who was to blame, actually,' said Audley. 'At Thornervaulx.'

'But I was the one who should have got the

317

bullet.' Mitchell examined the valley carefully, from the far-off white blue of the village, round the deceptive roll of the cornland between to where the track curved towards them. 'So it all adds up to the same thing, really.' He looked at Reg Buller suddenly. 'You were quite right, Mr Buller: if I'd thought of it . . . then I might just have done it, at that!'

'No, you wouldn't have done: you're not that stupid,' snapped Audley.

'Aren't I?' Mitchell's mouth twisted.

'Yes.' Audley looked from Mitchell to Jenny, and then at Ian. And then back to Jenny. 'We were working for Fred Clinton then, Miss Fielding. And he had a rule—a very strict rule. And Sir Jack has the same rule. It's what you might call our "Rule of Engagement", from the Falklands War—? Although it goes back much further: it goes back to Lord Mansfield giving judgement in the case of *Burdett v. Abbot*, in 1812.'

'Uh-huh . . . *Burdett v. Abbot*—' Mitchell swung towards Audley '—you know, David, I never *have* been able to trace that exact case—not even though Jack Butler's so fond of quoting it at us, at regular intervals . . . I asked a clever girl I know who works for the Law Society to trace it for me . . . and she couldn't. So, maybe Fred just made it up—to annoy us?'

Ian stirred. 'What did—what was Lord Mansfield *supposed* to have said—? In the case of "Burdett versus Abbot", Dr Audley?'

'Oh, it's quite simple, my dear fellow!' Mitchell annexed the question quickly. 'It's all to do with what you *can* do—and what you *can't* do—if you've taken the Queen's Shilling, as David and I

318

have . . . Which puts us in quite impossible situations, of course—'

'But "if you don't like the heat in the kitchen"—then you add that, Mr Robinson, eh?' Audley relaxed. 'No one ordered you to visit the battlefield of Salamanca, did they? You came here of your own free will, I take it?'

What were they both driving at? 'But we haven't taken the . . . the "Queen's Shilling", Dr Audley.' Their own old rule drove Jenny to defend Ian. 'We're just . . . journalists.'

'Doesn't make any difference, Miss Fielding.' A similar rule brought Paul Mitchell back. 'Not to you—not to Peter Wright, or Clive Ponting—or even to Kim Philby: whatever we are, or whatever we do, the same rule applies, according to Chief Justice Mansfield: *"It is therefore highly important that the mistake should be corrected which supposes that an Englishman, by taking on the additional character of a soldier—"* (but it doesn't matter what additional character you put on: soldier, or journalist, rat-catcher) *"—puts off any of the rights and duties of an Englishman"*. So how about that, then?'

Jenny thought, suddenly . . . 1812? Because now they were here, on the top of the Greater Arapile, where the Duke of Wellington had also ruled, on a military truth, in 1812, while Chief Justice Mansfield had ruled on this other legal truth.

'That's the second "hard-saying",' murmured Audley. 'Fred Clinton and Jack Butler, and St Matthew and Lord Mansfield . . . they all put us on our mettle.'

'Yes.' Mitchell was staring past him. 'And now Paddy MacManus is about to put us on our mettle, I rather think—what can you see through those

319

field-glasses of yours, Ian?' He pointed into the great open sweep of the valley. 'What car is that—?'

Ian lifted his binoculars, towards a distant dust-cloud on the track.

'Mr Buller!' Mitchell didn't wait for an answer. 'You go down and say "hullo" to Mrs Audley, and Miss Audley—okay? And keep them down there, in the rocks, until I call you . . . And do be a good fellow, and make a noise when you're going down, so as not to embarrass Mrs Audley—*okay?*'

'It's a little car—a SEAT, or a Citroën—or a Renault . . . a *little* car—' Ian read back what he could see automatically.

'That will do.' Mitchell was taking on his 'additional character' now. 'Off you go, Mr Buller.'

'I'm goin'—I'm bloody-goin'—Dr Mitchell!' Reg Buller was going.

'It's a Citroën 2-CV, Dr Mitchell,' Ian confirmed his sighting.

'That's just fine!' Mitchell was Field-Marshal Montgomery and Alexander of Macedon. 'You stay up here, Mr Robinson: talk to Dr Audley about the battle of Salamanca—tell him how you would have fought it from here—*okay?*'

'Oh—that's just fine!' Audley complained as he surrendered. 'We walk up and down, to give him a target—?'

'He doesn't want you, David. His payment is on Mr Robinson.' Mitchell looked at Ian. 'Are you prepared to walk, Mr Robinson?'

That was too much! 'Ian—'

'Shut up, Jen.' But he grinned at her. 'Like the man said—"*the rights and duties of an Englishman*"—? And . . . at least I've got a better chance than Mrs Fitzgibbon had, this

320

time—haven't I, Dr Mitchell?'

Mitchell picked up the rifle. 'Down there, Miss Fielding—on your tummy, by that flat rock—*there*? See?' He held the rifle to his chest with one hand and pointed with the other. 'The moment he gets out of the car, then I've got *carte blanche*, if he's got his rifle with him. And you can drop down then, Mr Robinson. And when you're down you stay down. Because I'm not at all sure that I can hit him, with this gun, at this range—not with my first shot, anyway.' He reached down into the open case, and scooped up a handful of the left-behind cartridges, and stuffed them into his pocket. And then grinned at Jenny. 'But . . . no problem, eh?'

It didn't seem like that at all, to her. But, then, it was quite out of her experience.

'What about behind us?' Audley's voice was cold. 'MacManus always operates with a partner—a back-up? And . . . my family is down there, Paul.'

'Don't worry about behind us.' Mitchell nodded at Jenny. *'If you please, Miss Fielding—? Go!'*

There was something in Mitchell's face which made any sort of protest contemptible, however much she wanted to argue with him, to assert herself.

So . . . over the dead grass, and the scatter of autumn crocuses, to where he'd indicated, and down behind a safe rock—

Mitchell was saying something, behind her; and so was Audley—but she couldn't hear what they were saying. Then he was beside her—first, on his knees—on his knees, but with the rifle carefully cradled in one hand, to keep it off the ground . . . and then easing himself carefully alongside her. 'No need to watch, Miss Fielding. In fact, I'd prefer

321

that you didn't—you'll only distract me.' He took a khaki handkerchief from his pocket and spread it out behind the rock and put two of his spare cartridges on it. 'Nothing to see, anyway. He's just stopped to have a final look around, just in case.'

She lowered her head, keeping her eyes on him. Because there was something to see, of course—something she'd never expected to see at all, ever . . . let alone like this, within touching distance: one man preparing to kill another man.

'And now there's a further delay—an unforeseen occurrence.' Mitchell was peering round the edge of the rock, keeping his own head low. 'There's a farm tractor coming behind him, towing a load of something. So he'll have to pull into the side to let it past, and wait for it to disappear. And he won't like that—not one bit.'

She could hear the tractor. 'Why not?'

'A witness.' He didn't look at her. 'Not that he plans to stay around afterwards, to be identified. And there'll be a different car waiting for him, another vehicle, anyway—maybe a lorry, or something like . . . Goods for Portugal, maybe. We're only two or three hours from the frontier, after all.' He looked at her suddenly. '"Quickly in—quickly out": that's his usual method. You can never tell for sure, of course—not with a wild animal. But it's always worked for him in the past.' He returned his attention to the front again as the noise of the tractor's diesel rose. 'And he certainly doesn't want to hang about in Spain, that's for sure. He's taken one hell of a risk already, as it is . . . Although his friends will have looked after him this far . . . so they may have other plans for him now, at that!'

'His friends?' The sound of the tractor rose to a crescendo, but then suddenly died away as it passed the headland of the Greater Arapile and continued on towards the ridge behind them. 'His friends—?'

'Now he's waiting again. And, if he's got any sense he'll turn round and wait for another chance . . . *Go on, you bastard! Turn round—there's a gap just ahead where you can do it easily! Don't be an idiot!*' Mitchell drew a deep breath and stared fixedly into the valley, with his chin almost into the dirt. 'No . . . of course you're not going to—are you! You missed out once—and the old juices are pumping now: this is what turns you on—' He stopped suddenly 'Yes . . . "friends", Miss Fielding. He did a difficult contract job for ETTA a few years back—one the Basques didn't fancy doing themselves for domestic reasons. It was a car bomb, actually. Although he prefers guns to bombs, himself. But it was a big bomb: it blew the damn car clear over the block . . . So they owe him one.' Just as suddenly he turned to her again. 'And a penny for your thoughts *now*, Miss Fielding?'

There was something not right with all this. 'I'd like more than a penny's-worth, Dr Mitchell—' She caught the edge of her own doubt: *why was he giving her so much, when he didn't need to?*

He looked away again. 'Well . . . we'll see, eh? I'll ration the pennies, maybe—*Ah! He's moving again . . . very slowly . . . and now he's stopped again, at the gap* . . . well, well! Does he smell a rat—does he?'

'How did he know we'd be here, Dr Mitchell?'

'Now *that* is asking.' Mitchell's chin was on the dirt now. 'We didn't know for sure ourselves, not at first: we did it by logic first—what *we* might have done, in your shoes, if we were stupid . . . before we managed to frighten one of Mr Reginald Buller's friends into confirming.' He slid the rifle forward, and applied the eye-piece of the telescopic sight to his left eye, adjusting its focus. 'It could . . . just be . . . that your Mr Buller isn't as clever as he thinks he is—' With a deft little movement, quickly and yet unhurriedly, he extracted a small screwdriver from the breast-pocket of his shirt and made an adjustment to the sight '—or . . . judging by the way he got out of England with his little fat chum . . . with a certain country's CD plates on his luggage . . . it *could* be that the devil you raised—Mr MacManus's employer, that is—is a very smart devil, as well as a very stupid one—' He applied the eye-piece to his eye again '—*that will do!*' He lowered the rifle for an instant, and looked at her squarely. 'We won't know until we ask him—will we, Miss Fielding?'

She wanted, quite desperately, to raise her head. And . . . *how could he be so cold-blooded, damn him!* 'How are we going to do that, Dr Mitchell—if you are about to kill him?'

'Kill him?' Paul Mitchell frowned at her for only a fraction of a second, before rolling back to his rifle, and bringing it up to his shoulder, and settling himself comfortably—long legs splayed out behind him, ankles flat to the dirt (one foot gouging away a swathe of autumn crocuses regardlessly). 'What d'you think I am—a *murderer* . . . not that it wouldn't give me the *greatest* of pleasures—the greatest of pleasure . . . and it'd be a bloody-sight easier, too—*don't look: he may spot your little white face over the top*—'

What stopped her from looking, even more than

his final shout, was that he wasn't looking at her: he had known, without looking, that she couldn't resist looking at the last—

The rifle kicked, sending a tremor through him and deafening her as he fired in the very instant that his order held her motionless, so that she witnessed the unforgettable professionalism of his second shot—*the practised bolt-action-empty-cartridge-flying-out-live-round-off-the-khaki-handkerchief-slid-into-the-breach—bolt-snapped—rifle-up—aim—FIRE!*

And then the whole thing started again—

But then stopped.

And then Mitchell's face momentarily sank on to his rifle, his unshaven cheek distorting it, with his eyes squeezed shut. *And with that all bets—all shouted orders—were off, and Jenny was on her knees, above the rock—*

The little car was moving again: it was backing, in a cloud of dust, down the track—*it was turning—swerving and skidding in its own dust into the gap in the track behind it, in a racing turn-about, to escape—*

'What's happening—?' As she spoke, Mitchell stepped up beside her. 'Did you miss?'

'Yes. I missed.' He didn't look at her. 'One does sometimes.'

The Citroën's tyres churned up the track, with its little engine screaming at them to get it moving, so violently that it rocked and bucked this way and that before engine and tyres were both fighting to obey the driver.

'My rifle fires high, and to the right,' continued

Mitchell. 'But *he* wouldn't have missed: he had a rather special gun, I think—a Voss Special, I think they call it.' He shook his head sadly. 'I've never seen one of them—I've only *heard* about them. They're like the old buffalo-hunters' long rifles, only better: on a windless day they can manage a couple of miles, supposedly . . . It's got a very long barrel and a marvellous sighting-device.'

Noise filled the valley, drowning out the rest of Mitchell's excuse: there were dust-clouds on the top of the cornfield, where she had trailed up behind Ian, with her feet hurting; and there was a dust-cloud coming up the track from the village, round the rise of the field which was deceptively flattened by the height of the Greater Arapile above it.

And—*God!*—there was even movement in the railway station, in the middle of nowhere, with men fanning out of the gap between its two buildings—and from behind them, with a single concussive *bang*, a red-winking rocket flared up, trailing a line of bright red smoke as it curved down towards the converging dust-clouds of the retreating Citroën 2-CV and the other dust-clouds—

'I smashed the passenger's window, in the car, with that first shot.' Mitchell's voice came back almost to the conversational. 'I was only supposed to frighten him . . . But he didn't come up towards us—he went round to take aim over the bonnet—that's when I saw the Voss . . . He was going to rest on the bonnet. So the second time I aimed for him.'

326

The dust-clouds still converged—even as the red smoketrail descended, to bounce in a final red spark as it hit the field: the spark bounced brightly once, and then the smoke drifted away from the point where it vanished.

'I don't know where that second shot went.' Mitchell paused. 'I aimed . . . *left* . . . and slightly down . . . I might have hit something—you never know . . . I couldn't guarantee to hit a tyre, after that first shot, Miss Fielding—do you understand? Not at this distance—?'

The further of the two dust-clouds stopped suddenly, the two vehicles which had caused it slewing to the left and right so as to block the passage of the approaching Citroën. One of them was large and black and civilian, the other drab and military-looking: their doors opened even before they had halted, and their occupants tumbled out—Spanish Civil Guards from the military vehicle, in their distinctive black tricornes, and bare-headed civilians from the black car—

Mitchell was still speaking. But she had been so intent on watching the drama in the valley, trying to imprint every detail on her memory—*this is something else I never thought I'd see!*—that she hadn't taken it in. 'What?'

'I said . . . they took their bloody time.'

The Citroën had also stopped now, but well short of the road block—a hundred yards or more away from the Spanish Police.

'You knew they were coming?' It was a foolish question.

'Too-bloody-right!' He stared at the scene, frowning. 'You don't think we play silly games on our own in other people's countries? Not *this* sort of game, anyway—*Ahh! He's thought better of it, by God!*'

'What—?' Something in his expression chilled her, in spite of the heat. But his words turned her away from him, back to the valley.

The Citroën was moving again, very slowly.

'His moment-of-truth.' Mitchell murmured the words. 'Just like O'Leary . . . it comes to them all sooner or later . . . later or sooner . . . But he's being—*no*! By God—*NO!*'

As he spoke the sound of the little car's engine changed, suddenly roaring in the great stillness of the yellow-and-red fields as the Citroën accelerated—with a new cloud of red dust, which had settled behind it, swirling up again as its tyres churned the track—

'He's making a run for it—*that's my man!*' breathed Mitchell.

The Spaniards at the road block were scattering—taking cover behind their vehicles.

'He'll never get through—' In a tank maybe, thought Jenny. But a 2CV was too little, too light—

Then the Citroën braked—its little red brake-lights were invisible in the dust and the sunlight, but it bucked and slewed sideways, until it was broadside in the track.

'He's turning round—'

'No he isn't—' Paul Mitchell cut her off as the distant sound of the revving engine reached them again *as the little car threw itself into the wire fence beside the road*—

The fence bowed and shivered, and stretched on

each side of the car for a moment, before the posts snapped and were pulled away as the car broke through into the corn stubble, throwing up an even greater dust-cloud as it started to climb the slope—the same slope down which she'd walked, thought Jenny, suddenly torn between what she knew, and the old instinctive sympathy for any hunted animal with the pack in full-cry behind it—the fox breaking cover out of the spinney into open country, knowing that it had been cornered, but going for its own run-for-freedom nevertheless—

The burst of gunfire, sharp and reverberating, with the echoes ringing across the valley from the Greater Arapile towards the opposing rocky plateau, changed the image: this was sun-baked Beirut again, with that same *knock-knock-knocking*—

But the dust-cloud was still moving. 'He's going to get away—'

'No he isn't.' Mitchell's voice was matter-of-fact, quite unemotional. 'See there—?'

Up over the top of the cornfield, out of the dead ground from which the Redcoats had once marched towards the French, another of those malevolent army vehicles loomed up, trailing its own dust-cloud. And this one had its own little turret, like a miniature tank: it stopped suddenly as she watched it, and the turret began to traverse.

The Citroën changed direction, no longer trying to breast the rise, aiming now to escape between two fires, along the curve of the field—

'Don't look—' Mitchell caught her arm '—*Miss Fielding*—'

She pulled away from him—pulled away just as

the long slender gun in the turret *banged* three
times—a different sound from the preceding
small-arms knocking . . . deeper and louder—and
probably the loudest noise this peaceful valley had
known since—

The Citroën was bowled over like a rabbit,
rolling and exploding in the same instant, its four
little tyres and underside visible for a last
fraction-of-a-second before it became an
incandescent ball of fire, shooting out flame and
black smoke as it became unrecognizable.

'Don't look!' This time Mitchell's grip was
irresistible: he swung her round to face him. 'He's
dead now. *He's no problem now*—it's called "Shot
while resisting arrest", Miss Fielding. So . . . *he's
got no problems now, either: no one forced him to run,
Miss Fielding* . . . do you see?'

It was strange how quiet it was. There had been
the loudest *bang*! of all as the Citroën had exploded.
But now she couldn't hear anything as she stared
accusingly at Mitchell. 'You knew that was going to
happen.'

'No. That is to say . . . *no* . . . I didn't know for
sure.' He was stone-faced. 'But you don't need to
waste any sympathy for him, Miss Fielding. He'd
never met your nice Mr Robinson, who goes to
church on Sundays. But he'd been paid to kill nice
Mr Robinson, so that was what he was going to
do—at maybe two thousand yards, and with a
soft-nosed bullet. And that *was* what he was going
to do . . . and it frightened the shit out of me when
he got out of his car, and the Spaniards hadn't
turned up, I can tell you.' His jaw tightened.
'Because then I had to decide whether I was going
to shoot-to-kill, or not . . . And this contraption—'

330

He lifted the rifle '—this was just supposed to be insurance. They said it wasn't really necessary, because they'd be here once he showed up. And then they offered me a handgun . . . But I didn't want to let him get that close. Because he's an expert, and I'm not—'

'No—?' She remembered what Reg Buller had said. And what, from her own observation of only a few minutes ago (so little time?) . . . she also remembered.

'No—damn it—no!' He showed his teeth. 'You don't know what you're talking about, Miss Fielding. Whatever you *think* you know . . . you-don't-know—' He let go of her arm, and straightened up 'But I'm not about to tell you.'

What she knew was that she mustn't let him confuse her with either sincerity or very good acting: for some reason he had given her too much, up to now, but she didn't know why. And that was no reason to trust him now.

He looked away from her, dismissing her.

The unrecognizable wreck of the Citroën continued to blaze fiercely, with its black smoke rising up in a mini-mushroom-cloud in the still air. And the uniformed men were converging on it . . . But the civilians were getting into their car—even as she watched the doors closed one by one, and then the car turned on to the track and moved slowly towards them.

Then she realized that she was alone: Paul Mitchell was retracing his steps, back to the monument, walking across the autumn crocuses as though they didn't exist—as though she didn't exist—

'Dr Mitchell!'

He stopped, and turned. 'Whatever you want to know—you ask Dr Audley now, Miss Fielding. And I wish you joy of it.'

There was a knot in her stomach. Just as Audley had so strangely reminded her of Philly, now Paul Mitchell recalled Ian—the new Ian, for whom she also didn't really exist as she had formerly done.

He looked past her for an instant, then at her, very coldly. 'I must go and make our peace with the Spaniards. Not that it'll be too difficult, I suspect.' His mouth twisted. 'Don't worry—they won't ask you any questions. Just so long as you go straight home now, and forget what you've seen.'

Her mouth opened.

'Oh yes—*forget*, Miss Fielding.' The twist became a travesty of a smile. 'A wanted man—a known foreign terrorist who has worked for ETTA in the past? And I wouldn't like to guess what's happened to his little fat chum, either. So *two* known terrorists, believed to be working for ETTA, have been shot by security forces, while resisting arrest. And that has nothing to do with any British tourists who may have been passing through, on their holidays: that wouldn't be good for the tourist industry, would it?' He flicked a glance past her for an instant. 'The Spaniards have waited a long time to close the MacManus file, and balance their books. So this way there are no complications—no messy trial, or anything like that. But next time ETTA may not find it so easy to hire outside talent.'

Jenny watched him bend down, to disassemble the rifle and replace each bit of it in its place in the case—right down to retrieving a final round from his back pocket, and putting it too in its box, with the two empty cases of the bullets he'd fired.

Then he looked up again. 'Of course, you may not want to forget—not after you've witnessed such a saleable event, eh? Pity you didn't have a camera!' He snapped the case shut and stood up. 'And the Spanish won't touch you, either. Because, apart from being your father's daughter, you haven't done anything—have you?' He stared at her. 'Which is funny really, when you think about it. Because that's all your own work—' He pointed into the valley '—that, and what happened to John Tully.'

'John—?'

'But you'll be in the clear there, too. He "surprised an intruder" . . . going through the files in his office. Only I'll bet there aren't any files on all this, because you'd only just started, hadn't you? And our chaps will not want to make a fuss about *us*, I shouldn't think . . . And I expect he was into a lot of other things, in any case. So, although they'll maybe want to talk to you, I doubt whether they'll ask any difficult questions. In fact, I guarantee they won't.' He gave her a dreadful reassuring smile.

All my own work! She looked down at the old-and-new battlefield for a moment, suddenly aghast. 'But why—?'

'But what?' He was waiting for her as she turned back to him. 'You don't need to feel *too* guilty, Miss Fielding. You have to earn your living, and this time you were trying to settle an old score—weren't you? And who can resist business *and* pleasure?' He pointed again. '*He* bloody-well couldn't, anyway—not even when he knew the risk . . . In fact, we're all in your debt for him—even though he wasn't the one you wanted.' He looked away

333

suddenly. 'But I can't stay here philosophizing about guilt—*David!*'

'No—' She couldn't let him go '—why—*why*—did he come after us? You must tell me, Dr Mitchell—*you must!*'

'No I mustn't—*David!*' He didn't even look at her. 'That answer's more than my job's worth. If you want to know, then you ask old David—he's the one you came to ask, isn't he? *David*—'

Audley loomed large. But where was Ian?

'My dear Paul!' Audley looked at her vaguely for an instant. 'You were right . . . but only just, by heaven! So . . . don't you *ever* do that to me again.' He focused on Jenny. 'I sent Mr Robinson to reassure my wife, Miss Fielding. And to make his peace with my daughter. He seemed . . . rather cut up about deceiving her—I don't quite know why, but he did.'

That sounded more like the old Ian, she thought. *But then . . . what had they talked about, these last out-of-time minutes—?*

'I'm sorry, David.' Mitchell shrugged insincerely. 'Being right never seems to do me any good . . . But I must go and make *our* peace with Aguirre now. And then I'll come back and put you fully in the picture—okay?'

'Yes—you do that.' Audley still stared at Jenny. 'Tell him that I'm booked into the Parador near Victoria tomorrow night. Because I want Cathy to see the battlefield there. And then we'll be gone the day after that—Hôtel des Basses Pyrénées in Bayonne, which is safely out of his jurisdiction. I want her to see the Vauban fortifications there.'

Mitchell's mouth twisted. 'I'll tell him that. But . . . you tell Miss Fielding—whom Mr Buller

334

always calls "The Lady" . . . or sometimes "That Lady" . . . or sometimes just "Lady" . . . whatever you want to tell her, David. She's full of questions.'

'Yes?' Audley didn't even watch Mitchell tread through the crocuses, as she did: he still seemed fascinated by her. But, although when she faced him she couldn't read his expression or his thoughts, she had the disconcerting feeling that he had been reading hers. 'He gave you a bad time, did he?'

'Not really.' More than ever he reminded her of Philly: Philly, not really in face or size, or even voice, but nonetheless indefinably Philly. So now she must really beware him. 'His rifle didn't shoot straight, Dr Audley. That may have put him in a bad mood.'

'I doubt that.' He regarded her steadily. 'Paul usually hits what he's aiming at. He has a natural talent that way. But he just doesn't like squeezing the trigger.'

'That's not what I've heard. But it's early days yet. So I suppose I could be wrong.' Philly, defending one of his friends, would have said exactly that.

'You could be. And you are.' He gave her a little sad smile. 'It was the mention of Frances that unsettled him. It always does. And I'm afraid it always will.'

'He loved her—didn't he?'

'Oh yes.' The smile twisted. 'But that's not his problem, my dear. His problem is that he knows *she* didn't love *him*. And . . . but we're not really discussing Frances Fitzgibbon, are we?' The sad smile faded. 'It's vengeance we're discussing—and publication?'

335

He couldn't have had more than five minutes with Ian—or had time tricked her? But even only five minutes would have been enough for the new Ian to put his question. And if Audley had demanded a price for the answering then the new Ian would have paid at once, without a second thought, even though he believed he already knew the answer to it.

'You've been talking to my partner, Dr Audley.'

He nodded. 'I have had that opportunity—yes.' He stared at her in silence for a moment. 'And I must tell you that he no longer seems so keen on writing about me, Miss Fielding.'

Surprise, surprise! But . . . there were plenty more fish in the sea, even if it would be hard to find one that swam so gracefully as Ian. 'I hope he didn't suggest that he was speaking for me?' It was the original Philly she must remember, not this equivocal copy.

'On the contrary. He made it abundantly plain that he was *not* speaking for you, Miss Fielding. And . . . he explained your commitment.' Suddenly he looked away from her for an instant, down into the valley. But then came back to her. 'But, for his part . . . perhaps he remembers that old Chinese proverb about revenge?'

Jenny didn't look into the valley. If he thought he could weaken her so easily, then he was much mistaken. 'What proverb is that?'

'"He—or, in this instance, *she*, of course—*she* who embarks on revenge should first dig two graves", Miss Fielding.' He tried the valley again. 'The way you're going, it looks as though you'll need more than two, though.'

She summoned Philly to her aid. 'There was a

grave dug before we started, Dr Audley. And we—I—didn't dig that one.'

No answer this time: he simply stared at her, testing her.

'You think we're digging our graves now?'

He tried once more, this time gesturing towards the new battlefield of Salamanca. 'Don't you think so, my dear?'

Now she had him. 'I don't quite know what to think yet. Except . . . at the moment the only people I know who might want to stop us are yourself and Dr Mitchell.'

'And that man?' He repeated the gesture. (Big, blunt-fingered hand, quite unlike Philly's: she must hold on to that dissimilarity!) 'MacManus—?'

She could shake her head honestly. 'I don't know who sent him. So . . . it could have been you, Dr Audley.' Now she really had his attention. 'To frighten us off . . . if Dr Mitchell doesn't like squeezing the trigger, as you say . . . Because you do seem to have succeeded in frightening my partner. And what happened to John Tully certainly frightened me.' The thought of John Tully came to her shamefully late. But, having come, it allied John to Philly and finally hardened her heart against Audley. 'John Tully was acting under my orders, Dr Audley. So what happened to him is my responsibility, St Matthew would say.' She clenched her teeth, knowing that she had almost betrayed Philly because of a freak imagined resemblance which had knotted her up. But now that was in the past, and she was herself again. 'And *Burdett* versus *Abbot* also cuts two ways, Dr Audley: if you think I'm going to walk away and forget John Tully, then you have the wrong

337

woman—' Even, in fairness, she must make it stronger than that '—and the wrong journalist.'

He looked at her for what seemed an age. But finally he nodded. 'Well . . . suppose I told you a story, then? How would that be?'

'A story?' Careful, now. 'Fact or fiction?'

'Just a story, Miss Fielding. An old Chinese story—?'

'With nothing promised on either side?'

'With nothing promised on either side—of course!'

'Then I'd listen.' Suddenly she had to play fair with him: that much, from their first sight of each other, she owed him. 'With all my "rights and duties" relating to Philip Masson and John Tully protected, Dr Audley?'

He nodded again, and the compact was made. 'There was this problem in this Intelligence department, nine years ago—nine years, give or take a few months, either way—'

'Research and Development—'

'*This department*—' He cut her off sharply— '—because its director was retiring . . . and his deputy had just dropped dead in his tracks, of over-work and a dickey heart. So the question was . . . *who was going to run the show?*'

The compact had been made, so all she had to do was to nod.

'It was an important job. Because, whoever got it, it opened up a lot of secret—*very* secret—*ultra* secret files to him—okay?'

Him wasn't okay. But she had to ride that, this time. So . . . another nod.

'So we had to get the best man for it—'

She didn't have to ride that. 'But there were two

best men, weren't there?' And then she had to pin him down. 'Philip Masson and Jack Butler. And you wanted Jack Butler.'

He looked down on her, and his face became quite beautifully ugly. 'It really is quite irrelevant now who wanted who, Miss Fielding. Or, anyway, quite unimportant in this context . . . so please don't interrupt.' He set his jaw. 'There was of course the usual manoeuvring and lobbying and fixing that one expects on such occasions—' Then his face broke up almost comically '—actually, Fred and I both wanted Jack. And we underestimated the opposition, too. And perhaps that isn't irrelevant, I agree! Because they started testing poor old Jack, to see how he'd measure up. And neither Fred nor I expected *that*.' He paused. 'And then, so it seemed, Jack nearly got killed on the job—twice in the same week . . . And the second time was within a hair's breadth, so we thought.'

'But it was the other candidate who died, Dr Audley—'

He stared her down—just as Philly had used to do. 'That was an accident, we supposed. And it wasn't *our* business to inquire into it: that was a police job first, and then Special Branch, with MI5 in reserve.' He drew a breath. 'And they didn't find one thing out of place—anymore than *we* did, later on.' He let the breath out with the words. 'Everybody did his job properly, believe me.' Finally he nodded. 'Whoever did it was a real pro. And, as Paddy MacManus was O'Leary's side-kick and junior partner then, maybe it was *him* . . . But we don't know, now . . . And *then*, when they'd given it a clean bill-of-health, we were quite relieved. Because it took all the heat off Jack Butler,

339

so he got the job. And because all *we* were concerned with was why they were trying to kill him, you see—do you see?'

Jenny didn't see. What she saw, in the next second, was that the little car was still burning in the valley: as always, it was amazing how long a collection of bits of metal burned, once they took fire. 'Why—?'

He shook his head at her. 'This isn't the Middle East, Miss Fielding: *we* don't go round killing their chaps. And *they* don't go round killing ours—it's bad for busines.' His lip curled. 'You journalists steal stories from each other, and that's fair enough. But if you started killing each other every time, then you'd pretty soon have a recruitment problem—especially if the editors started knocking each other off, as well, eh?' He shook his head again. 'No . . . putting O'Leary on to Jack Butler was too heavy to ignore: we had to sit down and find out *why*. Because Jack's a great chap. But he's not irreplaceable—even after your godfather's "accidental" death there were other candidates—' The lip curled once more '—including *me* even, faute de mieux . . . Except that I wasn't willing. Because I don't like the paperwork—the *managing*, as they say? Because I'm not a civil servant at heart: I'm a leopard who's too old to change his spots, Miss Fielding.'

Arrogant bugger! But then Philly had been pretty arrogant, too! But . . . *she mustn't interrupt—*

'So there had to be a reason.' He repaid her restraint by continuing. 'And we very soon came up with one. Because Jack was promoted, then he had access to a lot of highly-restricted files. So we thought . . . *once he sees those files, then he'll see something no one else has, maybe? So . . . they can't afford for him to see them . . . maybe?'*

He looked at her, and she realized that he wanted her to react now, to prove that she understood. 'Like . . . there was a traitor somewhere? What Mr Le Carré calls "a mole"—?'

He shrugged. 'Yes. Or . . . it could be that they'd deceived us somehow, with a piece of disinformation. They're damn good at that— feeding us with a great big pack of lies . . . or feeding the Yanks, or the Frogs, or the Krauts . . . or Mossad, and then they feed *us* . . . and we all believe it, and act accordingly—?' He almost grinned at her, but didn't. 'If you start off from the wrong place, then you usually end up at the source of the Nile, and you think you've made a great discovery. So you don't notice the boat they've moored on the Thames, alongside Westminster . . . ' He repeated the almost-but-not-grin. 'Don't ask me, Miss Fielding. Because I won't tell you.'

But he was self-satisfied. So he had come up with an answer. And all he wanted to do was to wrap up the question in the Official Secrets Act, so that he could shrug off his answer, in turn. So she had to get the question right. 'But . . . you had Sir Jack Butler there, beside you, after that. So . . . if he did see those files—?'

David Audley beamed at her. 'Absolutely right, Miss Fielding: we had him there beside us—' Then the beam dulled.

'What's the matter, Dr Audley?'

'Nothing—' He was uneasy for a moment. Then he was himself again. '—your Mr Ian Robinson is talking to my wife, with your Mr Buller . . . and to my daughter. And I was merely wondering what

341

they were saying down there—' He jerked his head '—in the rocks down there—?'

Jenny remembered the pointy-eared fox, which was also somewhere down there in the rocks. But it was beyond her imagination, what they were all up to now, down there: Ian and Reg and the pointy-eared fox, never mind Audley's wife and his daughter, after Paul Mitchell's two failed shots, and then that burst of gunfire, the turret-gun's concluding broadside.

But there was no one there in the rocks. 'What did you discover, Dr Audley?'

He made another ugly face. 'It took us a long time, Miss Fielding. And Paul Mitchell worked longer than I did.' He stared at her, and then nodded. 'Because your Mr Robinson is right—O'Leary wasn't enough for him: he wanted whoever was behind what happened at Thornervaulx.' Nod. 'And so did I, come to that.' Another nod. 'But for a quite different reason.'

'A quite different—?'

He shook his head again. 'But we didn't find anything—not even with old Jack alongside us: we didn't find a damn thing: not a happening, not a policy, not a name, not even a *smell*—nothing.'

Jenny junked Paul Mitchell with Frances Fitzgibbon: they had been, respectively, infantryman and infantrywoman who had fought and died in the front line, and of no interest to the historian's deeper truth.

'Paul worked all hours God sent—8 a.m. to midnight. Or later, sometimes, I suspect.' Audley tested her. 'I don't know . . . I went home each night. But he was always there next morning, when I came in, Miss Fielding.'

As with Reg Buller, so with David Audley. And as with Reg Buller, so with Ian Robinson too: whatever spell she cast across the years from Thornervaulx, Frances Fitzgibbon really must have been quite a woman, to ensnare them all like this, in all their different ways, thought Jenny enviously.

Except that Frances-*Marilyn* Fitzgibbon-*Francis* was dead now: *so sod her!*

So she waited.

'One morning, I came in . . . And Paul said "There's nothing here, David; the bastards have beaten us. Or Jack can't remember anything, anyway. So, even if O'Leary hadn't been so damned incompetent and done the job properly . . . either at the University, or at Thornervaulx . . . it wouldn't have made any difference. Because there's nothing here."'

Jenny still waited.

'And then it was easy, of course.' Audley nodded.

'Easy?' He wasn't talking about the woman now.

'O'Leary was the best—*the best*, Miss Fielding.' He nodded. 'Your Paddy MacManus wasn't in the same class: he was just a pale carbon-copy of the real thing.' He cocked his head dismissively towards the dispersing column of smoke in the plain between the Greater and Lesser Arapiles. 'O'Leary might have screwed up *once*, if he'd had very bad luck. And he did have very bad luck, when Frances Fitzgibbon turned up out of the blue, at Thornervaulx. But he didn't have any bad luck at the University. And he must have had Jack Butler right in his sights at Thornervaulx.' He stared at her. 'What my old Latin master used to say . . . God rest his lovely soul! . . . was that "nonsense

343

must be wrong!'', Miss Fielding.' Still, he stared. 'What if O'Leary *didn't* screw up? What if he did *exactly* what they paid him to do—to make us concentrate on Jack Butler—*and not on Philip Masson?*'

'And then it was easy', just as he had said: it was like the scales falling from her eyes, in the Bible story she'd once had to learn by heart, to take her O-level Religious Studies exam.

He saw that she understood. 'The irony is that dear Frances deceived us both: because of her we both had blinkers on: we couldn't think of anything except her—and Jack Butler. And we weren't getting any answer because we were asking the wrong question. But we got there at last, anyway.' Audley nodded. 'Your "Philly" was a great guy, Miss Fielding: we did him over after that, right from his birth to what we no longer believed was his accidental death. Although we still believed that he'd been drowned, of course—we never expected him to turn up again. And it took us a long time, I can tell you . . . Because we couldn't ask any of our questions obviously—in case we alerted the Other Side.' Nod. 'Because, either way—if he was *theirs*, or if he wasn't—we didn't want to let them know that we were on to them. Because that would have given the game away.'

Jenny felt her mouth fall open.

'No—he wasn't on *their* side, my dear.' Audley reassured her quickly. 'Your "Philly" was absolutely on *ours*, you have no need to worry.'

She wasn't worrying; it was insulting even to suggest that.

'They simply didn't want him to see one of our most secret files—that's all, Miss Fielding.' He

344

accepted her silence gently. 'And it took three of us—Mitchell and me, and someone I cordially detest—four months to find that file: three of us, and four months of hard labour . . . So that I know all about you, and your father as well as Philip Masson—all about the Korean War, and how he won his Military Cross . . . I know all about that . . . And about his career, after that. And his hobbies—and his girl-friends . . . and the girls he took on that boat of his—the *Jenny III* was it? . . . And when he took you for a holiday in France, that time—in that cottage in the Dordogne—?' The next nod was expressionless. 'Because your father was worried about that: because you were only fifteen years old, and he thought his old friend might just fancy you—? And his tax returns—*everything*, Miss Fielding.'

Jenny felt the sun burning her head, but a dreadful chill far below, where it hurt. 'That's ridiculous—'

His mouth twisted again. 'That's what we thought at the time, Miss Fielding.'

God! They hadn't quite got it right, even though they were clever—and even though Daddy had appeared then, out of the blue! Because it had been her—almost-sixteen-year-old-Jenny—who had had hot-pants for him, without knowing how to take desire further, when he'd discouraged her—God!

But she didn't even want to think about that now. 'Who killed him, Dr Audley?' She felt empty as she rammed the question at him. 'Who killed him?'

He relaxed. 'Oh, come on, Miss Fielding! You know I can't answer that!'

He was also like Mitchell: of course he was like

345

Mitchell! But . . . she would never have a better chance than now. 'Then I'll have to work harder, Dr Audley—to find out for myself. With or without Ian. And it may not be such a good book without him. But there are other writers who'll work for me.'

'Whatever the risk?'

She shrugged. 'Maybe I'll write it myself.' She put on her obstinate face. 'Someone had him killed. And I'm going to ruin the bastard—whoever he is.'

He nodded. 'You really did love him.' The nod continued. 'And not just like a good god-daughter, of course!' The nodding stopped. 'Well, then I shall have to tell you the rest of the story, Miss Fielding.'

He was too sure of himself for comfort. 'I'm listening, Dr Audley.'

He stared at her in silence for a moment. 'It hasn't occurred to you that your revenge has already been accomplished?'

Somewhere in the stillness of the valley an engine started up. Jenny was drawn towards the sound: the armoured personnel vehicle with the little turret-gun had started up; nearer to them, at the foot of the plateau in the gap in the fence beside the track, Paul Mitchell was in earnest conversation with one of the Spanish civilians; and the shapeless wreck of the little 2-CV was smoking now, rather than burning.

She felt quite empty. He hadn't mentioned a country, let alone a name. And of course he never would. And it didn't have to be a Russian name, or any one of half a dozen of their East European surrogates. Or it could be an Arab name. Or even an Israeli name. Or it could just conceivably be some clean-cut, crew-cut American. Or, as an ultimate possibility, a Saville-Row-suited Englishman.

'Are you saying that he's dead, Dr Audley?'

'No, Miss Fielding. That's a lie I'm not prepared to tell you. Because we're not into that sort of vengeance: it's not what we're hired for.'

She remembered what Reg Buller had said. 'You don't do wicked things like that—?'

A curious expression passed across his face. 'No, Miss Fielding. We don't do wicked things like that. Killing is too simple for us: we want more than that. Killing wouldn't give us our proper satisfaction.'

'More?' She couldn't read his face at all. 'Proper—?'

'Oh yes. When you've been deceived—as we *were* deceived . . . and for a long time before Philip Masson was killed—the trick is to continue the deception. But you turn it round the other way.' He smiled with his lips. 'It's like, if you find a traitor in the ranks, there's no point in arresting him. He'll only get a successor—probably someone you don't know. So you leave him where he is.' The not-smile widened. 'Ideally, of course, you turn *him* round—that's what Masterman did during the war, with his Germans . . . But that's very risky these days, when a man can be ideologically bent . . . So you leave him. Or you promote him, even: you make him even more successful, even more valuable to them . . . But this wasn't quite like that—' He raised his hand. '—no, Miss Fielding! That's as far as I can go there. So don't ask.' The not-smile became even uglier. 'Our first problem was to make them think that we were still deceived, back in '78—or '79, as it soon was . . . So we put out

347

rumours that the wicked Dr Audley had maybe had your godfather pushed off his little boat, suitably weighted. And had then stifled any sort of investigation by pretending to investigate the matter himself.' He nodded. 'All to ensure Jack Butler's promotion, of course . . . And you, of course, duly came upon those rumours—nicely matured by the years?'

She nodded. But the devil in the back of her brain leered at her. 'But I mustn't believe them now—is that it? Because I must believe *you* now?'

'You must believe what convinces you, Miss Fielding.' His mouth set hard.

She had cut deep, justly or not. 'I believe that Philly—that my godfather was murdered nine years ago, Dr Audley. And I also believe that John Tully is dead. And I need a much better answer to John Tully.'

'Ah . . . that's fair enough.' He agreed readily, almost like a judge taking an objection. 'As to poor Mr Tully, I can't answer you with any certainty—I can only hazard a guess there, Miss Fielding.'

'A guess?' The devil shook his head warningly.

'Yes . . . I think maybe we've not been as clever . . . or as clever for as long . . . as we thought, perhaps.' He made a face. 'Nothing lasts forever. And . . . we've been running our Masson deception for a long time, now.' One huge shoulder lifted philosophically. 'They may have tumbled to it . . . Or, they may suspect, honestly I don't know. But I rather fear I'll be working on that when I get back to London—while my dear wife and daughter are spending my money in Paris—?' The great once-upon-a-time rugger-playing shoulder rose again. 'Did they teach you seventeenth century

348

poetry at Roedean, Miss Fielding?'

'Poetry—?' The man was dangerous.

'No! It was biology, wasn't it!' Audley grinned. 'I remember . . . No—there was this seventeenth-century poet, writing his love-poem to chat this girl up—Andrew Marvell, it was . . . And he said, when you can't delay things, then you ought to hurry them up: *"Thus, though we cannot make our sun stand still . . . yet we will make him run"*—or something like that—?' He blinked disarmingly. 'It could be that they want to make a dirty great big scandal of it now, with questions in the House of Commons—? Because we're not going to reveal what we've been doing—never in a month of Sundays! So . . . your Mr Tully was a paid-up member of the National Union of Journalists. And you can kill soldiers, or you can kill "innocent bystanders" . . . But when you start to kill *journalists*—paid-up NUJ freelances, no less! That really puts the cat among the pigeons, Miss Fielding.' He raised an eyebrow. 'And your Ian would have been worse than Tully. Because he's well-liked . . . So "Heads, we don't win—tails we lose"?: the media will love another Intelligence scandal too, after Peter Wright and *Spycatcher*. And the other side's disinformation-people know just how to feed in a tit-bit or two of genuine scandal. Plus our original rumours, too. And, of course, the word will be out that Jennifer Fielding is preparing a shock-horror revelation—right? But not Ian Robinson—?'

He was playing dirty. So she could play the same game. 'Whereas in fact you were very clever? Is that what I'm supposed to say?'

He looked down at her, almost proudly. 'Not

349

very clever, Miss Fielding. But we did take your revenge for you even if we didn't kill him. Because we made a fool of him for a few years. And when his masters found out about that—which they've either just done . . . or maybe it was a year or two back . . . then he would have gone down a very long snake on the board, I rather think.' He shrugged. 'We can never do what we'd *like* to do. We have to settle for what we *want*. So our satisfaction is usually somewhat muted, you see. But we have asuredly ruined him, you can depend on that. And maybe worse.'

She saw. 'And I must believe all this—?'

'You must believe what suits you. Or . . . you can ask Mr Robinson what he believes, if you prefer?'

Jenny thought of Ian suddenly. 'Ian asked you a question, didn't he? About Mrs Fitzgibbon, was it—?'

'Yes.' She was rewarded with another of his odd faces. 'I must say that you did very well there: I'm surprised—and a little disturbed—that you got so close to her, after all this time. Because you wouldn't have got it from Paul . . . of that, I'm sure.' he frowned. 'But . . . you're certainly in the right job, anyway.'

He was flattering the wrong partner, thought Jenny grimly. 'What was the question?'

'The question?' he frowned again. 'Don't you—' A slight sound, as of a stone dislodged somewhere behind her, cut him off. 'Ah! I think that's my wife coming—'

'What was the question, Dr Audley?'

Audley looked at her. 'He wanted to know who Frances Fitzgibbon shouted at, that day at

350

Thornervaulx: whether it was at the man O'Leary, or at Paul Mitchell, Miss Fielding.'

'At—?' The scene Reg Buller had described suddenly came back to her, and with all the more vividness for its contrast, here on the top of the Greater Arapile: not fierce Spanish sunlight, in the midst of a brown rocky wilderness only softened by autumn crocuses, but the pouring rain, and the sodden grass and fallen leaves, and the great grey ruins of Thornervaulx Abbey.

'Yes.' He misread her expression. 'He knew the answer, of course. But it was still a good question. With a rare answer.'

The two places had nothing in common.

'When she saw O'Leary at Thornervaulx that day, she must have thought he was going to kill one of them—Paul, or Jack Butler . . . And Jack Butler for choice, maybe. But, of course, we don't exactly know what she thought. Because she died in Paul's arms, without saying anything.'

Or, maybe, there was something: there was violent death—here, today and long ago, and at Thornervaulx, nine years ago, on a wet November afternoon.

'But, even though she didn't have a gun, she was safe enough, anyway—'

Philly was the link—Philly and Audley—

'Only, if she shouted at Paul, that would have alerted him too late—either for himself, or for Jack Butler. Because O'Leary had a clear view of them both, by then—'

Mrs David Audley was tall and blonde, and a lot younger than her husband: obviously, she liked older men too, even though she was smiling at Ian as he helped her up across the rocks from below—

'So she shouted at O'Leary, Miss Fielding. And she must have known that he'd think she had a gun.' Audley glanced towards his wife for a second, to make sure she was far enough away. 'I didn't actually see it happen. But I saw something like it happen in the war, once . . . It's not a thing you forget: one human being dying for another, in cold blood.' He nodded slowly at her. 'She was quite a woman, was Frances. But I think she'd prefer not to have any publicity now.'

'*David!*' Mrs Audley didn't sound too pleased.

'Hullo, love!' Audley looked at Jenny for one last fraction of a second after acknowledging his name. 'What you must decide, Miss Fielding, is what your godfather would have wanted you to do. That's all.' He turned back to his wife. 'Love—I don't think you've met Jenny Fielding—? She's a friend of Willy Arkenshaw's, and she's dying to meet you.'

Jenny saw Ian behind Mrs David Audley. And, behind Ian, Miss Cathy Audley, bright and pointy-eared as the fox in the rocks down below.

And Reg Buller, finally.

And Reg Buller, knowing everything and nothing, had eyes for her only. Because she would sign his account, and agree his expenses. And they were both still alive.

'Lady—?'

Tomorrow was another day, he was saying.

EPILOGUE

ANOTHER CONVERSATION WHICH NEVER TOOK PLACE

'*I'm not at all pleased with the way this wretched affair finally turned out, Latimer.*'

'Yes, I do agree. It was quite unnecessarily violent. But that's the Spaniards for you. And they are actually rather pleased with us: they've wanted to settle with that Irishman ever since the Basques hired him to blow up that general of theirs.'

'*They left it damnably late, though. Aguirre could have taken the man long before. Straight off the plane, in fact—with no shooting. And no risk to Audley's family—I really didn't like that at all, Latimer.*'

'Yes. But we couldn't tell Aguirre what to do, Jack—could we? And, of course, I suppose he wanted as many of MacManus's ETTA contacts as possible: it was obvious that the man would call in their help to trace Audley once he knew where Fielding and Robinson were going.'

'*And how the devil did he know that?*'

'We're not quite sure, as yet. But he did have the Romanians to help him, of course. And they could have leaned on one of Buller's friends just as we did. But Aguirre assured me there'd be no risk to Audley.'

'*There's always a risk . . . And there's also the death of that fellow Tully. The Special Branch has already been on to me about that. They seem to think MacManus was responsible.*'

'Yes . . . well, that was a little rumour I let slip on the grapevine, Jack. So now that he's dead they'll most likely settle for "person or persons unknown", I shouldn't wonder.'

'*But Mitchell says it wasn't MacManus.*'

'No, I agree. It was most likely one of the

Romanians—the Departamentul de Informatii Externe doing its stuff . . . Mitchell's pretty sure that MacManus's minder was one of their officers. And it seems they're missing one of their trade attachés, so that fits. Plus Masson was their murder-victim originally, of course: the whole thing was their project, *ab initio . . .*'

'*And they've caused all the trouble now. Damned Romanians! I'd almost rather deal with the Russians, I sometimes think.*'

'Yes . . . well, I rather hope we can leave it to the Russians to sort out now, Jack. Because they're not at all pleased with the *Departamentul* as of now. In fact, there are going to be some heads rolling before very long. We may even pick up a defector or two—I have had a word with Jaggard about that, actually.'

'*Well, just make sure it doesn't get into the newspapers. Otherwise it'll only stir up that damn Fielding woman even more.*'

'She doesn't know anything about the Romanian connection, Jack.'

'*But she can put two-and-two together. And Audley's already told her far too much for my liking. I don't know what he was playing at, frankly.*'

'Oh . . . David was taking a calculated risk. And for once I must support him, Jack. Because we really cannot afford the publication of another book. And particularly a book about R & D . . . So he really had to stop her somehow.'

'*By telling her everything?*'

'He didn't tell her everything, exactly . . . But, look at it this way, Jack: the Russians will rein in the Romanians now—*they* know that no one will believe the DIE wasn't acting on their orders. And

356

they certainly wouldn't like everyone to know that the Romanians have been feeding *our* disinformation to Moscow all these years—'

'*I'm not worried about them. It's the woman Fielding I'm concerned with: she's well-connected. And she's tricky, like all journalists. And the man Robinson, who writes her books—he can't be trusted either.*'

'Oh, I don't think he'll write this one, Jack.'

'*No? Why not?*'

'He doesn't want to, apparently. And . . . he's about to get the offer of a rather nice research fellowship at Rylands College in Cambridge, I happen to know.'

'*How do you know?*'

'I have a friend there who is an admirer of his work. We've had a little talk, and we both think Mr Robinson will be happier in the groves of academe. And he has rather gone off Miss Fielding-ffulke, Mitchell says.'

'*I see. But that still leaves her, Latimer.*'

'Yes. But . . . well, I think we can leave *her* to David now, Jack.'

'*To Audley? But—?*'

'They've rather taken to each other. And David says that she could be very useful to us, in the right place and handled properly. And . . .'

'*And?*'

'And David also particularly wants to know who put her on to him in the first place. He says that Masson turning up like that again . . . that was pure accident. But the Honourable Jennifer Fielding-ffulke overhearing one particular piece of gossip about her beloved godfather . . . *that* was too much of a coincidence. And David doesn't like

357

coincidences. And nor, I must say, do I.'

'*You mean . . . it wasn't the Romanians?*'

'We're not sure. But we do have other enemies. And it's as well to know who they are, don't you think?'

'*Very well. But only on the strict understanding that no positive action is to be taken—is that understood, Latimer? Not by you—and not by Audley: no settling of scores—understood? We've had quite enough of that in this affair already.*'

'Understood, Jack. "Vengeance is mine, saith the Lord". I'll tell David that.'

Photoset, printed and bound in Great Britain by
REDWOOD BURN LIMITED, Trowbridge, Wiltshire